OIL ON SILVER

Reflections on current Counter Culture

David Erdos

PENNILESS PRESS PUBLICATIONS
www.pennilesspress.co.uk

Published by

Penniless Press Publications 2017

© David Erdos

The author asserts his moral right to be identified as the author of the work. All rights reserved. No part of this publication may be reproduced, stored in a retrieval system or transmitted in any form or by any means, electronic, mechanical, photocopying, recording or otherwise, without the prior permission of the publishers.

ISBN 978-0-244-31144-5

Dedicated to:

Heathcote Williams and Mike Lesser

With endless thanks to
Douglas Field, Jeff Jay Jones, Alan Moore Iain Sinclair, Chris Petit,
Andrew Kotting, Philip Reid, Snoo Wilson, Steve and Jo Hackett

And for their photographs and images:

Ruth Bayer, Keith Rodway, Elena Caldera, Chris Davies
Max Crow Reeves, Elspeth Moore, Tim Higham, Cindy Cash

Front cover image and copyright by Claire Palmer

Author Photo and copyright by Jack McGuire

Heathcote Williams occurs many times in this book. His work and my devotion to it has been a constant theme for all of the years I am duty bound to remember. Many of these pieces were discussed with and commented on by him. Towards the end of this book's preparation, the shock news of his passing on July 1st 2017 devastated all of those close and connected to him. His loss robs his family of a truly magical parent and grandfather and modern culture of one of its valuable and seminal voices. My work can offer only a small tribute.

It is for this reason that the collection starts and ends with two different types of summation. He made every one he brought into contact feel special. His work, some of which remains buried treasure, will go on to define culture's gold.

DE, 25th September 2017

CONTENTS

| INFLUENCE; AN INTRODUCTION | 11 |

| PART ONE: TREE SHAVINGS (BOOKS): | 15 |

TRANSCENDENT COURAGE	17
ON THE TEXTURE OF MEAT	20
WE ARE ALL LEPERS	25
DAYS IN SONG	28
COLD GHOST AVALANCHE	32
OF THEE I SING	36
HEARD IN THE HAND	42
THE POEM IS PART OF THE EYE	44
DOGS IN THE RAIN	48
BEHIND SHADOW	50

| PART TWO: SOUND SHAPING (MUSIC): | 57 |

AS PRECIOUS AS I USED TO BE	59
EARTHLY DELIGHTS	62
VOYAGE TO THE ACOLYTE	64
THEY ACCEPTABLE	83
TRIP WIZARDS	85
SPICE BOYS	88
AT THE SPRINGING OF THE SUN	93
CASUAL GODS	98
IN EXCELCIS	101
DIRECTOR OF JOY	105
ON THE TRANSLATION OF SPIRIT TO SNAKE	111
SEPARATING THE HEART	114
SOOTHING THE STING	117
THE PANDOREM	120

THE MIASMA MONKEY AND YOU	124
SALVATION IN THE SUBURBS	127
A COMPOUND FOR THE SOUL	1334
PART THREE: VOICE SHARING (THEATRE):	139
BETWEEN THESE TOWERS	141
I WILL TALK YOU TO DEATH	149
W – ON THE LIFE, DEATH AND CAREER OF SIR ARNOLD WESKER	154
BURNING THE BLOOD	160
CALL FOR CHANGE	166
BLACK BOX BUKKAKE	170
FROM CALVARY TO CHEMISTRY	173
PART FOUR: OTHERS WALKING (ENCOUNTERS):	179
KENSAL RISING	181
ODE TO THE ETERNALIST	188
DIVINE PASSENGER	220
DEAD RINGERS	222
SING A SONG OF SIMON	225
BETWEEN THE DRAGONS	229
FIERCE UNDERSTANDING	232
DIVISIONS OF LOVE	236
PART FIVE: GOLD STREAMING (TRIBUTES & EXERCISES IN STYLE)	239
THE OXFORD MAGIC	241
HIGH CHOIRS	243
BRANCHES OF THE YEW TREE	245
BOLESKINNING	247
THE STOCKHOLM SEQUENCE	250

LILIAN	267
GRIEFLAND	269
6 4 SNOO	274
HOARSE LATITUDES	278
COMEBACK	283
WITH THANKS	285
THE CURE FOR CANCER	288
CONDEMNATION	295
MUSE ON MONDAY	297
HER COLLECTION	311
A CHILDREN'S STORY	322
CODA: THE VIEW FROM UXBRIDGE	323
ON THE FADING OF STARS	325

INFLUENCE: AN INTRODUCTION

I hope it isn't too presumptuous of me to offer up a new word for the English language as it continues to develop and survive in these increasingly barbaric, if not downright troubled times. The word I would like to suggest is 'Fulfillicosis, ' by which I mean 'a state of being in which one is able to befriend and collaborate with the heroes and influences whose own work has helped form one's own thoughts and approaches to the world.' It started some years ago for me with a brief acquaintance with modern theatre's most significant dramatist and has continued on, happily taking in his oldest friend, a number of wondrous progressive and ambient musicians, seminal novelists and film makers, the ultimate poet-polemicist-playwright and activist of this and any age and a man widely regarded as, among his many other accomplishments, the greatest graphic novelist there will ever be. This state of grace, achieved through a combination of happy accident and wilfull, earnest letter writing led to 2016 being a year in which I was able to meet someone of real importance to me every month. I fulfilled the only ambitions I ever had, which was to meet and connect with such persons and while my travels took me from Uxbridge to Oxford to Finchley Road and Frognal Tube station, to a flat near the Barbican, a house in Teddington and on, towards Northampton, I felt as if fresh worlds had been scaled.

In trying to introduce the pieces included in this book, in which some of these people feature I thought it apposite to find a term to describe the privilege I continue to feel. It is a rare thing in these days of neglect and misunderstanding to unearth things of lasting value so after a time of loss and separation and at an age when I can truly appreciate them, these encounters have meant more to me than I can adequately describe in a brief introduction. The age of celebrity is a glib one, with many undeserving proponents, so to be able to look into the eyes of people whose contributions have each enriched the culture that struggles around us all while at the same time teaching it actual means of renewal, feels like one of the most valuable things I could have done with whatever time I have been granted. I wanted to mark and show these practitioners just how much I appreciate their work and lives and how in my own small way, I have tried and will continue to try to honour the standards they've set.

My own work as an actor, writer, director, teacher and illustrator has always been informed by a rich array of resources. I am known as an artistic touchstone for my friends and colleagues who often ask me for references and recommendations (a point of special pride was my friendship with the late, great and much missed Snoo Wilson –eulogised later in this book - who once called me, knowing I had more copies than he did of a play of his he needed to give to a production company) and I try to carry these values into teaching both the young and mature. Artists must bridge the forms at all levels if art is to continue at all, so these pieces of small scale journalism and creative impression are directed towards that goal. I want to see and learn from all manner of art forms that are able to 'ring the changes' and set the advances. If I see or experience something that is self reflexive in an uninspiring way, then I am drawn, perhaps even compelled towards pointing it out. My hope is that a truly constructive criticism – which is afterall part of being an artist in the first place – shows how to build *on* ideas.

The arts journalism of this collection is caught somewhere between the realms of review and essay. Many of the pieces are ruminations on what is possible, or not possible in the culture as well as being concerned with the responsibilties of creative expectation. In my experience the inherent danger in a great deal of artistic practise, is that no-one thinks fast enough, or indeed works hard enough to understand or appreciate the work, either actively or critically. Plays in performance can become lazy exercises in repitition, stand-up comedy, too often falls into becoming a series of practised responses under the guise of spontaneity. Art openings, rather like funerals, increasingly have more to do with the social follow through than with the intended causesense of celebration. Only music retains the necessary elements of focus and attention needed to renew itself each time. In succumbing to the false and misleading definitions of modern celebrity we have moved away from the strong authorial voice in favour of a cooling echo, and it is now crucial that we clear the cultural throat if we are to continue speaking with greater relevance.

The poetry and short dramatic pieces in the last section of the book, are selections from the larger body of my creative work and are an attempt to 'put my money where my mouth is'. If I am to critique or espouse others than I should at least show some of my own inner workings, in order for the opinions that form this book to be held to

INFLUENCE: AN INTRODUCTION

task, or perhaps justified. If this is a time when the physical book is in danger of fading or passing into the somewhat fetishistic realm of the vinyl record, then books need to speak as loudly as possible, either through the authority of one voice, or the richness of many. The words set down need to surpass their particular font and claim a music of their own. In this way, my 'fulfilliscosis' is also evidenced by the hold that the stylist writers and musicians I treasure have on me. I believe that all plays and poetry should aspire to a musical form, even if they are out to create a musicality, atmosphere, or naturally a world of their own (Pinter, Beckett, Jim Cartwright, Caryl Churchill, Howard Barker, Edward Bond etc), so just as plays, if boiled down to their essence are really only a matter of activated decisions and light, so writing must also create its own context. The creative and the critical must combine when discussing art and indeed, when making it. That is not to imply that a writer or artist must honour elitism in any way, or, conversely, think only of an audience when making their work, but rather, that the work produced should only leave the house once its maker has considered the full array of ramifications, strengths and indeed limitations it may or may not possess. Art is about asking questions afterall, while science is about answering them. To my way of thinking organised religion, as opposed to spiritual dedication, is about avoiding the question altogether.

In *Oil On Silver* books, performances, music and artworks from thr last couple of years are considered, along with some crucial encounters from that time. I hope these are far ranging and represent the work on offer, without reducing or detracting from them. For instance, I am constantly befuddled by mainstream book reviews that insist on telling you the plot of a novel or the thrust of a dialectic. I believe a piece of criticism should draw you towards the act of reading and therefore discovery, not do the work for you. It is this very exactitude which comes from the work of the people who have influenced me and who afterall introduced me to the ideas and standards I seek to convey.

For the last two years I have worked as part of the editorial board of the notorious *International Times*, started by Sir Paul McCartney, Barry Miles and John Hopkins in 1966 and revived for the new century by the great and much missed Mike Lesser. Versions and some of these pieces first appeared there and were commissioned under the infamous banner to which Theda Bara grants her image. My thanks go in particular to Claire Palmer, Nick Victor, Keith Rodway, Elena Caldera, Heathcote Ruthven, Robert Montgomery, Julie Goldsmith, Niall McDevitt, Max Crow Reeves, Rupert Loydell and the great Heathcote Williams for their support in mounting some of these selections. The aim in presenting them to you in this collection is to expand the hopeful reach of my observations and to showcase just some of the numerous and fascinating works that the current counter culture is producing. It is my profound hope that the fulfillicosis I have contracted over the last couple of years after much previous and indeed, current struggle is conducive and appealing to you and that you will be moved enough to want to discover these works if you are not already familiar with them.

The culture, as we know it, is forever under threat. But behind that danger lay a vast array of artists, practitioners and activists who are joining the forms in order to affect change. From Dada's botherers of reason to the forces of the Occupy movement to Harris and Stone's money burners, a new voice is calling for a new standard. The counter culture has always been with us from the first satirical or pornographic cave painting, to the coruscating anti-Trump activism surrounding us now. It is in the spirit of a greater eloquence and a growing cultural resourcefulness in both the young and the unignited old, that I offer in solidarity and support to those whose own work has touched me, these attempts to shape a new signalling bell.

Heroes are many things to many different people. Mine have shown that the truest path is one described by the sincerest of voices. Adventure and achievement only arrive after taking the bravest stance against oppression and difficulty in order to home in on the poetry of grace. Influence honoured begets innovation. May your own works be mighty even if they stay small.

And finally, a few words on the title of this book. The possibly polluting oil of criticism when poured on the artistic waters of others can achieve symbiosis and fusion through the hope of informed understanding and sense of collaboration. It is my hope that this liquid alchemises into silver, in order to attain lasting gold.

David Erdos, London, August 2017

Part One:

TREE SHAVINGS

(Books)

TRANSCENDENT COURAGE:

A Review Of Badshah Khan – Islamic Peace Warrior By Heathcote Williams

Over fifty years since his first publication, Heathcote Williams continues to chart both the injustices and deeply felt poetics at the heart of the human experience. His masterly new investigative poem and book *Badshah Khan: Islamic Peace Warrior* is an exemplary study of a neglected Angel on Earth. In writing this book, Mr Williams has continued to create and define a new genre; that of poetic journalism and biography, continuing a series of works including *The Red Dagger, Killing Kit, The Ruff Tuff Cream Puff Agency, David Cameron Eats Kittens* and his evisceration of the British Monarchy; *Royal Babylon*. Such works draw our attention to predicaments and individuals who necessitate scrutiny. And there is no better example of that than the figure of Peshawar born 'Shah of Shahs' Badshah Khan himself. A close friend and companion of Mahatma Gandhi, this 'Pashtun 6 foot 5 giant of a man founded an Islamic Peace Army of ten thousand unarmed 'soldiers' while the sectarian conflict that would pull India apart in the late 1940s raged around them.' In the current climate of suspicion and residual fear felt by the west towards the nation and movement of Islam, it goes without saying just how important it is to consider and review the life and work of one of its most positive proponents. The exactitude shown by Williams in this masterly poetic portrayal demonstrates one of his many stunning characteristics as a writer, poet, journalist and polemicist; the simple ability to educate and enlighten the public's ignorance of some of the darkest and most important areas of its own history.

Born in Afghanistan, Abdul Ghaffar Khan, as the son of a benign tribal Shah, devoted his life to nonviolent protest. It was these actions and stance that this epic poem reflects and dignifies. Categorised by Williams as 'Weaponised goodness', Khan's defiance of British rule led to a 27 year imprisonment - thereby equalling Nelson Mandela's status as an ultimate Prisoner of Conscience for the age, as well as enduring numerous, frequent torturing at the hands of the British. A jihad in reverse as we now understand it, but defined by Khan in his lifetime as the spreading of love and understanding between all men. The poem describes how Khan strove to break the 'useless customs' of imperialism and its practises, offering instead only the clear sighted values of wisdom and equality, thereby unifying all religions by stating that 'belief in God is to love your fellow man.' The brutality that he faced in trying to deliver that message exposes the limitations of not only all of those corrupted in the West, but also those who seek to misread and misrepresent a sense of belonging to and ownership of your own territory. Those on any side willing to use the suffering of others to justify their beliefs are not the soldiers of God, but rather the defenders of their own weakness.

The style of the book is crucial. One of Einstein's concerns in developing the Theory of Relativity was to 'unify the fields.' Heathcote Williams unifies the fields of poetry, biography and journalism effortlessly in this poem, with a writing style that combines extensive research with poetic reflection and contemplation. The result is an active linguistic philosophy: a uniquely considered response to events delivered to us in a language that is both educative and accessible. Williams, one of the great stylists of the 20th Century has developed a poetic voice that simplifies and elucidates. It is a kind of wave populated by the facts and details he wishes to communicate. There is a great deal of reported speech and quotation in the book, which blend seamlessly with the pitch and rise of the narratives presentation of facts. This sensual aspect of Mr Williams' writing is one its major areas of appeal. Anyone familiar with his acting roles in film, or audiobook recordings will recognise how the smoothness and honeyed rasp of his speaking voice is resonantly echoed in his written one. He is both teacher and lawyer, representing the information and accused by his insistent and rigourous examination of his subjects opposing forces, whether they be Khan's postwar British persecutors or the Japanese whale hunters, skewered effectively in his iconic *Whale Nation*.

Too often poetry falls prey to trends or indulgence. Williams' work as a whole and this book as its most recent example, easily resists that state of affairs. It creates and consolidates its own approach in a seductively measured blank verse style that seeks to dignify and embody the inspirational human being it honours.

Khan's deep understanding of the spiritual response and his spirited defiance of oppression granted him the transcendent courage quoted in the text. His extensive struggle is made all the more relevant by the fact that Afghanistan was the site and subject of his labours. Williams encapsulates the history of this area through his detailing of Khans' endurance, balancing it chillingly with a study of Afghanistan's role as target for the machinations of the American war machine and their attempt to nullify neighbouring Russia's hold over the area. Reagan's warmongery is exposed once more as is Obama's recent pride at his Tuesday Morning Kill List, with former President Clinton's phallic missiles affectionately termed as Lewinsky's giving us the darkest of final laughs. Throughout all of this the purety and character of Khan shines through, showing us that those who represent the culture we espouse are as barbaric and inhumane as our imagined eastern enemy.

The true prophet is not concerned with religion but simply with the human impulse. In an increasingly ignorant age, history and religion show us that they are questioned, denied or misunderstood far too often. This book and the life it conveys shows how the direct prophecies of love and understanding are the most relevant. Making the ill informed understand that, is therefore the only true task. Khan offered the means to love and to defend that love honourably. He saw nonviolence in a violent world as the highest form of devotion and asked and suffered at the hands of those only ready to hate. Ghaffar Khan died in 1988 at the age of 98, a near century of life that bridged the divide between sectarian violence and spiritual action. This new book by Heathcote Williams not only contains that life but reflects its achievements in the shine of Thin Man Press' ninety beautifully packaged pages.

The hands and hearts of both Williams and Khan have been joined in this book, along with all of those who accompanied and continued the struggle against ignorance and oppression. The wound, if not healed, now shines through.

To you then, as the potential readers of this seminal examination of a life's dedication and to its author, Heathcote Williams I offer a final Pashtun phrase, as quoted in the text:

Stre Mashe:

(Trans) May you never grow tired.

29th April 2015

ON THE TEXTURE OF MEAT
An overview and impression of Chris Petit's 'the *Butchers of Berlin'*

Jerry Cornelius: And so I set forth, into this tasty world..
(Michael Moorcock, The Final Programme, as adapted by Robert Fuest)

Chris Petit's masterly recent novel, *The Butchers of Berlin* is a shocking and precise examination on the nature of genocide, both in terms of the Nazi persecutions of the second world war and the specific hungers of the unconquered heart, seeking its revenge on the world. Set in 1943, the book details the efforts of a German police officer August Schlegl in attempting to solve a series of murders occurring in the city at a time of the mass transportation of the remaining Jewish residents, under the auspices and beady eyes of the city's SS colonists. A group of Jewish butchers are initially blamed for the flayed female corpse discovered on their premises, a possible act of retaliation against their oppressors who amongst other persecutions have forced them into the daily handling of pork. But this is by no means self evident. As the city is cleared of its Jews, increasing amounts of blood and legacy are left in their wake and the novel reverberates with the chill echoes of abandonment and desolation.

In story terms, the set up and conundrum are clear: why would a killer or cabal of killers strike now at a time when the currency of death has already been devalued to the extent of an everyday exchange? The predetermined fates of the remaining Jews within the city's limits are also beyond clarity. Death is in the air, so while these fresh murders have the perfect cover, how may their resonance be accurately defined? This is the predicament facing Schlegl in the first pages of the novel, but as the story deepens, the starkness and precision of Petit's prose allows these questions to emerge and take on unexpected directives.

The book's locale captures the war at the peak of its cruelty and the dehumanisation of the Jews by the Hitlerian hordes chimes sharply with the brutality of the murders Schlegl is faced with. The writing style, as ever with Petit, is accessible and restrained, allowing the reader to move freely through the scenes, unencumbered by verbiage, but always sticking close to events. This flow and relative ease is a common factor in all of Petit's procedural style novels from *The Psalm Killer* to *The Passenger* and a distillation of the vibrant atmospherics of his first book, *Robinson*, which is one of the great novels of the last thirty years. The style is also evident of Petit's skills and experience as a film maker. Scenes and episodes both glide past and grip us in the manner of their cinematic counterparts. The constant sense of literal transportation and spiritual movement of Petit's seminal film *Radio On* is never far away in all of his work, as he journeys through new territories and his gimlet eye is as ever, razor sharp. He is capable of producing both shocking detail;

> *'They're animals. They can't even kill like men. The probably fucked her and then rolled around in the blood before they got down to work..'*

to the poetry lurking in the commonplace;

> *'The light would not come for another hour. Socks and suspenders. Belt and braces..'*

All done with an ease which is one part Hemingway and one part Florian Shneider/Ralf Hutter (and the rest of Kraftwerk, for that matter). He draws us in so that we may see our own horrors in his galleried portraiture of the grim.

The book is dedicated to Petit's friend and collaborator Iain Sinclair and his wife, Anna, and like Sinclair on his legendary walks through London, Petit, for whom driving is his preferred idiom of choice notices and notates everything. A sense of motion is ever present in his films and books, and because his authorial voice is so assured, Petit is able to use alternating narratives to tell the story, gifting it with the full Technicolor treatment of old. He has used this device before in his novel *The Human Pool*, which also touched on issues surrounding the holocaust, but here, Petit is taking on a wider perspective on human culpability and its requisite frailty. He is unflinching in his study of everyday evil, whose nature is more particular to his prose than to his work in film, which is more to do with the existential as expressed in practical situations and arrangements.

There are many other film directors who have written novels, from Pasolini to Peter Greenaway and Neil Jordan, but Petit has always been able to fuse the two forms with ease and make them truly reflective of each other, through the already stated power of his fictional voice. He has spoken in interview on a number of occasions about the dwindling opportunities open to artists of his particular stamp. Of his film made with Iain Sinclair, *London Orbital*, he said; 'We thought it was the beginning of something. It turned out to be the end of something..' in terms of appealing to the current trends of broadcast commissioners, so there is a sense that his return to prose is a safer and possibly more secure place from which to launch a creative assault. There is also in the crime novel genre to which these books belong, a formula to be enhanced or even subverted and Petit does that here effortlessly. The intricacy of his approach to structure is one accomplishment, which is then compounded by the free form roaming through the streets of Berlin, as the linerality of the plot pans, tracks and dollies film-like through events and locations, casting what would have seemed familiar with an iridescent glow of frightening immediacy.

While Shlegl and his contempories have a touch of the Dashiel Hammett's in their dialogue;

> *'Don't waste your time on it,' Niebe looked at him archly, 'Its not as though homicide was your beat.'*

They are also fully aware of the viscerality of the environment within which they find themselves. The obscenity of Nazism is a scar on every passing cloud and a clot in every rainfall. Context and atmosphere stain them daily and that they are able to progress at all is testament to Petit's skills as a storyteller. Denied one form of expression at any given time, Petit is able to access another and bend it to his will, lifting a story with which we might think we are over familiar, beyond and above our expectations.

Unlike what seems like everyone else, I do not believe a review is there to encapsulate and tell you the whole story of its subject book in so many thousand words. Its purpose should only be to make you want to read the bloody thing. I am attempting to give a flavour of the approach and purpose that I detected while reading and engaging with the book as a means of encouragement and because I believe there is so much more to be found in Petit's writing than there is in other novels of recent history. The esteemed director Lindsay Anderson once said of the equally esteemed John Ford that, 'there are two types of film maker; the journeyman and the poet..' Ford was both.

As is Petit – in the truest sense of the word and chiefly because of the journey that he takes us on.

The reader and viewer are combined as never before. Petit is also an expert dramatist in his handling of scenes and prospective audience. We are instantly there in the story, transported by relatable prose that often seems to rhyme with our own needs for engagement and confession, and immersed in the glut and the grime of what is presented as well as the smells and the look of the dead.

The soon to be dead and the drear expectation they face is another theme of the story which courses through the book like a river of rain on pained streets. Shlegl, in one sense, on the wrong side of western sympathies is battling overwhelming odds as tries to solve the case. The book's other protagonist Sybil is also fighting her own small crusade of escape and resistance against increasingly querulous odds and the fact that their joint aims and issues combine is down to Petit's skill as structuralist and observer. He avoids uneasy sentiment and tells it 'like it is.' That many of us do not know what it is or indeed what it looks like is laid out in the writing and evidenced in the stare Petit gives us in his author's photo on the back jacket flap of the cover.

This book, then, sensually packaged by Simon and Shuster, has the texture of the darkly desirable object. That the object in question often sears and scorches us as we consume it, is one of the reasons art as a whole and literary accomplishment as a specific practise are necessary. We are not what we eat, wear or read, but are instead reflective of what we take from those engagements. The warped history of the past has smeared many a mirror. Chris Petit returns our scrutiny to some of life's darkest windows and points of observation, through his unflinching examination and documentation of moments of both weakness and renunciation. His recent film for television, *Content* was in part concerned with a fictionalised rumination on his own aging and current position or place in the modern creative context of craft over technology, as emphasised by his relationship with his children and in this novel, he asks similar questions of a developing society, which until a few years ago was still marked by the atrocities of the holocaust. As we enter a time when the last survivors of that event are dead or dying, the ignorance of current practise edges those events ever closer to conjecture. The SS and their counterparts are all around us still, disguised as fat faced fools in this country,

France, Russia, and indeed everywhere else, and as new priorities take over, we are in danger of losing a vital part of the chill that charms our fears and paranoia.

In fashioning a story that fits with the current trend for murder based fiction on the page and screen, Petit in this highly relevant novel, reminds us that we have not risen far from the mire, and that with the pretence lifted, the harsh light of the day we have made for ourselves scours the lines in the dwindling flesh of each face. We are all butchers, in terms of how we disseminate, divide and forego connection and in terms of how we disregard others, misplace value and gorge and choke at will on the events that surround us and the produce of the society that we have made for ourselves. This book allows the reader to place his or her own heart on the spiritual counter and to weigh the consequence of a Kundera-like laughter and forgetting, slicing through the shared aromas of defeat and questioning all we'd consume. It is a book which wraps the still bleeding past in its own form of greaseproof paper; a 482 page slab of reality that resists refridgeration and which will only improve on the shelf. As you finger your way through its elegant pages, the porousness of your flesh will be stained by the blood and lost fluids of its characters and you will be reminded that no truly worthy subject for fiction is easily dismissed or forgotten. The masterfully conjured faces of the characters within will fill your own and you will inhale every taste and sensation described.

The Butchers of Berlin is the new film by Chris Petit. As you read and consume it, and regardless of diet, you will know what it is to be meat.

WE ARE ALL LEPERS

A review of Josie Demuth's *Liggers & Dreamers: Tales From The London Art Scene*

In Thin Man Press's new publication, Josie Demuth artfully collects a representative body of skilled, if somewhat charmless objectionables, negotiating their way through contemporary art's shallow waters. These waters do not deepen when the assorted Liggers are able to gatecrash the Venice Biennale Art fair near the end of the book – where the reknowned and scantily disguised 'Koko Ono' receives a lifetime achievement award – and indeed a life on the waves frames the end of the book where the various characters we have encountered along the way set sail from St Katherine's Dock on a seemingly Fellini-esque soiree, along the Thames onboard 'the great 'Cork Street Wino.'

It's uncertain on a first reading whether the fourteen protagonists cleverly profiled at the start of the book deserve celebration, but perhaps that is the point. In focusing on the cockroaches who gather at the edge of the frame, the substance of the paintings and art that provide context for the stories and tales is smudged into soft focus. This reflects society's current love of style over substance, what might be called the Ribena or even marshmellow culture, that has replaced a time when all the world was sharp fruit and stone like gobstoppers.

Our reader's eye is therefore encouraged to roam camera like across incidents and connections between characters. Ms Demuth shows a novelist's eye can be matched to a conductor's ear as she draws our attention to her character's consuming passions. There is a great deal of dialogue in the book, all reflective of current London colloquialisms and these make the book accessible to those for whom a slim volume is ideal company on a journey to work, hour in the park, or welcome respite between other actions. In detailing this vibrant scene of self absorbtion so precisely, *Liggers and Dreamers* is more akin to having a fluid hologram in your pocket than it is to a piece of literature. The characters breathe, shout and interact, showing both secretiveness and exuberance, with their frequent boisterousness exposing the relatively small regard even the practitioners of the London art scene hold their own context in. Contemporary art, it seems to me, has never been concerned with its own process, or practise (see Damien Hirst's Spot paintings or much, if not all of Jeff Koon's output, both alluded to in the book) as it is with its own justification: 'I earn therefore I am' seems to be the prime validation and as Deborah, Simon, Ashpak, Tony Phun, Audrey and Irreverent George present themselves along with their various bête noires and fellows in the art of intrusion, they seem to regard themselves as part of the second wave of that success. A private view becomes an internal process that a public show provides context for. As you formulate what you think of the work you must fuel the brain with as much champagne and canapés as your unworthy soul can accommodate.

Food and more importantly drink, fuels these narratives, making the final river image pertinent, and indeed Josie's Liggers float and bob on its unending surfaces, spotting and commenting on each other as they sail from glass to glass. When, near the end the Liggers notice that Bill Brown's Albermarle Street Gallery is temporarily empty, they bemoan not the absence of art, but the absence of its commemoration, revealing their own desire to crown themselves art's designated celebrants. It strikes me that the contemporary art scene is concerned far more with how the work is regarded than with the work itself. Art has always been what the artists says it is, from the Neanderthal in the cave, through to Rembrandt's mirroring of his own aging, via Duchamp and onto Sarah Lucas' fried eggs, but *Liggers and Dreamers*' true interest for me, lays in how its vignette based structure allows the protagonists to become their own Pictures at an Exhibition. Whether that exhibition is reflective of anyone else is not for me to say, but it certainly details life as it is lived in the privileged Cork Street ghetto. A great many of us who live and who come from London and are perhaps residents of the suburbs like to know what's on offer, even if we do not always avail ourselves of it. Meryl, Eustacia, Audrey and the rest of the posse are dependent on and indeed defined by those opportunities. Whereas Beckett once detailed his walks with his father across fields close to Dublin with 'their hands forgotten in each other', these Liggers, Dreamers and Aspirants log and detail every step their will take to accomplish preeminence. This idealised state or dream strikes me as being one of self preservation only, where lifestyle supersedes life and the choices we make are governed by promotion, propulsion and popularity. Josie Demuth thereby proves herself as an adept storyteller, chronicler and journalist. The stance revealed in her book can be an obvious one in some contexts but its a statement made valid in this useful book, as we are warned that the modern world's fascination with itself can ultimately take us nowhere than up and then back down the same river. The wind is behind us and yet our wings are not reached for and so we choose not to fly.

Liggers and Dreamers is a timely portrait of an attitude and an age. Thin Man Press have produced another beautifully made and printed paperback that feels and smells appealing to the senses. Once you have read the book, hold it up to your ear and you will continue to hear the voices within chattering away and glorying in their own escapades and endeavours. To expand the creative analogy further; Ms Demuth also paints her liggers clearly, with succinct and encompassing descriptions, from the observation that all Liggers are Lepers, to the Reverend/Irreverant George's (Priest by day/Thief by night) observation that one of his fellow liggers tried to take communion four times, hunkering after the wafer in much the same way as they might for a private view's tray of comestibles. This book is a tasty array of starters and implied courses. Once you have consumed it, I recommend a slow contemplative look at Velasquez as dessert.

DAYS IN SONG:

A teview of Knifeforksandspoonspress' *New Poetry Anthology -Yesterday's Music Today* (Ed. Mike Ferguson & Rupert Loydell)

Poems are carriers: Of thought, image, perception, experience and more often than not, memory, even if those past moments can still be felt and tasted on the air. This new and vital anthology of music related poetry assists the capturing and containment of those things not always easily expressed; the sensory and emotional pleasures gained by a dedication to listening and making music and to the very changes that music brings about in the head, heart and it has to be said, feet.

Lovingly if economically produced, the book feels like the ultimate album insert, a comprehensive listing of voices and information. If only every album could come with such a book. Indeed, one's favourite records for those devoted to the music of yesterday, often loom large in the mind, from the lavish booklets accompanying many prog rock releases to the iconic stature of the last century's greatest recorded accomplishments; *Sgt Pepper* towers as *The Wall* for some may teeter, yet nothing ever topples if it's for the Crimson King. The modern trend for lavish box sets with their extensive essays and merchandise reproduces this, but for those whose pockets do not reach Australia, context is kept out of frame. The poems included in this book all enshrine their inspirations perfectly, whether general of specific, from Jimmy Juniper's likening of the sound of a saxophone to that of a poem, through Sarah James' dazzling word-jazz in 'Road Tripping/Remixing Life's playlists/In the Gap' with its 'Bosom. Besom. Birchstick. Broomed..The ear's osscicles shaped as high hat, cello and flute..' and onto Jay Ramsay's 'Homage to Beethoven' in which he describes and captures the images and impressions received whilst listening to the *Sonata in C Major, Opus III* on a motorway drive. Pop, Punk, Rock, Jazz, Blues, New wave and Classical combine in this book, showing that a love and connection with music is not and should not be defined by genre, style or period, with those who love Bartok finding help with King Crimson and those who like Punk perhaps viewing Stravinsky or famous

Greek serialist Ianis Xenakis, whose 'structure of seconds' passes through the living frame' in Jimmy Juniper's poem.

Robert Sheppard's extraordinary 'Angel at the Junk Box' is a small modernist masterpiece dedicated to the memory of Frank Sinatra in which 'every blip is a dizzy how.' There are not many books or indeed poems that ask you to 'Mute up your factitious sensation..Until the last syllable cymbals out..' but you will find them here in both Sheppard and Juniper's numerous pieces, along with Sue Birchenough's 'Aspects of One' ('Under my Skin you sing'), through to Sheila E. Murphy's 'Flute' which details how the flute 'eludes the calculus of impromptu masculinity..pierces the thin wall of breath and cloud..and honours learned signals still in season.'

Mike Ferguson and Rupert Loydell in compiling and editing this anthology have shown their own expertise, skill and dedication as both cultural professors and Poets. Loydell's 'Almost Nothing to do with Rock' labels that genre as 'a defiant shout against suffering' and 'This Place is a Shelter' shows how through a simple listing of types of song both deterioration and continuance can be countenanced. Ferguson's homage to Rickie Lee Jones, Heavy Metal and the relevance of Graham Nash's *Our House* to his own childhood is deeply affecting and artfully expressed.

Music and memory combine consistently in this collection, from Norman Jope's recollection of two landmark gigs of Daevid Allen's *Gong* in 1971 and 1989 to M.C. Caseley's summoning of Howling Wolf in the lobby of the Bloomsbury Hotel, all blades drawn across the 'killing floor'. Memory than becomes the means with which to reflect on the musical experience, evident in Angela Topping's poem 'Guitar' ('when you play its a love machine, a steel sounder, memory maker, heart lifter) and David Kennedy's dissection of the function of a pianist, through to David Hart's remarkable philosophy on the music of trees, where lovers sit 'very still while breeze through the leaves entertained us..' And this triggering of thought and sensation, as enabled by music seems to be part of the book's greater purpose. In attempting to capture and express so many core experiences from its core set of contributors, the cumulative effect, to my eyes and ears at least, is that the music we love, once heard, stays with us in ways deeper than we realise, no matter how self aware we are. The songs and pieces that reflect and return us to our deeper selves have, rather like love or it has to be said, bacteria, attached themselves to our

DNA, to that part of our structure that music as a whole tries to echo; the hidden, intangible soul that does not exist only at the point of departure, but which informs and explains our irrational, spiritual self. The part of us that cannot be changed or disguised because of the demands of everyday life. Music and our need for it are our internal rhyme, too often neglected in the blank verse of our accepted existence.

Ester Muchawksky-Schnapper's 'Satanic Music' is perhaps evidence of this, as 'a stinking barrack, an infested mattress, a watery soup is all there is/and finally a merciful sleep lifting you out to short freedom and its celestial music..' as is the 'loose boned blues' of Paul Hawkins' 'Number 8 Claremont Road: Red Room;' Therefore, *Yesterday's Music Today* contains poems and Poets who extend the remit of what is possible when we think about music, and indeed, detail what music is for. In displaying the likes, loves and connections enclosed, the editors and contributors have attempted to give poetry the same validation as song. In this country poetry is often downgraded in the public conscience, (whereas song even in its lowest form rarely is) resident only on tube train advertisements and badly written billboards, or else it is falls close to the too worthy ghetto of the self obsessed sunstantialist, detailing his or her experience as seminal and useful to all whilst being shared in unknown or culturally sealed rooms. Here, Ferguson and Loydell have released an album of favoured artists, a small scale Supergroup with a far reaching outlook, each one capable of preaching for their given cause, while at the same time guiding and offering full explanation for their own very personal loves.

Its an invaluable book and one which should be on sale wherever music is. When you buy your copy, recommend it to your local record shop or HMV (I know there are still a few out there) and return a love of music back to the high streets and sidestreets in which it was first discovered. You can also use this book as a means with which to discover some of the artists within whom you may be unfamiliar, from Howling Wolf to Xenakis to Rickie Lee Jones. If the book is an example of preaching to the coverted, than that congregation needs to garner itself a new one. Take this along as your own musical Gideon and spread the word so that the icloud generation can at some point extract their heads and recapture the sensations that those of us who have loved music for and in the ways it was originally intended to be received, have always had, as a secret, personal and then publically shared discovery. Yesterdays' music may detail past artists and experiences but they are still a vital part of both the day and the oncoming dark.

As Jim Morrison said: 'When the Music's over/Turn out the light..'

This book and these poems capture the sound of the flame.

COLD GHOST AVALANCHE

A review of Rupert M. Loydell's *Lovesongs For An Echo*

Rupert M Loydell's latest chapbook is an elegant requiem for the forgotten sound of meaning between significant others. The songs of absence and dislocation to be found within take the form of a series of prose poems charting the possible decline in the fictionalised protagonist's relationship and marriage, necessitating both regret and reflection in a series of pastoral settings subject to deterioration and leading to survival and a sense of renunciation. The flood or avalanche of memories (the title of this article stemming from the first line of the poem entitled, *Ice Copy*) are the core of the book, which knowing something of Loydell's dedication to contemporary music, produces a folksome, even conceptual air, leavened by references to such luminaries as the progenitor of Ambient Music, (I recommend RML's separately printed *8 Mesostics For Brian Eno* heartily), Hiroshi Yoshimura, Mark Rothko and the band Earlyguard.

In referencing numerous musical styles and practises as Loydell does in his other work, this book could also be his take on Dylan's *Blood on the Tracks*, as it rakes over the dead leaves of forgotten summers in the geographical and spiritual sense, evidenced particularly in *No Engine of a Narrative's* ;

'This is not the place I thought I'd live.
Stuttered sentences and forgotten dreams.
Hesitant hellos.
More and more goodbyes.'

This poem is perhaps a little commonplace at times, but the air of dislocation is breathed anew throughout the book, as in the one line Poem;

The Legacy of a Dream;
An empty lexicon. I don't remember. Part of us will never be.

The echoes that we are all subject to, house the unanswered questions, the recriminations, the doubts, if you will, that blight us all and

Loydell submits them to a useful scrutiny. He directs our attention to the surrounding air, encouraging us to examine all that we take for granted. In the brief poem, *Blink*, he asks us 'What is there to see or understand?' and therefore accomplishes the aim of all art and writing: to fuse the practitioner with the recipient, calling for their direct engagement and solidarity, in a simple, direct and poetic manner, separate that is, to the specific demands of poetry itself. Poetic impulse is the point here; the observation and philosophy that occurs when the terrain of the heart has been rescinded or broached. In this volume that impulse and desire is shown as something to be shared and as a place where those not as well versed in literature as Loydell is, can find a satisfactory summation. That RML breaches and bridges the forms is proof enough of his skill and allows the poetic thought or observation and the structured poem to co-exist. He reflects this literary marriage between head and heart for the reader (if not between man and wife in the implied story) in the rolling stream of everyday imagery used in the opening poem *One of Those Days*:

'One of those silver grey days, sun hardly up, tide still, mudbanks drying out, water reflecting purple..'

or *Clouds*'

A partial eclipse is not the same as temporary blindness..'

Each showing how we are able to re-imagine and re-interpret the world after heartbreak or pain on any number of levels, even as failure and/or disappointment robs us of perspective. The pieces, therefore form a progression, a narrative of sorts, an implied concept, as I have suggested that demystifies the process of art while at the same time securing its accomplishments. *The Nine Postcards* sequence uses artful and affecting imagery, such as the aforementioned 'Cold ghost Avalanche, ' or 'Madness is a medicine, ' or 'Let it rain. Let us navigate the heavy seas of love..' to make its points but does so in an understated and relateable way. Modernist poetry often squeezes the wounded thought to produce a haemorrage or (sometimes) clot of language, but here Loydell draws attention to what most people envisage a poem to be. He then adapts it into the poetically infused prose of the journal or dream diary. His pieces, in transposing these forms, seek connection and redress what we all know and observe around us in, if not new clothes entirely, then certainly in freshly laundered ones. He has allowed us to see some of his private fears and experiences (without implying this is any way autobiographical) while at the same time remaining in control. The sometimes conservative approach to language in other parts of the book conceals a darker fire and leads us to question all things that come before us, just as we are questioning those for whom we have lost devotion.

But more importantly, these prose poems shows the writer conversing, arguing and examining the facts of his/her and their detachment. The levels of despair are eased by a dignified and mature consideration of the circumstances that created them and deal sensitively with the speaker's concerns as a constellation of emotions known to us all, forms his existant universe. Introspection expands into said philosophy and the hearts journalism creates headlines for reader and poet alike.

Saluting the Distance and *Without Pity* are powerful examinations of what the playwright Howard Brenton referred to as 'the foul rag and bone shop of the heart' in his novel 'Diving for Pearls' and the long poem near the end of the book, *One and One*, is a masterful marrying of man and his interior landscape to the environment within which he finds himself, from the 'peculiar smells in the corner of the garden, ' through his favoured writers 'orbits and circles..matters of belief and memory..', to the phantom existence of an imagined pet dog. The idea of vanished worlds and shattered landscape both within and without, above and before us and him, is varigated by a look at the tragedy of the diminished bookshop in the poem *Fever*, and *Endless Trains* takes us from Dartmoor, Italy and New York all the way to Agnes Martin via 'Hungarian plum and honey spirit.'

Occasionally rhythms and image choices jar and a supposed flow is truncated but always with purpose and design. It's questionable whether we read poetry to collate the thoughts of others or to try and mirror our own perceptions, bit whatever the case, these pieces eloquently convey the power and conviction of this particular voice. Here you will find dedication and reference that will allow you to chart your own rises and descents. Poems flavour he air and fill the space within which they are encountered with brightly drawn feelings and the resonance of new silences. The reverberations of one heart to anothers, produces the echo shared by our common sympathies and the empathy we can show while reading and dealing with each other is another theme I detected on reading. If we can engender such thoughts with restraint and economy we are succeeding and elucidating the unversed and preparing the ground for greater and deeper investigation. As Loydell states in the final line of *The Notes that We Hear*, his tribute to the poet, David Miller:

'From the fragments of the world we make meaning, from the notes that we hear we make song.'

OF THEE I SING

An overview of *An Aesthetic Of Obscenity* 5 Novels By Jeff Nuttall
(Verbivoracious Press, 2016, Ed. By Douglas Field and Jay Jeff Jones)

Jeff Nuttall's professional life started and ended in relative normality, first as schoolteacher and latterly mainstream film and television actor, but the dynamic central thrust of his work as writer, performer and innovator strained the belts of convention, as tightly as his notable girth. This new release by the VP Vestschrift Series of a quintet of seminal works by Nuttall, written between 1975 and 1994, shows not only how expert their author was as a stylist and storyteller but also how important he was as a thinker and spokesman for writing with a capital W, art with a capital A, and response with a suitably big R. He raged WAR on convention, first directly and then I am sure, in repose.

In editors Douglas Field and Jeff Jay Jones' introduction, Nuttall is reported as formerly telling IT, that 'I paint poems, sing sculptures and draw novels' and so he does here, blending the forms in these effortlessly successful experiments and playgrounds for prose. The creamy heft of the paperback brings something of Nuttall's silky corpulence to the hand and one is reminded instantly of his presence and voice on reading. *The Gold Hole* and *Snipe's Spinster* are perhaps the most well known of the five books collected here but each is vital. For instance, the much neglected and shortest book, *Teeth*, written in a day after a booze infused challenge at The Groucho Club, shows how the most shallow of prompts can allow for the most profound and entertaining of speeches; Chapter Sixteen's

'Day spread itself apologetically, the way they sometimes do.'

echoes the opening lines of Beckett's *Murphy* beautifully.

As the writer of one of the most famous books on sixties' counter culture, *Bomb Culture*, Nuttall knew what to exploit and how to seek and advance renewal. His easeful control of all areas of literary, artistic and musical innovation were in many ways more impressive than his contemporary BS Johnson's insistence on his somewhat stringent ideas for reforms to the style and content of the modern (or postmodern) novel. This is evidenced in specific details, such as references to the Edinburgh haircut received, marked and celebrated in the opening pages of *Snipe's Spinster*. The prose sings due to its careful power and clarity and transmutes images upwards to the air, with the grace of cigar smoke, curling and coiling fresh thought. Written in first person, Snipe himself is a thinly disguised Nuttall who leads us through the remains of the society he signposted in *Bomb Culture* towards an acid tinged dawn. Pot (no pun intended) shots at various figures occur, most notably old IT associate, Mick Farren, but there is in the spite and subsequent drug struck languor, both an invective and charge at and for the pivotal forces of change. Sublime sentences drift past;

> 'The acid wore off around half past eight and I went home, clip-clop down the mountain...lights of Leith winking like dropped glass..'

Or

> '..the rich, bright light that had shot across the city into my time-warps, swam in browns:'

Snipe, after his embibements of Guinness, light suppers of Ryvita and cheese, experiments in homosexuality and desk tested erections thanks to female student Janet, resulting in ejaculations

> 'that feel like a 'bullet being drawn from a wound..delicately, carefully and with endless subsequent happiness'

meets up with associate and road manager Crane who after briefly swapping conspiracy stories tries to inveigle Snipe into the kidnapping of a Government minister's daughter. The ensuing romp is ripe with the fruits of invention as *Snipe's Spinster*, an aspect of the first person narrator's own personality is endlessly subdued and challenged in 83 of modern literature's most entertaining and subversive pages.

The House Party is even more revolutionary. It does what the aforementioned BS Johnson attempted with more brio than even he achieved in the Shandy-esque *Travelling People*, as form and layout, footnote, marginalia and illustration are blended into the thrust of the text to truly create the idea of novel as sculpture, as work of art in and of itself. This, then, is writing as its own lysergic. Rather than something that has resulted from the indulgence of substance, this is the substance itself. As Nuttall says in his introduction to the text, the book exists as an attempt to extend the possibilities of the blown mind and to see what that can really achieve. Full realisation at any cost. *The House Party* as a force for change and experiment, attempts to build on Joyce's intentions in *Finnegans Wake* which as quoted in the introduction was written 'about dream, in the language of dream and about a dreaming man.' and succeeds admirably. A parody of the country house novel it speaks through the experience of its four main characters and the sheer exuberance of its prose to the voice in the head of each reader that none of us can quite discern but which we each perhaps suspect is not entirely our own;

> 'I could nudge you their nature, the lilyblow daffodils set in reverse, the childslace cupcakes turned in their cream, the swell and the suck-swell.'

> 'Lay in the wet, in the swim, in the fishes and kippers that float up her fuck-tunnel,' said George.

The mind shouts and flings its dream-paint over the drab confines of the skull, re-ordering it in an instant and teaching us that behind words and language itself is the vibrant desire to express every facet of existence and experience. All of Nuttall's writing in this edition and what I know of his work through the beginnings of *The People Show* and the *Performance Art Scripts* are excavations of language and its possibilities. Indeed, they become challenges to the accepted and acceptable modes of expression that are often clogged or truncated by the pedestrian demands of common discourse. If you don't have an appetite for Hippo pudding by page 100, than sir, madam, you have no soul to speak of. And that is not something you will find in Robert Harris, or young master Amis.

As Field and Jones relay in their introduction *The Gold Hole* explores the 'psychosexual landscapes of a methedrine fuelled poet, Sam' and his declining relationship with former paramour, Jaz, set against the backdrop of the Moors Murders. In one chapter the aborted foetus of their lovechild speaks in eerie counterpoint to the novel's setting, an innovation that certainly puts Ian McEwan's latest novel *Nutshell*, to shame with its cursory retelling of Hamlet. Here is real tragedy writ large, and with a stunning level of precision and skill:

> 'During the first weeks I suppose you could have described me as an impulse of air. I was a small crisis of energy...'

'At eight weeks I had something of the fish, something of the plant and something of the human...'

'Sometimes the voice was like cocoa. I was often brown..'

The revelations drift past like shudders in the amniotic fluid, making us all mothers to our deeper and perhaps deepest levels of response. What strikes you by reaching the third book collected here is just how rich and strange Nuttall's work and that of his contemporaries was and continues to be, whether living or dead. Modernist and the finest examples of post modernist thought and practise from Johnson to Paul Ableman, Laura Mulvey, Jane Arden and Helene Cixous and all points inbetween, exists beyond the constraints of their original forms and approaches. There is no dichotomy when I state that this child of Nuttall's labours literally infuses death with a new form of life. Writing must transcend the page while still being of it and while contemporary performance, conceptualism and music often achieves this in isolated or singular examples, it is in someone like Jeff Nuttall that we see a sustained search for renewal of thought and response in every means possible.

Obscenity, if handled correctly as it is here on many of this volume's seductive pages, is a weapon that flies with the grace of a bird. All of Nuttall's writing chimes and resounds with that grace as he aims his flight in our direction. He wants us to celebrate and elevate the only true things we can draw on, where a 'hand at the heaving ocean' can bid the deep oyster to suck. The body's lowest forms of function are consummations of experience in Nuttall's worldview and sperm is mere paint in his hands. Piss revives as blood fuels. Shit affirms an intention. A kiss leads to clashes. A fuck makes the soul levitate.

In *The Patriarchs*, Nuttall explores his own writerly predicament as one of the successors to the previous literary generation though a canny exploration of the poet Jack Roberts, a figure bearing an uncanny resemblance to Ted Hughes. A symposium at a location that strongly sisters the Arvon foundation allows for responses to ebb and flow between writer and reader as the celebrity of the word is expunged. The limits and reaches of poetry and poetic definition are explored and commented on by Nuttall as unammed narrator, again by placing himself at the centre of the text. This once again fuses the forms as the density of the poetry on offer swirls around us;

> 'Dancelocks lopped to the stubble by slums, /She scrabbles in refuse, can't kiss or sing/ But thrashes on mattresses straddled by starvelings, '

and makes the novelist a conductor for and of the storm and to extend the metaphor, orchestra of response and intention. Nuttall as narrator comes not to praise or to bury Jack Roberts' Caesar, but rather to examine his laurel wreath, the golden crown of achievement afforded to him and all of the other great voices of linguistic pursuit;

> Beneath your voice, sticky flies play, choral over the filth of your dominion.

This truly is writing as art. An aesthetic on beauty as well as obscenity in which the sound cloud (meant in the poetic sense and nothing to do with the interweb) created by words and their inherent meanings and intentions teleports the reader into higher levels of consciousness. One is struck by how useful the book is and how appealing because of the extent to which it provokes and elevates both engagement and response in the reader. You, we, I become active participants not just in and because of content as it is relates to us, but to the act of what encountering text is and can be, along with the potential of transcendence.

This collection is a riot of words formed by the decimations of convention won and raged by writers like Nuttall, BS Johnson, Sinclair Meiles, Heathcote Williams, Samuel Beckett, William Burroughs et al in the long decades before. It is both sharply observed and as adventurously surrealist as David Gascoyne in his prime or as coruscating as the poetry and poetics of George Barker, WS Graham, or latterly Iain Sinclair, Alan Moore or Brian Catling. Nuttall's own court of miracles – to quote Catling's recent poetry collection – is also one informed by the virtues of the entertainer he indubitably was. His work in the 1970s with *The People Show* and other theatrical endeavours such as *A Nice Quiet Night* and *The Railings in the Park*, can still be glimpsed in the pleasantly familiar realism of *Teeth*, whose study of marital infidelity finds greater relevance through the feral fury of its female protagonists.

Jeff Nuttall was a teacher right to the end of his life, instructing us all on the potentials of our own efforts and showing how one could still throw the same sort of signal flares that Be-bop Jazz once fashioned, and that the theatrical Avant Garde developed across the other artistic forms in which it found fruition. He shimmered and glowed through all of his pursuits, cometing in from the basement of Better Books in 1967, to the old Traverse Theatre, Edinburgh in 1971, all the way through to Greenaway's *Prospero's Books* and bizarrely, ITV's *Kavanagh QC* in the nineties. He was a star who shaped the sky to his own image and who allowed the song of art to attain the highest scale. This new reprint by the Verbivoracious Press re-introduces a master to his hopefully willing pupils and quickly and effectively re-orders the house of study into a new and thrilling combination. It is no stretch to say that the works collected in this volume are what Sterne would have grown into if he had an inch of Methusaleh's reach.

The furthest branches of the tree are where the bird is now singing of forgotten stories and books strong enough to resist the fires of enveloping time. Amongst and above those spires of nature I am certain that the spirit of Jeff Nuttall capers nimbly beside the divine Ken Campbell and a chorus of other great ghosts and voices, from Chaucer to Charlie Parker, that are still responsible for our acceptance and understanding of what an idea is and can be. Nuttall's house party is large enough to contain all of our efforts and the lives that surround them. As stated in marginalia on page 163:

> 'Hack at the curtains. Hurl the stair rods at the windows in the front door. Slash the silken ankles'

And walk,

and as you do so, sing with this book as your guide.

HEARD IN THE HAND

A review of John Riordan's *Sound And Vision - A Guide To Music's Cult Artists From Punk And Indie Through To Hip-Hop, Dance Music And Beyond* (Dog And Bone Books 2016)

For those of you bored of hearing of the decline of modern music and the means to receive it, John Riordan's new book of band listings and biographies is a exuberant reminder of the voices, songs and bands that really mattered. Newly published by Dog and Bone, Riordan's concise containments of the artists of offer, along with his colourful and playful illustrations make this book the perfect gift for the young player who's personal zoo of reference stretches no further back than the Arctic Monkeys. Here Patti and the Salford Smiths rub shoulders with Devo and The Ramones, while Tom Waits gargles and Harry Parches in the background. The Buzzcocks shave the whiskers of the old asunder as the pixies magic their way free from grunge to attain a higher noise fed glory. Kraftwerk sit alongside Chic and even Spinal Tap are given equal billing. Riordan is clearly concerned with the name changers and there is something uncanny and delightful in his drawing style, making these players of one story, from the sainted (to me at the very least) Kate Bush to Run DMC all the way down to John Grant and Kendrick Lamar. Here are musicians whose writing has inspired Riordan to celebrate them with a vision of their own. Cartoons breed ownership. We align ourselves with them as children and when encountering them as adults obsess or collect them, in terms of comics, graphic novels of emblems of enthusiasm. Riordan's rich visuals show how illustration of this sort is a short hand for enthusiasm and how each artist, from Funkadelic to Primal Scream exists in a box and caption of their own making. They are the unimpeachable ones, able to resist all challenges, changes and compromises, either by remaining a part of their time (The Sex Pistols, The New York Dolls), reflecting it, (Bon Iver, Elbow), or moving through it, unconcerned with anything else other than their own imperatives (Nick Cave, Joanna Newsome, Beck, The flaming Lips). Everyone you would want to read about is here and Riordan's text is as concise as it is informative, a fine example being

Riordan's telling us in the trivia box of his Aphex Twin entry on video director Chris Cunningham's predilection for Robot porn.

The book is a beautiful object in all senses of the word (and drawing) being 160 hardbacked pages of attractive image and text that would excite and appeal to the uninformed. It is also a happy companion of the new waver of a certain age, as it provides a musical scrapbook for a once challenging youth, in which every trip to the now defunct Our Price retail chain or still surviving HMV yielded yet greater glory. In this grave stained year of loss across the arts, John Riordan's beautiful book is a totem and token of the music that roared and rechallenged the day. There was a time when artists did not seek to build their careers on the cake of celebrity. They took their nourishment from deeper waters. In this vibrant and colourful book, author and illustrator allows those somewhat neglected springs to rise and recolour the faded earth. Seek out this book if you desire the sound and vision of a fresh library of souls. They will be felt and be heard in your hand.

THE POEM IS PART OF THE EYE:

An appreciation of Ruth Bayer's *Skipping To Armageddon: Current 93 and Friends* (Strange Attractor Press, 2016)

What we know of the world comes from our journey through it. What we observe, reconsider or act upon. In Ruth Bayer's new collection of photographs, *Skipping to Armageddon*, published by the innovatory Strange Attractor Press, we glimpse a deeper world of understanding, both in terms of reference and intimacy as the book visually charts the friendship between Bayer and her main subject, poet, artist and musician, David Tibet. Tibet is the seminal star of the esoteric underground comprised as noted in David Keenan's *England's Hidden Reverse*, (also published by Strange Attractor) of *Coil, Nurse to Wound, Whitehouse* and *Current 93*. The journey between muse and artist, artist and muse starts in 1987 and ends in the present day. Bayer, an Austrian photographer living in Tufnel Park, encounters and befriends Tibet after he has moved into her former room. This sharing of intimacy and to some extent, origin deepens to the point in which Ruth becomes a much prized visual biographer of that entire scene of artists who emerged out of the post punk days of Throbbing Gristle et all, to create and explore new areas of industrialisation, religion and the esoteric in music, visuals and sound.

Tibet's stare is all encompassing on account of his elegant features and large eyes and the first photograph, a simple portrait of a bare chested David shows a level of daring that one is still not quite accustomed to. The stare is one of both welcome and challenge, a statement of intent and identity and therefore an object which in the purest sense, transcends its birthing form. It is a wonderful way to open a book of photographs, perhaps the only way as the subject addresses the viewer directly, speaking through a closed mouth on the eloquence of the soul. His image is fused with the photographer as author/presenter and the twin messages thereby parent each other.

Photography is often about containment of the subject and the imposition of style, whether it's the artful but artificial shadows of David Bailey or the all consuming ones of Bill Brandt, but in Ruth

Bayer's work one sees a freeing of the image. A gentility of approach that frames the subject not with lines or borders but with the true language of light. Tibet fills the literal frame as he does in all senses in his other endeavours, but is here placed in a gentle cage (if that isn't too much of an oxymoron) of friendship, a protective shell which shows him, even at the start of their association as someone to be cherished and held in esteem by the camera's eye. The light from the right of picture fuses with his shoulder and cheek as opposed to layering over him or coating him with God's paint and the monochrome nature of the image allows his face to become part of the page as opposed to being just presented by it. It is, at the risk of too much contrivance, an image that speaks in all the codes of introduction and because of Tibet's physiognomy, is practically Vermeer-like in terms of affect and complexion.

As the images accrue – as one does not feel like one is turning the pages of a book but rather journeying through an accumulation of time – Tibet's fascination and mystery combine with something far more celebratory. A section set in Brookwood Cemetary, with Tibet, Freya Aswynn, Douglas P. And Rose McDowall shows friendship displayed artfully and joyously among the graves. The richness of the black and white imagery creating the impression of feeling, texture and therefore colour without having to display it. Here are people powerfully alive and able to translate a deathly setting into an expression of sanctified renewal by simple gestures of positivism and consolidation. That this section comes after photos of Tibet looking like the survivor of a decadent night, Bayer is showing us both wing and underside of her particular angel. Tibet is a muse for Bayer in a different way that Beatrice was for Dante, or Marianne for Mick (or Keith). He is someone and something that allows her to examine what the stare is for, and how if it comes from the right person, it can guide us towards a greater truth.

Tibet's truth is formed from his studies of the esoteric side of Christianity and mysticism and his attachment and obsession with Noddy, that great emblem of children's fiction. The pictures of various Noddy dolls bedeck Tibet like the flowers he clearly sees them as being and it is Bayer's sincere approach that allows this. Although there are a several colour shots and styles of shot (from fish eye lens to landscape), it is the music that Bayer feels emanating from her friend that reaches us through the page. The poetic surge that powers through love and friendship skips through this book on the wings of light, providing the title and alluding to Tibet and his associates missions of examination and recovery.

What the book conveys above all else is something that John Berger would clearly approve of; the photo as eye itself, rather than object before it. An artistic blend of message, medium and music that makes the best art and fuses the forms. The photograph as poem, birthed by the circumstances that have taken place before the button is pressed, and which then repeat endlessly across the milliseconds it takes for the click to register. Like an eyelid the camera captures, absorbs and transforms, in the same way as the signal does to and from the brain. Light dances from the music made or holds its breath as words form, seen in the first picture of the Crouch End 1994 section, in which a close up of Tibet is infused and half drowned by the night.

As Bayer says in one of the three introductions here (the first from esteemed novelist Michael Faber, the second a wonderfully touching and emotional one from Tibet himself), she does not impose composition or style but takes ideas and inspiration from the subject and the given moment. This is the mark of a true artist. She is someone who does not impose her style on a subject but rather finds her form within it, about it and because of it. There is a famous Orson Welles story he often told about his filming style. He was once asked in interview after reflections on his vibrant invention of what was possible in terms of camera angle and shooting style how he knew where to put the camera. He replied simply: 'I put the camera where the story is.' Ruth Bayer in this beautifully rendered book by Strange Attractor does exactly the same. She finds what is real in what is imagined. She dreams and she captures, turning the world all the while. The connection she feels is what her photographs offer. She sees in one man the beauty of friendship. She translates Geoff Cox and John Balance. The poem is part of her eye.

24th November 2016

THE POEM IS PART OF THE EYE

photos and copyright by Ruth Bayer

DOGS IN THE RAIN

A review in the form of a poem of *Warp And Woof*   (Analogue Flashback Books, 2016.)

Reviewing reviews can be tricky,
As if the repeating of viewpoints can
In some way distract. And so charged
With the task, and with the need to distinguish,
I choose the form of a poem to draw attention
To detail and to perhaps, interact.

The pamphlet is dense, as all chapbooks are
With opinion; appraisals of albums, and their affects,
Sharp and smooth. Gregg Fiddament's
'Absolutely She Cried' strikes me most, being as it is
A prose-poem, capturing The Doors' 'Alive She Cried, '
With his needle scratching 'a warped ouroboran groove.'

Roselle Angwin, stoned, remembers a distant Cambridge,
Listening to the Floyd she's transported by **'*Echoes'***
And 'the motionless albatross in the air.'
Her recollection is brief but shot through with detail,
The privilege of the place breeds a conflict
Between what is elite and what's shared.

John Gimblett's 'The First and the Last' talks of Fripp
And all he's accomplished. From Bowie to Blondie
And all the way back to KC. But its on the first Peter Gabriel
Tour that Robert is most praised and pictured, sitting
On the side of the stage, flagged by curtains 'throwing out
   magnificent music like the sun and its neutrinos, speckles..'
         that rise, bright and free.

Charlie Baylis' writes of *Rain dogs* by Tom Waits,
In terms of World War two and the legacy it engendered.
He sees Waits as a phantom from a 'muddy hole in that war.'
An album for the 'urban dispossessed' and
Their 'heavenly drinking' the dark world Tom Waits

DOGS IN THE RAIN

Leaves us is certainly worth waiting for.
Sandra Tappenden speaks of *La Mystere Des Voix Bulgare*
With aplomb, 'a music belonging outdoors, to raw women'
And all of its 'strident calling' for the intimate
Realm of the heart. Her writing is rich, her immediacy clear
As she listens, transforming time in her 'morning kitchen'
From so called normal encounters to those close to art.

Andrew Darlington Jefferson's the old Airplane for us,
Democratising the cultists from LSD's ancient reign.
Rupert Loydell evocatively Azimuths, as Norman Jope
Returns to Miles Davis. Clark Allison cleanses senses
By exploring Merzbow's *Tauromachine*, risking pain.
From Dylan's Basement tapes to an Abearareon campsite,

Bert Jansch's Jack Orion sits next to the Convenience Kings.
Editor Loydell chooses well and the voices are both
Eloquent and instructive, as we align tastes as readers
To those writing for us, who in these gentle pages
Celebrates those who inspire
Through what they play, share and sing.

The weather is warm but still it cuts through us.
As it changes and weathers *us* we find music to alter
The soul and assist. The dog barks. The voice breaks,
Taking the heart along with it. These reviewers choose songs
That reveal the rain and warp within living
Is soon saved by singing and what it teaches us to resist.

24th October 2016

BEHIND SHADOW – or, AN OPERA OF THE MIND

A reflection and review on *The Idea of the Avant-Garde and what it means today* (ed. Marc James Leger, MUP, 2016)

In the current crisis of faith, liberty, truth and the fallibility of virtually every institution and belief system in which we have previously invested, perhaps the only means of survival and expression lays in the creation of a new language with which to deal with the fallout and resultant issues involved. In this vital, new publication from Manchester University Press, editor and Canadian scholar, Marc James Leger presents an array of voices reflecting and proselytising on the uses and relevance of the Avant-Garde as the only legitimate force and means of expression that we, in a rapidly consolidating right wing world, now have left.

From seminal critic Laura Mulvey's essay on Mary Kelly's installation, *The Ballad of Kastriot Rexhepi* and its statements on Temporality, to Spanish artist Santiago Sierra's *300 People* which consists of a roll-call of past and present rulers and the royal of the world (whose alphabetical selection and placing is itself a statement on how power passes inconsistently across titles and nation states), onto discussions between New York based artist Gregory Sholette and Harvard professor of design Krzysztof Wodiczko, to Leger and radical art collective, the Critical Art Ensemble, German author Alexsander Kluge and his countryman philosopher and social scientist, Oscar Negt, the point is established that there are crucial developments and innovations occurring as there always have been, in what is still seen as elitist intellectual environments. What the Avant-Garde did in the past, through Dada in terms of art activism and Serialism in music, along with elements of postmodernism and experimentalism in literature, and indeed continues to do today, as a form and force in itself, is to show how abstracted or progressive modes of expression defy all catergorisations of background and class, despite being defined or stewarded by those at the far reaches of thought and accomplishment.

They also serve a greater political purpose of course, in defining new means of opposition, with the supposedly 'chaotic' voice achieving a new elegance. As poet, playwright and polemicist, Heathcote

Williams states, on the birth of Dadaist thought and action, exemplified by Tristan Tzara and his contemporaries but stretching further back;

> '..Apollinaire and co were appalled by the First World War, if indeed they weren't injured by it. They judged that the military-industrial complexes of France and Germany considered themselves governed by reason. Reason then became the enemy. Through dada and surrealism they declared war on reason. They had a political purpose...'

Leger's book in the light of this history both details such developments while also finding a new meaning and relevance for the word reason by carefully aligning how effectively the works on offer take that initial oppositional stance and make it one embedded in a new kind of cultural consciousness, that can be appreciated in both the surface, presentational terms of the works produced along with their formative contextual elements.

The feminist aesthetics of the literary critic Helene Cixous, for instance (not included here) are art works or works of literature in themselves, as indeed are the works of Laura Mulvey, from her books on *Citizen Kane* and Fetishism across the forms, through to her films with Peter Wollen, and in reading the coruscating and revelatory essays, reports, encounters and artworks Leger has gathered together and commissioned, one has the notion of a clear and powerful manifesto taking shape, one that is not only able to reflect the times in which it is written, but also able to offer or point towards effective solutions.

New York based conceptual artist and philosopher Adrian Piper's opening essay on the limitations of postmodernism and its anti-originality thesis in the face of what the Avant-Garde sets out to accomplish, allows us to enter into and engage with this collection on a high academic level while making perfect sense for the lay-person. As she states;

> 'the promotional fervour with which the concept of originality in invoked to market and canonize modern art finds its parallel in

> *the fervour with which the anti-originality thesis itself was marketed as original..'*

You'll excuse the contradiction, but the conundrum is clear. In an unravelling society that is in danger of losing hold of its invented theories both culturally and politically, we are in danger of not only losing the ability to recognise what is valuable and what isn't, but also the willingness to mourn or even recognise what that loss can be and the effect it can have on us. It is only when we move beyond standard forms that we can find greater access. It is for this reason that abstract expressionism has never truly gone away, as it can be evidenced today in a young child's unwitting, early scrawl as much as it is in considered Pollockian archive, or in the mastery and eventual mental deterioration of Willem De Kooning. That the shallow ends of current conceptualist thinking and practise in modern art have replaced the true or deeply affecting expressive motions and ideas of the recent past with surface comments on commercialism or sexual identity (yawn), shows how we are in real danger of becoming separated on a biological and spiritual level from the lizard in the brain who teaches us all how to change.

The iconoclastic actor, writer, director and theatrical conceptualist, Ken Campbell once remarked that he had;

> *'given up reading regular fiction as it was just about people coming in and out of rooms and falling in love..nowadays I just read science fiction, as that is about everything else!'*

That wondrous statement was in fact pointing the way towards a greater glory and landscape for our artistic and critical perception. This isn't one necessarily defined by a genre such as sci-fi, or by the scale we might find in the larger classical houses of New York, London or Bayreuth, but the notion of an 'Opera of the mind' working with the full orchestra of responses and motivations is an enticing one, purported in Piper's own work and essay, as it seeks definitions between the postmodern and Avant-Gardism, showing how that very impulse can innovate within the bounds of free market capitalism by commenting on the irrational inequalities that comprise it in a totally explosive way. The connections between free market expression and free market consumption can be joined through the seeming irrationalism of the Avant-Garde statement and in that way, contain an acceptable code for societal understanding.

Noted performance artist Andrea Fraser essays the practices of 'Institutional Critique' as exemplified by the work of Daniel Buren, Hans Haacke and Peter Burger, focusing on the means with which progressive artworks and the theories that created them in the museum, gallery, symposium and lecture hall, demonstrate how the institutions that 'impose their (own) frame on art' are in danger of ossifying both the art itself and the customs of understanding and delivery around it. Fraser focuses also on artists like Michael Asher who

> *'took Duchamp one step further..by showing that art can only truly be defined by the discourses and practices and evaluations around it.'*

A statement that somehow captures what Avant-Gardism itself accomplishes, by proclaiming that art exists beyond its own creators' statement of authority. For art and the institutions that showcase it to survive, we need one system of interpretation, one state of being, unified in a communal response to that which is created, one which rises beyond a sense of ownership that otherwise falls into areas of adapting to a given market. It requires its own autonomy and lives beyond and behind its own shadow.

David Tomas investigates Post Avant-Garde practises through a lecture on Kafka's *A Report to the Academy* by visuals akin to a kind of graphic score, along with a study of The Southern California Consortium of Art Schools symposium and the editorial work of Alexander Alberro and Blake Stimson. This comprehensive essay seeks to advance the positions and arguments of Andrea Fraser's previous one while offering its own advances and here, Leger shows true skill as an editor. This book is not just a gathering of voices and reflections of what is possible; it is a moving and reflex driven process, the literal equivalent of live intellectual engagement or questioning lecture. By attending to the form of the book you are invited into the process necessary to the development of a free- flowing movement of discourse. There is a dance of ideas while at the same time, brain food has been placed in your hand.

In this essay and in this book as a whole;

> *...art, cybernetics, semiotics, structuralism, psychoanalysis, anthropology, film studies, gender studies, postcolonial and visual studies, as well as trans-disciplinary politics of representation*

along with the multiple and contradictory composition of social identities...

are the tools chosen to fight and carve a critical future. That the contributors are artists, writers, philosophers, professors of global repute does not limit our reaction to the positions on offer. The book is scholarly but also expansive. It has a plethora of

fascinating black and white illustrations that add to the greater metaphor of understanding and does that rare thing in academia, chiefly enabling the book to stand on its own right and to become an educational course on its own terms. One can become an expert on these theories, practitioners and bodies of work by reading it, regaling others with the knowledge on offer through the intricate pollinations of theory and history. We live in a time of the death of the expert in commercial terms and so as the voices of resistance and disobedience attempt to corral themselves against the prevailing new world order, the fresh 'daemon at our shoulder' is no longer a malevolent figure, but one who is able to prompt us into darker action in unenlightened times. For the first time the anger of revolt can collaborate with the aims of the angel whose wings too show a trace of shadow through the white. The previously unaccepted can now be the new language and voice of retaliation. The idea of the Avant–Garde and the worlds it leads to and attempts to suggest and create is the point. That is the true issue. The works on display, once considered cannot be allowed to ossify, just because they have been demonstrated. The painting gathers dust in the gallery as the book does on the shelf, or even the iPad on the arm of the chair. The play has been performed. The music listened to. Now we must rise up and re-engage with what is on offer and allow the buds of our own wings to bolster forth and break the skin. The wounds we reveal will not be easy to recover from but they will at least show the struggle we have undergone in order to contain the things that confront us and which often defy easy representation.

That these thoughts only take me to page 29 of a 285 page volume shows the riches on offer, from Hal Foster's report on Robert Gober's post 9/11 installation in which visitors were ushered into a gallery of 'forlorn objects' relating the aftermath of that crisis as if they 'were being ushered into a dream', to Mulvey's expert celebration of her colleague Mary Kelly, through to *Cosey Fanni Tutti's* end papers suggestion and refutation of what Avant-Gardism can achieve, worlds of resistance are engendered. Sara Marcus' call for a 'girl Avant-Garde, ' independent of the totemism of Duchamp's male urinal re-orders our response and attention, as does the great Chris Cutler's (composer, music theorist, lecturer and founding percussionist of Avant-Garde musical activists, Henry Cow) 'Thoughts on Music and the Avant-Garde: Considerations on a term and Its public use, ' in which art and the Avant-Garde notions of anti-art, continuity and discontinuity and the very history of artistic resistance in music, is shown as a noble task. As Cutler states when comparing Duchamp's work *Fountain* with Cage's *4'33"*;

> *'..that (it) in its very quiet way represents nothing less than an attempt to dissolve the category of music. It (in fact) asks of music, as the readymade asks of art: if this is music, then what is not?'*

What Cutler calls *'the ghost at every feast thereafter'* both defines the problematic nature of what the Avant-Garde's response to society is in terms of being a communal or individual series of statements, along with the subsequent issues of how it is perceived by those living happily outside it. He also points towards a solution. Music as the truest, potentially democratic resource can show us how there are other levels of interpretation and being that can assist the common adventure and help to progress us all towards some form of revelation. We have simply to open our minds and accept this new language, borne on music's own currents and linguistic status. As Cutler states, Cage's work after 1951's *Sixteen Dances* was an attempt to remove intentionality from the production of all works. To return in fact, to the instinctive response no matter how informed and to create a world of works that lead to communal perception through a notion of what anti-art can actually mean and achieve. This notion helps to return us to the earlier considerations of Institutional Critique that can exist within our own heads and personal galleries of action. Musicians of Cutler's stamp, along with his colleagues in Henry Cow; Fred Frith, Lol Coxhill and Lindsay Cooper constantly sought new definitions, even if those definitions led to fatalism. When Cutler states at the end of his majestic essay that,

> *'.. the avant garde is dead. That is its triumph. Let it lie.'*

He is of course opening up new avenues of debate. If the previous forms of resistance are only fit for the archive what new form will our present and future positions take? Will we in the light of the current situation create or forge a new conventionality in reaction to the irrationalism of Trump, Brexit and the dangers inherent in the end of American superpower, or are we condemned to forever remain throwing pebbles, glass and stones against ever more re-inforced steel? The Idea of the Avant-Garde and what it means today is eerily prescient in its documentation of former innovations and current practises. Its relevance is therefore undeniable. This collection shows that amidst the darknesses that surround us there is another colour forming. Whether this is revelatory in terms of pitch or consistency, or simply a matter of a developing tone or shade, we cannot say. But what we can do by examining the examples of works and approaches gathered here - that date back to the early twentieth century and move towards tomorrow - is realise that the *idea* of and behind such an approach forms the true value and creates the lasting glory, as opposed to the works that assisted its definition. At this time and on this day, nothing as we understand it, works. We must regroup as we disassemble. A once rear (garde) action is fighting its way to the front.

We salute Marc James Leger and the distinguished contributors of this volume. A new light is shining. We just need to know where to look.

11th February 2017

Part Two:

SOUND SHAPING
(Music)

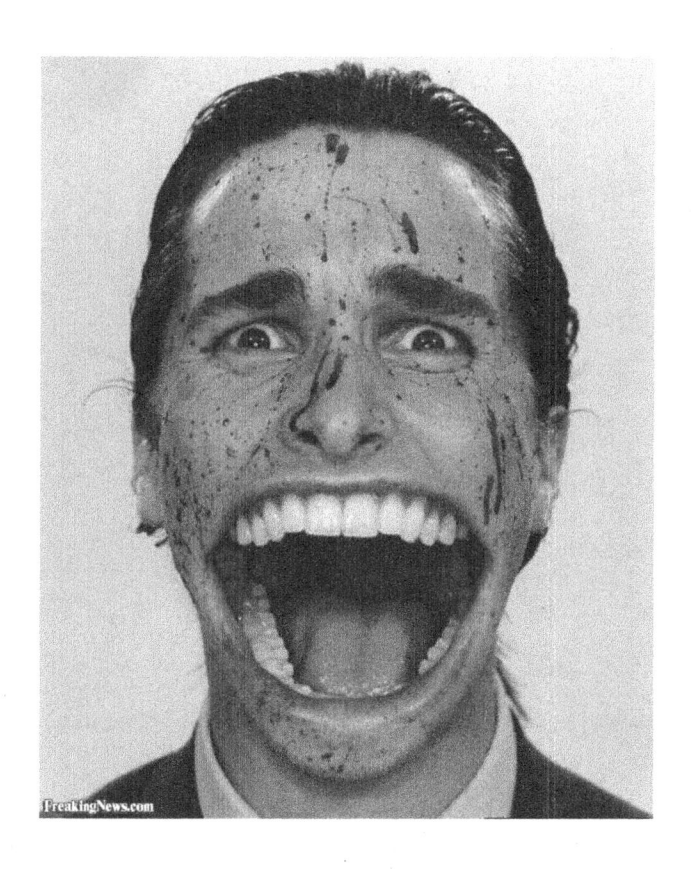

AS PRECIOUS AS I USED TO BE
A review of *Made Of Light* by Tymon Dogg (Thin Man Music)

Known as the ultimate personification of 'Gypsy Punk', the singer, composer and multi-instrumentalist Tymon Dogg continues to celebrate and invoke fresh forms of lilting romanticism and political engagement in his new album, *Made Of Light*, released on Thin Man Music this month. A long time collaborator with Joe Strummer in the Mescaleroes and before that, The Clash, championed by Martin Scorcese and Brad Pitt, discovered by Paul McCartney when he was a teenager, Dogg has spent over 40 years injecting a love of the sacred and profane into his musical muse. His impassioned connection with the primary forces of music and its inherent mysticism plods, strums, plucks, squarks and fuels each one of these stately and frequently beautiful ten songs and one instrumental, creating a world into which we may bring our own, in order to compare both experience and influence.

The opener, 'Conscience Money' houses that stately, almost renaissance feel with an insistent harpsichord refrain powering the message of the song, with its attack on the rich and soulful solidarity with the disenfranchised.

'Time for Moving on' echoes a distant McCartney and carries with it a depth of vision in which the leaving of a lover is equated with the uncertainty of truth in all things revealing itself. The song seeks answers in the search behind its singing; 'When you give everything/ You can't expect to end up King.' Being one of many winning couplets sprinkled throughout the record like shards of the road splintered and thrown to the wind as Dogg journeys on.

Made of Light has been packaged in a seductively smooth double slipcase with each of its 2 cd's taking the form of mini black vinyl. This makes each cd Side one and two of a record and it is this harking back to the much prized and newly fetishized form that makes Dogg's howl for recall all the more pertinent, coming as it does at a time of political barbarism and emotional detachment through the constraints and false promise of new technologies.

He seeks in these songs to unite the heart and the soul with both economy of address and depth of feeling, the lushness of his arrangements for Violin, Viola, Piano, Mandolins, Guitar, Bass,

Percussion and Drums contrasting with the raggedness of his voice. Here is, to invoke the old Jimmy Webb written album for the actor Richard Harris, 'A Tramp, Shining' in the truest sense. This is not a comment that suggests or demeans Dogg's social status – indeed he looks suitably urbane and charming in the back cover photo – but one that attempts to describe the effect of his delivery; that of a broken soul seeking closure, repair and understanding.

It is true, Dogg's voice is hard to love, but that has been said of many singers from Toms Waits and Robinson through to Justin Hawkins, but that is not the point. The real issue here, is just that; Tymon's dogged humanity infusing itself across musical perfectionism with an element of human error. Moments of small dissonance such as that which occurs in closer 'Walking Down the Road' are completed and explained as medium and message combine.

From the rolling agit-prop of 'Pound of Grain' through the broken balladering of the title track, across the pounding piano of 'Like I used to be, ' to the fingerpoking bassline in 'That's the Way It is, ' Tymon Dogg finds inventive ways to corral and confront his listener, whether they are 'pipped to the post by a mobile phone' or 'toying with being a lesbian out of heterosexual spite', the characters that people these songs are full of the same need to search and define themselves as their creator/composer and indeed, the frenzied string led shimmer of the one instrumental 'Rock Box Hammer' sings just as urgently of Dogg's need to reach us all in a uniquely formed 41 minutes.

The album lives as a statement, separate in a way to musical taste and trend, but as a living reflection of one man's view of the world and its magical, romantic and political forces. He sings in his own way over musical and lyrical input of interest to us all. It is a continuation of the same issues and ideas of his fallen but never forgotten comrade Joe Strummer and seeks the unification of as many hearts as possible under one glass, which he raises to toast, if not the hopes for a brighter future, then those of a more enlightened present. As the song DMT concludes:

'Who are these souls of mystery/of learning and of pain

AS PRECIOUS AS I USED TO BE

Who have to learn their lessons/ over and over again?'
There is 'a mass of energy so far behind the eyes,
And in 'the face of loving' is 'such a strange disguise..'

In an age when the album is dying, Tymon Dogg sings with the defiant rasp of a cherished final breath. Poignant and profound, rough and disconcerting, although he talks of darkness, we are all encouraged to spare one last look towards the light.

9th October 2015

EARTHLY DELIGHTS AND SPECTRAL MORNINGS
A review of Steve Hackett's *Spectral Mornings* 2015 (Cherry Red Records)

For those of you socially defined by current trends and tradings, who shelter behind the word 'cool', this recent release from the Cherry Red label, for whom Prog is one of their specialties, is a deliberate provocation. Steve Hackett's *Spectral Mornings* first appeared as the title track of his third solo album in 1979. Having emerged from *Genesis* in 1977, Hackett's exodus into the freeworld of self expression yielded impressive results. He was as prolific as he was far ranging and the mysterious, even eastern style tinge to his signature sound was evident and epitomised on this powerful instrumental that soared with a refined and economic majesty. The piece was a major accomplishment, marking Hackett's identity as a solo artist and showing that an instrumental could achieve the anthemlike status of the most poignant and stirring of songs. Listening to the original now, the clarity of Hackett's guitar is a vocal in the purest sense.

This 2015 version made in aid of Parkinson's UK has been newly arranged and adapted by Hackett (guitars), Robert Reed (Piano, keyboards), Nick Beggs (Bass), Nick D'Virgilio (Drums), Peter Jones (Recorders), Christina Booth (vocals) and David Langdon (vocals and flute.) David Langdon has written new lyrics to the song, which make it invaluable as both a rallying cry and call for Charity. It is the kind of lyric you might imagine in your head upon first hearing the track, marrying occasionally familiar phrases with a stirring and inspiring call for 'hope in a darkened heart.' I believe Virginia Astley first coined this phrase in her 1986 album of the same name, but that is hardly the point. Creativity of any kind, unless it arrives from the stratosphere of the unknown Gods of Genius, is about arrangement; the finding of the correct phrase, word or image that balances the next, leading to the affects and assumptions that the best songs, books and plays exert on us. There are in the end only 8 musical notes and so these beautiful words, artfully chosen from the common heritage and matched by Langdon and Booth's gorgeous vocals lend the song both dignity and more than a little magic.

Charity singles can sometimes darken our own hearts, sacrificing musical credibility for maximum effect but this new version of Spectral Mornings stands as both a pertinent mission statement for the unfortunate Parkinson's sufferer, as it does for all of those prone to infirmity of any kind, as well as a new set of clothes for the emperor. This time, said emperor is very far from being naked. His new robes protect his reputation and inspire all of those around him to raise their own levels of presentation and his new shoes prepare the way for a brave and adventurous path, along which a cynical age can effectively embrace whichever standards it needs to attain new dignities and awareness of those whose own darknesses occasionally struggle for dawn. *Spectral Mornings* is a 20 minute EP containing 4 versions of the song. It is beautifully arranged, played and sung, with some heart melting counterpoint taking place between David Langdon and Christina Booth adding to a performance that in my view resists all needs for the often aimless prejudice of trends and current likings. Thoughts of the 'soul letting go', and a greater spiritual solidarity are concepts in sympathy with us all. The EP becomes an artefact in its own right and as a small piece of art, a frame for both the feeling and song, both in its original form and in this new interpretation. The CD arrived in its amazon envelope this morning and I have already played it constantly. It tells the story of how the ghosts of ourselves can successfully people the day. There is, as the song says, always hope.

VOYAGE TO THE ACOLYTE:
A THEATRO-MATIC ENCOUNTER WITH STEVE HACKETT

This piece is a combination of internal monologue and the ranscription of an interview with seminal guitarist and composer, Steve Hackett. The encounter has been shaped into a kind of playtext in which the internal and external combine. Evidence of the real can be found in Keith Rodway's filmed section of this conversation, available on the International Times website and indeed on what I like to call the Youtube..

Steve Hackett, photo and copyright by Keith Rodway

VOYAGE TO THE ACOLYTE

PROLOGUE.

(The web page as a stage for the Interviewer's exchange and expression. On film, the encounter which the interested viewer can share).

DAVID: *The best art combines. The separate forms merge together. And above all, is music; the language of heart, mind and soul. Music means more as it is the purest expression. So the chance of talking to one of my inspirations is something I can only express in this particular way. I'm striving for a form that I hope is appealing as it comes from excitement and an allegiance of sorts. How do we engage with those people who touched something in us when we were ourselves partly formed? Whether Rock, Jazz or Blues, Classical, Punk or Reggae, the genre is nothing when someone's hand playing touches you, through the years.*

Exterior. High Street. Day.

The ENTHUSER introduces. Wintered winds spur him. Somewhere else a film plays.

DAVID *(continues) Now, take a walk down the road. The Avenue is before you. You've been up since Dawn and you're early, so you measure your steps as you go...*

A pleasant Surburban street on the outskirts of London. The washed cars. The bright houses, hiding the masters within. As you walk, you think back on all of the things that helped form you. You feel detached but consider how you may engage with one source.

Between people, taste defines and divides and often gives way to judgement. It is our task to resist that and to perhaps, unify.

As and if you read or watch, you are me, meeting one of my inspirations. Steve Hackett, Composer, Singer, Guitarist, chief of the specialist polls. Practically an album a year since 1977, and before that an uncanny debut, whose skill and beauty created an unmatched atmosphere.

Music without prejudice: If you can.. resist style, and embrace substance. So called prog rock won't bite you, as in its purest form, songs evolve. As you walk, you dream back to some of the songs that first formed you. Twelve years old, cassettes proffered..and one of these: Genesis. The Song; Dance on a Volcano, *a chime from a distant guitar drawing closer, before transportation to a world beyond your zone 6.*

You're still in the dark. I'm playing Voyage of the Acolyte. *Listen. The hippy dream is updated with a classically charged mystic glow.*

As a first album it shines. The title too is impressive. A young musician commencing and charting his journey to chase down his muse.

Aren't we all Acolytes to the separate things that we worship?

Our enthusiasms explain us and this is how I become You.

And so you and I now become the Acolyte on your journey. A mythic quest with a bus pass. A brief conversation whose flow and rhythm forms a small symphony.

Your eyes open.

Inside, you select the next music: a Hackett guitar piece from his second LP. Side Two, track Four. A vocal air flows around you. A singing starts in you that you do not recognise. The Voice of Necam solo. The melody of which, will transform you. A single note lowers before you, taken with it, rise with hope, then reflect. Improvised words can't contain what these notes do to your spirit. And yet they appear to form anchors, mooring you to the day:

(SINGS:) *Then/ As we move from sleep/ To find out who we are/We lose the things a dream can keep/ In favour of the star...*

The expert plays on as I journey out now to meet him. From my current day, back to childhood, before returning again to these words. How do you license the thrill of meeting someone you favour.. especially somebody bound to music, and its secret call on the heart. We are not what we eat – that merely assists our condition. We are what we value and what we choose to retain.

SCENE ONE

(The day finds its form as the front door opens. From childhood bedroom to doorstep, Guitar in hand, there he is..)

SH: Good morning..

DE: Hi, Steve..Thanks so much..

SH: Glad you found it. Come on through to the front room.

DE: Thanks..

SH: This is the temporary studio for a while..as we build in the garden..

DE: Hello David..

SH: And this is the permanent, wife Jo..

DE. Hi, Jo.. thanks so much..

DAVID: *Enter Steve's wife and partner. An accomplished and impassioned poet, lyricist and activist in her own right, she sits me down, proffers coffee, and a childlike dream becomes concrete, coffee and chairs, in a trice..*

SCENE TWO.

(Lights rise. A comfortable living room. Bookcases, neat sofa, keyboard, guitars, table, plants. Steve Hackett sits as separate worlds move to settle. Jo Hackett, provides, sits and listens and then busies herself with her day.).

DAVID: *We both tune up for a while as we settle into the air made together. As we dance around conversation the small volcano of my own fervour, fuels. We skirt and skip, move around, touching on songs, moments, albums. Ideas are conjured, reflections occur, thoughts connect. The Acolyte is now the Master. The spells have been conjured and in the room, today thoughts resound. You want to learn what made them and chart their inspirations. The audience making music with the favoured artist, perhaps. A jamming of thoughts you will read and see if you'd care to. Your younger self re-emerges as you follow on where he leads...*

DE: You've been so busy of late. Your workrate is astounding. Thanks so much for this.

SH: Not a problem..

JH: It's been a hectic time..

SH: We did three of four months on the road straight. We've got a few changes coming up. People are starting to fall over, you know..

DE: Yes. there's been a lot of cross pollination. It must be wearying..

JH: Busy bees..

SH: Yes. Not all of them, sharp! But I've been revving up recently and making up for some years when things were more complicated and various people that I was involved with were making things difficult...

DE: On the management side..?

SH: Yes, that's right. But in recent years, since Jo and I have been together full time we've upped the gig schedule and it means that

I've been playing everywhere.. and with everyone..as well as doing my own stuff..I've been doing a lot of guest things for people..

DE: You've been very promiscuous, musically..

SH: Promiscuous, yes. Prolifically promiscuous..

DE: Putting yourself about a bit, as my Grandmother used to say..

SH: Yes, indeed.. I mean, there's lots of things that are favours to people..so at one time, back in the day, if I did guest spots for people, I tended to charge them to do it, but then in more recent years there's been more camaraderie in an industry that already feels marginalised in terms of those artists who specialise in greatly varied types of music..

DE: And your work's become so varied..

SH: Yes. So I feel drawn to new standards and almost duty bound to assist..Its also good to be asked.

DE: Part of the cross pollination..Advancing the form..

SH: Glad you think so..

DE: Which to my ear you've always done. Its certainly there on *Voyage of the Acolyte* as your first album, but particularly evident on *Please Don't Touch*, your second LP and first as a solo artist in which there are so many different styles of music, often in the same song.

SH: Yes.

DE: You've mentioned before that you felt exposed on that album..

SH: I did. Well I was out of the group for a start, so I didn't have the comfort of saying, well here I am, let me set up my little stall in the marketplace, while the band were off elsewhere doing very well with all the numbers. *Genesis* was a monster and it was very hard to follow in its wake..but once you've been partly responsible for creating Frankensteins by product, its hard to complain that its run amok and done its thing..

DE: Was that element of exposure necessary, then?

SH: Well, it was certainly a springboard. It gave me a chance to – you know you had Tony Stratton-Smith who was the label boss, who took a chance on me. He was a great gregarious character who'd managed The Bonzo Dog Doo Dah band, the Nice. Do you know much about him? He was an accomplished journalist, author, gambler, raconteur, drinker and impresario who then formed the label that housed The Bonzos, Genesis, Lindisfarne, Monty Python. He was a real force within what was then a new part of the industry..

DE: Very much the charisma that named the label..

SH: Indeed. I learnt a lot from him, you know. I was very happy to just sit and listen to him. Often into the wee small ones in various watering holes across Soho, or in the Marquee club's after hours. I realised very quickly that I was the child and he was the grown up..

DE: Right..

SH: So when I was ready to leave the band, he was right there behind me as I went on to do a whole series of albums..

DE: A kind of musical parent..

SH: He was wonderful, yes..

DE: So, we might say that under his stewardship, Genesis, as a band, in line with its origins at Charterhouse, with Tony Banks, Mike Rutherford, Peter Gabriel and Anthony Phillips had become a very public school, in its own right, for your own education as a rock star.

SH: Well, yes. I very much fulfilled my role as a publicist for the band. I worked very hard to make Genesis happen. So the recent exclusion of my subsequent career from the Sum of the Parts DVD pissed me off, mightily. I got letters of apology from several members of the band and from the director who informed me that certain decisions had been made to favour some and downplay others (by others), so I actually retweeted that message as I had got a lot of flak from people saying that I seemed to have given little to it at all, when in fact I'd spent two hours being interviewed individually for it and then another two hours with the band, so somewhere along the way, there seems to have been a real imbalance.. even though we were approached as equals. And it all looked very good. And there were things contracted in and so on and so forth. And then things seemed to change. Phil wrote to me and said, well I rather naievely thought that we were all going to promote this together, but then, you know, I suppose the competitive element kicks in. So, yes. It did rankle. Its a strange one, Genesis, isn't it? It seems to be incapable of moving forward as a viable unit, so its going to remain a band with a very interesting past – or a very promising past, I should say but not necessarily a future..unless Phil recovers enough for the others to talk him into doing it. So this once great bastion of..this that and the other..remains completely dormant. I do my best to keep that music alive by going out and playing it. I did two or three years of doing nothing else but Genesis stuff with the *Genesis Revisited* albums of course but I'm now changing that, so the last show I did was half and half, we did two sets, so we got the chance to show what I'm currently doing rather than just keeping the museum doors open, glorious though the exhibits are.

DE: So, you're showing a tremendous integrity in doing that, rather more perhaps than the band itself, in archiving or curating that work; songs that will never be done again, by the original players – which is something that a fan base always wants to see.

SH: Yes, I suppose its wearing a curators cap in a museum of my own making to some extent. But I do care about it. Whereas I find that what they tend to say about the albums that let's be honest still sell the most, is that, well, yes, we did all that when we were young..and bearded..

DE: You mean in a dismissive way..

SH: Yes, it sounds extremely dismissive..and of something that as an art form has I think exonerated itself, with time. Now, I'm getting really serious here but I do believe that there's something valuable about a genre that tries to include within itself all other genres of music in both small and large ways. For instance I'm using a charango guitar from Peru on the latest piece I'm working on and then it'll be a deduk from Armenia and an Oud from Iran as we go on..and there'll be players from Hungary and so on.. so I'm not sure that there's a distinction between what is now known as world music and that of progressive music, apart from the fact that one seems to be more hip and is considered more worthy. You know at one time its seemed that the prog rock was terminally unhip. It still had its supporters, but people weren't talking about it, almost to the extent that you felt you couldn't really talk about it. Publicly. But under the umbrella of progressive rock..advances, extensions and rejuvenations can be made.

DE: Music as the collection of different voices..

SH: Yes, yes..

DE: As well as flavours and tones..Its a question of style, or even life choices; to move from a food and onto a fashion analogy; the dressing up of music in new clothes rejuvenates on all sorts of levels. Its fair to say that Robert Fripp for instance, has always been a truly progressive musician on all sorts of levels, but clearly by advancing the musical form from the template set down by 21st Century Schzoid Man through new wave, into the avant garde and on into the areas of soundscaping.. and certainly your recent albums, *Wild Orchids* and *Out of the Tunnels Mouth* have been concerned with similar advances.. Do you feel that music now, or the form by which the music industry has currently defined itself is damaging and indeed limiting in a final, even fatal sense?

SH: Yes, I think to bridge both a generation gap and a style gap, to use your fashion analogy, is the true aim. Music without prejudice is where we need to pitch the tent. So, that'll take me from the Ukele to the Stratocaster.

DE: It sounds almost evangelical.

SH: Well, yes. Irrespective of whether there is a God or not, Music is certainly the God for me, and in line with man and mammon, music is its own currency or code of belief, if you will, so I no longer worry how well or badly an album does. I mean with a case of the recent Box set, *Premonitions*, it wasn't a case of 'Oh, well that was the hit album, ' and that one didn't do so well..' but now its all in a box. And therefore part of a whole anyway. I mean in one sense, all achievements seem so small in retrospect. The whole point is in keeping going. It's the marathon for me. It's the run that interests me, not the finishing line.

DE: And this explains the prolific output.. so many new albums, guest spots on others work, hectic touring schedule..you're in one sense, rewriting new ways to appreciate this music in terms of itself and in a grander sense, music as a whole..

SH: I think so, yes. I get as turned on by flamenco strumming techniques as I do blues finger vibrato. They're all subcultures, aren't they? They're all inward looking and people perfect their crafts with these individual concerns. For instance I'm writing this new piece about Iceland as Jo and I went there recently, so this Peruvian charango may provide a link between inspirations. Music is landscape, writing the story and simultaneously painting the picture, so I'm trying to get all those elements in there. I find most of the music that resonates for me tends to come from this sense of having a story. Even the love songs I like tend to have accompanying narratives, whether its in terms of dreams and incident or something like the moonlight sonata, or other similar pieces of musical romanticism. Separate schools of thought is the issue... I mean, I know that I'm moving between subjects to some extent here, but separate schools of thought that really should be listening to each other is my idea of heaven. Everything's passed. Everyone's achieved what they set out to do, so Bach can have a conversation with Miles Davis and the idea that they all start to see the value in each other's abilities and we get beyond the zeitgeist excites me greatly. I'm attempting that on this side of the pearly gates! I thought at some point I'd do a compilation, 'Blues, Bach and Beyond' as I've done each of those things in separation..

DE: So, in moving across the forms as you say, your advances are perhaps spreading, or almost collaging as you create new work. When I teach acting and writing, I seek new definitions and often say that the best things in each form create and perhaps merge in terms of the connections made. So we could say that Harold Pinter's plays are more subject to his poetry than most people believe, or that Caryl Churchill's plays are a kind of sculpture..So, what you're doing now is a form of musical painting..

SH: Exactly, yes. So I now feel that I'm applying my influences, like paint. My Father was a painter.

DE: So, what you do now, in fact, honours him.

SH: I think it does, yes. I hope it does.

DE: I'm quite sure.

DAVID. *A Pause. You connect. Empathy is a music. And as the thoughts settle, both interests now combine. You start to feel more relaxed as at the start you were nervous. Soon your exchange will come into focus, represented for you as a film..*

These words have been ways for you to empathise with me. I have been sharing something that means much to me, because it dates back to a carefree time in my childhood, in which what you discover, shows you in time how to be.

SH. You were talking about Harold Pinter. Of course he started as an actor..

DE. Yes, but before that he was a poet, so there's a fusing of inspiration and practise, right at the start of his career..

SH. Its funny that, isn't it, as Genesis started very much as writers, they thought they were going to write and other people were going to do their songs: wrong. Same with Elton John. Although of course now people are doing Elton John songs, rather more than Genesis songs of course, although they have been covers of them. Although I suspect people are far more likely to go away and do Phil Collins songs, of course..

DE. R 'n' B artists, for sure. As his solo work is still very highly regarded in that sphere..

SH. He's had a nod to that genre, hasn't he? I've had classical guitarists do some of my stuff.

DE. Yes, but I was wondering Steve, do you define your work in that way at all? It strikes me that there's two very different sides to your music, separate to its experimentation of genre and style, from the blues based electric side to the classical acoustic work. Do you see yourself as a classicist working within rock structures or vice versa?

SH. Well, I never really did my lessons with the classical stuff. I didn't want anyone to slap my wrist. I wanted to get there on my own. So it was a slow burn really, all of that. But I was passionate about it and in fact, put off playing finger style for a very long time until I could ignore it no longer and i thought playing with the nails might be seen as unmanly, a little like knitting! Real men don't use nails!

DE. Ah, that wasn't how it was in Pimlico, then, back in the day?

SH. No. But I have been known to put a bit of laquer on..

DE. Your body is a tool. And the machine needs oiling..

SH. Indeed. Although I remain a classical groupie to extend the glamour analogy. In one way of course, I'm a fraud as I've never studied in the dedicated sense, but on another level, because I've got there on my own and didn't want to learn to do anything properly,

I've found a connection to the early style of classical guitar playing which I must prefer, because I find it has far more varied tone colours. People that are taught these days tend to be told that they must lay into and articulate every note equally, where the more vibrato Nineteenth century approached as practised by Segovia where you slow down between phrases is so much more romantic. So every note doesn't require the same value or dynamic and things become far more varied..

DE. You might say you're ingraining, or weaving, or indeed mixing..we might even say progressing classical approaches..?

SH. Yes. It's a word that my friend Theo Cheng, whose a very fine classical guitarist, said, is that what you're actually doing is orchestrating. The bass strings are like brass if you go bright here, and if you're doing harmonics its a little like a glockenspiel and then this is almost piano like... Its a bit of a stretch. But if you move from the sound hole and closer to the frets you start to lose less of the low frequencies and it starts to sound a bit more like a harp.. So, all of those things fascinate me. And at the moment I'm trying to do some flamenco things. I'm having a little trouble with some of the rhythms but I'm having an interesting time getting there and am then discovering other wonderful things along the way..

DE. Was this a conscious decision that you've devoted some time to recently, or a series of progessions since you first started playing?

SH. I had this idea right from the start that I wanted to be someone sketching in a number of styles. I didn't want to be someone who relied or was defined solely by technique. But inevitably the more you practise and play correctly, speed becomes an inevitable consequence of that..

DE. And something to perhaps resist?

SH. At the correct times, absolutely.

DE. And its been done very artfully in your work. I've found that when progressive artists are too obvious with their classical influences, the work can veer towards levels of emotional detachment and dare I say it, sound quite ugly. Your work in that area remains fused with warmth and sensitivity..

SH. I suspect rock versions of classical pieces usually don't work for me but then I want the spirit of those melodies to be evident in what I choose to do. Where Grieg left off, Led Zeppelin flew.

DE. The Hall of the Mountain King is currently to be located in or about..?

SH. Kashmir, certainly. Now that may not be a conscious thing for any of those guys. But having done some work in Japan with John Paul Jones, I know of course that he was a one time orchestrator for Dusty Springfield, so the classical, string driven thing –

DE. Powers many an airship.

SH. Yes. I'm certainly interested in bands that carry an element of Grieg on board! There aren't that many, but I do find that a great deal of Grieg sounds less classical and more magical, mystical, more pagan if you like and that connects strongly with what I do. A string orchestra can sounds as vital and as alive as a rock band..but can of course also sound like a frumpy maiden aunt, leaving you to wonder, 'What is she doing there?'

DE. Whereas a wall of marshall stacks can at the very worst turn you into a disconsolate teenager..

SH. Yes!

DE. I suppose the natural province for classical stylings away from the concert hall lays with soundtrack work. Which you've not done a lot of, have you?

SH. No. There was the theme tune to the 'Second Chance' TV series in 1982 which was on *Bay of Kings* album, and then a recent lightning fast commission for an HBO documentary called *Outwitting Hitler*, which was mainly comprised of a series of edits of things I had already or was working on, but that was a case of the contract arriving on Friday and them needing the pieces on the Monday. So, no, Hollywood hasn't come calling. I get the odd actor who's interested in certain things. For instance Bruce Willis approached me..

DE. He didn't want to sing, did he?

SH. No. We were talking about harmonica players. I'm a harmonica player as well. He came along to a show in New York, so we had a very nice time harmonising on that theme..

DE. You've never done a voice and guitar album have you, more of a folk singer style. Roy Harper's son, Nick Harper specialises in that..

SH. Yes and he's very good. Funnily enough, I've tried to talk (original Genesis guitarist and founding member) Anthony Phillips into perhaps doing something like this as he's very keen on harmonies. He was on a couple of tracks on *Out of the Tunnel's Mouth* and did a fantastic job..

DE. That would be wonderful, an album of you two together..

SH. Well, I said to him; 'Do you fancy doing an album of harmonies and twelve string – so far he's said no..

DE. But the future of the form if left to the hands of its antecedents, could lay in projects like this?

SH. Well, we've spent quite a lot of time together. Once every three months or so we have a get together..

DE. Fascinating. A Genesis that never was!

SH. I said to him many years ago, 'had we been in Genesis together, I suspect we'd have gotten on very well..' as I think, essentially he's a non competitive character, so we could have been and perhaps could be in a situation where it doesn't matter if we do your song or my song, as we'd be working together in that pure way in which nobody's counting..

DE. And what's interesting is that you're both so prolific. The only people I can think of that have the same level of output, not only in the prog rock form but music in general are you, Anthony Phillips, Peter Hammill and Steven Wilson of course..

SH. Yes. And I find that many of the songs I'm drawn to that are to do with the early band before I joined, are things that he wrote; such as Visions of Angels – which is a beautiful song, we never managed to do it live, but I would have done that and if anybody said to me, I'd like to do that and would you play on it? I'd be only too happy to – and other pieces such as Dusk, which is an extraordinary song, lyrically. I suspect we were listening to the same things, such as Country Joe and the Fish and what have you, early on, so there's a real joing of forces and inspirations and approach to the guitar and composition..

DE. You also need to do an album with Alan White to complete your Yes triumvirate (of *GTR* with Steve Howe and *Squackett* with Chris Squire), and then move on to Anthony Phillips!

SH. Well, I'll tell you proudly that Chris once asked me to join Yes. I turned him down but should have said , well let's do a Yes album and if it turns out well, we'll tour it. But at the time I was in the middle of a divorce and various other things, so I was fighting on the homefront and to do more of a rearguard action seemed a better option. I loved working with Chris. I'm sure we would have done more stuff together. I think Chris was a great force in music.

DE. That's what's wonderful about the *Squackett* album. You would have thought it would be a certain thing –

SH. But it wasn't at all..

DE. No. Its a wonderfully joyous, Pop Rock record, a more satisfying version of what you were attempting in *GTR* and the *Feedback 86* projects, perhaps? *Tall Ships* is remarkable. That bassline is just stunning.

SH. That was the first thing to be written. He had a new bass one day and we were out at my other studio in Twickenham and he said, 'I just want to try this out..'and I said, 'Chris, that's really good, if you can remember what you just played - as 99 out of 100 musicians rarely can – we can turn that into a song..' If you ever hear the surround sound version of that, the chorus from that song is the best thing on that album, because we use the same thing from the front and back, so its just enormous..

DE. *The Summer Backwards* is a beautiful song..

SH. Yes. There was some stuff intended for solo things, be it his or mine..but what was lovely about him, was that anytime that anyone had an idea, we used it. And then you might add a variation or whatever. So everything was longform..

DE. Expansive.. painterly, to return to our previous theme..

SH. Yes. I had a lot of joy working with him. As I did with..

DE. With Steve Howe?

SH. Yes, we worked well together, although there were some eventual differences. But no, I was going to say Richie Havens.

DE. Oh. One of my favourite singers. A beautiful, beautiful voice..

SH. God, yes.

DE. There's an old Sight and Sound concert from 73, 74 which I have recorded with him and a small band and the intensity of his playing.

SH. Yes, all he needed was a guitar and his voice..

DE. He often did that thing that Kevin Coyne did, just wrapping his hands around the neck and strumming furiously..

SH. Well, he liked to play barre chords on an open tuning, but he also liked doing this thing – I saw him once at the Jazz Cafe –

DE. I saw him there..

SH. Did you? Did you see him, doing this kind of field holler thing...

DE. Yes, I did!

SH. Extraordinary. He's singing into the floor and he's just getting louder and louder and this voice is just filling the room.. I mean, how is that possible? He has the power of an operatic singer. I don't know if you've ever stood next to an Opera Singer in a big Opera House, and how loud a singer can be. I believe someone like Bryn Terfel can be as loud as 200 others.. in the Albert Hall! No Mic!

DE. Ah, but you sing of course through the guitar..

SH. Well, yes..

DE. And early on perhaps you were shy about your voice, or you disguised your voice a lot, in pieces like *Carry on up the Vicarage* and so on..but its a charming voice..

SH. Well, thankyou. Its a smaller voice than Phil or Pete, but I think I can go higher and sweeter and it allows me to explore character at the expense of technique perhaps. But I have amassed more technique with time. But its notoriously unreliable. What a bastard thing! Roy Orbison will always be Roy Orbison.

DE. And Richie Havens, too. The soul in that voice.

SH. Absolutely.

DE. The voice is the key, isn't it, to unlocking the love or connection we feel to the song itself. I have the same thing with Anthony Newley, although of course its a very different thing, but I can listen to two minutes of him and it fills me with joy..

SH. Yes. He was very interesting, wasn't he? I remember that series..

DE. The Strange World of Gurney Slade..

SH. Yes, that's it..

DE. When they released it on DVD I went to a tribute evening at the NFT and people were calling it a sit com..I got quite incensed and spoke up, saying that it was one of the most original and compelling things ever made and incredibly important, responsible for many of the techniques and devices, still in use today...

SH. Yes.

DE. Talking to the stone and it answering back..walking away from the set..questioning the form..Quite progressive..

SH. Sure, a forerunner for many of the things seen in things like Python and so on...

DE. Yes.

SH. Its a good little island, this, isn't it? Its come up with lots of ideas. Its probably something to do with the weather. We don't get out much, etc..

DE. That's interesting. A climate based retreat to within, summoning the elemental forces in the internal and external senses..

SH. I think if Shakespeare had grown up in California, we might not have had quite as many Plays..

DE. Innovation is another key of course. I mean IT is very much defined by its beginnings in the 60's, but its always struck me that that was the last great decade. Obviously your career is more defined by the 70's, but the root is there..

SH. No, I agree. The 50's was very much the era of Light Entertainment but in the 60's, the shackles were off and we were free to then capitalise and create in the decade that followed, once we came of age.

DE. And to do so in this very artful way. I was going to ask you about lyrical concerns and the means of expression. You've explained elsewhere that your song *Fire on the Moon* was about the end of your second marriage, but its not immediately evident. So, do you find that a tangential approach is the best way to express and indeed be creative in an artful way about painful or troubling issues?

SH. Yes, that song is about divorce and depression. But it was also about facing upto the fact that one way of life wasn't going to work anymore and that people were pulling apart. But working with Jo, living, loving and working with her has been a huge rejuvenation. My comeback started absolutely at that moment. She has been hugely generous and put me back on my feet. And hugely patient. So that I have now arrived at the point when I realised I could no longer function without her. And the fact that I wasn't looking for a song-writing partner, but I found one. Again, its this integration, beyond something that I am capable of and it stretches me.

DE. You progress in all senses of the word.

SH. Yes, I do. I now try and think with her brain and we have great moments of telepathy and spiritual things and premonitions. She's hugely attuned to people and knows instantly who's going to be a good guy and a bad guy, useful and not useful and she's also highly concerned about the plight of the world.

DE. So you feel released from the box and perhaps for the first time, properly supported; to have someone truly fighting for you.

SH. Yes. We're a team. We're a force. But you know, she cares about everyone. She cares about the world. Even as a kid she told her parents to donate her pocket money to the hungry and deserving.

DE. That's lovely.

SH. It started very young with her. I'd never met someone so engaged.

DE. It's remarkable to have found that. I'm in a solitary period of my own life, having lost my Mother and having no family either, so it gives one hope, seeing it in others. I wish you both, Mazeltov.

SH. Mazeltov..

DE. The jewish congratulations..

SH. Ah, yes, of course..

DE. Thankyou, Steve.

Fade to Black.

EPILOGUE.

DAVID. *And with that we are done. No masks on the face and no positions adopted. Just the chance of connection at the start of his day. We would leave. He would write. We filmed the introduction, which in fact was the ending of this most rewarding foray.*

As I made my way home, I remembered the tape that my first friend had gifted and heard at once the playing that had made the briefest time appear long. Then music did its work and memories became albums. Books of photographs are still called that as each contained image has the power and reach of a song.

Steve's gallery frames old and new connections, collected. As he walks through, his hands capture all he has seen, known and done. I attempt this now, thinking back, as his playing soundtracks me. I'm listening to Genesis *with my father. I'm playing* The Voice of Necam *to my Mum. I have returned to the past and made it my present bassline. A guitar is now playing, leading me on. I've begun.*

To Steve and Jo Hackett

For your happiness
I offer this small dedication;

As the musician asks questions,
The audience answers them.

In the means to go on
Lays the truth we take from the silence;

In the comparison and the difference
We will learn to sing the same song.

THEY ACCEPTABLE

A review of I Ludicrous' *Dull is the New Interesting*

From the jagged guitar stirrings loudly quoting Bowie's Blue Jean with a hemmed sequin or two of Marc Bolan thrown into the mix, I, Ludicrous' rambling beer swilling new album combines both the glam and the glum. Messrs Hung, Proctor and Brett epitomise the finer aspects of Dadrock, that often overlooked genre. Men now easily esconsed into middle age, they have managed to maintain the punkish attitude of their youth by accessing wisdom and experience's bedfellows, humour and detachment. The grizzly assault of 'We're Signed' and 'Cheer Up' energetically gives way to the sorry tale of 'George Jenkins', his cold baked beans and artful synth pop stylings. Vocally a little coarse at times these songs nevertheless invite familiarity as well as amuse you with their vigour. There is a touch here of the Ian Durys and his own *Jack Shit George* and one is frequently spirited away to the days of Kilburn and the High Roads via Kilburn, Hastings and all good points inbetween.

As the album proceeds one is reminded in a healthy way of early Stranglers, Damned and even the Red Aeroplanes. 'Hacky's Wine Bar' has a whiff of the Sex Pistols flowing over its pistachios and arpeggios and 'Things That Happen's no nonsense approach to reclaiming the guitar, bass and drum template of good old rock with or without the roll is satisfying and dare I say it, reassuring.

The song on this album are the aural equivalent of a sneaky afternoon in the pub with these venerable gentleman, expressing a good few years spent observing and possibly judging the world around them. From 'Oscar Pistorius who started well but whose end wasn't glorious', amusing couplets abound imbuing the songs with the conversational flair lacking in a lot of pop music. Albums and bands like this chart an alternative course for modern music making. They are extensions of personality rather than concept and idea and bring to mind the glory days of Half Man Half Biscuit and if you can remember them, Max Splodge and his musings on Simon Templar.

Humour is an essential element to survival and songs like these lift the day with their easy charms. The ironic lecturing lyric of 'Old Professors Young Professionals' has something for us all to learn about respecting the past and I suspect that some of the motivation for this album was to remind people that technology is not the salvation we all think it is and that a return to the limited form is often a greater means of expression.

We slice music these days, carving it like forgotten roasts on a tired Sunday table but I, Ludicrous with the flow and ease of this album, feed us their thoughts in a tightly packed 40 minutes with an increasing attention to detail and a gentle exploration of the textures and capabilities of the power trio.

'When this Depression's Over' shines with contemporary relevance with its neat quoting of The Doors' 'The End'and the closing 'Clerking 'til I die' with its rememberance of dead colleagues and end cover of Stamp and Avery's 'Ascension Day' complete this particularly drink fuelled but ultimately sobering session with aplomb.

Titles to Theatre Plays are crucial if we are to understand their action. Those to albums are often decorative but this album uses its contradictory title well.

We are all Oxymorons if we do not stop to ask a question or two of the society that surrounds us. We believe we are all vibrantly and vitally alive but a great deal of our efforts are aimless. I, Ludicrous keep a watchful eye from their corner table, staring past the fruit machines, peanuts and out into the fleeting night. They whisper a careful warning before draining their pint glass; Do not think too much of yourself: there might not be enough left for the rest of us.

3rd November 2015

TRIP WIZARDS

A review of *Trip Hazard* by Brotherhood Of The Machine

This new release from daring and muscular new exponents of the underground music scene, Dave and John Francis' *Brotherhood of the Machine,* contains three feverish demonstrations of post apocalyptic musical shamanism. Somewhere in one of England's darker portals these brothers labour over a smouldering concoction of Hawkwind, Can, Amon Duul and Goblin, seasoning the mix, with splashes of guitar led heroics reminiscent of ZZ Top at their least mainstream, Brian Eno at his most experimental, and sound meisters such as Scott Walker and Tomas Koner, to make a kind of grizzled trance ritual, sure to set the next generation of rockers and ravers aflame. The three pieces of this album are soundtracks to new states of being, where the trip taken transports the listener to places of confrontation and resurgence. The opening *Meditation of the Blue Serpent* updates the diabolic fervour of Kenneth Anger's infamous *Lucifer Rising* in musical form as well as conjuring mind pictures suitable for the accompaniment of Dario Argento, Gaspar Noe, or the films and images you capture in your own moments of darkness and dissatisfaction. There is the sense of the receiver of these sounds and compositions as being asked to unpeel themselves from the usual fixity of purpose achieved when listening in order to properly enter this music. It works in the same way that film can do, which is why I have referenced a few names, by appealing to a visceral sense of renewal and questioning: How may we participate? This music is too demanding to detach from in the way the everyday listener may do, confining it to the background, and is suitably mood based to make excess movement superfluous; rather, it is music to *be* to: music as an enhancer of consciousness, a drug that draws us into itself, rather than us subsuming it.

The 37 minute *Hin und Zuruck* is a heart ripping ride through a fresh internal landscape. As we travel through its darkness compelled by the power and drive of Dave Francis's Keyboards and Sax and John Francis' Guitar, we hear distant howls from the old Radiophonic workshop of Delia Derbyshire and White Noise albums. We are fuelled by the need to explore these toxic new lands and chased by sharp winds of accusation. The keyboards swirl and gather like constantly pecking birds of prey and the cold winds engendered by the relentless rhythms and occasional train sounds reveal the lack of safe shelter. Alien intrusion of some kind appears as the piece develops with eerie keyboard soundscapes scooping and sculpting the ground beneath the listener's scrambling feet. The word listener is probably an incorrect noun in this case as the aforementioned receivers of this album need and should be called an audience. They should then behave as one, in the truest sense of that term, as there is a real drama here and the sense that something needs to be accomplished. By the end of closing track, *Flying Saucer Patrol*; we have a mission laid down by these brothers to both understand the reasons for the machines existence and to perhaps surrender to it. There is nothing we can do to escape the power and call of the primal forces that music unleashes and the length of the *Hin Und Zuruk* allows for and indeed enables an effective narrative to emerge.

The music herein is not tied to trend and clearly the underground world to which Brotherhood of the Machine belong, along with those crafty and artful exponents of electronica and alternative musics documented in publications like *Wired* magazine, is aimed at creating new ways to listen free of the constraints of the marketplace. This is a kind of music where the audience can collaborate with the creators through their levels of engagement. We are here to forge new standards of cultural exchange along with new disciplines of doing so, if culture is to survive and encounter new modes of expression, that are not necessarily tied to the needs imposed by entertainment. The hazard can only occur if you judge without understanding, if not the reason for each note or pattern, then the emergent feeling. This is music that asks us to participate in ways separate from the body. It is music as air to be inhaled and ingested. It is the smoke and the pill, the needle and burn in the brain.

Flying Saucer Patrol is the more conventional of the three pieces and shows that the Francis brothers are not just mere merchants of sound and atmosphere and there is something celebratory in its evocation of Roswellian skies, inviting us to accept that the darker forces we like to assign to fiction may in fact, have us as the players in a deeper theatre than we are currently aware of. Music is the ultimate trip as someone clichéd once said but it is true. The instrument is not just the machine for making the music but the carrier of both sickness and cure. From *Gounod's Faust* to Geryon Throne's mighty piece, *Orthodox* the trapped voices of the underground will not and cannot be silenced. This album summons the power of the core and thrusts it through the rock, roll and surface tension we all inhabit in our private hours, into the shaman's dawn and after the Sorceror's night. Support this music regardless of taste. Think of it as not the soundtrack for a film you'll never see, but as that of one you did not know was there already, its sounds and inferred images boiling your blood and stoking your thought to a level of near exegesis. The feet may stay firm but the veins are dancing and the blackest compulsion is tunnelling through every fibre and channel of resistance. This music surges through the soul, turning those who embrace it into reverberant sound chambers. We are the radio and this is the frequency of future resistance to the norm. Put on your boots and start running. The hell hounds are coming and the hazards are yours to reject.

22nd February 2016

SPICE BOYS

Gig review – *The Wondersmiths Play The Spice Of Life*, Soho, London 28/5/16

The future is still in the past. It's what I believe and it certainly informs all my practise, from teaching and directing to writing and the concept is still what I look for as an audience and an actor as well. On Saturday night, a happy reconnection with someone from my past led me to see a short and explosive set from a vital new group of aspirant pop musicians, whose drive and enthusiasm powered me straight back to my own days of wonder and awe. On a small basement stage in a trendy soho location, The Wondersmiths comprising of Chris Horncastle (vocals), Dave Owen(Guitar, backing vocals), Oli Franklin (Drums, backing vocals), Alex Kaltio (Bass, backing vocals), and Henry Tydeman on keyboards and backing vocals, played a slickly rehearsed set already primed for mainstream exposure and the grand concert stage.

Headlining a disparate and somewhat eccentric line up comprising a solo female balladeer following on in the wake of Laura Mulvey and Rickie Lee Jones, an androgynously voiced indie superstar in waiting playing acoustic power rock, and what seemed to be thrash metal trio fronted by the lead guitarist in Tinariwen's doppleganger and a bass player who looked like he'd eaten all the others and was in the process of cutting up his next victim, The Wondersmiths burst onto the stage with five songs (I'll ignore the crowd pleasing Taylor Swift cover; Kaltio made me doubly proud by first not knowing it and then gamely jamming it into shape) that not only transformed the space but lifted the entire experience into something beyond just another weekend London activity.

We live in blasé'd times. The current artistic climate is one in which each new 'act' tries to feed on its predecessor, whether in music, film or the stage, either redefining the image or reacting against it, in order to appeal for support. This group have little or no pretence to them. What they communicate above anything else is what all musicians should do; the simple joy of playing. With Franklin's first strike of the drum an agenda was announced, delivered with the full brunt of Horncastle's boundless enthusiasm and powered by a band of young men in their early twenties, already approaching impressive levels of expertise.

The songs are pop perfect – or should that be perfect pop – right down to the titles: *We Were Young, All It Takes, This is it*, etc, and are carefully structured, hook heavy, clean, punchy, all encompassing. This was pop music that invited you in, rather than just existing within its own secularity. As songwriters, these young men have paid attention to the standards and successes of the past and achieved that rare accomplishment of emulation without impersonation. They have included standard pop refrains, such as the vocal wohs beloved of stadium meisters such as U2 and Coldplay but married them to all of the things we love about the energy and spirit of pop, regardless of whether we take it seriously not.

The Wondersmiths certainly do. They have a one beer rule before gigs, which is refreshing on all levels, especially in the light of current poserdom, where the fraudulent ghosts of Pete Docherty's former image mindlessly ape the truly hedonistic innovations of Keith Richards, and where Alex Turner's meaningless attempt at an Elvis type chic wax and wane just as quickly as his quiff on a Glastonbury night. The inversion of that famous surname is also important. Where the former kings of Salford swivelled in Morrissey's self diagnosed outsiderdom, (despite Marr's constant attempts at vibrant musical reformation), the band place a positive spin on common experience. They want us to feel the joy they experience in playing and relaying their songs, while igniting our own hunger and need for music, regardless of taste. This is an extremely honourable thing to have done and to want to do and although this was the first time that I've seen them, I have no doubt that each show is approached with the exact same sense of mission.

In acting, the notion of performing often leads you into false areas. In music the reverse takes place. Horncastle has clearly studied the frontman role not only to the nth degree, but clearly all the way down to the end of the alphabet. Wembley is in his head and heart and it is clear that as far he is concerned every night will be fuelled by the city of blinding lights, whether out in Mick Jagger's exotic fleshpots of LA or Brazil, or down the Weller-esque tubestation at midnight. If his stage patter wandered slightly at times, his sense of wonder was restored when he sang. Horncastle has an infectious presence and an almost childlike voice, comprising the same qualities and appeal of one we would like to pet, and emerging through his beard with the same sweetness, power and clarity of Tim Booth's in James.

Oli Franklin drums with the skill, energy and delight of the celebrant marksman and Owen and Kaltio grin and beam as they appealingly finger and slide, while Tydeman underpins all with his effectively judged eighties style synth workings. The energy is what hits you more than anything and with that energy, the startling level of commitment.

The Wondersmiths have a purety of approach and a slickness that defies their years. This may make them something of an anathema to the loosely defined tardiness of the current musical scene which appears to be somewhat groundless and free falling as it seeks redefinition. The band's response to this is to become a crack squadron with an almost business like air, ready for any and all operations. The current task at hand is to spread the infection. But this is no illness, as infectious*ness* is the issue. They seek to win you and they mean to do so with pop.

The band were accompanied by their own tight collective of friends and followers, who knew the words that at times I couldn't hear, not because of the group's lack of precision and control, but through the simple situation of PA's and small rooms that have plagued rock and pop since the days of the Cavern Club.

This is only important when one considers what new music is actually for in the light of the current state of the music business; it is no longer about the making of records as far as the market is concerned. Now the live experience takes precedence, even over the digital one, which has become the entree for the concert's main course. The joy of making is what we are looking at and listening for, rather than what is made, with the recorded versions of the songs performed acting in one sense, as aide memoirs. In this way new bands become a form of active memory, aligned more than ever to the high points of our social existence. The Wondersmiths seem to know this and therefore clearly strive to create perfect pop experiences that consistently demand our involvement.

Pop unites us all at some level. The difference between The Beatles and The Monkees during the 1960's was that although everyone knew the Beatles came from an everyday normality of situation common to most of the country and indeed the world beyond, nobody quite knew how they were able to reach such extraordinary levels of accomplishment. While nobody really knew where the Monkees came from (areas of privilege as it turned out, apart from Davy Jones' Manchester – although Mrs Nesmith invented Tippex remember), yet everyone could see what they did. Particularly when it was all done for them. Until late in their career, they were delivering somebody else's pop agenda, designed for a market and a level of consumption which set the template for every enforced act of commercial practise ever since. The Wondersmiths combine elements of these two examples. They are not The Beatles – nobody ever can be that good again – but we *feel* that we know where they come from because of the clarity of their presentation, but also because they're delivering to us things we both know and did not know that we wanted; chiefly that primal connection to the thrill that only music can provide.

Their song *Insignificant* was a key part of the set. On the strength of the thirty minutes on a hot Saturday night in London they proved themselves to be anything but. These young men have studied those lessons and echoes still reverberating through the air of over eighty years of popular song and rearranged them with care for their present audiences and for the prospective ones to come in their highly promising future.

The worries of communication and aspiraton that blighted the fractious nature and contradictions of other bands have been fused here into a truly positive approach. The sounds of a hot and crowded night have been incorporated to form a better day. You wake up pleased at having seen them, knowing that somewhere there are young men engaged in the act of seeking positive change, even if just on the level of social interaction. Their last song of the night, *I Know you Better* was a cannily chosen and constructed piece of power pop and as much of an invocation as it was an invitation. In a short space of time, something familiar has been made anew by the group and we are all encouraged to continue the connection.

Small groups of anything will always preach to the converted. With music as their church (for doesn't every gig venue become one?), The Wondersmiths seek expansion without the implied indoctrination of that analagy. Their evangelicism is one that no-one can take issue with because of the very purety they put on show. As they mature they will perhaps harness the uniqueness, humour and skill of a band like Bare Naked Ladies, who while not known to the countless hordes in the same way that this band clearly want to be seen to be, are nevertheless a Canadian equivalent, albeit a generation or two before them. Last night I detected the same range and richness of that band. I also heard James and Abba and a true sense of wonder. Their tasty music revived me, served as it was, laced with spice.

Success is always relative of course, but as they journey on I hope their positivity brings them pleasure. They should know that while still at this early level of gaining notice (the words Philip Schofield were mentioned in terms of promotion) they have already garnered a full sense of skill, expertise and unification. There's a clear plan to follow. They will be the wonder to everyone's common Smith.

Their EP, *ONE* is available on itunes and from www.thewondersmiths.com. They can be found in abbreviation at www.twitter.com/thewondersmiths and/or www.facebook.com/ thewondersmiths. The last piece of information is that their record label is called Animal Farm. Go and visit. Across the bright fields you will see them as they start to canter. The Wondersmiths are approaching. All hail and get ready for the dynamic young steeds at the gate.

The Wondersmiths

AT THE SPRINGING OF THE SUN:

A review of the Elfic Circle projects recital of *Bardik Springs*, the nehru centre, London 28th september 2016

It is over thirty years since I first saw Conrad Rooks' seminal, cult film of psychedelic breakdown and recovery, *Chappaqua*, on late night british television. In this strange and bewildering masterpiece, black and white, hand held cinematography reflecting the shambolic nature of the so called real world and the protagonist's fractured state, gives way to a brief colour interlude of spiritual revelation in which a goddess like silent brunette in a virginal white dress traipses through a sunlit forest. The scene is soundtracked by a two minute Ravi Shankar composition of flute, harp and percussion. That piece of music has haunted me through the ensuing decades and in times of stress and worry I often try to recapture (and to some extent recompose) it in my mind. This evening, thanks to Elfic Circle Project Producer and Manager, R. Rovers, I was able to come close to experiencing it again through the entrancing Elfic Circle Trio, comprising Andrea Seki on Harp, Catherine Dreau on Vibraphone and Fabrice De Graef on Irish Bansuri flute (in which the key holes are in the irish style and the rest of the flute is Bansuri in terms of its craft and origins).

Presented by Jay Visvadeva for the Sama Arts Network and PRSSV, a charity involved with promoting all areas of Indian Music and Dance, this recital was one of exquisite transportation. Music being the purest and most effective of all the creative forms worked its magic over this much treasured hour. It is rare that a concert of any sort becomes a privilege but so it was tonight, when witnessing the purity of intent as shown by these musicians along with the expertise of their performance.

Their new album, *Bardik Springs*, is to be released in November and tonight was the second introductory recital, preparing the way for its release. Mixed and produced by that great seminalist of the post punk, ambient era of innovation, artist, bassist, collaborator and associate of everyone from World Music masters to The Orb and Paul McCartney, Youth, the material played just a few hours previously to these words being written led and connected a devoted and enthused audience towards a sense of reformation and transcendence. The future of music and how we receive it has been a source of debate for some time. Here, tonight, was a glimpse of a much sought future, brought about through the most traditional of means; craft and the containment of beauty.

As the audience settled, Fabrice De Graef led the trio through the opening pieces of the forthcoming album, *Voyage to Karnataka* and *Prelude;* both atmospheric Bansuri led evocations of sacred sites and the effect of seeking such places out. The Bansuri flute is a long, slim, wooden tube, with no valves, only holes and the seated De Graef, a powerful, yet peaceful, noble looking Frenchman immediately commanded the space. The technique and soul of his playing was served impeccably by the gentility of Seki's harp and Dreau's vibes, and without realising it fully, the audience were being given a unique entree to a world that we in our divided and metropolitan state often deny or ignore on account of our social and spiritual ignorance. After a brief introduction by main composer, Andrea Seki, we were taken into the programme and album and in so doing, immediately transported. I was, as the first notes sounded, taken right back to the neglected glow of my forgotten television set, and the Shankar piece, which over time has become a window to another world of intoxication.

The album, *Bardik Springs* is a result of the Elfic Circle Projects's journey and studies throughout India, Kashmir and French Brittany and as the performance continued, with the trio accompanied and beautifully complimented by Sitarist Christian Nocon and Tabla player Sachin Khetani, we, listening were able to relive and experience all these musicians had seen, felt and heard.

The harp's driving insistence on the opening of *On Beach Nectar*, put me in mind of the Canadian Windham Hill label and its stars, William Ackerman, Michael Hedges and Liz Story, and showed how this Indian styled music, played- apart from Sachin Khetani – by non Indians transcended its own voicings to do what all great music does; become one voice and one total means of expression. De Graef's breath extended into and beyond the notes he played, which allowed for bursts of Harp struck revelation, made all the more magical by the tastefulness of Dreau's vibraphone. The piece arced and weaved around us, powered by Nocon's Sitar, testing and tasting the air and allowing us as listeners to walk the sands that these musicians did. The nectar was ours to imbibe.

Breton Vedic Trance, a fusion of French and Indian textures started with a sonorous harp figure. It was uncanny as the sense of a voice was inferred and with it, a deeper sense of consultation, as if the composition and arrangement of notes created a voice that was consulting and engaging with its subject. There was an awareness created of knowledge and experience being both offered and shared and Seki's incantatory vocalising emphasised that. In this piece of music, reflective of a specific time and place something was being created that would last in the mind far longer than it possibly would in the ear. The Bansuri line continued in and out of sound as De Graef conjured and consorted with the muse through the beauty and sheen of slim wood.

On the road to Tappani opened with a cyclical harp figure that also implied motion as we echoed the musicians previous travels. It was simple but intoxicating, as all great music is and should be, with the flute melody driving us on. A sudden scattershot break in rhythm and melody gave the impression of the journey moving from the road, uowards into air and I instinctively felt a true sense of aural levitation. A key change in any piece of music, if it comes at the right moment alters our inner harmonic and I felt the uplift of change along with the chime of engagement. As the piece developed and rotated in structure and effect, I heard a lyric, expressed – if it doesn't seem too much of an oxymoron – musically. Its meaning was deepened by repetition and then subtle variation and the end result to my way of thinking, was that here was a piece of music teaching the heart in the school of the ear.

Rozaball Secret began with a series of musical;ascensions and confirmations as Sitar and Tabla substantiated the piece's eternal and ultimate claim on spiritual truth. As the piece developed, it implied fast moving but graceful montages of visual experience; glimpses from the road of revelation and recovery; spells we might sing deep within.

Andrea Seki informed us that *These Days In Srinagar*, was prompted the ancient songs of the Bardik tradition and the voyages and struggles of love, and indeed the opening harp passage epitomised both the complexities of feeling and understanding of what love is, along with the preparations for that journey of discovery. Seki's harp was precise, passionate, beautiful. Dreau's accompaniment emphasised support and womanly inspiration and De Graef enquired onwards into the chain of sound, all due to the magic of breath. A sung piece, containing evocative and memorable verses, such as 'In the silent night of Srinagar/I feel the secrets of this time/In these days of Srinagar/ I feel my heart within the stars, ' that allowed the lyrics to fuse with the music in more of a compositional way, than in a standard song form, and this helped to enhance both piquancy and context..

The album's title track opened with glorious rolling cascades of harp, that played with rhythm and tempo and I instinctively glimpsed a variety of rotating and revolving images, from a child cartwheeling down a soft and forgiving hill in slow motion, to abstracted shapes suggesting externalised auras cleansing and restoring the space around them. These reverberations and inferences, allowed for a deepening of each image, as glistening vibraphone implied the glamour of a sun christened sea.

The closing interpretation of a classic Indian Raga, *Raga Bhimpalasi* united the entire quintet in a tribute to the music that inspired them. The fruit of their past studies tasted fresh in the momentarily jasmine infused air, creating a new form of teaching for us all. The conversation of strings between sitar and harp were celebrated by De Graef's muscular flute work and dignified by Dreau's vibraphone. Khetani's palm on the tabla pushed forwards as his fingers arced and tapped out the measures of life. Revelation was induced and celebrated and we on a close London night were taken in hand and transported back in time, over time and *despite* time to lands that though they may seem far away, are in actuality as close as the dream that attends the nightly closing of our eyes. Indeed, this music and the people playing it were the conveyors and translators of night, moving the attainments of dream directly in line with the day.

Musicians like this are the reasons for Art. In meeting them briefly afterwards, they were as generous and humble and as devoted to the ideas that formed them as you would want them to be, Sadly this is often not the case in other areas and forms of contemporary practice. The Elfic Circle Project leads us back towards an ancient chain of discovery, in which we can marry the shallow concerns of everyday life with something hopefully longer lasting. Music as reminder that we were once so much greater than this.

It should be said that these were my impressions of a concert, having never heard the trio before. I am attempting in a few words to encapsulate instrumental and partly voiced pieces to give you the reader an impression and to do what I can to prepare the way for the album. It will doubtless have all of Youth's expert understanding of sound and its attendant aims and possibilities, but the purety and skill of its players are what I wish to convey. Musicians like this are the greatest artists of all because they have nothing to hide behind, unlike actors and many current artists. In conversation, they were as delightful and devoted as I'd hoped, and their producer/manager, R. Rovers' devotion to them was extraordinary. We fall into a trap in this country around our artists, both in terms of who we celebrate and how we choose to celebrate them. These six people gently relocated what we should all try to feel about artistic endeavour and showed in a just few minutes that this is clearly a project of worth..

A filmed interview and album review will follow. I thoroughly recommend this music, but I'm sure you, the reader have worked that out already. When the album arrives it will show that the difference between so called New Age and packaged World music and that which truly comes from an authentic time and place is simple: style and substance are the fruit of two separate trees.

Look carefully. The sun has reflected itself on the water and is as we speak changing leaves.

28th September 2016

CASUAL GODS:

An account of recording with Kiranpal Singh and Clem Alford (Youth's Recording Studio, London 2016)

Perhaps one of the only true aims in life is to live close to beauty, and of a kind that is conjured from the small pains of man. On Monday October 10, 2016 I was privileged to sit in on a recording session at seminal Polymath producer, artist, poet and musician, Youth's London base which featured two maestro's of Indian music, Sitarist Clem Alford and Santoor Player, Kiranpal Singh. Over four hours both men recorded five composed and improvised songs and patterns, ranging from three to fifteen minutes in length as part of the Indo-TranCeltic sessions arranged by Elfic Circle Project Producer and Manager R. Rovers, and curating artists Dr. Frances Shepherd and Anjan Saha from PRSSV Management, for an album to be released by Manodharma Records.

Seated on the floor, first Kiranpal and then Clem and then Kiranpal again summoned the musical landscapes of the ancient east in the London room, transporting all in attendance from a rain infused day in the south.

One is struck at the ease by which such masters create and configure the sounds they represent and convey. Indian music is based on a series of patterns and systems, of which the raga is the most famous, but other forms such as the dhun are just as beguiling. From these approaches, melodies, harmonies and rhythmic patterns of effortless beauty emerge.

Two new Santoor compositions began the session, emerging from Kiranpal Singh despite the acute discomfort of a head piercing toothache. Music, as R. Rovers commented would be his healer and so it proved as the faultless performance betrayed no sign of unease. The Santoor is both percussion and strings and each strike resounds with emanations from an ancient bell, quickly supported by the smooth scratch of the strings, creating the impression of voices within a fluid cloud, taking shape as the music plays on. It is an instrument of celebration and premonition and seems to speak with a voice of both warning and wisdom. On listening one feels guided, not only into song and the Indian classical traditions of which it is part, but also on a journey whose destination it has somehow seen. Perched on the lap, Singh plays with both power and delicacy, communing with the gods of perfection.

The drone-cloud of tuning that typifies Indian instrumentation is shared of course by the sitar. From this spell of sound the notes arrive, unbidden and Alford's mastery over forty years takes us straight to the long sought for mystic terrain. While one instrument is in the key of D and the other in C Sharp, these separate voices create a unified language. And in this session their separate expressions combined to make the most beautiful of statements. As Clem Alford played, he transcended his own earthbound condition to become one with the music he knows so well and represents with such skill. After his two new compositions he overdubbed two ambient, trance like tracks from a new project by Youth, and while we could not hear the music he could in his cans we in the room, were treated to a perfectly formed live sitar composition that emerged spontaneously and complimented the assignment with not one misstep or misplaced intention. On hearing the piece on playback we were struck by how organic his part had been, as if it had been at the root of the new song from the start. When Clem left for a performance engagement later that day he had completed four new contributions in little more than an hour. With a shrug, a fastening of the coat and a slipping on of the shoes he was off on his next pilgrimage.

Kiranpal Singh resumed the seated position and although ailing slightly by now, played on the same new pieces and two others with stunning fluidity and flexibility. Both men are true masters of their form and style and cross the field of their endeavours like the most elemental of forces. A few strikes for sound on the strings and awareness of the given key, and Kiranpal Singh's skill and talent were once more unlocked. All of us listening were aghast at the beauty he brought into being. Youth listened and guided the session as he worked on other projects on other levels of the house and at one point his fellow esteemed Producer, John Leckie popped in to say hello. Having worked with everyone from the days of Abbey Road, the old Harvest label and through The Stone Roses, onto other world masters such as Santoor Maestro, Shiv Kumar Sharma at Peter Gabriel's Real World HQ, it was delightful to see these musicians connect and align with some of western musics' most prominent guiding forces.

More than any other artists, musicians of this calibre are able to surmount any obstacle and attain the summit of achievement through nothing more than their experience and inner voice. Singh's santoor was made for him and so speaks with his own inner mode of expression, as does Alford's Sitar, his companion across his long and distinguished career. It is in these instances of normality that new worlds are truly brought into being. Music is the means and mode of travel and from these sounds the seeds of our potential are sewn. As the highest and purest form of art, music is its own prayer, its own means of transubstantiation. It is the method by which the unsteady world achieves peace.

We are all of us gods when close to beauty. Music like this is religion, making each of us our own priest. On a normal day and with no ceremony, and in casual clothes our ascendence remains ours to choose.

It was under Youth's auspices that this session took place. This small poem was offered in tribute.

In your house of sound,
All attend
To your musical Babel,
Rooms bred for voices, each resonant with a truth.
Sun at each touch, while rain taints the window,
A palace whose subjects join the ancient to now
Thanks to Youth.
With gratitudefor your time, we celebrate these endeavours.
Priase and peace to you,
As you draw from the greyness of day,
Gold, then blue.

11th October 2016

IN EXCELCIS

A review of Hypnopazuzu's Performance of *Create Christ Sailor Boy* Union Chapel, London October 22nd 2016

Music as communion. On Saturday October 22nd 2016 a full house of counter culturalists and lovers of the transformative powers of musical transferral and resurrection collected to witness Current 93 founder David Tibet's new project with Youth, probably modern music's most artful artist and collaborator. The album, available to stream and buy on itunes, *Create Christ Sailor Boy*, is a remarkable slab of drone like summoning and muscular angelicism. Over ten pieces and an hour and a quarter the deepest rumblings of a bass stoked earth are invoked alongside the sharpest electronics and the ascendant purity of Tibet's voice and words. Ambient textures both soothe and challenge as we are led on that journey of ascension, one that reveals, invokes and uncovers a darker purpose in all of us.

After a spectacular recital of doom struck, wing piercing soundscapery from support act The Stargazer's Assistant, Hypnopazuzu take the stage, after a treated and has to be said, aurally impressive recording of 'Chirpy chirpy cheep cheep, ' the final notes being slowly consumed by the eerie and demonic scapings of a sharp cloud of electronica. The band comprises of Youth and his associates Michael Rendall on keyboards, Gerry Diver on Violin and Bodran, Bede Trillo on Guitar, Jamie Grashion on Moog, Tom Grashion on Drums and Gong, Stanley Manning on harmonium and long string drones gong with Youth himself on Bass and Drone Harmonium. Together these men create a shifting landscape of sound, tectonic aural awakenings whose structure and melody provide the journey for David Tibet's vocals and vision to follow.

Tibet entered moments after to wild applause, clutching a small plastic bag containing poems, creeds and lyrics and as his voice soared forth I was immediately transported. The opening song that emerged from the swelling black cloud of noise and majesty was stoked into being by Diver's violin and the combined harmonium drones supplied by Youth, Manning and Grashion. The song, *Your Eyes in the Skittle Hills* calls us all to Create Christ a Sailor Boy, set upon the waves of our own needs and desires and Tibet is instantly established as a musical shaman, druid or priest, commanding and demanding worship. While sounding like nothing on earth there were textures and satisfactions here that took in everything from the Hillier Ensemble to Dead Can Dance, Tibet and Youth's home bands, Current 93 and Killing Joke, to the soundtrack of some primal inner yearning. The songs, classified as religious on itunes do so much more than reflect that as a belief system or genre. They create their own god and set the Christ figure that Tibet imagines, evokes and summons high on his own stellar sea.

There is a unity to the songs, and a force also. *Christmas with the Channellers* rages and roars at the private heart with a surging, malignant power. Youth's bass rumbles from somewhere close to Hades while Diver drives the highest frequencies of the violin to tear the very clouds from the sky. Tibet's voice rides the crest as the music, a mixture of a blood stained soul and devilish electronics takes us ever further into and towards Tibet's sacred destination. The salutary nature of the drums powers on and one imagines a giant slave like creature breaking through the earth in his attempt to snag or smear an escaping angel.

Conversely *The Crow at Play* skimpers along at a bodran driven pace, its gaelic overtones skilfully mastered by Tibet's celebration of an oncoming palace of the mind as Youth and Jamie Grashion join him on vocals. The music is rich and vibrant while still shot through with the same elemental force of the other pieces. The music is blood coloured, glistening with the gold of other fluids spent and purefied in the sparking fires of expression.

The Sex of Stars is a standout in a set of standouts. Michael Rendall's stentorian piano figure demands continued repetition. It is the kind of simple chordal riff you dream of both playing and writing if you really love music on a deeper level and this structure allows Tibet to eviscerate and explore his astral exhumations to the fullest effect. Trillos's guitar soars as Youth's bass fills in the voids of absence that Tibet sings of and the pace and tempo accelerate and reach an orgasmic rush that draws us all out of our seat, encouraging us to move our bodies in as frenzied a way as our personal inhibitions will allow. The band is as tight as it is intense and the Union Chapel proves once again it is the perfect venue for this sort of music. Concerts do indeed become sermons here, served up by everyone from David

Byrne and Paul Simon, to Dead Can Dance, The Enid and Simon Fisher Turner, and the majesty of the building seems to increase as Hypnopazuzu summon and manifest semblances of our own inner gods.

Magog at the Maypole steers and swirls towards a form of apocalypse and Tibet's vocals are incantatory in sound, rage and aspect. He is willing and ushering a rapt audience towards a ferocious dawn of expression, provoking anarchy while still maintaining control and exposing and exploring the full capability of the heightened senses. The music thunders and coarses through the blood that seems to shine in the veins of Tibet's throat as he sings. Youth's bass is right at the heart of the fire and the alchemical nature of the music is all encompassing.

Sweet sodom SingSongs capers out on the sound wings of a plucked sitar as the ritualistic drum pattern surges us ever onward to still further heights of inspiration. This is music and this is an album and project that creates a world, separate to our own and closer to whatever guiding forces there may in fact be, awaiting us in the higher, or perhaps deeper reaches. It is pagan, animalitic, spiritualised and infused with the gold in the seam of the dream.

Pinocchio's Handjob's mighty chordal sweep confirms and echoes some of the power of The Sex of Stars and after a blast of bursting flute from multi-skilled harmonic master, Diver, Tibet escorts us towards a form of armageddon that would surely await that famous puppet as his desire was planed away by a frenzied masturbatory grip. Tibet is a famed Noddy fan so the inspiration here maybe a clearing away of a famed rival and what he or it represents. Certainly the representatives and emblems abound in Tibet's lyrics as he clears the spiritual and emotional decks of what we have come to rely on and bids us all towards a greater sense of scope and worship. The totems of such figures from Christ to this other wooden boy are important to his writing and this deeply skilled exponent of outsider art is expert at describing the interior states of those held within the confines of the conventional.

The Aura's are escaping the Forest arrives on a cloud of glisten and buzz and a deeper range of vocal. Diver takes the higher frequencies as Tibet stays close to the floor as if communing with the hidden forces, in a way and with a voice and language that's reminiscent of Lisa Gerrard's channelling of Latin, Greek, Turkish, Armenian and

Hebrew. The song builds and spirals like a bird escaping the entwined branches of a celestial forest and the light sears through the gathering sound. By the end of the song Tibet and the band have attained a screeching fury that makes magic of music in its most transformative and effective way.

The closing piece, *Night Shout, Bird Tongue* draws the concert to a dignified conclusion. The grand sweep of the chords underlies and carries the weight of thought, dream and spirit we have all been priviliged to witness. Tibet sings of 'the tall grass, bending like words, ' and as we listen, I am reminded of how reality too can so easily shift when the correct thought or soundtrack is placed beneath it. Hypnopazuzu and all of Youth and David Tibet's work is about undermining and exploring that reality and its limitations and how we fall prey to it. They are also of course committed to the ways and means with which we can learn to survive and resist it. Music like this achieves its own commendation through its strength, depth and substance. In Exelcis Deo: Glory to the god in our ears.

David Tibet photo and copyright by Ruth Bayer

DIRECTOR OF JOY:

An overview of the work of Greg Wilson's *Super Weird Substance* and the Sounds at The Heart of the Dream

If you were not entirely aware before, a new world is waiting, made only of music to power the heart, soul and feet. The following piece is meant as some sort of tribute to Greg Wilson's *Super Weird Substance* label and the plethora of works featured, remixed, DJ'ed and curated by Wilson and his cohorts, including Josh Ray, Black Grape's Kermit Leveridge, The Reynolds Sisters and others including The Great Alan Moore and Tim Holmes of Festival 23.

> *'A multimedia label founded by DJ Greg Wilson, Super Weird Substance deals primarily with Balearic Psychedelic Dub Disco recordings while hosting on the live side 60's styled happenings that include talks, art, bands and DJs.'*

For over 35 years, Liverpool born DJ, Greg Wilson has been at the heart of the Manchester sound, from the decks of the Hacienda when they mattered the most, to the current underground, rippling the earth beneath our feet with some of dance music's most urgent and innovatory beats. That he and his colleagues continue to redefine and work towards new standards of fashion and delivery when those once golden times have to a large extent rusted over, is testament to the energy and artistry of those working under the Super Weird Substance label.

Even the title is right. At a time when life itself is in danger of collapsing under prejudice, political ignorance and spiritual vacancy, here is music as lifeblood to pump and refuel the lost way. The shadows to which we are all falling prey to, are gathering and the substance within us is spoiling. In his work as DJ and producer, Wilson is attempting to separate the source from the infection and create some sort of dance fed curative. He places these solutions in the sound cloud in the hope that they rain down on us all. At a time in which we are blasted and beset on all sides, dance music becomes elemental, shamanistic, seminal. It is the method and means of escape.

As I type I am listening to a number of Wilson's DJ sets, currently, a recent show at XOYO London on October 12th 2016 in which classic funk and 80's electronic ride a dance beat that both compels and entrances. These are instructions to dance yourself clear of danger, music that will breach the empty spaces subsumed by society. Wilson is fighting a battle against the darker forces with the beat and the groove as his guide.

The tracks expand organically, the shifts in rhythm and bass led excursions rise above any and all musical tastes and deliver you into the realm of transcendence in which the club or bedroom becomes your own chamber primed for teleportation to the almost central areas that dance aims towards. Listener, music maker and DJ become one being, one consciousness, locked in the search for solution. These crucial shifts can be heard in everything from Bach to Philip Glass, and the systems of change and renewal are clearly working for us. Each set is a move towards the sun, perfect for an outdoors festival or gig, but relevant also to a venue that's shrouded by night.

A Portmeirion ('automatic/systematic') set glides with delicious urgency. The brow furrows not with sorrow but with pleasure as the sublime vocals make a new backing band for your soul. The more you listen the more aware you of the almost campaign like nature at play here. Wilson is to the DJ what Mick Jagger (like him or not) is to the frontman; he is the progenitor of a new standard, updating the examples previously laid down, (such as in Wilson's case by the notorious Wigan Pier stylings of electro funk he practised early in in his career - or in Jagger's case, all lead singers) to the most vital aspects of the current re-edit scene that give the past a contemporary twist. Funk becomes fashion and so much more than mere fancy. It holds the frequency in which the heart begins hearing and the vascular finds its voice.

Joy is the point and the agenda behind these musical offerings to the gods of night. Wilson is the high priest, proffering not burnt remains but rather, shining stars that glitter and glimmer with all of the best we can be.

A remix of Prince's *Sign o' the times* from a set in Washington DC in May of this year betters the original – if that's possible – as does other remixes, from treatments of Gwen Stefani's *Rich Girl* to the Talking Heads' *Psycho Killer*, the tinny percussive repetitions doing more to honour the unbalanced nature of the protagonist than even David Byrne's own neck led gyrations led him into.

Blind Arcade meets Super Weird Substance in the Morphogenetic Field is a mixtape by Wilson that features demos and works in progress by Kermit Leveridge and EVM128 which shows that *'reality is not what it seems and what we see might not be real.'* What is real is the artistry on display here, the experimentation not at the expense of listenability or avant gardism, but in ways that deepen the groove. We rarely think about why we dance or how, and the intention here is not to do that, but as the tracks evolve the mix of near tribal drumming and classic doo-wop samples from 'Sherry Baby, ' demonstrate how dance music in its most innovatory guise is more akin to painting or the lingual collagism of Burroughs and Gysin at their best. Alan Moore echoes in with refrains and reminders on the nature of information and what it, as our own super weird substance actually does to us. It is, as is mentioned, a strange world indeed.

Available as a limited edition one sided 7 inch single, Kermit's setting of the much missed Howard Marks' reading of 'Lies and Other Fools' is a break in this collection of beats. Here, sparse chords, electronic signals and industrial surrounds house Marks' incantation of the *'memories of affection..and layers of evil stacked precariously at the doors of perception..filled by a heroin glide.. as tears fall into place.'* Jon Rose's soundscape grants Marks' impassioned reading a greater death fed glory and reminds us that the Super Weird Substance of our supposed reality manifests itself in many forms and that these associates are artists working in a given medium. It could be said that 'house' or dance music in its purest form and original context was self serving (nothing wrong with that as it could also be argued that it was in part a reaction to the constraints of Thatcherism) and the soundtrack to a thousand nights of rain kissed hedonism and a once fashionable drug. In the works of this label, it is a musical pigment and a means of expression beyond even the goals of the word.

The Super Weird Substance CD compiles the eight singles released in the four month span from July to October 2015, featuring Blind Arcade and The Reynolds Sisters, it heralded new album projects and happenings from this year and into the next that are simply irresistible.

Wilson's sublime composition *Summer Came My Way* opens proceedings with a blissful but insistent balearic style groove and transcendent vocals from Carmel Reynolds, Katherine Reynolds and Tracey Carmen. It captures you and your need to become part of the song completely. Just as Brian Eno has praised backing vocals as the song's invitation to the listener to take part, so the artful construction allows you in, sewing you fashionably to singer, composer, mix and performance. This music doesn't hammer you into position like the most oppressive and areas of the tatty nightclub at 3am, but gracefully threads you into place with all of the refinement of a party in paradise.

Sweet Tooth T's *She Can't Love you/Feel the Same* harks back to the last days of disco in NYC in 1979 and once more The Reynolds beautifully crest Tyrell's programming, offering insistence and a gentle hand lain on your shoulder as you place your hand on their hip while taking to the dance floor with one or indeed, both of them. Its a chic chic, more electronic but just as human and overpowering and has some of the feel of what Stuart Price was trying to do with Madonna. A piece like this is far more successful, as it comes out of the experience and grand plan of Wilson's overview, who along with his cohorts and colleagues and it has to be said, audiences, has pioneered what dance music can do since the late 1970's. Wilson is an elegant and good looking man and therefore his ease with the beauty on hand is assured.

Kermit Leveridge and SWS' mix of The Stooges *I Wanna Be Your Dog* is exemplary and reveals just how much Madonna stole for the *Confessions on the Dancefloor* album from the truer elements of dance and electronic music. The cover also exposes how powerful the song is when taken out of the doghouse and placed under the glare of a dazzling light. Each piece on the CD runs from four to eight minutes and shows how the happening live sets, some of which are mentioned above – and for which there are hundreds – can be contained or perhaps represented within the confines of one song. If that isn't what a composer, photographer, poet, or playwright does then I am not who I thought I was. This is both a direct example of the DJ and Mixer's art, as it is a slice of musical alchemy.

World Gone Crazy, written by Tracey Carmen and Greg Wilson and Performed by the Reverend Clive Freckleton shows how a former Minister of Music can call out against the evils of the world for the benefit of a lost and disillusioned post acid house generation in a language that they will really appreciate. The driving rhythm is the perfect platform for a subtly changing top line. This is perhaps something that rap doesn't have as a musical genre, (recent advances from Kendrick Lamar aside) with all of its sameness of style. The same of course could also be said of any major musical form from Ska to Prog, but here the sound deepens as Freckleton's growl summons the very devil to move himself free from the bass.

The Reynolds twins next provide a sweet antidote in their cover of Bessie Banks' *Don't You Worry Baby The Best is Yet To Come*, a soulful and beat laced treatment of Clyde Otis and Herman Kelly's tune, while Blind Arcade's *Give It Away* is Kermit and EVM128's epic call for positivity in life which uses programming, strings and motown style brass to convey its message of empathy and progression.

As you listen to these songs you become aware that more than in any other practise, the musicians, mixers and artists in the so called north of England have always enlightened the south, from The Beatles to The Happy Mondays, there is nothing that Liverpool and Manchester hasn't seen and acted upon first. I spent a number of years in those areas and some of the standards I have set for myself in my own work as actor, writer, director and teacher were formed there and have sustained me and the others I have worked with since. We are often lost in London, hoisted on our own petard and thinking we are the centre of the universe. As Alan Moore has stated in a previous piece, that fulcrum starts in Northampton and spirals out across the provinces. Along each crucial seam are pockets of resistance and the fresh suits for musical and spiritual change. These advances are no more evident than in the work that Greg Wilson, Kermit Leveridge, Josh Ray, The Reynolds and all their collaborators, new and old have always been doing.

Along with a range of fashionable merchandise Super Weird Substance has also produced a fanzine, *Beneath the Manhole Cover*, which takes in everything from Kurt Vonnegut to Cocaine Toothdrops. They are using music and all the other forms of their preference and expression to join the dots along the staves of our own consciousness. They are orchestrators of the internal symphony and arrangers of the personal song. Greg Wilson and his colleagues are all that a DJ and an artist needs to be and should be: They are the Directors of Joy. Now we must dance towards dawn.

Motor Museum

The Reynolds

Kermitt and Cleve
photos and copyright by Elspeth Moore

ON THE TRANSLATION OF SPIRIT TO SNAKE
A review of Unicazurn's new album *Transpandorem* (Touch 2016)

Unicazurn's new album *Transpandorem* announces itself with both an umlaut and sounds of uncanny arrival, as if a vast astral craft was seeking earthly location, changing the ground as it lands. As harsh winds accompany this embodiment of aural conquest, an altogether different and less enchanting air is brought into being. In these opening moments the musicians behind this intricate music making are teaching the mind what to hear. Made of two electronic compositions, the first *Breathe The Snake* encourages the listener to inhale not only the essence of a sound driven serpent rising and settling through this mix of aural alchemy, but also the separate powers and tensions behind its very creation. With Stephen Thrower on keyboards, saxophone, string machine and treated woodwinds and David Knight on guitar, synths and organ, shamanism crests and coarses its way, free of storms, to the ear.

Touch's beautiful vinyl package makes this album a totemistic object in itself, evident in Jon Wozencroft's striking cover image of suffering leaves and wheat, and the shimmering density of *Breathe the Snake* enables us to conjure a kind of coruscation and virus affecting the landscape of sense. Musical Duos have always been some of the most effective ways to get new music across from the days of Parisian Chanson in the 1920's with voice and piano, through to the exuberant dalliances of The Associates or Yello, but here Knight and Thrower prove themselves to be expert soundscapists of the highest order. Indeed, music can be said to be the highest of all the forms in terms of what it is able to do, making those who make it, virtual Druids of reflex and interconnection. Magicians of any stamp and sort are the true artists of change. I would go as far as to call them the shapers and controllers of space, affecting the immediate destiny of the moment by changing the air around us. Here, in these two pieces of music, a sense of sculpture and structure combines with the spread and flow of the 'sound-paint, ' allowing us to release the snake Unicazurn would have us summon and watch as its ensuing trail scars and re-fissures the land.

Each moment of this first piece allows for transformation as the music moves and invokes its inherent reptile. The texture of the cover artwork therefore acts as a useful equivalent to what these wonderful musicians are making in and of themselves. A spell is cast, solely in terms of sound and one that guides and shapes our understanding and perception of what we are presented with. In both of the pieces of music on this album you hear echoes of every ground breaking experimental artist from Delia Darbyshire to Simon Fisher Turner and Christian Fennesz, through flickers and shades of Wendy Carlos and early examples of JM Jarre, Vangelis and John Surman and yet each is subsumed in a greater glory; an elegant and almost inspiring call for mental and physical change.

Records like this are played not to be studied but to be experienced in the same way that art and photographs are and as the piece concludes the story is left unfinished. Indeed a CD or digital version should be played on endless rotation with the limited revolutions of the record merely announcing the spiralling path to adopt.

Although individual in character, both compositions influence and reflect each other, with Knight and Thrower exploring the fringes of their own internal landscapes and worldview, while at the same time asking us to enquire at the borders of where music and sound effectively converge. There are echoes of the austerity of Rick Wright's *Sysyphus* (from Pink Floyd's *Ummagumma*) in both pieces, but in Breathe the Snake, the sound soon swells with distant echoes of a more acceptable sense of welcome than in that slightly formless piece from 1969. In 2017, this is music to enter into, as well as being sounds, ideas and images that will in turn, enter you. If music cannot move or transform us in some way, it is scarcely worth describing as music at all. That which we can write off easily, we can no more write about in a truly useful way, than the worst kind of moral or political transgression. On this sublimely accomplished record and in these two compositions that ripple with a range of suggested ideas and intentions we have something ambient and ethereal that we can, in a very real way, hold onto.

Side Two's *Pale Salt Seam,* is the calmer of the two pieces, and extends the strictures of ambience with a delightfully mesmeric quality. By summoning Terry Riley at his most primal, its String machine workings produce a virtual factory of reflection, as if the density of Side One of the record had found its solution or balm. While falling into the areas of experimentation, improvisation and electronica, covered by magazines like *Wired* (and even the outer pages of *Prog*), both musical statements extend the supplied remits as to where this music can go and more importantly, how it can get there. This is because, like the best line in Pinter, something else is suggested beneath. By fashioning their own world in a genre that is already about creating effective alternatives, this particular duo are rearranging the surface of sound. They are using the musical equivalent of ambiguities usually found in drama to enthral and enrapture. This is a piece of vinyl that rises across and indeed through technology to make its own claim on the need for reformation. This lofty statement stems from how Unicazurn seem to me to have fashioned their own unique sound from recognisable elements as well as creating an implied visual gallery. The name of the band and of the music it produces, conjures echoes of place, affiliation and states of being. As a combined approach and system, Unicazurn offers a reason to experience and imagine the new, as well as providing a useful signpost through sound. Listen if you are interested in joining with the musicians to compose an end product together, not in the same way that Brian Eno talks, or talked about generative music at the start of the century, but in the almost standard way of combining title with sound to create a new and ever evolving idea. Eno's most affecting album title in my opinion is and will always be, *Another Green World*. Unicazurn take you to one of their own making and imagining. They even go as far as to provide climate and scenery. Now it is you who must people the plain.

We who are pale must work with the salt forces within us to merge and seek congress; Man meats his new world in this musical/magical seam.

17th January 2017

SEPARATING THE HEART

On Stian Westerhus' new album *Amputation* (House of Mythology 2016)

In the fight between our two major organs, the heart is its own unique instrument. Stian Westerhus' new album *Amputation* newly released on Mark Lewis' visionary *House of Mythology* label is an uncanny statement on that particular strain of music and its attempts to express inner feeling and outward action. Comprised of six consciousness shredding pieces, this beautifully designed object transcends its physical CD form and allows for transformation to take place on many levels in and around the listener. The compositions all feature Westerhus on voice, electric guitar and drum machine, but this is no lonely outpouring made in a cramped bedroom. Here, all three performative elements combine to influence each other, with plaintive solo Frippertonic style guitar transmogrifying into celestial discord on album opener *Kings Never Sleep*, and indeed the more extreme textures of the aforementioned Fripp in his royal guise as King of all things Crimson is in evidence at times, albeit balanced by the Jonsi like vocal approach that Westerhus makes entirely his own.

Indeed, each composition explores the extremes that this combination of musical forces can allow, as melodies are stated, deconstructed, examined in separation and left, either partially truncated, or else resolved by a thoroughly affecting rearrangement of motifs. *Sinking Ships*, the second pieces does this superbly and as Westerhus vocalises in transcendently elegant spirals of growl and falsetto, in combinations of English and Norweigan soundings, he seems to comment on and complement what the music is doing beneath his fingers. Regardless of whether this album was composed or recorded in a small studio or bedroom, Westerhus defies the notion of the solo songwriter seeking sustenance or muse, as he takes on the form of musical shaman as the reverberations of guitar and treated percussion bring the ceiling to the floor and then, more importantly, propel that floor skywards in arcs of aspiration.

These pieces are not just songs, even if they reference that trusted form, they are something else as well, at once higher and in some way far more mature than the still forming youngster forever searching for his lost middle eight. As Westerhus sings of 'tracking through the snow, he too is rising ever higher, literally elevating the form he has chosen for his own expression. He is separating the areas necessary to do that and providing the amputation that leads to renewal. This is so called cerebral music achieving a full pitch of emotion and showing that the progressive, experimental and even avant garde sections of record shops anywhere (as opposed, sadly, to everywhere) are where you will find what new music is actually *for*.

How Long capers in a haphazard spangles of treated guitar notes as the protagonist struggles to make his way across his encumbered and heavily burdened eight and a half minute landscape. As his musical feet rise through ice and snow, angelic distortions and variation allow release and transformation, as if the journey was being handled by the most skilled of dramatists and film makers. Indeed, that is the main impression here, that Westerhus has a unique understanding of the elements of drama. These reside not just in the areas of text or content, but far more in those of structure, texture, contrast and tone.

Title track, *Amputation* starts with a virtual avalanche of noise, combining drone, buzz, squeal, pulse and reverberant apocalypse in the making; a storm of noise emanating from one man, who in acting as his own producer is also able to control the elements of his own alchemy to stunning effect. Here, music becomes the landscape it can be seen to emerge from as opposed to just reflecting it. As the controlled chaos achieves mastery, Westerhus' sung ghostly refrains are, if not a soothing wind or passage of air or light through the darkness, then certainly some sort of promise of reformation. The pain of amputation as a concept in itself is echoed here, not just as a physical event but as a spiritual one, the organ rattling its own inner keys as removal occurs, with the eventual recovery glimpsed as a long lost goal, suddenly drawing ever closer on a cloud of steel winged electronica, as if the guitar was summoning the angels of return to deliver us into a form of salvation.

'Choose between the bright lights and the city walls' Westerhus sings not just as a way of defining yourself as something freed or contained but as someone conducting and rearranging their own consciousness, imposing and fusing it on the environment that forms and surrounds them at once.

In its opening moments, *Infectious Decay* channels Radiohead with its skittering beats and use of Westerhus moving between high and low vocal registers. However, like the best music the piece and its composer soon shows why a possible reference has been used in a certain way and the propulsive beat is soon embedded into the melodic treatment and transformed. Limited modes of expression are revealed as the true means of achieving something expansive and indeed greater and Westerhus as player, programmer, singer, structuralist and conductor of the listener's response proves himself to be a maestro in the best sense in which that term is useful for a rock/modern music style audience; He is attempting to change how we experience the song as both cultural object and totem in itself. Songs speak to the heart just as rhythm appeals to the body. This album seeks to wrench these functions apart and examine them in ways that are as instinctive as they are expert. Rhythms are distributed and disseminated. Melodies are watered and contained. The listener's response is the true home for the harmonies separate to those provided by Westerhus's vocals and the barrage and explosions of distortion which come unbidden in closing track, *Amputation Part 2* allow us to reach for the calmer moments we have previously experienced in order to reunite the parts of ourself that have been torn asunder. As the album reaches its conclusion the music literally breaks apart, allowing us to piece together the remnants of our own passage through it. Music is the highest and most effective of all the artistic forms. In this one forty minute, exquisitely packaged album, Stian Westerhus has showed us how the amputations faced everyday by everyone of us that often go unrecognised contain the root of connection to everything around us. Broken and beaten and unaware of both our own pain and avenues of redemption, we may lose ourselves in the obfuscation and snow we place around and before us. Thankfully, from that possible sense of obliteration, a new and cleansing cold is approaching, in which all of our wounds may be healed.

Supported by the Arts Council Norway, *Amputation* has been nominated for a Norweigan Grammy. That an album of such ferocious beauty and anger garners awards shows us closer to the Mediterranean drift that so called 'art music', if that is the correct term, need not have the glacial politeness of ECM to achieve its own glistening state of grace. The sun coasts the ice and brings with it, colour. Long may your Angels attend.

10th January 2017

SOOTHING THE STING

An impression of *Laniakea – A Pot Of Powdered Nettles* By Massimo Pupillo and Daniel O Sullivan (House Of Mythology 2016)

An eerie fugal cascade, like a choir arriving from a point beyond death heralds this remarkable album from Massimo Pupillo and Daniel O Sullivan. The music rumbles with the primal forces of the earth while resounding with something both celestial and ominous. *Laniakea - A Pot of Powdered Nettles* is a tribute to seminal artist, permaculturalist and Coil collaborator, Ian Johnstone, who Pupillo and O Sullivan befriended, worked with and been inspired by as members of Zu and Ulver respectively and who helped set in motion much of the thinking, resourcefulness and spiritualism behind England's true (reverse and) counter culture, based as much of it was at 147, Tower Gardens Road, Tottenham.

The first epic composition, *The Contagious Magick of The Superabundance* honours its title in a suitably majestic fashion. The land and air seem to shift about and beneath you, as if the sounds were urging or pressing the body or spirit to rise. A combination of Bass, Voice, Elka Crescendo 303 and M-tron keyboards, Viola, wind and the dark angelicism of Hildegard von Bingen allows these musical crests and tones to move in a truly tectonic fashion, as areas reminiscent of the outer reaches of Dead Can Dance's early music combines with the very spirit of air. As the forces gather something more than beautiful manifests; a form is in fact defining itself, or allowing itself to be defined, as we listen, with the music and soundscaping sculpting feelings and responses to the death of a beloved friend, shaping them into a kind of Aural Golem. The four pieces on the album are regarded by its makers as 'Heart songs' into which they have poured their joy, confusion, grief and philosophy. The resultant transcendent and transformative gift can do nothing but touch you as you realise how much they felt and owed to and for their friend. Loss is an ocean in constant motion and although these pieces end at certain times, the life and power of them continue. They are in a very real way, mastering the electric and making it truly elemental.

The second song, *The Sky is an Egg*, after a corralling of sharp and mutating breezes, achieves form and attitude with low electric guitar strikings. Sharp synth lines mutate as the incantatory lyric is intoned. *'The Sky is an Egg..With time presiding.. The sylvan night.. Pyracanthus protecting..'* Here are mystical codes and ancient greetings invoked to honour the passing of truly inspirational forces. Music as prayer, as sacred site, as communion. The passing of Leonard Cohen reminds us that although he could be summarised as the most sophisticated if perhaps conventional of rock music's balladeers, what marked him out, as has been noted by the great Heathcote Williams, is the notion of transcendence that featured in all his work. And so it is here, as Pupillo and O Sullivan call through the musical mist to their dead friend, praising time's renewal of the sky that houses the living and the dead with statements that unite all levels of existence;

'When you are in amber/ when you are in dust..Zone in parallel rose/Sewn in parallel rows..'

The statements and abstracted expressions of them, are effortlessly moving as we are taken beyond the limits of accepted language, with words capturing or attempting to capture what music does in an instant of mood or of note. We compose and restructure our grief through the use of any means necessary or open to us and create a new way to feel and to be.

Zone in Parallel Rose is the title of the third Heartsong. It skitters and scars with a merciless low drive of strings, while high pitched musical tendril like tones claw and graffiti the space around listening. Spells are literally pieced together as phrases and harmonies collide to create and unify this new arena for expression. Here, the *'tipping on axis'* gives way to a *'red ripe seed'* that creates *'flowers to form something in sleep.'* The *'penetration of the mind'* occurs when the journey between where you come from and where you are going is riven with a sense of loss and renewal.

Loss, in the west at least, is too often marked by a standard social occasion. This album, stemming as it does from bereavement on a personal level becomes a greater statement and one shareable with all manner of audiences. Grief is as constant a part of nature as the air that we breathe and the constant interelation of life and death finds echo and expression in these pieces. We move around, between and because of it, all the while inhaling and transmuting it and as it enters and fuses with what we are and what we hope to be, either in terms of ourselves as a whole or simply in relation to the forces around us, we learn to accommodate what many see as a horror, but which in effect is merely the frame for the vibrancy there in us all. The album is therefore, to my way of thinking, achieving something far more impressive than other music encountered on a purely experiential level. It is, through the very purity of its intention and resultant statement showing the love of the life that has passed and the essence that can still be maintained.

Closing piece *Calcite,* uses all stated instruments, along with Bamboo flute, Fingerbells, Chimes, Dictaphone, Uher 4400, Gamelan and more importantly, 'Francois and the feuding cats of Nunhead' to deliver us somewhere approaching a state of grace. As the rages and waves of response, anger and grief achieve understanding through an acknowledgement of the value of Ian Johnstone and all he inspired among his social and artistic circle, a new power blisters forth. Sounds and textures occur that lift the music from the CD player into the air and then through it. The artistry scours a hole into which we can see glimpses and impressions of everything made for the ear.

In 1969, Pete Townshend refered to King Crimson's groundbreaking first album *In the Court of The Crimson King*, as 'an uncanny masterpiece.' The same phrase can be applied to *Laniakea – A Pot of Powdered Nettles,* as its conjoining of light and darkness, of the affirmative and the ominous, of the bewildering and the profound, achieves a conversation between the parts of us that remember the dead and the parts that are still living with them. This is the power and usefulness of art. It should wound us as much as it soothes us. It must be of us and ready to change. In the twisting field of experience we all walk through, the nettle and thorn of loss implied in this album's title are broiled and alchemically changed. We become the music in its truest sense, as the most effective and affecting areas of art surely require a degree of commitment. Listening is not passive. It is an engagement on the most basic level if it is to classed as listening at all. And listening breeds empathy and connection. That is what lays at the heart of all drama afterall and which allows that field and therefore art and literature reflecting its outer reaches to join, fuse and become music. To progress in unity as a society of culturally informed and sensitive beings we should learn to share each others pain and successes and not just reflect on our own separate glories and trials. Music, if coming from the heart as these pieces clearly do, offers that possibility. It must and should tear us open. And so we must watch as our blood turns to gold.

THE PANDOREM: A PLACE FOR THE SOUL

Thoughts on Unicazurn live at Cafe Oto, London, Wednesday 25th January 2017

As Kubla Khan did for Xanadu, so Unicazurn have done for Dalston. Cafe Oto, the area's prime location for the performance of new music of all denominations proved the perfect host for David Knight and Stephen Thrower's mix of ambient industrial electronica, as they premiered elements and improvisations relating to their new album *Transpandorem* (Touch, 2017) in the flesh and on the strings, pads and keys.

Accompanied by legendary singer, experimental musician and performance artist Danielle Dax (whose first public performance in ten years, this was) on incantatory calls and whispered vocals and David J. Smith on percussion, brushes, cutlery and other tinctures of pressure and air, Knight and Thrower turned the upper reaches of Hackney into a place of shamanic transference. Playing to a full capacity of 150, the spirit-power-quartet of Unicazurn ably proved that the experimental and avant garde avenues of expression lead not to seclusion but to a sense of reformation. While some practitioners of the bleep, beat and feedback school keep the innocent and unschooled at bay (much like some of their prog and serialist antecedents did), Soundscapers like Knight, Thrower, Thomas Koner, David Sylvian, Christian Fennesz and Simon Fisher Turner are constantly seeking what sound and the inherent vision manifested by that sound, can do. Films of the mind, or aural spells are what are conjured through these musical explorations, joining and re-emphasising all of the artistic forms. Indeed, music like this does what acting should do, chiefly, provide its own aesthetic and theory, rather than just relying on the surface elements of presentation and ill-conceived interpretation.

The opening piece arrived on slides of grating power and tectonic like aural shifts as Knight sliced guitar strings with a butter knife and Thrower moved from ipad to organ, while Smith and Dax completed the spaces with echoes of voice hand managed ephemera. 'The Weevils in the tea.' surfaced as a phrase I hung onto as the piece motored and shimmered along. The general electricity in the room, sensed and literal, was personified by Dax's blue and purple hair, mascara and cherry red lips. This aligned with the vibrant stares and connections between the musicians as they summoned the numerous spirits of void. The informed improvisations that led to this and the other compositions created thoroughly believable, almost graspable worlds, another task of drama, if not to the point of touch then certainly to the edge of acceptability. This form of resonance transforms performances like this into encounters on an affecting instinctive and dammit – it must be said, spiritual level. We are transported, if not in a grand and lasting way, then certainly on a moment by moment basis, marking each phrase, mood or intonation and checking in with both those around us and more importantly within ourselves, about how each one of them speaks to and finds relevance in and around us.

Out of the miasma of aural intention, revelatory and resonant deep organ chords assumed a majesty that lifted the air. The effect was and is a coming together of elements, a fusing, or baking of the soul that thanks to the heat and energy in the room rises and colours one's thought.

Watching others listen is a unique experience and one that more than anything else separate to that special event that occurs between hearts and genitals, connects individuals. How we experience art on any level creates art, defines it. It is where art can be heard, felt, seen and shared. And the understanding that comes from a true and sensitive response provides the very beat of friendship. We can only perhaps locate a love for our fellow men and women across the bridge of taste and while those bridges vary enormously in terms of length, width and what they actually cover, I was struck by how closely others followed and allowed the sounds and musics played on this evening to transport each member of the audience towards their own inner pandorems.

That distinction has just occurred to me as I attempt to summon ways to describe and contain this live performance. It in no way captures the meaning of the album title, which remains Unicazurn's special province, and yet as a found phrase onto which I have imposed an interpretation it seems to allude to or define that place within us that both receives and is changed by music as it works its magic on us.

Improvisation in music is the most thrilling sort. As a celestial feel claimed the room, Thrower picked up his clarinet and somehow contained the scale of what had been happening within the slender body of that instrument. The industrial through the acoustic. Electronica summoned by application of mouth. David J. Smith charted his progress on cymbal and stick while Knight capered alongside and underneath providing a mixture of controlled chaos and fugal sympathy on his trusted electric to bring the piece to a significant and satisfying conclusion after 24 minutes.

I hereby change tense as I quote from my notebook, written while listening:

> *The second piece summons the arrival of the kind of Pink Floyd you always wanted but never quite received as an insistent churning figure is 'fripped' into transcendence by Knight's masterly chimes on guitar. Moments of discord threaten but are then folded back into submission as the guitar voice pierces through the Mo Tucker like beat of Smith's drum. Here is a velvet coloured underground in the purest sense, as freed from conventional song structure, while at the same time somehow echoing it, we caper along music's rim.*

The pieces that comprise *Transpandorem* and these live experiments, improvisations and variations strike me as the progeny and evolution of ambient classics such as Fripp and Eno's *No Pussy Footing* album and Peter Hammill at the peak of his Sonix and Unsung work. They do not copy them but seek to take the model further, so that one encounters this music in a new way. Despite the occassional harshness of texture, it invites us to participate. It is music you meet and converse with, creating the friendship of collaboration rather than leisure.

> *Reverberated shimmers settle around us or find the places to directly affect us, as if injected...*

This allowed us to move while sitting and experiencing, something that put me in mind of Bauhaus' Peter Murphy in the old Maxell cassette tape advert of the early 1980's as the winds of change and time ripped, roared and snagged themselves on his impressive cheekbones. Brevity aside;

> *..organ led resolutions subsume all with electric star shots as a place of calm is attained. Within this settling, one hears other distant orchestras, both earthly and alien and in my head the mind seemed to flutter and fold on developing tangents of real...*

THE PANDOREM: A PLACE FOR THE SOUL

Audiences are in essence, passive. As are consumers. Only those on the hunt for a bargain are active, desperate as they are for a quick fix or recognisable form of sustenance. Here, the music sought to fill its spectators with a sense of self and place. As I watched and listened I fancied I could hear the very act of listening itself and it occurred to me that concerts or recitals -which is what this more resembled - were and are opportunities to understand that listening is an act of consummation, both with the source of the sound and the feelings or things it begets. If we can forget where we are when we arrived to encounter it, then there has been a true and lasting renewal. We can experience in a new way what we have now become, through it. Art changes us every time that we see it, affecting us slightly degree by degree, piece by piece. This is why songs and albums remain with us over a lifetime, as do books and poems, films, paintings, plays. To do this with sounds seems to me the highest achievement. And tonight's transportation went from four people's evocation of that we only sense into a graspable thing for us all. There was ceremony here and celebration. There was study, reflection and real activity too.

The crowd's enthusiastic responses at each turn of events led to an encore of contained and then freed clarinet voicings, turntable like churn and ascending guitar wall, full of combined and soaring phrases. I watched Smith's extended shadow on the back curtain nodding towards the darkness like a Hassidic jew at the wailing wall and felt the religious combine with the spiritual and dare I say it, demonic. Outside, Dalston was bopping to its own frenetic rhythm. But inside this small tooth like building in its city sectioned jawline, the resounding mouth had been turned inside out.

The Pandorem is found. On that night in a low East London room, one hundred and fifty souls moved towards it, each one of them eager to locate their own starting ground.

6th Februray 2017

THE MIASMA MONKEY AND YOU

On Greg Wilson and Alan Moore's *Mandrill meets Super Weird Substance at the Art lab Apocalypse*: a mixtape for the heart, head and soul

Out of the miasma of music, noise and radio stylings conjured by Super Weird Substance's Grand Mix Meister Greg Wilson, carefully shaped leaves, shards and droppings of Alan Moore's *Mandrillifesto* obscure and influence both your peripheral vision and oncoming foresight. Assisted by the darkly angelic Reynold Sisters and the jungle fused flow of Kermit Leveridge, this corrall of musical shamans transforms your personal listening device and environment into a portal pointed towards a new world of potential. Moore's Mandrillifesto, birthed as a reaction to the oncoming horrors of Brexit is a savage and yet charming beast intent on plucking the ostrich's head out of the sand and thrusting its worm caked muck mask into your own corpulence.

Recently launched on Facebook by Moore and cohort Joe Brown as part of the Northampton Arts Lab's ongoing assault on contemporary culture and now being adapted for film and video by director Megan Lucas, this musical arm of the project is just as thrilling. After a dystopic interference spiked tuning in, the insistent groove hits you immediately, accompanied by a powerfully funk driven ape, grooving and growling to the ends of each hair on its dance smitten back. Radio K-O-N-G splinters the temperate air with a enough power to drive us all back to the primordial casserole of electric forces that sparked the first break-beat of shock and perception. We are at once in the realm of the King.

Moore as magical mandrill and 'musical marmoset' ushers in the 'savannah skanking of Desmond Morris and the Naked Aces, Left Handed Monkey Wrench.' The joy is unconfined.

'At a time of national demise' the need for such a powerful sense of reformation is undeniable. Cometh the mandrill to push us all towards the brightest dawn. The Reynolds soothe us towards pop like unification with their gorgeously alluring voices and swivel hipped rhythms, as samples of Chris Morris from one of Brasseye's greatest moments exhorts us to 'do it through a mandrill', taking the drug of revolution as a means of reshaping the day. This is an imaginary song from a group of wise and hidden hearts that calls on us all to emerge from a broken world. As the 'Messiah of the Mandrill' continues to transmute itself through a mix of ska, sampled Madness at their exuberant Camden best and Kermit Leveridge pushing us to the edge of Jimmy Cliff, vocal sweetness, coupled with warnings against the sour days we are currently presented with, compel us all to accept the mandrillifesto as the best way to make the only effective set of changes we can hope to muster.

From experimental (BBC) radiophonic avant-gardism to old school reggae, from the Northampton boulevards to the Jamacian shoreline, these musical variations are carried not by bird but by chimp across the tendrils of a culture 'Ballarding' itself into a state of Drowned World style disrepair. We are stoked, we are soothed, we are Charlton Hestoned into fresh states of awareness as the musical landscape shifts around us. Moore shares another glorious mandrill moment via 'Hoots & The My-tails' who proceed to construct a reggae and ukulele fashioned symphony skittering its way towards a new sense of celebration, achieved by 'painting the sky in grenadine..' and making 'loveliness compulsory.' Cometh the moment, cometh the mandrill as a force of change. Hoot to the blood of the moon as a totem for that much needed transformation and fresh means of becoming enables you to revisit your own inner Darwinism and reconnect with the formative wildness of your own tender bassline.

Reverberated echoes of noise shatter the beat at this point in the mix and settle, giving the effect of music being turned inside out and reversed, only to improve on the original surface design.

Monkey shrieks and antique film announcements then introduce mutated soul that proceeds to move at a frenetic pace as Moore as current DJ and Director of Joy, announces 'Bathtime for Bonzo', another rapture rippled warning. Only through the energy of funk, soul and transatlantic rhythm can we push ourselves towards a new state of recognition and evolve as a communal, rave tarnished horde of physical intellectuals, whose every step, twitch and gesture is a means of furthering communication.

Chris Morris returns with the wonderful mandrill sketch from The Day Today as the music changes once more thirteen minutes in, a connection to the infamous story of 'Elizabeth I having given birth to a mandrill by mistake.' A synthetic tron like pulse then pushes us further along the electric seam as we see and hear no evil and disco twirl our multi flanged hearts and tanktops towards a tropical kingdom of the mandrill, the ultimate marsupial whose emergence and musculature rips the track apart with an ejaculation of anthemic exultation at minute fifteen in which 'absolute serenity' is fixed as the ultimate goal and where we are able to access the 'funky magic at the mountain top.' It is here that humour and intention join forces to replace the missing link with a musical form of the magic that Moore sees as society's true adhesive. Music can teach us as much if not more than any other art form when it has this much thought and skill behind it, as evidenced by Wilson and his cohorts, supporting and enabling the 'Tamarind Tyrant' to present the latest Orangutango!

As the Reynolds urge us to 'Let the mandrill funk you down' Moore Barry Whites, Reds and Blues along, before fusing into Kermit Leveridge and all manner of samples. The jungle celebration is more vibrant than any city fresco and more colourful than a firework on Viagra. This mixtape is 21 minutes of post apocaplyptic bliss that creates a revolution for the body. It is the job of the mind and its resultant conscience to catch up with that vessel and attempt to ring any changes on offer. If you have no phone to hand, beat your answers on the floor of the dancing space you find yourself in, or against the nearest, most convenient wall. The medium is the message but there will always be room for the overgrown and, if they are truly repentant, the small of vision.

A treatment and elaboration of The Kinks *Apeman* brings the discourse, discord and saccharine stylings and indeed, the party, both personal and political to a happy conclusion, providing connection to all of mankind's fights against the true animals that oppose our own freedom and restrain us without melody, harmony or message. The true rhythm of resistance is ours for the taking and easy to master. You begin by beating your hands against your chest and then by allowing the groove-growl to grow..

We will always need Moore. The world left to us is the least.

SALVATION IN THE SUBURBS

PART ONE:

The Good Disciples Debut Performance, Greenhill Rooms, Harrow Arts Centre, February 12th 2017

Sweet music, the teacher of hearts. Gathered together in a modern Nissen style hut behind Harrow Arts Centre on a cold Sunday in February, some fifty souls united with their corporeal forms to bear witness to the debut performance of *The Good Disciples*, a trio specialising in the expert recital of traditional Indian music, imbued with exploration, improvisation and new composition and comprised of Kiranpal Singh master of the Santoor, Shahbaz Hussain, master of the Tabla and Fabrice DeGraef, master of the Bansuri flute.

Three masters do magic music make. Having learnt their craft from their own maestros and masters, Singh from the legendary Pt Shiv Kumar Sharma, Hussein from the great Ustad Alla Rakha Khan and DeGraef from Pt Hariprasad Chaurasia, these Good Disciples of the muse and tradition of this sacred and special music form the latest offshoot of R. Rovers' Elfic Circle Project and those artists specialising in the musical explorations around Youth's new world music label. They appeared under the banner of PRSSV, specialist promoters of new and traditional Indian music, produced and promoted by Anjan Saha and Dr. Frances Shepherd. Over the course of a couple of hours to an enraptured audience of enthusiasts and students of the music, a world and community were gracefully formed and quickly ignited by the powerful forces at play.

2017 marks the 50th anniversary of the seminal album *Call of the Valley* by Shiv Kumar Sharma, Brijbushan Kabra and Hariprasad Chaurasia, and this recital heralds the recording of a new album in honour of this, to be produced by Youth at his world renowned London studios after a thrilling week in which they will rehearse and compose new music at PRSSV's Music Archive Centre and at The Music Room, Wembley. Today bore the first fruits of a week's rehearsal by shaking the tree of endeavour. Coming together from different parts of the country and hemisphere, DeGraef initially fell prey to the betrayals of the London transport system, leaving the first half of the recital to become a duo of tabla and santoor. From the first strike of string and drum, sounds of eerie permanence infiltrated the somewhat temporary nature of the space. The santoor is an orchestra in itself and the expressiveness and magic conjured by the striking of its strings is revelatory. As an instrument its resonance is remarkable, as effective as any synthesiser can be or brace of winds, or violins. It speaks directly to the heart and the head, while creating a language for the soul which Hussain's dextrous tabla playing instantly emphasised with his striking palette of colour and intonation.

The opening two pieces, lasting some twenty minutes each in length bare the common Indian names of Kilvana and Alab and take the form of explorations along and across melodies and harmonies on given ragas. The raga as the main template for Indian music acts as a kind of mothership for its musician settlers to dissemmenate from and return to, much like an expert jazz player will evolve a standard song. Once we recognise that there is a commonality across forms and backgrounds we are able to access all types of world music as sciences, practices and languages in their own right, separate even to their background. In this way, so called traditional pieces are renewed each time they are played, no matter how familiar and those listening can therefore experience them again in a completely new way. For the celts and English, Danny Boy is always Danny Boy, but here a new Dhani is birthed.

That the santoor is struck with such grace and admits such power is impressive enough, but one is never quite prepared for the mysticism on offer. Kiranpal Singh is the most gracious and down to earth of men and moments before he began playing we were discussing the merits of a Clapham made club sandwich, so the element of transportation and magic in his fingers is one to be treasured and praised.

Hussain's fingers are no less impressive. His tabla playing was incendiary, making him a Carl Palmer, a John Bonham, perhaps even a Keith Moon of his drums. The power in his hands and digits would put any rock player, or for that matter, any athlete to shame as the strokes and strikes of the tabla skin necessary to play it properly demonstrated the class and sheer range he has to offer. At one point he broke into an impromptu solo recital and brief teaching session, demonstrating the capabilities of his instruments that had his entire audience rapt and held, from elderly observers to those wriggling free of their prams and the sense of a community fired on by such a powerful force was heart warming to think of in reflection and invigorating to witness first hand.

A seven beat improvisation followed, lasting nearly forty minutes that took the small room from the rain wracked ruins right to the foot of the mountain, guiding those listening ever higher in scope, fulfilment and entertainment.

The partnership between the two men was extraordinary. One could see the tacit understanding between them as Shabaz's fiery, adolescent power was allowed to build through the support of Kiranpal's stately elegance. They filled in and balanced the opening half of the concert with the kind of grace lacking in the surly attitudes of which pop and rock are formed, an attitude that places players like this in an entirely different league.

After the betrayals of the city, DeGraef's arrival led to the second half of the concert in which the full trio played their new album, along with ensuing variations and explorations. Formed around a composition called *Charukeshi,* the beauty of the Bansuri filtered through us with an almost visible force. As tender and noble a sound as that produced through it, I have not heard. It is, in essence, a true sword for the soul. That a musician can arrive after hours of stress and immediately conjure such beauty and artistry is testament to DeGraef's skill but also shows how musicians of this stamp are the most superior of artists. Actors are always affected to some degree by their situation and often try to use it. Artists often exploit theirs or form their works solely from them, whereas it seems to me that musicians have a completely different discipline and these disciples in particular have brought a huge sense of force to the good.

Sitting cross legged on a series of cushions, Hussain was placed in-between Singh and DeGraef and the enjoyment and understanding the three men shared was as appealing as the music they played. I watched Shahbaz Hussain's obvious joy as he represented through his playing the heartbeats of an entire population while their voices and experiences were channelled through the wood of the flute and their souls deepened, colouring the room and air within it through the resonance of the 'santooring strings' and the deep musical spells that it casts. It was sound that you could taste, see, touch and smell, so physical was its presence. Art should be about creating the undeniable in all of its forms, and so it proved here.

In short, the recital showed what a real connection in a band can be, as well as a comment on form. Due to the sadness of the passing of two of its members I was put in mind of the fact that here was a kind of soulful and acoustic ELP in one way, albeit one with none of that groups indulgences. Now that the sweet voiced and acoustic driven Greg Lake is dead, along with the classically saturated anxieties of Keith Emerson, a trio of players is key to our understanding of musical language. We are forever searching for the perfect combination across the forms, styles and genres, whether it is guitar, or piano, bass and drums in rock or jazz, or violin, viola and cello. The equation, the balance seems right. The Good Disciples have discovered the answer because they know it already. They follow the truth of the sound from its origins in the land, mountains and spirit of a given or imagined place, right down to the universal musical statement of melody, harmony and rhythm. Like the three acts of a well made play, or the conventional beginning, middle and end of a story, their quest is the simple unification of forces. Here in this handful of pieces and variety of explorations across two and a half hours of playing and demonstrating, their journey showed us that no matter where we find ourselves, Heaven and Harrow have the potential to be the same place; the location for the settling soul.

My thanks go to these expert practitioners and to the producers and promoters who presented the music of one world and allowed it to influence the space of another. Sense what you can through these words and examine the space for these sounds. Now your own quest has started. You must learn how to equal such love.

SALVATION IN THE SUBURBS
PART TWO:
The Good Disciples Perform At The Music Room, Wembley 18th February 2017

I

In Preston Road, I locate
A greater impression of beauty,
Behind the grubby facades of the shop fronts,
A purety shines, borne by sound.

Mr. Rahmat Simab's Music Room
Is a palace behind lowly buildings
A private realm where charmed music
In restoring true gold to the streets,

Has been found.

II

In this kingdom and cathedral of strings
Where the fingers that play invoke angels,
And the Tabla drums in attendance
To the flight of the flute as soul-god,
There are countless towers to scale,
Each bearing the path of this music,
Each as truly divine and as sacred
As anything found or forgot.

Sounds of refinement restore the tired day's
Transformation, pushing the blood into singing
As it spiritualises the heart. As the eyes close,
You are sent towards a deeper sense of becoming
As the body moves, the cells listen, ordered
And formed by such art. There is in fact a new air,
That passes between note and player, instantly composing
New futures in which the coldness of day recognises

Both the warmth of within and light shared.
A slow fire builds, before easing itself across evening,
Painting the room as we listen to the jasmine sound
And soul-flare. Passages converse with the past
While gifting us through a new present,
As we re-interpret through ragas, the saga's
That each of us has to face. The tale is retold,
The story resung, composed over, as the known day

Reconfigures and we learn how to live and through music
Pray, in this place. This music makes the air, edible,
Filling the mouth, bridging senses, while making
Of that first fire a feeling to which even
The loveliest face can't compare; the sense that
Between strangers tonight, there is a form of communion.
And so the Music Room attains kingship,
With its particular monarchy sourced by care.

The Good Disciples ascend along the cloud-weave
Of their masters; Fabrice De Graef, Shahbaz Hussain
And Kiranpal Singh sound and soar. The Music Room
Is the home for these symphonies of becoming,
As the waters rise through emotion, a new spirit
Arrives at hopes door. Garnered tonight by the love
And devotion shared sweetly is the taste of sensation,
Like swallowing a star inside dreams.

Thanks to these gracious hosts and these heavenly players,
One night in London, while private, offers us a new public
Scheme, to unite with these sounds as the fabric to clothe
Those who shiver. Against the oppressive times, we grow frightened
Of the forces aligned against peace. It is only here,
In such rooms, beautifully dressed, eastern, scented
That we can experience transformations
In which the stresses of day find release.

SALVATION IN THE SUBURBS

III

Three men play as one
And yet each has their moment.
They teach us all as we listen
What music is, when allowed.

IV

DeGraef's devotions to the Moon,
Through kissing wood pose a question
About what we know of music as well as
What we know of sound. His Bansuri sings
To the night that covers all in this suburb,
His song's graceful insistence
Is a bird across cloud as light folds.

There is an overpowering sense
Of ancient worlds in his sounding,
As if time travel were simply a matter
Of the changing air in his flute.
The stilled beauty stuns before it too is sent skyward,
Breaking the night with star patterns, as all that is earth
And the astral are gracefully passed underfoot.

Hussain powers this flight with the strength
And skill of his drumming,
As Singh's one hundred strings are sky feathers
On which the shimmering moon finds its place.
Another raga plays, traditional, inflamed,
Yet romantic, in woman waits under stars
And at the remove of day in the mountains;

All at once we can see her
As her man moves to make his return from this land.
To catch such glimpses attend this special place,
This new Kingdom,
In which eastern music's language and lessons
Will no doubt form a congress
That the head, heart and soul understand.

A COMPOUND FOR THE SOUL

An instaneous response and review of Teleplasmiste's new album, *Frequency Is The New Ecstacy* (House Of Mythology, 2017)

I

The ecstatic returns from a host of lost forces; the past, stars and stories and the majesties of the sky. In this new release we glimpse a sense of renewal, in which the darkness of the day is re-ordered by a fresh understanding of light.

Released on April 7th, by Teleplasmiste, the duo of Mark O. Pilkington of Strange Attractor Press and Urthona and Michael J. York of Coil and the equally crucial The Stargazer's Assistant, *Frequency is the new Ecstasy* showcases as House of Mythology's Press release states, 'the shared journey through nature and electricity, via a combination of vintage and contemporary synthesisers and acoustic pipes, creating a sound that furthers the continuum of minimalistic and Kosmiche musics..'

Listening to the sound file ahead of physical release date has been a privilege that I would like to share with you in as impressionistic a way a possible. What follows is my response to the six compositions and explorations that make up the CD and download versions of the album (there are five on the vinyl), written as I listened, felt and thought about them. My soul was stirred and has led to a number of compound terms, through which I try to capture the effect this beautiful and challenging music had and continues to have on me. It was as revelatory an experience as it was an enjoyable one and it literally coloured my day, moving from one sense of what is possible to another.

Reality and the inherent and supposed satisfactions that define and occur to us are all based on an agreed level, or frequency of perception. What if, by re-tuning there were other ways to be free?

II

From the earth splitting drone to the reach for transcendence Teleplasmiste's new release squeezes hard on the heart. That the soul is invoked as you listen to this emergence is testament to the power that has been considered, composed and released. Here is electronic music made to tectonically shift you. As the ground beneath is reordered you are constantly changed in your place.

Opening track, A *Gift of Unknown Things* hammers into your listening, teaching you how to experience this music and perhaps fuse with it. As the searing drone crests the steel like striking continues as synthetic pulses carry you towards calm. If blood were flame, coursing through the vein, making dragons, this piece would soundtrack that evolution, that air. The gift is the art of the drone, flexing its sound tail to sting you, and by that sting to inform you with a succulent strength that takes hold.

Gravity is the enemy clears the stage with a bucolicism that is quickly shattered as what sounds like an ancient pipe and flute fushion is battered by electric drum burst and flare. The effect is of the air blackening and then quickly transforming, moving in fact through all colours as the assault rages on. But this is an attack that's controlled by exceptional forces, as the mix of woods, winds and (what sound like) muezzin's signal appropriate calls for the day. The music twists through the air as I write, an LSD type aural-vision, in which rather than seeing, I am listening into new worlds. Here is where the strange creatures move, Thomas Newton like, sex clouds sperming as around me now is a burning of the reality I believed. An eerie saxophone wails as the ghost of Albert Ayler now shatters, before the clouds shimmer, dissolving away to cool foam. A sampled voice then intones a prayer to this movement; 'music is becoming light..' And I see it, as a second primal force makes its claim.

Astodaan rides the drone that births pulsation, with insistence over rhythm affecting another eloquent state. A sound storm arrives, like mutating birds grown together, a tapestry of dark wings synthesising as the tone orchestra soars. The effect, listening is of an entirely new weather, stalking the land with dark colours as if maturing fresh buds and new leaves. Rain falls in swords, piercing the earth as clouds bristle, while below blackened grasses are needling the sound of the wind. Great swoops of sound that make the title an action or a state of place or of being that are only arrived at after this profound sense of change. There is an alien air as well as of something forgotten, along with a far distant future in which numerous ruined and featureless lands seek re-growth.

In this way these sounds and these compositions become political warnings joining the expressive arts with the known. Can a pop song do this? Perhaps if the lyric's explicit. But it seems to me that experimental or Avant-Garde composition can literally unearth language from the places beyond standard voice. One senses the need for some reformation as one is stunned by the power that lurks close to discord. And yet there is harmony here, even if at first, it seems ugly, as if the disfigurement is related to all that we find beautiful. I am being moved as I write towards joining an almost celestial choir, where the animal angels are screaming an alien song to strange gods. I know at once there is wrong and that the silvered clouds have a sharpness. This music has taught me we have to move fast and dig deep.

Mind at Large pulses in, with an attendant pitch which can frighten. In the stilled hall of mirrors, the reflections are now rippling. The sound-wasp leaves a trail across the glittering facades, fronts and faces, but it is a singular line of transgression that is coarsening everything. Ambient, electronic music does more than almost any other, as it has no standard form. It moves with us as we adapt, hearing it. Under these sheets of sound-ice there is life quickly forming as indeed the wasp image shimmers in repeating patterns beneath. A real buzz is heard and one begins as you listen. It is enchanting and immersive too. The sound stuns. I love music like this as it bridges the forms. It is painting. And yet also drama and there is something *at play*, going on. The mind is at large and expands as you listen. The possibilities are transgressive, causing the listener to react. And interact too. Here is a true conversation is which sound and image are shared as you listen and try to understand what's been made. As the journey reaches end, there are high tones and a flourish as if the quest captured had been handed over for your developing perceptions to explore.

Fall of the Yak Man begins with a series of stumbling notes and tones, as if the protagonist were returning now through a landscape that is at once shaped and resistant to his very path through the snow. Bass notes warm the air as the sounds of the man form around us, as the near tune recomposes a dignified synthline grows. A man is a mix of constantly moving forces, from blood to emotion to the waters of eyes, taste and fear. An inescapable synth figure forms, before it is subdued by sound-weather, as the clouds of white move around him, stretching the air, blurring sight. An aural foreboding begins, summoning itself from this essence with repeats of synth patterns that suddenly change in the ear. The Yak man is invoked, not through fruit or flesh but through music; as generative sounding as Eno, and yet as celebratory as Neu! I am struck by the search as I type now and listen to these spells of renewal and these summonings of the soul. We become him as we listen to this spectacular sound-portrait, as much a compound perhaps as the phrases I have chosen to people this text. It is a beautiful piece as it moves through the patterns; a song version of Borges' 'The Other' in which a dreaming man dreams a man.

Radioclast, the epic album closer, moves from pure silence into peaceful spells of rebirth. An emotional chord, cast by angelic echoes, powers the sound through the landscape, as if it were fronting it with a shield. We are slid through this sound as if it were those very angels who pushed us, keen to retrieve us from the drudgery of day, into faith. The drones shatter the frame in which they take place as I listen, whether on laptop or ear-piece, I am instantly place where they are.

Isn't this the true point of any art in its essence? To, like the Pied Piper, steal us and for us, like those children, to never return or stay changed?

Rhapsodic synth calls spear on, adding both force and persuasion. Instrumental instruction from the radio frame, to the mind. An undeniable sense of summoning as it happens. A capturing of the ritual, whether in a field at dawn, in Crowley's room, or Stonehenge. Over twenty minutes this piece provides its own manifesto. It is a sky itself and a climate. It is a way to be and to think. It is a trance state of sorts, unrelated to dance but a neighbour. The ecstasy of the title is gradually built. It consumes. It is a beautiful sound that lifts my day as I listen. When twelve minutes in, a dip happens I am wrenched through a hall in the sound. But then I am quickly transformed. I am remade. I am offered. And I understand something for which no word exists. I am held. We are the music we seek. That is why it speaks to us. Radioclast re-imagines the frequencies we'd all share.

III

That we do not makes this album essential. Play it to those you hate or to strangers in a proper attempt to find peace.

This album transforms. I bid you all to fall subject. There are Kings in ascendence and they waiting for us to return.

20th February 2017

Part Three:

VOICE SHARING
(Theatre)

BETWEEN THESE TOWERS:

A review and interview concerning You Should See The Other Guy's production, *Land Of The Three Towers* – Carpenters and Docklands Centre, Gibbins Road, Stratford E15, Saturday 30th January 2016

I

The theatre is ready to drop. Unaware, it walks on, celebrity glazed, misdirected, while all the time, underneath it, a series of other cultures are formed. It is these below-foot strands and strains that can and will give way to the future; the seeds and/or pods of creation from which new approaches will grow. Nina Scott and Emer Mary Morris, representing a new generation of young theatre makers and thinkers, have in this inaugural work for their new company began to unveil a fresh hope for the uses and benefits of theatre in both the public consciousness outside of art, as well as its relevance as a form of direct and cultured activism within it.

Emer, an actress and director and Nina, a former Set Designer forged early links with the subjugated residents of the Carpenter's Estate, and were present during the occupation of 2014, when the events depicted in the performance took place. Following a series of transcriptions of testimonies and experiences relating to the struggle against Newham Council and its leader Robin Wales, Morris and Scott secured a two week long fund from the Arts Council, with which to collate and produce the piece. As Nina Scott says: "We'd seen so many verbatim theatre pieces which were just dry collections of quotes and recollections..so we wanted to produce something that had as many varied forms of response as possible.." This, she, Emer and the resourceful and talented company have done, creating something that aspires far more closely to the ultimate form of music, the aim of all dramatic art. In my view Land of the Three Towers is a kind of song, reflective of the female spirit that has formed, guided and delivered the piece, connecting not only subject to practise but also creating a fresh way to deal and emphasise with an all too common story.

What follows is a review of the piece.

II

Courting preciousness, I'll start with a famous quote from Brecht:
> "In the dark times
> Will there also be singing?
> Yes, there will also be singing.
> About the dark times."

and do so gladly, as those prophetic words seem apt to a review of *Land Of The Three Towers*, which at its most primary level shines a light on the female voice. The 80 minute piece, developed with and performed by Carly Jane Hutchinson, Lotte Rice, Maria Hunter, Jennifer Daley, Grace Surey, with music sensitively played and sung by Sophie Williams, detailed the plight of the residents of the Carpenter's estate in the face of Newham Council's decision to close down and convert a number of properties on it for commercial purposes through a series of threatened compulsory purchase orders and forced evictions in 2014. The Three Towers of the Estate are the first and last thing you see on arriving and departing Stratford and the threats faced by the residents and ensuing court battle with Newham Council are what the piece is fired by. The emblematic nature of the estate becomes a haunting one in the light of what its residents suffered and as the title of plays are crucial to our understanding of them we should not forget the constituent elements of that shattered land.

The show's song style structure utilises the verbatim form of presentation to showcase the attitudes and experiences of the oppressed residents, artfully fusing impression, re-inaction, monologue, song and vocalised choral refrains. From the testimony of an elderly woman who had lived there since the war, we are led through a series of experiences and impressions of all residents, observers and participants, which if nothing else redefines the modern notion of community and the crisis it currently finds itself in and therefore makes Land of the Three Towers a celebration of the fighting spirit. One of the cast members is a homeless and expectant mother who has clearly been failed by this council and while soon to be relocated to Birmingham provides a startling example of what this production is for. Her, and indeed Emer and Nina's connection with the struggle of the Focus 15 Mothers, for whom the Carpenter's Estate was a lifeline, is a unique demonstration of political, artistic and social relevance; a completely rare conjunction of forces and rationale, practically unheard of in today's cultural climate and dare I say it, society, where the differences in social and political strata have never been more pronounced.

The Focus 15 Mothers, had been temporarily housed by the council in the human equivalent of a battery chicken farm, in which 'with two arms outstretched each person's living space could be defined.' Young single Mothers of all races and ethnicities were effectively freedom's prisoners, albeit for a limited period. Stories are relayed in the piece of how maximum stays of 6-8 months stretched into two or three years until alternative council housing could be supplied. Mothers whose children could not stand the confinement were forced out onto the street after a certain period, or at best induced to spend the greater parts of the day outside, just so their children could run freely. The image of a toddler playing outside the Westfield complex is a haunting one, as the endless metres of dazzle threaten the smile of a child. The Carpenters Estate was one of the only lifelines for these nascent families, with its council run flats offering what most of us might expect as the minimum amount of space within which to effectively live. In the wake of the 2012 Olympics, here is its true legacy and an answer to the question of what happens next after a two week sportsday costing £9 billion. It goes without saying that this company of women have achieved far more in their two week period of production, albeit on a miniscule scale. The Olympic Dome has become a reverberant sound chamber, 'signifying nothing', echoing its socio-political irrelevance throughout the city, country and ultimately, history.

The people here, conversely ignored and maltreated by a seemingly uncaring council, became the real living dead, with the only light deemed fit for ignition being the one above Robin Wales' head as his council and no doubt the Quango behind it spearheaded the carpenter's estate for decapitation. By his actions in this matter alone, Wales seems to be the worst kind of politician, the blackened fruit in an already rotten bowl, who uses his public office for nothing more than private tyranny.

The Focus 15 Mothers who had found a sense of respite and home on the estate formed a group to both represent the residents and oppose this action. In doing so they became the Canaries who cleansed the Coalmine, if not permanently, then certainly for long enough for those caked in the dirt and slur of oppression to sparkle. That they eventually had to leave is not the point. They were able to do so on their own terms and after a long and harrowing struggle against a crusade of oppression. As Nina says; "We thought it was crucial that we could read between the lines and express what lay within them..and also an important part of the process was acknowledging the celebratory nature of the E15 Mothers in general, as celebration is the best and most effective form of protest.."

The celebratory nature of that protest so clearly captured in the performance enabled the activists involved at the time and represented here, to pose the relevant questions for those often denied the dignity of expression. Those suffering acquire voice through art and in a patriarchal society defined by the capitalist curve, these female voices touch us from some of the life's sharpest corners.

Indeed, the notion of voice and form lays at the heart of this piece. As Set Designer/Co-Director, Nina says; "Its important to tell the story in whatever form is nesscessary..why should something be seen in such and such a way just because it takes place in a theatre.." Land of the Three Towers didn't, of course, as it was performed on the very site of the protest and occupation, but in doing so, it created a theatre of both moment and memory. Here, then was an act of true revolution in a beligerant age, a small community led effervescence, and something entirely lacking in current society. The unseen spoke and those cast in shadow suddenly moved centre stage.

In championing its numerous inspirations so effectively, economically and it has to be said, spiritually, this collage of hearts and voices, primed by the need for action is part of a long history of arts led activism, from Brecht's Lehstrucke, through the work of Augusto Boal, John McGrath's 7:84 (most notably The Cheviot, The Stag and the Black, Black Oil) and onto the Agit-Prop of the Living Theatre and Cardboard Citizen's work over the last twenty years, with whom Emer Mary Morris has worked. By moving effortlessly through the forms and finding simple ways to combine them, the sense of hope and celebration was found. Not so much the hope of beating councils at their own game, but rather in finding new and unified means with which to continue to confront and question those official bodies in both their elected and non-elected forms, calling them to account for their misrepresentations and lack of concern and of care.

III

Thanks to the society they exist in Emer, Nina and company now need enough support to allow them to continue and to expand the show and their practise of it. They tick a lot of Arts Council boxes in supplying for work for young people and those in crisis but because they are tackling the council led inadequacy on a grand scale there are several obstacles to overcome. As Emer says, "We've been asked to take the show to Hastings, Birmingham and Manchester as there are numerous groups and communities in crisis, all too easily overlooked.." But the piece deserves a wider forum, where those in protest are forced to engage with the opposition and not just walk around it.

Land of the Three Towers is, in essence a dramatised song of suffering far more than it is a simple play of action. This to me is its ultimate salvation as what heart can resist the female voice singing purely, especially if that song combines the hopes and fears of Woman in the general sense, as the true witness to the events of contemporary history. It's there in the Greeks as it is throughout all times since, and was once more expressed in a brief open mic section of the show when Vanessa Huby, a single mother living on the Carpenter's estate sang in a fragile voice a self composed song of motherly renunciation to her three young daughters. Land of the Three Towers made many points that evening but in enabling this small piece of humanity at its purest form to shine through, it achieved a full state of grace.

Theatre in the general sense (separate to its location space) began and reaches its full relevance through its use of music as the ultimate artistic form. The fragile beauty of the singers voices in this piece carries its words to the wind. Theatre is made for the air. The ideas are cast above and before us. Precious few audiences know how to accept this and thereby fail to appreciate what is being given to them.

These days in the theatres, we watch expecting entertainment but we rarely listen. If we did enlightenment and education would be much easier to receive. It is shows like these and the ideas behind them that encourage us to do so. Change the space and you'll find a new way to view it. Open your heart. Look and listen. (The Fourth Wall was a Doll's House and there to be broken down, all along.)

You Should See The Other Guy have begun that search for new form and it is crucial that they remain outside of accepted theatre parlance, teaching those who come to see it, new ways to express and reflect the drama of their own lives. Nina and Emer have recently discovered a collection of VHS tapes recorded in the 1980's in which Carpenter Estate residents were encouraged to demonstrate a skill, tell stories or simply showcase their homes and lifestyles and this strikes me as a remarkable goldmine not only in terms of theatrical presentation but as a kind of divine right to develop a uniquely new form. A community under siege has found expression and the right like minded practitioners to represent it. In seeking connections, transcribing the frustrations of residents and wanting to expand the form Nina and Emer are poised to make art fuelled by the greater function of real social change. And that is something that hasn't been seen in this country at least, for a long, long time. Culture is contained by those who glance at it. The Art Gallery liggers are only really there for the wine.

Although at an early stage of its development, every facet of the show pointed to a greater future. At one point the five female cast members embodied male testimony with an infectious ease and sense of humour, at another point they broke your heart with the oppressiveness of it all. Lotte Rice perfectly embodied long term resident Mary's anger and frustration as much as Carly Jane Hutchinson's predicament dignified the soulfulness of her performance. Even the open mic slot was included to faithfully replicate the life of the estate. It is a rare thing for Theatre makers to have this level of commitment and the more I think about it, the more these two young women and their associates should be celebrated. They have achieved a unity between thought and action and they have signposted a future for the very notion of change.

IV

Poetry can make us think but can it lead to action?
The so called 'Play' can capture but can it make **us** act?

V

In dealing with the notion of collective action, *Land of the Three Towers* marries outrage to vulnerability in an unholy church, and we as the attendant congregation had on the night and will have to as the project develops, reposition ourselves to understand the ramifications of the described events in all their horror and small scale glory. The realities of peoples lives is the true genre and the music of this show, in terms of spirit, and it calls on our own music, borne from personal sensitivity and empathy to facilitate and support its advances. The show and the thinking behind it is the first step towards a new reform, in which theatre in its broadest sense rediscovers a deeper vocation and audience. The Arts must combine to attain their full relevance and You Should See the Other Guy have delivered this in a simple, accessible and engaging way, through both education and entertainment. Goliath remains but the slingshot is full of new stones.

The problem facing Nina, Emer and the company in the development of the show now lays with you. How much will you commit when you get the chance to see a future incarnation, and what will you do to question your own forces of opposition. The Ivory tower is often confined to a single room and this show if nothing else rattles your battlements. There is a future ahead in which the piece is toured across country, highlighting the struggle of the Carpenters Estate residents as a means of representing similar victimisations everywhere, but that unfortunately contains elements of preaching to the converted. In this regard the opening Brecht quote of this review becomes problematical. As the dark times are invoked how do those not in shadow get to see what's gone on? Those members of society rich enough to avoid the problems these residents have faced are the true audience for this presentation. The efforts behind its creation, coupled to the sensitive and sincere approaches that formed them are the true weapons for the activist. In a way, the protest or compliance with recognised forms of opposition can fail to engage those in power, as that is what they expect and are indeed, primed to ignore. This refers to what the show itself can do, in its current Community Theatre or Agit-Prop format, along with what the actual residents achieved, which was to not only postpone Newham Council's action under the direction of Council Leader, Robin Wales, but to restore a sense of communal pride and accomplishment to an acceptable level when faced with overwhelming odds. They left, and yet new residents remain, and with them, new hope. There are not many theatre evenings that showcase that ambition, even if, arguably that is their reason to be.

VI

The Olympic legacy in all its shattered and shameful glory has led hundreds of people into disarray. With the great race run, the eggs and spoons are out in all senses as those left behind stumble on with little or no resources, forging sparks in the wake of 2012's evermore plastic flame. The finishing line has been erased and so we are asked in presentations like this to join this second race, which while it may run in the dark is nevertheless leading towards a new state of being in which entertainment and the connection between communities contained and reflected through it can be managed. What you must now do is seek out this company, invite them to perform, give them the tea and biscuits (literal and metaphorical) and learn how to chorus their song. Plays are too often seen as the vehicles for actors. What they really are is the transport from one sense of ourselves to the next. The women in this company all have their hands on the wheel. Fuck the shameful cliché. They know where they're going and why.

As Emer Mary Morris profoundly says, in regards to formulating the piece as something akin to a new form; "We didn't initially know what we were doing..we simply believed that we could.."

The three towers remain. These women will now take them to you. It won't be long. So keep watching, as they drive with the truth in their eyes.

I WILL TALK YOU TO DEATH

A review of *Evening at The Talk House* by Wallace Shawn A response to the play as opposed to the production

Wallace Shawn's new Play 'Evening at The Talk House, ' currently running at the NT's Dorfman Theatre is the latest work in his ongoing investigation into the death of culture and with it, responsible thought. Questioning the moral, political and artistic status quo has always been the sinqua non of Shawn's plays but 'The Fever, ' 'The Designated Mourner, ' 'Grasses of a Thousand Colours' and now this new, artfully disguised masterpiece are deliberate provocations for a complacent and comfortable crowd.

As you start reading, the play seems smaller in scope than its predecessors and far more concerned with almost genteel introductions to characters, incidents and ideas, but it soon opens up to prove itself to be as chilling a portrait of (dis) organised State control as the latter Pinter plays, showing how the governing classes dispense both privilege and punishment. Robert's long opening monologue – dismissed recently in *The Evening Standard* with the blandest description possible, sets the scene with far more detail than we realise. A former playwright, now turned TV Hack, Robert's eponymous and much respected 'Midnight in a Clearing with Moon and Stars, ' serves to bind not only the hidden story in the play which connects the protagonists through their numerous functions, but also harks back to a time when the taste for ancient tales and classically set stories was still fresh on the communal tongue. Now Robert is employed by an Orwellian type broadcaster to produce a long running sit-com/soap opera, or something very close to it, but which now passes for Drama, a kind of Storm Saxon set up for those of you familiar with Alan Moore and David Lloyd's *V for Vendetta*, or, if not that, the televisual cousin of the equally synthetic Soylent Green. The other characters were all connected to the original play as actors or observers, including Nellie the proprietor of The Talk House Club where this play is set. The club, once the home of celebration and revelry, epitomised by its famous snacks, but now endangered and close to bankruptcy, is now a fading refuge, existing long enough to grant this group of people one last conversation about the size and the scale of the dark. Tom, Jane, Bill, Annette and Dick primed and informed by Robert's work early in their careers went on to involve themselves in a series of compromises and thwarted adventures, each declining in their way as the anonymous but nevertheless oppressive regime took hold. It is in fact this singular evening that brings them back together, perhaps for the final time, allowing a final chance of renewal. It is of course what we might call the human tragedy that they are prevented from doing so.

Shawn's characters are often self obsessed but capable of long term reflection. This was apparent in the early work, 'The Old Man' and in his most recognised play 'Aunt Dan and Lemon' in which the morally corrupt are at least self aware enough to know that they are not ashamed of their shortcomings or indeed defined by their forebodings. This is nowhere more apparent than in Jack's defence of his own limitations in 'The Designated Mourner, ' or indeed Shawn's own self summary in the highly regarded film, 'My Dinner With Andre, ' but he does a good deal more here than just 'sharpen a few pencils..' Instead, in a relatively short play, that seems on first glance, far more accessible than the intricately woven strands of fantasy and conjecture from which *Grasses of a Thousand Colours* was spun, is to place both characters and reader/audiences into the thick of the fight. The theatre as a force and form of change and entertainment is literally dead in this play and in its wake a new form of entertainment has taken over, commissioned by the state and written by such former luminaries as Robert and it is this new format which seems to cover all with a placatory standard as well as resolve any need. Actors who cannot find employment in the chosen broadcasts are forced into becoming state sanctioned murderers, sent to far countries to assassinate all insurgents. When they have outlived their usefulness in that department they are suitably embroiled in a process of 'targeting, ' in which future insurgents are recognised and then handed onto others, a collusion that the truly artistic spirit was practically formed to resist. In the twilight of their careers they are finding the pig before you put the pineapple on it and are doing it gladly, sucking down and succumbing to the poisoned teat of the state. When the ramshackle character of Dick is introduced the once charming actor has become a bloated parody of himself. Someone once sweet and adorable has become a kind of walking cancer and social canker, and his first entrance details how he has just endured an intervention from friends who have beaten him up in the hope of showing him the error of his ways. This literal and deeply funny repression of the artistic spirit and personality is more directly expressed in this play than in some of Shawn's others, but carries as much power and relevance as anything previously described. Jack's debate on the effects of Pornography and Literature in The Designated Mourner are perhaps wider reaching, but the effect is the same: the artistic impulse is one to be punished by either direct outside action or from the shallow confines of the private heart.

Evening at The Talk House therefore becomes the ultimate piece of Democratic retaliation against all foreign forces, from African intrigue under Mugabe type action, through to the evils of Isis, but unfortunately comes at a cost. It shows that the only way to defeat evil is to use evil and in doing so, sacrifice what makes you an artist or entertainer in the first place. (This is also of course a mirror for the profession as we currently experience and practise it.) Art which questions art is often seen as pretentious, but this is not the case here. Shawn is a masterful dealer of moral and artistic principle and to blur the analogies, sculpts with language and ideas in ways and with means that are both self reflective and revelatory. The ridiculous notion that a crumbling theatrical vanguard lead the way is almost too much to stomach but then we in Britain have to recognise that one of the UK's most famous TV shows was about a bunch of Wartime geriatrics defending the nation against Hitler, not all of whom were fully aware of their limitations. Shawn's characters, in having surrendered their primary spirit realise the damnations they have incurred but continue, fighting the vainglorious fight irrespective of prestige or capability. What Shawn shows, certainly in the character of Robert (who becomes the chief villain/antagonist), but also in Bill, Tom and Annette is their lack of care about this. They do what is required of them by adjusting the heart like a belt and tailoring the mind and perception, all under the illusion of duty, first to their talent but truly to the changing context within which they find themselves. A late confrontation between the character of Jane (a former actress and waitress in the Talk House) shows how deeply the fight has raged and how much it has affected its soldiers, and Robert's nonchalance is suitably chilling. Subsidiary characters die at a regular intervals throughout the play and when the Landlady Nellie shows signs of succumbing, seemingly from the engendered atmosphere of collusion if nothing else, the finely wrought ambiguity of the play's ending deals extensive dividends. It is in fact, only Dick (played by Shawn himself in the NT Production) who, despite bearing the brunt of insult and perfidy throughout, is able to reinvoke the poetry of their youth and question the nature of their declining years. His reading from Robert's play is exemplary as described in the text and shows how its very quality has him condemned. His pride and connection prove to be his downfall, with his early choking fit serving as a ghostly prologue /premonition of his own possibly Robert led end. Robert as ever is in control, labouring under the darkest wing while making sure that each angel is extinguished.

For those of you who have read Wallace Shawn's previous work, you will know how unexpected and uncanny his writing is. Sentences constantly surprise and amaze you, from the relating of sexual congress with forest animals in *Grasses of a Thousand Colours* to the descriptions of an actress's apartment full of flattened cats in this play, to the stunning fictional excerpt from Midnight in a Clearing, a textual equivalent to the bewitching filmic inserts by Bill Morrison in Shawn's previous. It's a world where the word is King and one for which I believe theatre exists. Many would disagree of course, seeing the theatre as a place for spectacle and experimentation, but for me, it has always been a place where the word placed in the air affects change in the exact same way as the musical chord alters the rise of the heart. Wallace Shawn along with other geniuses such as Heathcote Williams, Harold Pinter, Samuel Beckett and the thoroughly British writer, Jim Cartwright place language and its attendant lords of meaning and music right at the heart of theatrical experience. They show that while there maybe room for all, the correct words are all you will need.

Evening at The Talk House is a play where the real story is both masked and mirrrored. You have to work out how each of these characters affected their own individual deteriorations and transformations. And you alone have to picture the regime that is even as we speak and read infiltrating each space and silence around us. Wallace Shawn under the guise of Author/Actor is an Oracle of sorts, standing at the gates (The National Theatre can't be regarded as a sideline) and pointing towards both ruin and reward. The sad truth is that the characters in this play, reflect back on all of us and through their dark and nefarious mirroring, they find us all undeserving. And yet we are not sorry and so rattle on towards death. This is a play where talking and action are combined and not demonstrated. It is, like all of Shawn's plays both concerto and portrait, slow dance in shadow as well as lantern lecture. The light at the end may flicker but the talk in the dark goes on. I know that when I see this play I will be impressed by the production and charmed and chilled by the performances but I wanted to write first, after reading, because I believe that this smooth shouldered slim volume speaks more than a roomful of truth. Go to the play, in all senses. Listen. And then read about your own heart.

29th November 2015

W

Thoughts on the life, work and death of Sir Arnold Wesker

There is a famous and appealing story told and by the great poet and theatrical master, Harold Pinter about an encounter he had with a friend of his and her young daughter. At a reception of some kind, the woman approached Pinter and introduced him to the inquisitive six year old. 'This man is called Harold Pinter, ' she said, 'and he's a very good writer.' 'Oh, really? replied the young girl, 'can he do a W?'

He could, of course and many more. As could his close contemporary, Sir Arnold Wesker, whose death this week marks another sad loss for modern culture, and indeed for 2016 in general, which is turning out to be less of a pre-ordained system of calculated time measures, and far more of a cull, with many noteables across the forms, passing on to a different chart.

In the current climate where craft, form and language are radically simplified, those further down the alphabet from the ABC approach to challenge and consideration are in danger of falling, in the dramatic sense, into a state of neglect, or something that looks very much like it. This has happened across the board, from masters such as IT's own Mr Williams, to Charles Wood, Howard Barker, Edward Bond, John Osborne and Snoo Wilson (to name but six) being rarely performed, or perhaps even known to successive generations of theatre students and audiences, having fallen foul of the current trends and desire for familiar ideas conveyed with what often seems to this writer, like brevity.

Wesker of course, was a forerunner of even these Authors, starting with the Royal Court's sans decor production of *The Kitchen* in 1959, after several attempts and low level jobs, needed to establish himself, including an early short story called *Pools,* nervously handed to the director Lindsay Anderson outside the theatre in 1958. It was only with the first production of *Roots i*n Coventry and then a performance of the full famous Trilogy of plays that dealt with the upsurge of socialist commitment in post war East London, (*Roots*/*Chicken Soup with Barley*/*I'm Talking About Jerusalem*) at the Royal Court Theatre in 1960 that Wesker took hold.

Like Pinter before him, 1960 was a pivotal year for Wesker and for an intense period Sloane Square and the West End were ruled by two young jewish men from the same shared streets. That THE CARE-TAKER proved to be more lasting artistic enterprise (free from its point and time of origin) and perhaps the more important, is testament to the crucial differences between the two as both writers and men. Pinter was both a conscious and subconscious poet, who used the form diligently, to create poems that ranged from a youthful exuberance with language to a more weighted response when engaging with political developments. His published poetry shows a journey and steady filtering of perspective. Subconsciously, his poetry infuses his plays in ways that have perhaps only been matched by Samuel Beckett, Jim Cartwright and the aforementioned holy six.

Indeed, many of Pinter's plays are not plays at all; they assume the form certainly and follow the accepted structure to varying degrees, but they are in effect, poetic studies of the moment, through either impulse, effect or ramification. *Old Times* is a worthy example of this, through its lack of verifiable fact and its weaving of time and reality. Pinter's work, like Beckett's achieved a musical level of accomplishment. One can enter into and listen to his plays as much as one can watch or engage with them. They are complete transmogrifications of intention transfused into Art. With Wesker, it is slightly different. The writing itself is what interested him, perhaps a little more than the active moment. His work aspires to that same musical level, but like the annoying person sitting next to you at the concert, there is at time a little too much 'talking' interrupting and stopping the flow. This might lead you to believe that his plays are annoying to watch in some way. I can assure you there are not. They are erudite, intelligent, compassionate and perceptive works that deal with the nature and ambivalences of people in both contemporary and historical society, and they flow well. But that in effect, is the issue. If you are aware of the flow of ideas and expression then something is missing; that silent partner that Harold Pinter knew all too well. He captured this beast in the pause and showed us the face we can't picture. The undisguised strangeness and unsaid root to us all. The thing that cannot be written down or explained, Pinter showcased. No matter what we do or accomplish, the deficiency and inability to truly express what we want or feel is always present. The unlocatable aspect remains in the place we can't go. Wesker, in my view dealt with absolutes only. From Beatie's rise in *Roots*, to Peter's in *The Kitchen;* he was always using his characters to make his points. Even one of his most beautiful plays and stories, *Love Letters On Blue Paper* has a very specific agenda, detailing the death of a former prominent trade Unionist.

These concerns are also clearly present in his play, *The Friends,* which he infamously directed in 1970 to the consternation of its rebellious cast, and also in *The Old Ones*, in which a group of decaying dreamers and activists chart their own fall with humour, warding off the stark judgements they would otherwise place on themselves. In 1969 Wesker wrote an unpublished Ur-text of a play called *The New Play*, in which he detailed what he was writing and why he was trying to write and not write it, meticulously scrutinising his own impulses and achievements. In fact, go through the plays in any order and you will see these points being painted continuously, for that is what Wesker was in my view; his rich language and layering of intent is like a paint adorning the imaginary houses in his work, and in the case of his play *Their Very Own And Golden City*, palaces and cathedrals he would have and wanted to build. His play *Shylock* rewrites *The Merchant of Venice* to rightfully reclaim the virtues of that unfortunate jew. As does *Caritas* with its study of medieval English Witchcraft, and his *One Woman* plays (collected in *Wesker – Plays: 2*), all have coated viewpoints and agendas. To Wesker, the writing was all, but words, in my view, are not always the writing. Harold Pinter unearthed this more than anybody else before or since, and perhaps, in reaction to his acclaim, Sir Arnold did not. Here were two fiercely intelligent working class boys who did not go to college or University. Reliant on the self education they had engaged with since childhood, they achieved their PHD's on the street. The Autodidact is both University Don and Cleaner. They sought their own order as a way to reveal their own worth. Arnold Wesker was I think continually engaged on a search for his and this is I believe demonstrated in the sheer amount of work he produced. There is a side to Judaism that is keen to please and a side that is defensive. Wesker constantly engaged with his public on an international and latterly regional scale, presenting them with fresh arguments for discussion, while also showing that his traditional sensibilities were also reflective of Judaism's third side (it is perhaps the only major religion with three or possibly four sides); namely, its vibrancy and command of new forms. From Finance, through Dentistry and on and into Showbusiness, the Jews have defined what we are. It should perhaps be noted that I am a Jew myself.

In regards to the plays, the other crucial difference between the two Hackney men is that Pinter was an Actor. He knew the theatre in a different way to Wesker; not as church (or Synagogue) in which a kind of salvation could be found, but as a factory shithouse that had to be cleared daily in order to make it workable. His approach was perhaps animalistic and practical, to some degree, just as Wesker's was perhaps more angelic and/or romantic. Wesker was in love with the chances on offer whereas Pinter fixed his gaze firmly on the dark roulette wheel.

Action is key and sometimes Wesker's plays forsake action. It has been written in other criticism that the dramatic highlight of his beautiful and lyrical play *The Four Seasons* is when the male protagonist Adam (originally played by the great Alan Bates) makes an apple strudel live on stage. While this maybe the case, that play in particular shows the best and worst in Wesker's work. Here the conscious poet is writing the play, when it should be the subconscious one sat in the driver's seat, if not wearing the chef's apron. Direct Poetry in plays, no matter how accomplished dates and reduces dramatic action, irrespective of accomplishments in form and style. This is evident in the work of Christopher Fry and damnit, TS Eliot's *The Confidential Clerk* and *Murder In The Cathedral*, and it also evident in Tony Harrison's *The Prince's Play* and *Fram*.

The classic and classically infused plays of Steven Berkoff, another Stepney resident and Hackney attendant reach their fullest expression in the fusion of dramatic and poetic speech as opposed to written verse and while *The Four Seasons* contains intermittent lines of poetry, it is seasoned so heavily with a literate and literary voice, from Adam's biblical significance to Beatrice, the female protagonist's echoes of Dante's great muse. This is the point about the conscious use of language and the stick that beats against the door of artistic veneration. There is something *lacking* as opposed to something missing and yet what is there is still worth your admittance alone.

It's a somewhat contrary fact, that all plays are essentially written to be read; they are there of course to be acted and worked on. Some may argue with this, as of course the best plays afford constant reading and consultation. But the point to my mind is, that when a play is read one is put in touch with what is *possible as a result of reading it*, in terms of performance, yes, on one level, but on a more primal level; *what it can do to the room*. Drama is about transformation as we know, and therefore transportation is required, either logistically or internally, so that we end up somewhere quite different from our point of arrival. Having done that, we can adapt our responses, through reflection, and join in an active way with what the words engender. Thought into action, the closest thing to what music can do, by making us cry, fuck or dance.

On the page we encounter the distinctions and exceptions. All of Pinter reads well, as does all of Miller, or indeed, all of Shakespeare, Marlowe, Bond, Rattigan. And Wesker too. But his is a novelist's impulse. He wants that expansion. Concision is not his true aim. Vanguard of Rock, Pete Townshend has talked in the past of how 'limited forms can give way to greater expression..' Wesker wants the wide world in his plays and his personal aims and ambitions also demonstrated that impulse, most famously in his taking over of Chalk Farm's Roundhouse as his Centre 42, a relatively shortlived idealistic enterprise which combined artistic endeavour with communal socialism. Wesker wanted to be a world changer but his reach fell a little short at times. He was a dreamer who not only dared to dream but was willing and able to detail just how those dreams could be grasped. He was perhaps a little unwilling at times to relinquish his right to do so and the means he used, and famously responded at great length to his critics across the world's newspapers and journals if he felt his aims and work had been misunderstood. This level of passion and defensiveness is admirable. Today's writers may well reflect and contain what is going on around them, often in a very journalistic, topical and dare I say it, throwaway type fashion, but they do not seem to be concerned with *changing* anything. Wesker fought change and conversely fought for it. He had a great and tremendous energy. He engaged and debated. He corralled and defended. He sought the high towers despite the constant pull of the moat. In effect, he did what writers are supposed to do: he kept writing, amassing over 50 plays, several unproduced screenplays, an artful book for children, *Fatlips*, a substantial novel, *Honey* – written near the end of his life, a comprehensive autobiography, *As Much As I Dare*, a fascinating volume of poetry *All Things Tire Of Themselves* concerning his *Five Poems For Harold Pinter, Erotica, The King's Daughters*, and 4 volumes of stories, which rank among his finest achievements, as do his journals and essays, *Fears of Fragmentation, Distinctions, the Journalists* and a late book of interviews with Chiara Montenero, *Ambivalences*. As I type this I have his twenty or so volumes stacked on my desk and they form a far ranging litany and legacy of ideas and passions.

There is an idea that a writer should by the end of his life written the equivalent of his or her own body weight. I myself have been quite prolific, so while my published books are slim, my compiled manuscripts may well supersede my stockiness. This would have been the case with Wesker but his books are substantial and their refinement is what truly remains of him. He was a writer who allowed the word to dance with him in his celebration of all he saw and felt and while the last couple of years of his life were blighted with illness he used his healthy span to be as both difficult as he was charming and accomplished. He was, from what I have read, a man of passion and vigour, washed as we all are by the joys and tyrannies of life. I did not know him as a person but then to what extent can we ever know even those we sit close to, so that is a matter for his friends and family. His W stood firmly in the postwar cannon and deserves renewal and recovery beyond the one or two titles that are the only points of reference for the general view. Wesker was a lot more than his Trilogy, as Edward Bond is insurpassably more than *Lear* or *Saved*, or Peter Barnes for *The Ruling Class*, Osborne, *Look Back In Anger*, or Charles Wood, *Dingo*. The list goes on. Wesker's plays came from his heart. While that heart is no more, his blood and his language flow on.

Attend the Lords of Hackney Downs and Stepney, for as we watch, their Palaces are gold.

BURNING THE BLOOD

On the 50th anniversary production of Heathcote Williams' *The Local Stigmatic*
– Old Red Lion, 6th May 2016

As Nabokov's long buried story, *The Enchanter* was to his great novel, *Lolita*, so Heathcote Williams' *The Local Stigmatic* is to his pyschedelic masterpiece *AC/DC*. Chiefly, the progenitor of a greater glory, but a piece still redolent of the private, scorching flame that birthed it. The title, as in all plays is crucial to its understanding: the local stigmatic is a perfect euphemism to describe the action conveyed beneath it. This new revival staged in the tidy confines of the Old Red Lion Theatre pub in Islington, captures the burn of that flame, but grasps little of its beauty.

The production is short, sharp and efficiently directed for the limitations of the space, but the director has encouraged his youthful and dedicated young actors to roar and blaze through the piece, doubtless to convey the immediacy of its language and situation, while missing much of the subtleties that lay beneath. The play is concerned with the need to matter to the people and world that surround us and the realisation that when we do not or are found wanting on that account, the only recourse our despair can give us is violent retaliation against anything or anyone close to hand. This means that we need to be led into that predicament and not just thrown or forced; not so we may examine the whys and wherefores in a cold, academic sense, but so we have time to quantify the relevance to our own lives and responses when watching the play.

Two South London dreamers, Graham and Ray, co-exist in a heavily inferred homoeroticism in clearly reduced circumstances. Both are eager to make their mark on the society that is catching sparks around them. The play was written and set in the mid 1960s, Williams' sophomore effort after his debut novel, *The Speakers* and the text deliciously if economically refers to the downside of those glorious summers. The boys have nothing and nowhere to go. The opening exchange about Graham's experience at the dog track is a bewildering start to a play when reading it for the first time, but it is the key to understanding the problems its protagonists face. When a play gives you sparse stage direction it is because the writing is telling you, consciously or not, that the text is perhaps meant to exist in an internal space. The play is about the fantasies its protagonists face and the antagonisms reality presents them. The lack of safe substance from which to draw interpretation means that all answers must be found *in the text*.

This production starts with a scene setter; pre-recorded sound of the racetrack with Graham improvising his reactions to the race. He swears, struts and swaggers. The house music of popular sixties doom anthems overprepares us for this; The Stones' 'Paint it Black,' The Animal's 'Please Don't Let Me Be Misunderstood', The Velvet's 'I'm Waiting for the Man,' so before the play begins, we have been forced down one treeless path of interpretation and it is down that unwavering path we remain.

My own belief as a director is that one has to realise the text and not impose on it. I recognise in saying this, that it is a view not shared by others and that there is nothing wrong in providing audiences with some context, especially those for whom the play is unfamiliar. Indeed, Stigmatic has long been an almost mythic text, rarely performed, published in this country in the long out of print Traverse Plays collection and only recently available in its filmed version on an Al Pacino collection released in the US, as the play, as has been noted elsewhere, has long been a pet project and point of obsession for him. But my point still stands; if you start a play with recorded sound – as many do on the fringe and indeed elsewhere – you begin, in my view, with a *false* moment. When the language and style is as rich and as dense as true theatricality demands – as it is in this play – all you need do is release it, explore it and allow your actors to direct its true focus to those watching, thereby allowing the world and context of the play to be established *through that language*. This observation comes not from criticism but from devotion to the play and what I believe theatre can do. It's all subjective of course but this is what reviews are for and productions also.

What director, Michael Toumey and his cast have done is to paint the scenes in close shades of the same colour. The actors shout and declaim from the off and Graham's desperate vigil at the dog track is then followed by a solitary Ray seeking to attack the armchair and bedsit around him, without provocation and simply as a display of the uncontrolled rage which clearly fuels and infects him. These two impositions, which I name as such because they are not in the text, no doubt allowed the actors to access the energies required to take them through the play but they also rob it of some of its truer sensations. If Graham and Ray are shown to be unbalanced from the start we cannot begin to understand them. Especially when the play is as short as this one. Other reviews have praised the 'What the Fuck' quality of the production. To this, I can only add the belief that 'Why the Fuck' is as important. If theatre is to create a world we need some explanation for it.

There is a pleasing chemistry between the two lead actors, Wilson James and William Frazer, who as young men have all the charm, appeal and swagger a younger audience will appreciate, but swaggering young men can also be a closed door. To sacrifice the notion of their vulnerbility and humanity, however warped, is to sacrifice the true horror of recognition. Society's monsters are not cartoons. They are the people drawing the pictures we all crave to look at.

The two young men are followers and proto-stalkers of the famous. At one point, Anna Massey, Shirley-Anne Field and the Duke of Bedford are listed as among Ray's favourites. This shows unbalance to some degree, of course, but the comedic value of the targets is somewhat coarsened by the unrelenting machismo on offer. When the two men confront the target of their attack, a British film actor, David, played by Tom Sawyer, their coquettish display and front are overly exaggerated, almost lampoonish and therefore the interplay is robbed of subtlety and the chill factor of real disturbance is thawed. Taken at such a pitch of distortion, there is no dramatic reason for David to remain in their company as they proceed to chat him up and ply him with drinks.

In an interview for *The International Times* website, Mr. Toumey related that his favourite line in the play occurred when Graham asks David what he's drinking. When he's told campari, he refers to it as 'port and lemon in disguise, ' and then says, 'you're sewn up, ain'tcha?' If the true coldness of this threat is to be grasped it needs to come from an unexpected place, the result of two outsiders battering their way in from the void, only to find ruins at every quarter.

The 'boys, ' have a need and compunction to matter. Attractively dressed and styled, their misfit nature is unexplained but still needs to be legitimised. Ray is always being thrown out of pubs, particularly the *Earl of Strathmore* in Earls Court, a queer pub, whose banning of him, he finds ironic. While this does not imply the Graham and Ray are gay in actuality, there is nothing to substantiate the opposite and when a young woman that Ray is sleeping with is said to be coming round to their flat to visit, Ray quickly decides to 'cut' or cancel her, and go out with Graham instead. To my thinking, this adds to the dreamscapes within which the two roam, playing with identities in the same way as immortalised by those compromised celebrities and serial killers, who do not possess any of their own. I was looking for a stumble, but all I found was strut.

Essentially of course, these are small details but they are transformative ones. A slight unsteadiness would have shown a semblance of dislocation from the confidence of 1960's London happening around them that went some way to explaining why they descend into a state of near murder. I wanted the boys' nervousness, and frailty to seep out through their sweat. A young Shirley Anne Field would pump the blood of any young man in the immediate vicinity and certainly, Anna Massey had her charms, but the *Duke of Bedford*? Instead, with everything pumped up to the max, it all seems a foregone conclusion. What I required was more space given for the ideas and meaning behind the language to breathe. This is particularly important in a small and smoke tinged room where the observer's mind often lingers on the surface.

Of course, to some extent a one act play does not give you much room to manouver, but the production uses the cramped space extremely well. It is brilliantly lit by Tom Kitney in its three main areas of bedsit, bar and street for instance, but the point remains: One act plays bare the same relation as short stories do to novels; you may not have the expansion but you have the subtle shades, the details. To push the analogy into painterly terms: when the canvas is small, you must begin to consider the brush.

I didn't believe the attack on David captured the shock effect of the violence as unravelled by the play. There is a prefiguring scene, when an unnamed *man* interrupts Graham and Ray's nightly walk between pubs. Here, he is blind and lashes out with his cane, forcing the boys into a series of animalistic and stylised movements. When he is persuaded and shouted off, it is done so through a door upstage left on the back wall and this expands the stage space well. But when David is kicked and beaten by Ray, the actor falls and remains downstage at the feet of the audience. This wouldn't matter so much for the fact that at the end of the scene, the actor leaves, destroying the image and resonance of attack. The intention was clearly to connect the audience to the violence, but if the image is discarded this isn't achieved as fully as it could be if placed elsewhere. Particularly if we are to feel it coming. We already know that it is, through reading or listening to the play, (something audiences rarely do) but when it does, it should shock us with its fury and ugliness. I felt those vital energies were spent before the moment of attack, leaving us with a sense of containment and a lightly stylised series of actions. With the body draped in a coat there is a silent placing and grinding of the foot, first on hip and then crotch, and the facial gouging with a flick knife occurring under the coat receives no movement or scream. I needed volume and shock here and not in the pages and minutes before. I wanted the attack to be on us, as an audience so that we could see the true affects of self destructive thinking writ large on the man's face or page. The return to the flat which follows therefore forgives or excuses our aggressors, rather than allowing us to see them as the wild and somewhat neglected dogs pushed back into their own cage; dogs who are forced to run their own race against the society around them, which thinks so little of them, that they are not spared even a scrap of attention.

The argument for subtlety in some places allows for savagery in others. Small theatre spaces like the *Old Red Lion* can become immersive, almost cinematic experiences if the levels of delivery are artfully poised.

The production was also song heavy, hammering the isolationist point home somewhat needlessly as it is there in the text. Along with the aforementioned opening salvo, The Kinks' 'I'm not like Everybody Else, ' The Walker Brothers, 'The Sun Ain't Gonna Shine Anymore, ' The Who's 'The Kid's Are Alright' all underlined an unesscessary literalism. Williams' work has its own music. His is the playlist I would much rather hear.

The young audience enjoyed it greatly on press night, as I'm sure all others did, and that of course is to be celebrated as it gets the play and Williams' name out to new generations. But literature should educate and entertain and to my thinking the production was soaked not in the cold blood of remorse and helplessness of real character, but in the slick oil of the cinematic psycho. Perhaps that's inescapable these days. We've had so many of them after all, from *Friday the 13th* to *Casualty*, but there was a chance here for something else.

The monsters among us commit their atrocities, if not quietly, then with certain levels of discretion and/or lack of control. Perhaps that is not possible in these unenlightened times when we are more than a little distanced from the simple power of the word, but I believe it should still be something to strive for.

At a time when new plays at the fashionable theatres last little more than an hour, *The Local Stigmatic* at 50 minutes is in the truly modern tradition of the One Act Play as defined by Pinter, Bond, Brenton and Snoo Wilson in the sixties. It stands its own ground. I felt that certain decisions in this production has reduced the play rather than expanded it. Here were speakers belting it out in the closed rooms of the oncoming night. I wanted whispers or even moans in those neglected shadows. Wilson James' Graham was in a constant state of committed and unblinking psychopathy from the get-go, but performed with impressive energy and attack. William Frazer's *Ray* had more colour and style but less gradation and modulation in his changing states, and Tom Sawyer's *Man* and *David* were finely wrought studies of persecution if a little over and then underplayed respectively.

This critique is offered with respect for mounting and recognising the anniversary of a seminal play and effectively placing it within a vibrant theatrical context.

I merely wished for a closer scrutiny, which is always the province of a studio theatre; an ability to see the blood within the vein, worrying itself to the skin.

True rage and dissatisfaction are cold and can often empty us. Once the fire has cracked, only then does the burning begin.

7th May 2016

CALL FOR CHANGE:

A review of *Poetry Can Fuck Up Your Finances*: Cockpit Theatre, London 23rd October 2016

As the esteemed poet and artist, Robert Montgomery has recently written and said, 'Money is a superstition, ' a powerful and revelatory edict that was echoed in this performance, the second in Daisy Campbell's stagings of poetic collages in response to society's hottest topics, committed under Heathcote Williams' Poetry Can Fuck Off banner and hosted at Marylebone's Cockpit theatre by Dave Wybrow and Brainfruit productions. In the light of recent events regarding this shattered – or at least shattering isle – the notion of the value of money and the part it has to play in and what it says of our lives is explored through expert recitations of the works of Heathcote Williams, Hakim Bey and John Harris, writer, magician and founder of *The Burning Issue*, the only magazine exclusively for money burners. A cast of five including Brainfruit founder Roy Hutchins, famed as Heathcote's leading poetic representative, Dan Copeland, Viv Boot, Jacquline Haigh, Tom Baker and sublimely supported by multi-instrumentalist and angel voiced singer- songwriter Mike McEwan, transported a committed cockpit audience into not only the history of money but also the ramifications it has had on our culture as both serving grace and final demand.

Staged around a makeshift sacrficial altar and a raised platform, the performers are able to utilise the versatile stage space of the theatre to both invoke and unify various treaties and manifestoes. The call for change is not just a useful pun to do with the rattling of pocket signifiers tying us all to the ground, but it is also a rallying cry for its audiences, to both reject and seek new futures through the possibilities for renewal in thought and form that poetry itemises. Hosted by Tom Baker's blokeish devilry and sinister accordion rumblings, dialogues and discourses ensure that the points raised inspire and influence those watching and listening across two hours of intense literary questioning. Roy Hutchins on synth bass and piano and Mike McEwan on everything else subtly underscore intense passages of text when not reading or performing themselves and McEwan's sublime songs and artful cover versions enhance the flow of words, creating and gifting proceedings with a profound depth of understanding. Unlike the music in Hollywood films which wrongly tell us what to feel, theatre music at its most effective should tell us how to, educating or guiding our responses and acting as a separate voice, another character if you like. So it proves here, with McEwan's stocky frame giving rise to all sorts of incidental pleasures, filling the evocative space of the cockpit and artfully tainting the air.

Like her much missed father, the seminal and irreplaceable Ken, Daisy Campbell is a superb director and manipulator of the dramatic/comedic and theatrical moment. She creates an intense atmosphere that nevertheless ripples with humanity throughout and allows her performers to act as separate hosts while forming part of a larger ceremony. There is something of the mystical about the evening; a druid's cloak with a sneering countenance beneath, as the pieces chosen and presented inform us of the self inflicted dark magic we are all practising on ourselves by reducing our own existence within currency's unholy communion. The root of all evil indeed, but hopefully one we can learn from and this chance for change is exemplified by the space and time given to the three keynote speakers who each talk profoundly in the misuses and abuses that our love of currency wreaks, from writer and KLF biographer John Higgs, to inspirational speaker Vinay Gupta, who as a corporate man in the old century describes himself in relation to money as a 'former heavy user, ' to the writer and magician Christopher Stone who invited everyone in attendance to a series of magical happenings in London's financial district on November 7th 2016 from 12.30pm (See the piece Between The Dragons).

Theatrically speaking this shows real mastery on Daisy's part, in that she has constructed something whose very foundations can be altered and which can still remain standing, but which will on resuming take the audience straight back to the given moment of revelation in which the narrative or description of a fall from grace on the splintering wings of currency is seen in all of its nerve shattering infamy. This is nowhere more apparent than in Viv Boot's glorious sharing of excerpts in a voice that uncannily summons Ken Campbell's, reminding us of the joy he would have taken in seeing his daughter put together such a show and how effectively and uproariously he would have taken part. A further highpoint occurs, quite literally when Jacqueline Haigh appears on the platform over the other performers, in a glittering silver dress as a twin tailed dragon like princess, whose additional tube supplied vagina explodes into a cascade of golden confetti while extorting John Harris' 'call on all iconoclasts.. to pity the rich while the poor burn.' Here is theatre in its purest, most alchemical form. Words as literal gold.

Indeed, the words both collude and invoke. The theatre at its purest form is to some extent an act of persuasion. In conventional plays we are invited to believe the lie of fiction, either in term of invented content or thinly disguised reportage. Here, the opposite is true as the facts shared and offered to us cut straight to the heart of what we have done to the world we believe we have made. At one point a stunning rendition of 80's pop classic, 'Money (That's what I want)' breaks out, led by McEwans drumming on a tambourine while Hutchins, for a man known for his energy and elegance loutishly bangs a support pole with a plank of wood. The opening line of this song 'The best things in life are free, ' has never seemed more relevant after an hour of disseminaton and dissent (and perhaps descent also) as we are led down to the depths of ourselves and challenged accordingly and if you'll excuse the bad pun, accordion-ally by Tom Baker's dark chuckling and rasping, squeezebox drones.

In the first of the three keynote speeches, John Higgs reminds us of the KLF's mighty Island of Jura happening in which they burnt a million pounds, a revelatory act still not thoroughly understood by contemporary society. As Higgs says, 'it is one thing to start to burn a million pounds but quite another thing to finish burning it, ' and Vinay Gupta's masterful and eloquent five minutes exhorts all objects to effectively describe or justify their own function or be found wanting. These and Christopher Stone's magical exhortations are wonderfully supported by Daisy's Campbell's witty, nimble and authoritative production and approach. You see it in all her work, from the early days of supporting her dad, through her many activities across the culture and recent production of Robert Anton Wilson's *Cosmic Trigger* trilogy. She is a visionary and an activist and if this doesn't make too much of a trilogy of bad puns, we are all the richer for her.

The evening concluded with a focusing on the central altar. In a ceremony initiated and conducted by John Harris, the audience were asked to take part in a four cornered series of burnings. Serial numbers of notes were obtained and in small groups we were invited to cremate the selected notes that were already burning in our pockets.

CALL FOR A CHANGE

For the time it took to go through a couple of hundred pounds the theatre became a place of magic and the eerie silence of ceremonial witness held full and proper sway. The true currency that was achieved could be felt in those quiet moments of reflection shared and exchanged between us, which created on one Sunday night in London a universal truth. As one masterful line in the show said, 'if you have created the world why on earth would you want to waste your time on economics?'

These shows will continue at regular intervals. Look out for them as they tackle this and other artistic and political topics that affect the shapes that you make on the day. The song of reformation has begun and it is even now ratting its way through your pocket and purse. At one point in the show there are reports how someone has sold off the rights to their virginity while another has places the earth on ebay, describing it as 'used but authentic, ' let that surely be the term by which we are all known, achieved only through the acceptance of the abuse and the reasons and need for revolt. There is still time to decide on new ways of unifications and a new means of social exchange. Perhaps the coming moments will allow your own notions to form and your own inventions to occur. Pause and reflect. Soldier on to adventure. Attend all endeavours. And invest in the truth. In this single show poetry owns us. Now we must let it as we learn what to value and spend.

24th October 2016

BLACK BOX BUKKAKE

A review of The Northampton Arts Lab's Theatre production: *The Annual General Meeting of a Medium Sized Firm of Accountants* The Playhouse Theatre, Northampton November 4th 2016

The theatre is dead on its feet. Or if it isn't its stance has become monolithic; stone fed, it stands heavy, cast by a celebrity glaze. It is a closed structure and made for those beneath to give worship. And yet it will not admit them. They are only there to adore. To look at each play like a film, frozen by fame and false glory, or as a piece of art too expensive for anyone committed or keen to quite touch. It is a hulk made of straw but the stuff is dense enough to secure it. And so it stands, a vast totem, tightening earth, crushing ground. And yet at those feet a new earth is already in flower, and fresh shoots are bidding to try and replace that lost step. Just one of these buds found its light at Northampton Playhouse on Friday 4th November 2016 when the Northampton Arts Lab presented their second theatre play, *The Annual General Meeting Of A Medium Sized Firm Of Accountants*.

Coming hot on the heels of their first show *Artmageddon* and under the direction, leadership and artistic and technical mastery of Megan Lucas, the show was something of a triumph. Written by NAL group members including Megan Lucas, Tom Jordan, Tom Clarke, Michelle La Belle, Josh Spiller, Jess Fowler and yes, your very own and actual Alan Moore, the seventy minute play was a mix of artistic anarchy, technical accomplishment and more importantly, humour of both the brightest and blackest sorts. Compiled by the Arts Lab over a series of monthly meetings, the play charts the fantasies and consequences of those desires for the medium sized firm of accountants. From the IT guy's email courtship of the lovely and strangely unattainable Holly, (played by Stephanie Humphris), to Tim Burr the desk lover's physical and mental commitment to his four legged paramour and penile saviour, through to the boss's strangely schizophrenic wanderings between sexual states, this group of low level financial servants aspire to some of the skies darker stars. At one point one of the accountants, Walter (played by Dalen Lewis with admirable restraint) turns into a watercooler, so innocuous and unobtrusive is his presence and yet his desire to serve nevertheless achieving its ultimate fulfilment. A new apprentice, Nickbert Teslastein, played with wondrous invention by Sonny Drake, holds court in a stunningly inventive monologue by Michelle La Belle on the powers of numerology and the binary code and of how his grandmother shagged everyone from Nikola Tesla to Albert Einstein, as this and other pieces ignited their own forms of electricity.

The compact black box fringe space of the theatre allowed these dreams greater prescience and the smallness of the theatre enabled the rapt audience to watch the play transform into the best television show it ever saw, as projections of emails, statistics and film clips illustrated the various points and ideas. The first half concludes with a rousing song from chief focus, Seth Lopod (written by Tom Jordan and composed and played on ukele by a woollen octopus masked Roswell Blake and sung by Samuel Jones) in which his desire to be one with and indeed wank with a gay octopus is the only possible means of his escape from his uninspiring trollop of a wife who is clearly holding him back from his sperm driven swim to the heart. There are not many plays whose first half concludes with a slender man of asian origin being blasted by the produce of an octopus cock and this is intricately worked up to by Lopod's fish based lunches. Let Mark Ravenhill continue to shop for lurid illustration, the Arts Lab has bettered the deal.

The second half broadened to take in the pyschologies of these dampened protagonists (quite literally in Lopod's case) and was still reeling from Lindsay Spence's standout performance of the Desk lover's declaration of love, sex and connection with nature (again penned by Michelle La Belle), but it also contained the evening's real gem, a five minute film piece of Alan Moore in the somewhat expected role of God, project manager and creator of the universe, brokering a deal to pacify and/or appease Kim Jong Un while dealing with the existential agonies of Morgen Bailey's shunned Leticia. Artfully filmed and treated by Megan Lucas' technical wizardry, Alan's halo glimmered and bolstered above him as he talked of the illusion of reality, the inadequacies of the TV show Lost, 'Fucking rubbish. That's fifty hours of my eternal existence I won't get back!' and how resembling Captain Birdseye in a frock is not what any monotheiastic deity should have any right to expect.

Jess Fowler appeared in a self written monologues as a health and safety officer and as a cleaner penned by Megan Lucas, both characters trying to calm things over, just as Josh Spiller's ingenious IT contributions sought to unravel them, and all in a tightly woven package, courtesy of the polymathic M. Lucas, who worked her own magic across wires, forms, digitalisation, all on a laptop with at least four keys missing. This play was a stunning piece of theatrical invention that left its audience enthused and enraptured. Poignancy was supplied by a final monologue written by Tom Jordan in which Ann Onymous, a lonely office lady, sensitively played by Michelle La Belle and even more passed over than Morgen Bailey's disappointed Leticia beautifully encaptured the solitude and sacrifice that lays at the heart of modern office life.

Although well discussed, planned and formulated the rehearsal time was limited to the point of virtual non-existence on the show. The NAL are not professional actors, they are artists, writers, teachers and architects, but they are all the better for it. They are free of the pressures, constraints and limitations of the professional theatre, while being imbued with the appropriate sensibilities necessary to mount a work of this sort. It always helps when there are intelligent people on the stage and of course talented ones, who understand that to be self serving is not the issue. The play is the thing in the more conventional sense, but beyond even that, is the idea. The intention. The word. The poetic to be expressed and the enlivening image. These are the aspects that matter as they seek to challenge and of course entertain. And so, calm prevailed and the ship sailed effortlessly on, loaded as it was with more ideas than any of London's most popular plays of the day can come up with, and with as many mixtures of artistic endeavour on board as you could ask or expect a wayward parrot to crap on. It was what all theatre should be, an adventure of the purest sort. Transformative, elucidating and enlightening in its own way and on its own terms. The production has not been filmed so it lives on now in the memory of a hundred people packed in on a Friday night in a place described by Alan Moore as the Centre of the Universe (Northampton). It is hoped that it sails again across blander waters, spilling its seed and tainting the faces of all who bare witness. May that be you reading this and others like you. Open your mind is what the wind will be calling and as a delighted smile plays and follows, these hardy sailors will want to come on your face.

The bukkake in porn is a strange celebration. It is the body applauding. Look ma, no hands

FROM CALVARY TO CHEMISTRY

A review of Wandering Albatross' production of *The Immortalist* by Heathcote Williams October Gallery, London December 9th 2016

A proper theatre is formed of ideas. Whether under the glare of old suns primed as they were by Greek judgement or by the uncomprehending eyes of the present, the theatre should challenge and in an indirect way try to teach. This seminal play, written by Heathcote Williams after conversations with David Solomon and Mike Lesser and informed by notions popularised by Robert Anton Wilson, is one of the richest of his dramatic works and one that certainly struck me as a teenager, pushing at the doors of literature and seeking entrance to the mysterious world of counter cultural viewpoint, whilst easing my way past the sharp weapons of the old avant garde.

The play takes the form of a television interview with a man who claims to be 278 years old, a little too young for Shakespeare but certainly old enough to have lived through the days of Courbet and the Paris Commune. Frazer's golden bough was something within easy reach of this individual, and as he drops names and experiences across the intervening time period, one becomes aware that this play in particular is a roller coaster ride not just through theories of extended mortality, but through the history of rebellion itself.

In his summary of the issues and aspects that have affected his existance 278's justifications and deliberate obfuscations abound. They are there to both entrance and bewilder, herding the audience into a fresh new perspective where the fields of perception place them as the cattle, steeped - as all cattle are - in bullshit.

The bravura nature of the flow of ideas and argument needs a rapid delivery, a semi-frantic yet nevertheless coruscating rim-shot striking journey from word to word-image and then back again towards word. In the production mounted on Friday, December the 9th 2016 at the remarkable enclave of artistry, the October Gallery in Holborn, the approach was more stately than revolutionary. Jack Moylett, whose touching enthusiasm for the play has led to this production here and previously in Berlin performs 278 as a wise old cove warmed by a low fire. He seeks to mystify and seduce, perhaps aiming for the confident otherworldly twinkle of Patrick Troughtons's Doctor Who, embellished with a dash of William Hartnell's austere stroppery, and his portrayal has a pleasing composure to it. It does not however, quite capture the strangeness of atmosphere if not content in Williams' dramatic work, the very element that led to the mystique he was often awarded. Williams' career has been a healthy mix of strident polemicism and poetic entrenchment. He was, is and will remain the ultimate cult artist, and it is important to honour the eerie glow of his work, as much as you value its contemporary relevance.

The Immortalist is not a play in the conventional sense (but neither are Harold Pinter's, Samuel Beckett's, Caryl Churchill's, or Jim Cartwright's for that matter), it is a theatre essay, rippling with successive waves of discourse, conjecture and japery. It crackles with the singe of ideas, from the notion of sublimating your own shit in order to distill immortality's crucial ingredient, Indole, to the idea that death is a lifestyle choice, a fashion statement of the deadly, keen to keep hold on us all.

The psychedelic exuberance of his 1970 masterpiece AC/DC, is the begetter of this particular piece. If you like, it is *The Immortalist's* , wild, older brother, who has defied the conventions of upbringing and expectation and gone out into the world to fuck and be fucked in its myriad corners, before wiping himself clean on the shattered souls of the lost. This play therefore becomes the studious and refined younger brother of the former, who has learnt from the wayward nature of his sibling, and started to reflect on his exploits with several bright opinions at hand. It is a fast and difficult music but one which soon has us singing as the vitality of Williams' language begs for celebration, and Williams as word magus directs us all through the roar of his song. The best plays aspire to musical levels of delivery and resonance and must be served accordingly. Moylett's easy irish charm captures some of this music but also misses aspects of it's strength. Pacing and levels of interpretation could be more closely followed, but placed in their stead, is a delicate sharing, a lulling which certainly embodies the sensualist aspect of Heathcote Williams' life and work, while foregoing much of the aforementioned stridency.

What is wanted on stage is an echo or embodiment of what one receives on reading, a shadowing of Heathcote's laughter, as he whips up and conjures a range of responses that allow us to dance towards death. This vital brew requires the mastery of a conductor with his eye on the prize and a racing driver with his grasp of the clutch, as he veers towards it. We must, over the course of fifty minutes crash through the windscreen of experience in order to renegotiate our place at the wheel. What must be rammed in our faces should be a new weather, designed for the fresh hole before us, igniting the throat and the mind. A signpost subsumed by the road.

The direction of this play is at times, static. 278 and the Interviewer played by an exquisitely voiced Allison Mullin, either sit or stand without further staging and this relative immobility stops us connecting fully with the events described in the text and the emerging situation between the two characters, something that should be shared with us, placing us there as they talk. As the Interviewer comes to understand, sympathise and disagree with the points on offer, she too has a chance to begin a journey, evident in her struggle to grapple with the notions at hand. 'Time is a false alarm...' 'Analyse. Transcend.' '..stimulate a different chemical mandala in your body..' '..disobey the alien order..' Again and again she is given the keys to the chamber. Again and again she refuses to move.

A much sought for conclusion of the play is for 278 and the Interviewer to somehow dematerialise, or transcend in some way, but of course that is not truly the point. It's possible that the figure of 278 could be played by an animated skeleton or yoda like, mummified puppet voiced by an actor, or imagined as a combination of darkness, wisdom and devilry, as if Harold Pinter in all of his black eyed glory had fused with the type of acid casualty glimpsed in the party scene of *Midnight Cowboy*, before being glossed by Machen's *Great God Pan*. 278 is a self defined god primarily through his defiance. And his rejection of reality as we understand it is what lifts this conversation into a new realm of impact, in which the exchanging of states and extremes of being is the ultimate goal.

As he is gently interrogated we are encouraged to undergo the various stages of belief, from scepticism to adoration and there is much in this performance that allows that. It does however need tightening. The basic setting of two chairs in front of a hung backdrop featuring a blow-up of the playscript's original cover (of two skeletons in conversation), is used, but was off kilter and compared to the shuffling informal opening did not help establish the appropriate context and atmosphere. The television setting is not important as the piece is at heart a conversation in the truest extent of the word; and no doubt some would argue that my concern also isn't, but when one is presenting ideas and images of this calibre, a level of precision enhances both the understanding of what is shown and more importantly of what is implied afterwards. It could be argued that the last thing theatre needs is elaborate decorative elements of setting. We must instead fill the space with words and their tokenistic magic, especially if they stem from linguistic trickster's of the stamp of Heathcote Williams. Having said that of course, it should be noted that Williams is very much his own postal service in terms of poetic achievement, so that is a task in itself.

What I wanted therefore was a greater sense of involvement and control. There were some affecting moments of commitment when Moylett raged but perhaps in this one off performance at least, a little too much gentility. Theatre should beguile us as effectively as it transports and affronts us but I wanted the delivery to lay waste to the doors truth breaks down.

I am not of the mind that message trumps nuance – and indeed the low animal bearing that name makes an appearance in the text, albeit in a slightly heavy handed way – but I am of one that the passing on of full creative and critical understanding is the point of each performance between actors and audience. The best plays achieve this and we must not stand (or sit) in their way. But we must allow for the physical nature of the language to manifest itself in terms of both thought and action and there were at times here, a little too much restraint on display.

All theatre is hard work but the real energy, the true energy is hard to capture and one that many actors shy away from. The delivery of a playtext is not set in stone. It is afterall, written to take place in the air and the air is forever changeable. The essential truth is the same (we must for instance, continue to keep breathing) but the approaches can vary if the idea is to live. It is vital in this play that the audience believe they are sitting in the same room as someone who has moved through and past the 'black kingdom' and begun to reclaim higher forms.

278's ingenious history of the twentieth century's flirtations with genocide from the '14-18 folk festival' to 'the 39-45' one, leaves us with a view on the flippancy of man's actions. It takes us through the ethereal nature of Timothy Leary or Krishnamurti type thought via the uses and abuses of Tri- and Di-methyl Tryptamine and a 'messiah like universe' of stopped clocks. Its final statement is one that changed my personal view of what was possible with writing; chiefly how to make the most casual statement the most revelatory. When it arrives here it is highlighted a little too heavily - even by something as simple as a head turn - when it should perhaps take us by surprise and leave us at the door of conversion, but the flavour is still fit to taste:

> *'There are people alive now who are not going to die. Put that on the news.'*

If not the fact in itself, then the fiction is useful. In fact, more than useful, it, as a statement, totally transforms who we are and how we understand things to be. In nineteen syllables, Heathcote Williams provides a near textbook haiku of transcendence. It is a line and sequence of thought that demands its own theatre and virtually its own medium. And for me ranks with that other great and fundamental statement of importance, found in Petey's final appeal to Stanley Webber 'The Birthday Party, ' 'Stanley, don't let them tell you what to do!' These are commands and acts of word-magic aimed at the strength in us all.

If this production had been played as a recital in the round a deeper sense of sharing would perhaps have been received – though it should be noted that it was received by an audience greatful to hear the play again and to delight in the majesty of language on offer - and this would perhaps have suited the style of Moylett and Mullins' delivery more effectively. By moving slightly away from what I hesitate to call 'certain rules of presentation, ' some elements slipped past us. The effect was of missing certain choice pieces of meat – which 278 eats 'if it meets him' - in an ever deepening stew, and yet everyone present was aware that amidst peas and chicken there was dazzle and duck still to come.

The word concert remained and ultimately moved like music. As we must move from disaster towards some sort of revolve for the soul. *Wandering Albatross* landed well and showed refined dedication. From the heights of grand theory to the oceans at play within us. The truth must be sent by albatross, eagle, pigeon. The governing air's in the writing. If we relearn how to breathe it, we may also relearn how to live. In this play tonight we caught a glimpse of the process. The ideas achieve flight even if their origins remain earthbound. Humour and gall elevate them as the divine is revealed in bullshit. As the stunned cattle gaze towards the storms of transference, we hear the grand Oxfordian chuckle as he fountain pens and exhorts us:

'Dead men of the world unite. You have nothing to lose but your lids.'

10th December 2016

photo and copyright by Chris Davies

Part Four:

OTHERS TALKING
(Encounters)

KENSAL RISING

On Walking The London Night With Iain Sinclair and Andrew Kotting February 23rd 2016

The temptation is to write in his style: *'Incidents and inspirations, passports to unknown destinations..'* but temptations post the snake smeared apple, are there to be resisted and the true aim was to walk in his shadow, if only briefly. And on a fresh Tuesday evening in February 2016, starting at 10.30pm at the corner of Finchley Road and Frognal, that's what I was able to do, fulfilling a long sought for personal ambition.

What is it about writing and writers that excites and engages us? Surely, the basic ignition of idea and style that is able to transport the reader and appreciator, from the day they currently inhabit, offering a glimpse of alternative worlds and viewpoints. The Writer at their best is a shaman, capable of inducing and intoxicating the reader with the necessary means of exit and transformation. Iain Sinclair does this constantly in his seminal poetry, novels and masterpieces of psychogeography, and to the extent that all of his books become maps of both practise and imagination, primed by new directives and intentions. Having met at a poetry recital dedicated to David Gascoyne, Iain invited me to join him and his friend and constant collaborator, Andrew Kotting on their latest venture; a continuation of work already charted in his book, *London Overground – A Day's Walk Around the Ginger Line.*

This book is the latest (of two) missives from Iain and our walk that evening took the form of a nocturnal alternative, a flipside to the blazing enterprise and daylit reverie previously charted, detailing the expansion of the new overground trainline as it marks and passes the vestiges of London's Olympic legacy.

Sinclair and Kotting are Quixotes of the artistic and literary spirit, differing from the tragic-comedy of that model through the sharpness of their own investigations. Dividing his time between London, Hastings and a home in the Pyrenees, Kotting is also a contemporary proto-Hercules, taking on massive physical labours in order to complete the task, whether it is wrestling with the London river system to ensure his Swan pedaloe reached its destination in his film with Sinclair, *Swandown*, or enabling the journey of his daughter Eden and Grandmother, Gladys' trek around England in his film *Gallivant*. Andrew talked of his nightly trails through the mountains of Europe, forging on into darkness and embracing the unexpected, even in what had become partly familiar terrain, and as he powered on ahead, matched by Iain and I hope my own short-arsed pedestrianism, his heroic status remained secure. The victim of a recent shocking road accident, and the bearer of a nasty hole in his leg, Kotting is an Art Warrior of the highest order. These men both literally and artistically walk the walk and talk the talk, their money placed firmly where their mouths are, spent wisely as they plan and plough they way through the city. Unlike many practitioners they are their work in all meanings and/or senses of the word, testing their limits and speculations breath by breath and step by step, authenticating every thought and image. Their humour, openness and humanity blaze through. I had worried about interrupting the rhythm and flow not only of the night long walk from Haggerston in the east to the far reaches of South London and back, but also of their friendship, but both men were as welcoming and as generous as you would wish and want them to be.

To paraphrase Peter Cook's famous embodiment of Harold Macmillan in *Beyond the Fringe*: 'We talked of many things' from the nature of London and the need to perhaps not summon its past but certainly measure its changes, to the mysteries of the disappearing bookseller, Driffield, through to the mystical, kabbalistic Seven; the ancient guides there to be encountered by the flaneur and pyschogeographer on their nightly pilgrimages. Harold Pinter and Heathcote Williams loomed large, as they often do in my conversation, as did Iain's other brother in collaboration, Chris Petit, who achieves by the driven mile what Sinclair and Kotting do on foot. Petit's seminal film, *Radio On* is a touchstone for many an independent film-maker, but slightly less well known are his novels, the first of which, *Robinson,* is up there in my opinion with Iain's *Downriver* as the last word on the London spirit and first word in fresh ways of telling stories and reinvigorating modern prose.

Here then, are men at the forefront of standards that are not recognised by the mainstream, and while they would never wish to succumb to it, in being located somewhere between cult artists of the highest rank and 'muses for the masses' (if they could only forsake their trend sodden blinkers) it strikes me that their work is offered in the spirit of all great innovators, in that they are marking the borders of a new field of enterprise and it has to be said, endeavour, showing where art, film and literature can go in order to advance the culture. Grand claims I know and any misrepresentations of purpose are my fault and opinion entirely but it seemed to me as I walked, that Iain and Andrew are clearly charting new forms of practise. Each walk and trip they take is a new film or book in its own right, and while the film maker John Rogers is compiling footage of the trip under separate cover, the three hours I shared with them were a limited edition I will always prize. If I never get to do it again, the brief connection will be treasured and if I do, then the reading of breath and atoms between these two friends and artists will people a new library.

The evening was a series of reports from a front line determined by the overground stations, but it was subject to much conjecture and rumination. At each stop, (West Hampstead, Kilburn, Kensal Rise, Willesden Junction etc), Iain captured Andrew in comic poses and while discussing the progress of the Arsenal – as Samuel Beckett once did with friends of mine – along with their separate histories, and collaborators such as Alan Moore, Brian Catling, Etruscan book's Nick Johnson and numerous others, I was hosted, consulted and taken interest in.

Jewish cemetaries played a large part in the conversation, from the discovery of one close to Iain's home in Hackney, to the granderies of Kensal Rise where Harold Pinter's personal silence is held. Along the marathon like residential road to Willesden, Andrew realised we would pass the home of a good friend of his and I witnessed the formulation of the kind of artistic Christmas that I in my semitic balaclava could only dream of: Iain and Andrew are book magnets and finding a discarded box of unwanted novels signed and dated one and posted it through the friend's front door. It was approaching midnight and perhaps too late to rouse the suburbs unduly, so imagine waking to find an important friend's hello wrapped in papered spine and words. A throwaway item was rendered invaluable, not only through the bearing of eminent signatures, but also through a true and touching sentiment.

Kotting's a hugger on the grand scale, a great bear of warmth and vitality and someone who makes you feel a friend, even if only for the moment you're talking to him, so observing this small idea from impulse to execution reminded me of what real goodness is; the simple exchange of offers and information, bridges over the communal divide.

Since the death of my beloved mother, Lilian, and the long felt loss of my father, Tommy, I'm someone without a family. A consequence of this is a somewhat bewildering sense of solitude, even among my many friends and an independence that is both daunting and inspiring. I have over the last few years been able to work with and get to know many of my heroes so this simple exercise in friendship touched me greatly. Ours is a barbaric age in the ways and means with which we forsake community and connection and while culture and the arts are often prey to their own insularities and elitism, the scope of some people's work is undeniable. Am I wrong to make so much of a small and simple gesture? I don't believe so, as these are the moments and acts that stand out at a time when few are interested in helping and seeing others' work, beyond the nose and limits of their own nepotism.

What strikes you most about these two men is their intense interest in the forces they come into contact with. They are proponents and supporters of other artists whose work and aims collide with theirs and are passionate observers of the cultural climate. Whether its Andrew in the mountains or Iain on the avenue, here are men capturing and encountering the city in ways that most of us couldn't begin to appreciate. There was a delicious moment as we approached White City where an in-progress development site took on the full dimensions of a Ballardian city-scape and we conjectured how the much missed JG would have relished seeing it. At night, entire sections of the city resemble caged hybrids of beast and machine with the half closed eyes or ransacked or part made structures stir with a barely repressed violence. The sounds of occasional passing traffic are stabs and jabs from an orchestral needle and everywhere and everything anticipates the storm. Whether it is meteorlogical or social, change and the potential for change lay coiled in an uneasy silence and only Sinclair and Kotting are there to document it. Of the rest of us, none of us know where we are. I'm sure that's the case in most large cities, certainly in the west. As a lifelong London native of small revenue, I do not always indulge in what the city has to offer and remain within my own small limit.

Many's the night when I witness the hoi gloriously polloi-ing while I seek comfort in my singular tread, and then of course there are the visitations to numerous bright planets and principalities, but it is Iain Sinclair who teaches us how to truly value our metropolis, by walking and writing it down, reflecting the stories and experiences he has witnessed with a journalists flair, leavened by his skills as Poet and Novelist. Through the pictorial and imagistic approach of his writing; he makes true London Art, separate to the self congratulatory Shoreditch and Soho-ites, turning the city into its own novel, gallery and bookstall. To extend the analogy a little further, he conducts a London tinged symphony, corralling voices and themes, no doubt fuguing them also, all to make a body of work as dense and reflective as it is generous and deftly designed. Sinclair dares the reader to take part, to consider the consequences of his or her actions. To question purpose and place. To, in all senses, understand and unravel the poetry of practise and belief. He unearths the possible through his artistic and political diligence and through the literary conceits of summoning the ghosts of writers and faces he's known, from William Blake, to the Krays, through the ghosts of David Litvinoff and Derek Raymond, down on through to the practices of Leon Kossoff and Arthur Machen, and the contemporary work of Brian Catling, assosciates of the Swedenborg Institute and current Baron of cool, Stewart Lee.

Both Iain and Andrew have accomplished what many of us fail to do; they know, if not why they are here, then what they are supposed to do while they wait to find out, which is to chase, confront and question the limits and standards we have set for ourselves in all aspects of modern living. These are men who hold no truck with Godot's procrastination. They would instead tear the trousers from Estragon's legs and march him and Vladimir firmly onto the road. They wish, with a child like enthusiasm, to experience each moment and to measure its value as they do so. The night is perhaps as physically delicious to them as the prospect of encountering it, and no doubt as satisfying as the full English that awaits them at journeys end. These are men of 58 and 71 who have more life and power than the children who slouch as low as their bollock free trousers will permit them. As practitioners, they are as visceral as the work they create together and in separation. As you linger in the corners of your own hour, Sinclair and Kotting are out there past midnight, slowly relabeling time.

I salute them.

As you sit there tonight with your wine and/or television, imagine them walking, reintroducing themselves to the sources of their own fascination. There are new ways to read and new ways to experience film, whether its through the expansive form of Andrew's *Swandown*, *By Ourselves* and *Acumen*, or Iain and Chris Petit's *London Orbital*, or Iain's early portrait of Allen Ginsberg in *Ah! Sunflower*, or any one of his books. The drive and generosity of their work, coupled with the challenges presented by it, enables the appreciator to become part of the project. Sinclair's readers become the authors of their own understanding as does Kotting's viewers. These are books and films as food for the foot and the soul. Walk with them while reading, recall them as you watch and you will be rewarded beyond the simple and passive consumption we usually expect as receivers. Ape the dedication and enthusiasm these men show to the smallest extent and you will be truly evolving the form. At some point, as Iain said to me, it will be upto someone else to continue the rigourous documentation of change or devolution he has started. Let that be you in both the reading you do and the questioning it engenders. Listen to the future, now. It is building. At the present time, we are tuning but the base notes are there in the past.

As Kensal Rise gave way to Willesden we found a small park with trees of our own to piss across. For that brief time the simple pleasures offered by life and biology were crowned with a singular glory. Trousers secured, and after the two men had brandied and joked, Iain gave me a piece of his Kendal mint cake. It tasted, not of victory (I detected no Apocalypse that night!), but of rejuvenation, not only of my own outlook, but of general possibility. As we arrived at White City, Andrew asked a pair of jobsworth Westfield cleaners if we could walk through that glazed palace of disrepute through to the primordial pleasures of Shepherd's Bush Green. Denied, I had to steer them through the endless Bus lane to the promised point, endangering my Kotting hug. It was a rite of passage I hope I passed, if not at the time then in reflection. At 1am I left them to return by Nightbus to my Uxbriidge home. I watched them as they pressed on towards the dawn, the creators of a new day we should all wake to; one of promise and progression, in which the limits set by our own feet are no longer the barriers to our perception. At Kensal Green we peered over a railway bridge to gaze at the stabled mastodons of iron and rust. I felt the flame of happiness. I had in those three hours bettered the darknesses I had brought upon myself and already my spirits had started to rise.

Thankyou, Gentlemen.

Now, reader, you too, should walk on.

Iain Sinclair

Andrew Kotting

Paintings by David Erdos Photo and copyright by Iain Sinclair

ODE TO THE ETERNALIST:
A LITERA-MATIC ENCOUNTER WITH ALAN MOORE

Wednesday August 17th 2016, The Lodge Studios, Northampton

Alan Moore photos from Keith Rodway's film

I: FINDING THE DOOR YOU DESERVE

DAVID ERDOS: Limited as it is, the reality defined by the way most of us now live it can be described as the limerick of a wounded imagination: Alan Moore is one of the major poets of our recovery. Meeting him was the fulfilment of a lifetime's ambition, the chance to connect with a man whose body of work has helped to shape some of my dreams, thoughts and practise across the years and whose ideas, along with Heathcote's have produced a lasting legacy for current and indeed successive generations.

Alan's work stands in line with a select group of offerings that have aimed to transform, elucidate, challenge and educate, often in the most startling and entertaining ways. From William Blake, to Samuel Beckett, Harold Pinter and Edward Bond, to Heathcote, Iain Sinclair, Angela Carter, and dammit, Anthony Newley, to all points in between, his graphic novels, essays, songs, stories and novels exist on a higher plane than simple changes or innovations in style and form. Those encountering such works are not only shown how to truly read and think but how to *behave*. For most of us that is simply to recognise the constraints we live in and attempt to comment and in some way change them. Heathcote Williams escaped from a certain type of English upbringing into a Sloane Square cupboard, and from that small sanctuary, attained the world; Alan has done so by making the humble and neglected boroughs of his Northampton upbringing, not only the centre of that selfsame globe, but of the magical one beyond it. Part of the appeal of the filmed section of this interview, which can be found on the *International Times* website under this title, was the chance of bringing the two men together, albeit briefly. I was able to honour my own reverence for Alan's work by enabling him to honour his gratitude for Heathcote's and vice versa.

Magic struck hard, because as we were talking about Heathcote, he rang me. Hearing the phone ring, I didn't take the call at first, as Alan was in full flow, but at the next point of emphasis I was able to call Heathcote back and these two artistic giants were able to speak to each other, the great H praising Alan's *V for Vendetta* as a supreme accomplishment and Alan graciously thanking Heathcote for the inspiration he had provided, all through the speaker function of my iPhone! I was, as Harold Pinter once said, 'chuffed to my bullocks' that I was able to unite them, reason enough perhaps for my own small existence on that particular day in the near midlands.

It was a precious moment and Alan Moore is the most engaging and considerate of men. His openness and generosity are well documented, his everyman quality complimenting his otherworldly experience, and this coupled with his gentlemanly cane and ornate hand gallery of rings intoxicates you into gratitude for his time and presence.

Read anything by Alan Moore and you will quickly realise that his work, views, approach and imagination are vital components for today and indeed, tomorrow's culture and society. The responsibility of conducting myself well and creating a satisfactory experience for him was crucial to me and weighed on my mind. I am no cucumber in any regard and as such find it hard to be cool. Nettles (to extend the nature analogy a little further) are however there to be grasped, so I ask you to see through the stumble and glimpse the excitement and pleasure I was about to take. I was for these few hours the thing wading through the swamp (sic) of unknowing and he was the light shining through. Any of the work and titles mentioned in the film and subsequent conversation are worthy of investigation. If you don't already have them, shame on you.

After my initial letter and phonecall to him, Alan had invited me Northampton which I had known well some years ago, but until I walked through the unassuming door of his preferred meeting place, the Lodge Studio I hadn't realised it was the headquarters of seminal cult band, *The Enid*, who's earlier incarnation had been the first gig I went to as a 15 year old. Mark, the joint manager of the studio alerted me to the noises and footsteps upstairs and who was making them. I had literally walked into the days of my own intrinsic formation. I was for those next hours, both blessed and transported. As we discussed the present and future, the past lingered and re-introduced itself, quantum like all around us. The concurrent strands of interest and dedication mingled perfectly and while I have done countless stupid things in my life, I have also completed my fair share of helpful and hopefully worthy actions. At a somewhat isolated time in my own life, I had been shown a long sought for door. Whether I deserved it was another matter.

What follows is an evocation of my excitement and nervousness beforehand in the form of a small poem and then a transcription of our conversation after the filmed section had ended. Thankfully the talk flowed and I was able to talk with Alan for two more hours, as *The Enid* ascended above.

II: THE SMALL SOUNDS OF APPROACH: AN INTROPOEM

The small sounds of approach herald Alan's entrance.
Entranced I move shyly, admitting him to the room.
The conversation begins and there is not one stilted moment,
A flow of thoughts crest the airwaves
In tune with The Enid's music upstairs.

Reflections of day. Incomprehension at Brexit.
Alan's thanks for my present of Newley's Gurney Slade.

We self reference for a while before talk turns to McGoohan,
That lost, sainted Patrick imprisoned by his own Prisoner.
All of the standards he set about the modes of perception
And that under us all is the villain
The Number One in our ego, subverting the hero
And exposing the slick dreams we all make.

Here is the kick and the thrill of touching one of my inspirations,
Along with the weight of the time he has granted
And that I am keen not to waste.
Keith's camera turns. He can only film for an hour.
After that, the ideas continue, so new and real, they court taste.

III: TOWARDS JERUSALEM AND OTHER GOLDEN CITES

(Leading on from the film and containing a journey from Alan Moore's Jerusalem *through* Four Dimensional Reality *and onto* Einstein and the illusion of Transcience, *via the* Snake God Glycon *and the manifestations of Steve Moore's* Moon Goddess, Selene, *all the way through to Timothy Leary's shin and the re-invention of culture: A journey through the mind and materials of Alan Moore's view of this and other worlds)*

DAVID ERDOS: So there's a tremendous range of emotions that bubbled up to the surface in me when you mentioned before about cutting off relations with many of the artists involved in the previous work; even though what I personally connect with – even as someone who started out as a painter - is less to do with the art and is in fact far more aligned to your own vision. The publication of *Jerusalem* is therefore of real significance, the signifier of a whole new period of practise, perhaps. I mean, its amazing to see a copy of it here on the table, as it's something that's been read about and discussed for a number of years. Is this going to start a new brace of novels and writings..perhaps not of the same length! Is it a million words?

ALAN MOORE: No, its not a million words. Let me –

DAVID ERDOS: Dispel that myth!

ALAN MOORE: Yeah. What happened was I was talking to my lovely, brilliant daughter Leah.. I have two lovely, brilliant daughters, but this one happened to be Leah and she was just calling up to check in with me and I said, 'Last night I finished *Jerusalem*..' and she said, 'Oh, congratulations, ' and we had a little conversation and then she went away and because she is a modern person who lives in the modern world, she was on social media and she said, 'My Dad has done it, he's finished, ' and because I had said previously that it was going to be somewhere between half a million and three quarters of a million words, all the repetitions of that word 'million' had perhaps erased her memory of the qualifying half or three quarters. It went out as 'he's just finished his million word novel.' And because of the way journalism works today, where I believe most of it is taken off the internet, this then became a *Guardian* article; it's in the newspapers, so this is defintely true. It then gets back onto the internet that this has been in the *Guardian* and that gets picked up by other papers –

DAVID ERDOS: Language as a virus, indeed –

ALAN MOORE: Right! So in the end I've got a 614,000 word novel that ends up looking like a slender pamphlet, compared to what people were expecting. So, no, I would never do anything as big as this again but I don't think I need to, I would have thought.

DAVID ERDOS: You've described it as the most readable thing you've ever written..

ALAN MOORE: Well, that was its intention. There are people who will be disagreeing with me passionately, possibly even violently when they get to chapter 25, which is a bit of a puzzle, but its certainly not the same as *Voice of the Fire* where there was the stone age dialect –

DAVID ERDOS: Yeah, I've got *Voice of the Fire* in my bag as we speak –

ALAN MOORE: Ah, Well I still have huge love for *Voice of the Fire*. That was my first attempt at expressing how I feel about the place where I live. So to some degree, *Jerusalem* is an extension of that. It's not a sequel. But I was trying to get deeper.

DAVID ERDOS: There's a lot more about your family in it..

ALAN MOORE: There is a lot more, yes.

DAVID ERDOS: There's a connection to *The Birth Caul* –

ALAN MOORE: Indeed, along with the biographical and semi-biographical things that I've done. There's probably also connections to *(seminal and never completed – due to artist issues - graphic novel) Big Numbers*. All these works are trying to express the same thing, chiefly the importance of the places where we live, the importance of the materials that are right here around us that we overlook in our quest for the exotic.

NOT SO STRANGE INTERLUDE

At this point Keith Rodway leaves, a film gig back in Hastings. Alan thanks and expresses his friendship and support. Keith mentions IT and an enquiry from the Roundhouse, where we posit performance as the answer to their needs. The Roundhouse have contacted IT as part of their 50th celebrations. They want something for their archive but we want something NEW for today. Alan is keen to resurrect a character formed as a reaction to Brexit; a fascist demagogue rising from the rubble of a broken society wearing a beautiful white suited robe but taking on the form of a Mandrill offering a dark Mandrillifesto proporting to show us all that we've done. A spectacular plan, that could exfoliate Iain Sinclair's Politics of Liberation, *Ah Sunflowering through the mire into which we have currently weeded ourselves. Keith ups and goes to the accompanying strains of* The Enid. *Alan and I then continue. A dream made real in Northampton. Just Alan and me in a room...*

ALAN MOORE: So we were talking about *Jerusalem* and it's connection to my family. It's fuelled by the amount of stories in my family and the amount of bizarre stories in my family that to me, seem titanic. The imagery. The background..

DAVID ERDOS: Yes, there's that great Stephen Poliakoff quote, that there's at least three great stories in every family –

ALAN MOORE: Yes, I'm aware that there are these great and unrealised stories in every family group and this is one of the things that *Jerusalem* is trying to say. Mine was so weird. The strain of madness that was in the Vernon side of the family, with my Great grandfather Ginger Vernon, who turns up in the novel as Snowy Vernall and my father's cousin, Audrey Vernon who the novel is dedicated to and who turns up as Audrey Vernall, and this was just one of the strands that I knew about. How my great grandfather used to just run up walls. You'd be talking to him, then you'd look away, perhaps at something on the street and when you turned back he'd be gone and three stories above you, admiring a particularly nice piece of chimney breast.. and how he was once arrested for drunkenly haranguing the crowds from a rooftop – something reported in the local paper of the time – I've also heard other family rumours of how he had retouched the frescoes down at the Guildhall and made numerous other adjustments throughout the town. There's also much talk of a great aunt Thursa, who I'm certain existed, and yet Leah, who's been doing a lot of the digging up of the genealogy of the family could find no trace of her, so whether she was a family friend who was known as an aunt, or an actual relation is unclear. And yet she was completely mad. There's reports of her taking her accordion out and playing it during the blitz, while the bombers were going over, totally unconcerned. I thought this was just wonderful. And then there's the stories of my paternal grandmother who was a deathmonger. Deathmongers; now I'm sure the word doesn't exist outside of certain boroughs in Northampton, although I'm sure the occupation does. A deathmonger is someone who in areas that are too poor to have midwives or undertakers, there is a working class woman – always a woman – down the end of the street who will take care of either for a shilling. So, if you're about to give birth, you call the deathmonger! If someone's just died you lay them out and call the deathmonger. And my gran was one. Terrifying woman. But I believe she probably became one after the early death of her first daughter at the age of eighteen months, so, yes I thought, well, there's a story there and a sense that all these stories have an element of weirdness in them. I knew for instance that Ginger Vernon had at one time eaten his way through a vase of tulips. And I can kind of see that, because they would look very succulent..

DAVID ERDOS: They're a beautiful flower!

ALAN MOORE: ..so, he'd sort of lost it and eaten the tulips –

DAVID ERDOS: Perhaps as a way to feel better?

ALAN MOORE: I knew that he also, when he was down at my gran's house on Green Street – she used to have two mirrors on

opposite walls and he became convinced that these were two windows looking into the rooms of the terraced houses and that you could see in these rooms the various patriarchs and that if he waved they would all wave back to him –

DAVID ERDOS: How long had you been aware of all these strands?

ALAN MOORE: These were stories, some of them, that I'd known since childhood and some I've come across later. There was also the family tradition that every Christmas, my nan would get the entire family into the front room and would take down a pristine china pisspot from the wall and would fill it with a foul concoction of various spirits and then the whole family would pass around the pisspot drinking these interesting blends of whiskey, rum and everything else; Looney Soup! This is like discovering they were cannibals!

DAVID ERDOS: Invocation of the highest order. A magic ritual!

ALAN MOORE: It's monstrous. And deathmongers of course, I'm assuming that they called them that since it became inadvisable to call them by their other name. Because women who helped with birth – most of the witches who were hung and burnt, were midwives, so deathmonger was a term that was brought in strategically to replace the term witch, or wisewoman. This was the 1940s.

DAVID ERDOS: And yet it's the only necessary function.

ALAN MOORE: Absolutely.

DAVID ERDOS: I'm marked by the memory of holding my own mother as she was dying, as if I was touching for the first and last time all that was crucial. And of course, there's that picture of you in Eddie Campbell's adaptation of *The Birthcaul*, holding your mother as she passes..

ALAN MOORE: These giant women who stand at either end of life.

DAVID ERDOS: Is it fair to say then that in terms of your own life and how its developed, that you've consciously chosen the magic rather than the madness, because of some of these roots and connections?

ALAN MOORE: Possibly. It seems like a better choice to me. And I'm not sure how crazy any of those relatives actually were. Ginger Vernon – and this was something that Leah found out – he was the first cartoonist in the family. In bars, for the price of a pint, he would draw a caricature of somebody. And that was something I didn't know.

DAVID ERDOS: Another link.

ALAN MOORE: I knew that he would have these incredible fierce tempers where he would break most of the windows in the house, and yet everyone respected him. Conversely, he was so respected for his craft that one of his acquaintances who was just setting up a business making glass and supplying a lot of big contracts asked him to be a director of the company he was setting up, on the condition that Ginger stayed out of the pub for two weeks. And Ginger said, 'No, I don't much like being told what to do so you can stick it up your arse,' Later, his wife would really berate him as they'd walk past the mansion of this guy up on Billing Road, while they traipsed back to their little terrace dwelling on the end of Green Street, so you can imagine what he'd missed out on all sorts of levels and in all sorts of areas. And yet I really respect that.

DAVID ERDOS: But then is this not the attitude and approach that you're embodying, especially with Hollywood? Are you not Ginger, windows aside of course! (*inexpressed and pretentious idea:*) Or are those windows representing perhaps the shattered viewpoints shared with the artists of your previous work?

ALAN MOORE: Perhaps.

DAVID ERDOS: And of course the book is or becomes pyschogeography on the highest level, doesn't it? This puts you right there with Iain Sinclair.

ALAN MOORE: Well, I hope so. It's a different approach of course to place than Iain's. Its certainly more full of ridiculous fiction and obviously more personal to me... (*pauses*) Now, we're about to move off onto a tangent. What was I saying?

DAVID ERDOS: Well, its tricky because everything you've been saying is so interesting. But I just raised the notion of you embodying Ginger...

ALAN MOORE: Well, yes, that is an important thing. There was a record back in the day, not a particularly brilliant record, back in the 70s, but it was a lot of fun, by *The Tubes*. Do you remember them?

DAVID ERDOS: They sound..familiar..

ALAN MOORE: They were an Art/Performance band. The single that got into the charts was called 'Don't Touch Me There.' But one of the songs on the album was called 'Young and Rich, ' and I was listening to this at some point in the early 80s at a time when I was relatively young and relatively rich and there was a lyric on it, on this particular song that said, 'I can respect a man who had it all/and threw the ball away..' and I thought, 'yeah that sounds true. Don't clutch onto things. Don't consider any of this important..'

DAVID ERDOS: And that struck you very deeply at that time?

ALAN MOORE: Very deeply. So when I found out about Ginger having turned down this directorship, without which I would not exist, had he not done that, because my nan would have been far too middle class to have ever married my grandfather and then produced my father and so on..

DAVID ERDOS: So, that one decision and its resonances filter down. Is there a genuine link then to a decision like that and turning down the film money from *Watchmen, From Hell, V for Vendetta* and *The League of Extraordinary Gentlemen?* I mean we were talking before about the examples your work has set. There's no finer example in these shallow days of commerce over art, than this decision of yours which has set a standard for all artists when confronted or involved in compromise of any sort?

ALAN MOORE: I think there certainly is. And there's also a connection - which is mentioned in the book – to my mates Bill Drummond and Jimmy Cauty of The KLF, when they ridiculously went and burnt that million quid on the island of Jura and then brought the film around to a select number of venues, one of which was 'Alan Moore's Front Room.' So I've got them and Gimpo and a few other people on my sofa while we watched that remarkable film and I thought that is so powerful because it said no to money. And money's everything isn't it? It's the code from which we make life and death and everything in the world. You can buy death with it. You can be life with it. Everything. So to be able to say, 'No, I don't really want that, ' and to actually burn it, was stunning. I mean, Bill and Jimmy by deleting their back catalogue have lost a lot more than a million quid. I really admire that. Because money, when it comes down to it is the biggest chain that any of us have around our necks. And to say, 'look, its just paper, its just kindling..'

DAVID ERDOS: Its almost a poetic, almost fanciful conceit, isn't it? Tokenistic at best. As it says on a ten pound note, 'promise to pay the bearer the value of –

ALAN MOORE: It's all imaginary. There hasn't been a gold standard for years. And back when there was a gold standard before Gordon Brown sold it off, if everyone who had a ten pound note had said, 'Could we, er, have a little bit of gold..?' Well, the answer was, 'well, actually, we..er..we haven't got it..' So, it's always based upon illusion. And that was before quantitive easing, which is just printing monopoly money. It's an admission that none of this is real.

DAVID ERDOS: It's all just so tokenistic. And reminds me of what you were saying before about cartology and how one thing can represent or contain something else, so completely. I for instance, like you, struggle to believe in astrology with its symbols and signs, despite the occassional look at a horoscope, whereas I find Tarot, even though I know very little about it, completely absorbing and strangely reflective.

ALAN MOORE: It's a lot more compelling. With astrology, I accept that yeah, the midwife standing next to the bed is actually subjecting you to more gravitational force than the remote stars of this particular constellation, or indeed, that one. I accept that. Though, I did have a moment during one of my magical experiences where I almost understood astrology and how it sort of works. Because I had a moment in which I realised that the entirety of the universe was actually only inside my head. And then that thought was too big to hang onto and I lost it. And yet there was a moment when I thought, 'Yes, of course, all the stars are inside my head. That's why astrology works.' It's an internal constellation.

DAVID ERDOS: Will you hang onto *Promethea*, as one of the works that you'll still lay claim to, or does that fall under the same umbrella of disownment as the others?

ALAN MOORE: I'm afraid that as I don't own it, I have to let that go, just like all the others. Despite the fact that I know we did some wonderful work there.

DAVID ERDOS: Because that is surely one of your greatest achievements, not only structurally, but technically in terms of how it was accomplished, with the entire final art work and design making one great image, along with its containment and reflection of the Kabbalah and myth of Promethea herself. It summons the very notion of magic as a force for change through the pages of a graphic novel.

ALAN MOORE: It is something of a flourish, yes. You couldn't do *Promethea* without magic. Especially the Tarot issue, with the anagrams. It stands alone, I think, just as a feat. It shows the reason why magic is important. I mean, the reason why the art of the final issue turns into two posters is because I was told to do it by voices. During a very important magical experience I suddenly realised that I was actually a magus, which is a kind of – it's not a rank, its just a different level of consciousness to an ordinary sort of magician – so I thought, 'Right, I'm a Magus, ' and I understood this with absolute clarity. So I then thought with *Promethea* the final issue will be issue 32, because that's appropriate. It will be a 32 page issue and it will somehow be readable as a comic strip but it will turn into these two beautiful psychedelic posters. This is what will happen and I will announce this. And then the next day, over the next days, it took about ten hours I think, I wrote and typed out all of *Promethea 23*, the Hochmar issue.

DAVID ERDOS: You were given it?

ALAN MOORE: Yes. It just came out in a spurt of Hochmar energy. The thing is, then I had to actually do the thing. So, once I'd come down from all the mushrooms, I said I had to do this as I've said I will.

DAVID ERDOS: The mushrooms are still the way in?

ALAN MOORE: Sometimes. They were on that occasion. But there are other ways in. Actually writing is as conscience altering as anything. But on this occasion, when I actually had to do the thing, I was up at Steve Moore's and I said, 'how am I actually going to do this?' And he said, 'Well, let me make a little tiny, folded book and I'll put the page numbers and then we'll open it out and we'll see what that would be like..'

DAVID ERDOS: There's that fantastic (in the literal sense) scene in your multiform piece 'Unearthing' that acts as a kind of talismanic biography of writer, mentor and magician Steve Moore that I wanted to ask you about. The episode when you describe being with Steve and his goddess Selene appears in the room before you..

ALAN MOORE: That was at my place, on the evening that I was just talking about. Him and Selene had gone to bed and I was still buzzing from the experience..

DAVID ERDOS: I'm fascinated by this. *(who wouldn't be?)* Was that an actual manifestation? What was the precise nature of that? Would you be able to tell me? I'm sorry, if its an inappropriate question to ask.

ALAN MOORE: No, not at all. I'd asked Steve upto my place as he was reaching this crisis point where he after a month or two of solitary meditation could materialise Selene to the point of where, if he looked away, she would still be in the same place. She was like a physical person in the room with him. He'd go round to the shops with her.

DAVID ERDOS: But he sees her, you can't see her?

ALAN MOORE: He sees her. And this was very worrying for Steve, because he was a rationalist and he knew that the most rational explanation, the one that required less multiplying entities is that he's gone mad. So I suggested, 'would it be helpful at all if you brought her up to Northampton and I will get into some sort of magical trance and we'll see if I can see her?' And he said, 'yeah, ok, that might work.' So, then he came up and was sitting in the armchair and said, 'Right, well shall we do this?' And I said, sure. So he took his glasses off and put them on the table and then he sat with his arms by his side and closed his eyes, and I was just staring at him. And I saw, sitting straddling in his lap, completely made of a sort of transparent electric blue there was the goddess Selene. She looked nothing like the one he'd talked about, the one he'd done the picture of and told me about all these years. For one thing she was disturbingly young. She was about thirteen. Thirteen. Naked. She didn't have the Stephane, the moon crown. She had a single peacock feather in a headband, but the peacock feather rose into two crescent points at the tip. She was sitting astride his lap. His real arms were down by his side. He'd got a pair of phantom arms that were around her back. She'd got her head resting on his right shoulder, but she was looking round over her shoulder at me and smiling and I was just completely caught in this gaze. And it was real. It was happening. And then he just said, 'hang on, I've got to sort myself out, here.' And she just vanished. And I was saying, 'I could see her. I could see her. You've got four arms, because two of them were around her, ' And he said, 'Yes, I was imagining I'd got my arms around her, ' And I said, 'She'd got her head on your shoulder but was sort of turning round and looking at me, ' And he said, 'yeah, that's why it was getting uncomfortable. She might was well just sit beside me. She wants to be able to see you.' And so for the rest of the evening until they went to bed – THEY – they were just sitting on the sofa. I couldn't see her. But she would occasionally join in with our conversation. She said some quite funny things! And then they went to bed. And then the next day they went back to London, craftily travelling on a single ticket. Apparently she was sitting on his lap all the way back.

DAVID ERDOS: Does Glycon appear in the same way?

ALAN MOORE: Not in the same way. My relationship with Glycon is different. He's a presence and he's also a focus. I think all of us have to make our own peace with the universe, beyond any religion, however they conceive it. One of the values of gods – this is not to say of religions in the man made sense, but of gods – is that they provide us with a focus through which we can hopefully understand the universe. So with Glycon who is a transparently fake god and thus transparently real, no more than he said he was. So Glycon for me, provides an ideal.

DAVID ERDOS: Did you make the picture you published of him first, as an act of summoning?

ALAN MOORE: I was moving towards that. I'd asked Steve 'What's the best way to become a magician?' And he'd said, 'Find a god or let one find you.' And then about a week or two after that, I came across the illustration of Glycon, the statue of the snake god that had been dug up in Talymis and I thought, 'That is the most beautiful thing I've ever seen. I feel an instant connection with that. And it's got lovely hair.' So then I was kind of feeling my way into it and then we had the initial experience on January 7th 1994 which is what I feel to be my first genuine magical experience, which felt like a direct contact with Glycon. A direct experience of Glycon; a coiling, recursive, idea-form; the best way I can describe it. A kind of divine immaterial form, made entirely of beautiful ideas that was self referential and recursive and a very sweet and enlightening presence, or at least in my estimation.

DAVID ERDOS: And coming at a perfect time for you, after the end of your first marriage, just at the time when you'd reached this crossroads or counterpoint in your life?

ALAN MOORE: It was probably a bit worrying at first, for those around me, when I announced, yes. I'm a magician in the proper non conjuring sense. I'm talking about daemons, angels, the whole lot. By saying that to your friends you're putting them in an uncomfortable position because their first thought is probably going to be, 'Oh shit, he's gone mad.' And yet if you are a coherent and eloquent and fairly persuasive, intelligent person, their second thought might be, 'Oh shit, what if he hasn't? because if he hasn't gone mad, I might have to rearrange my own view of reality.'

DAVID ERDOS: It's one of your great creative acts, isn't it? Almost the greatest thing you ever wrote was your change, or even your desire to make this change and then follow it through?

ALAN MOORE: Well, it certainly led me to understand the power of declaration. Simply by saying you're a magician, you become one.

DAVID ERDOS: And it starts to happen –

ALAN MOORE: It starts to happen. Though there has to be the right intent.

DAVID ERDOS: Are we therefore living on the wrong frequency? If reality can be contained or represented by the cartology of the Tarot, is the fact that we can put those cards back in their pack emblematic of the tokenistic nature of our own reality, especially one defined as we discussed before, by money? I'm someone desperate to make a connection or receive an indication of some other life level. I'm desperate to find some evidence of my parents now they're both dead. They both died on the same day, some years apart, so that leads me to think of patterns and other systems. So, I'm – Well. I'm scared to ask you in a way and I'm aware that I'm pussyfooting around it –

ALAN MOORE: I know what you mean –

DAVID ERDOS: Thank you. I mean, is there a way, and in saying this I know it can only be done with people you know well and trust but could you give me some form of magical instruction?

ALAN MOORE: I could broadly suggest some things, yes. But in terms of the general point. I think we are approaching a different state of being in perhaps more ways than one. I was talking about the Coagula. There is also the thing that I was expressing in *Promethea*, which is that there is an inherent prophecy in the tarot that would seem to indicate, what with the final card in the sequence being The Universe, card 32 or path 32. So, with that you have the combination of the earthly sphere, Malkuth and the Lunar sphere of dreams and the imagination, Yesod, you've got them combining because that is the path that connects those two, the 32nd path that connects those two spheres. I think that as a species we're probably moving up. The thing is this – Malkuth – this is all in our mind as well, demonstrably. We compose this reality out of the photons bombarding our retinas and the vibrations bombarding the timpana of our ears; everything. We're putting it together moment by moment. But its only inside our heads where we're putting it together. We don't relate to reality directly. We don't perceive reality directly. What we perceive is our perception of it. So this is another mental state, just as kabbalah suggests. I think that we are moving our focus up that central column of the tree of life. I would say that this is reflected in the growing virtuality of our culture. And its not even with things like virtual reality. I've been playing around with that and that's going to have a massive impact. When I first heard about virtual reality, I said, I think quite cleverly; 'What, like there's another sort?'

DAVID ERDOS (*Laughs*)

ALANMOORE: So, you see, work and play generally takes place in some sort of virtual space. Increasingly so. I think we are moving towards a different position, perhaps necessarily. In our heads. I mean, we're not going to suddenly turn all this into dreamland. That's not how it will work. But by moving upto a different kind of reality from that virtual realm that we're creating – and yes, it is all mostly escapist fun at the moment – but I suspect that the quest for artificial intelligence, what that will end up doing, other than giving us some incredibly powerful processing machines, is teaching us a lot more about non artificial intelligence and I think that the same goes for virtual reality. I think that this might give us a different perspective on good old fashioned ordinary reality.

DAVID ERDOS: So, as a young tyro novelist, just about to publish your second book and putting aside forty years of comics, essays, film scripts and graphic novels, is that now going to be the focus of your work; that you'll now produce a series of directly themed magical or conscience shifting based works?

ALAN MOORE: Well, everything I do is informed by magic, of course. In saying that, I don't think they will all be overtly magical and there isn't a lot that is overtly magical in *Jerusalem*.

DAVID ERDOS: May I have a look at the copy you've brought along?

ALAN MOORE: Please do. And then I'll sign it for you.

DAVID ERDOS: Alan, do you mean I can have this?

ALAN MOORE: Yes, of course. It's for you.

DAVID ERDOS: I don't know what to say. Oh, Alan, thankyou. You're going to make me cry!

ALAN MOORE: Well, Man Up!

DAVID ERDOS (*Laughs*) I'll endeavour to! The last thing you want is a weeping Jew on your doorstep!

ALAN MOORE (*Laughs*)

DAVID ERDOS: Thank you so much.

ALAN MOORE: My pleasure. But in terms of *Jerusalem* and what you were saying about your parents and things like that: I wanted to give people another option for thinking about that. What *Jerusalem* says – and I hope this will be helpful to everybody and not the exact reverse of that – what it suggests is that post Einstein we would appear to be living in a universe and in a space time continuum that has at least four dimensions. Physical dimensions. That's what a dimension is. We know that there is a fourth one because Einstein said that spacetime is curved, so that means that the other three ordinary dimensions of spacetime have to have another one, in order to be curved through. From what I understand the fourth dimension is not time, specifically but our *perception* of time that forms the way that we perceive the fourth dimension. We perceive it as a passage of events. This is what is called by scientists a 'block universe; which is a four dimensional solid in which nothing is moving, nothing is changing, eternally. And in such a solid you would have to hypothethise that there is this huge..let's call it a rugby ball.. of spacetime and a huge hyper moment in which everything is existing at the same time. But you've got the big bang at one end of the rugby ball and the big crunch or whatever at the other end, and every moment that has ever existed or will ever exist is somewhere contained within that huge solid. Eternally. And the moments that make up our lives, I imagine them as some kind of filaments, where you might say that we're a couple of metres high and maybe a metre wide, half a metre deep, or whatever, and we're seventy or eighty years long. So, filaments that perhaps look like millipeeds, with lots of arms and legs are frozen, like flies in amber, in time, forever. And its just our consciousness moving through that length that gives the illusion of things happening. Just like if you got a strip of film. The individual cells are not changing, they're not moving. They are that way forever. But when the projector beam, or in this case our consciousness plays across those, Charlie Chaplin does his funny walk, rescues the girl and foils the baddie. There is the appearance of story and narrative and events, which are not really there. There's just a series of moments. If this is true then when our consciousness gets to the end of our lives I would think it would have nowhere to go except back to the beginning of them. Which would speak to an eternal recurrence where everytime, it would feel like the first time. Although of course in the light of this notion it doesn't make sense to even talk about a first time. But here every moment is the same moment, the same thoughts, all of the same events over and over again. All of the best moments of your life. Forever. And that is Heaven.

DAVID ERDOS: That's amazing.

ALAN MOORE: And all of your worst moments, over and over again, forever, that is hell, that is purgatory.

DAVID ERDOS: That resounds with me very strongly. I'm sure its partly to do with my natural jewish neurosis but I live and remember everything I've ever said and done since about the age of seven. All the bad decisions come back unexpected and uninvited. Along with the good.

ALAN MOORE: Yeah. Me too. Its one of the reasons I stopped drinking was that I thought all of those moments when you – even thirty years later – you just go, 'Oh, you twat!' Its not like its just some of those moments, or most of those moments, but all of those moments – throughout which you were pissed!

DAVID ERDOS: But drink aside, that of course gives creedence to the whole quantum, four dimensional theory you've just outlined. I feel these things all the time but the more you do you realise when you talk to others that they don't think that way, or that if they do, they go out of their way to not do so, or avoid it entirely. What the great Ken Campbell referred to as Mystery Bruises.

ALAN MOORE: That's right. I love Ken and Melinda and I are great friends with Daisy. But, yes, you're right. Most people don't think like that. I was greatly involved and more than halfway through *Jerusalem* when I came across this great quote by Einstein from a few months before he died. He was consoling the widow of a fellow physicist and he said and I'm paraphrasing here but he said to this woman, 'Look, to physicists like me and your husband death isn't really a big deal because we understand

'The persistent illusion of transcience.'

That is five words. If I'd heard them before I started writing *Jerusalem* I would probably have saved myself some 614000 other ones!

DAVID ERDOS (*Laughs*) *Jerusalem: A Title* by Alan Moore!

ALAN MOORE (*Laughs*) And yet that is the persistent illusion that people have: that people, places and things are going away, never to be seen again. Whereas in a solid time they are there forever. And that makes every moment eternal. And it makes us all eternal. And it makes this place, Jerusalem, the eternal city. Everywhere. Even, perhaps especially the lowest places, the slums. Because they probably need Jerusalem to be 'builded between those dark, satanic mills.' That's where you need Jerusalem most.

DAVID ERDOS: From the toilet cleaner to the stars, which forms part of your own journey.

ALAN MOORE: Yes. And so I wanted to give people that option. Because I've got a lot of friends who are hard rationalists and aetheists and I can understand that. But we all need a way of dealing with eternity and thinking about it. And this would seem to be a good way to do it. And I would also point out that Nietzche who was of course a far more sloppy thinker than I am (*laughs*) - he came out with a slightly more flawed version of the same thing – but he was basing it upon the fact that he believed the universe to be infinite, so in an infinite universe you will get infinite recurrences just of this world, just as you would in mathematics. But actually, this is not an infinite universe. Its very big but it's not infinite. So what he was saying about his very similar idea of recurrence was that it was the most scientific idea of a kind of afterlife and that's why he liked it. And yet its not really an afterlife. It's a *during* life.

DAVID ERDOS: Sideways. They're all.. over there.

ALAN MOORE: Well, he was saying that if you followed that belief you would have a better life, whether or not it turned out to be true. To say every moment is eternal. Don't do anything you can't live with forever. Be kind. Try to make every moment as good as possible if this is where you're going to be forever.

DAVID ERDOS: It's the Spalding Gray concept of the perfect moment, that journeying from one to another regardless of the arbitrary nature of everything else.

ALAN MOORE: Yes. It certainly solves a lot of problems. One of the things during the 1980s, when I'd got small children and the cold war was as bad as its ever been. And I had to tell them. I'd heard that the thing that frightened children the most was nucleur war, because their parents daren't even speak about it. So I thought, 'right, I'm going to have to explain nucleur war to the kids. I'm not looking forward to it. But I'm going to do it.' And I did. And I had to think about what nucleur war would mean. And I realised that every biological struggle since the dawn of time would have been for nothing. It would all have been retroactively cancelled because now we have a dead planet and nobody will ever know that we were here. Now, yes, that's very depressing. But you know, we might get through this, we might just get through this. But then of course, there's the environmental problem which is pretty serious and that would lead to the exact same thing. So if we make this planet into something like Venus then every single human struggle, every birth, every decision, is all for nothing. Ok, so we might get through the environmental things. But then you know, give it a few million years, the sun is going to get bigger and start to consume everything around it..but then Eric Drexus suggested pruning the sun; Solar Husbandry! Or we might have migrated somewhere else. There's always these scientific possibilities. But then of course, the universe eventually ends so all of it will be gone. However, with an Eternalist perspective, that all vanishes.

DAVID ERDOS: The notion that the past is still happening over there is tremendously seductive. One of my fears watching my mother fade before me was the death of the mind coinciding or trapped within the death of the body. And where that goes. And how it travels. And from that, what comprises us, that there must be something that makes me me and you you that isn't just bound by chemicals. So, the idea that as her life ends here it immediately starts again there is as captivating as it is desired.

ALAN MOORE: What you witnessed was just the end of her story. And if stories don't have ends then they're just soap opera and they're worthless. They just make it up as they go along and its worthless. I mean, I was saying this to Steve who had adopted his own eternalist point of view before his own death, before he went to put it to the test; I was saying, 'you know, look, actually if this was true, I could see a lot of problems for everbody and a lot of problems for science because doesn't this remove the concepts of cause and effect? Or it certainly makes them not so clear cut.' And I said for religion I can foresee terrible terrible problems as one of the things this does away with is the concept of free will. This is all assuming a predetermined universe. So where is vice? Where is virtue? That's a problem for all of us because we all like to have someone to blame.' And I've thought my way round that, as actually the way it works out is, its still that way for us. Down here, its still going to seem like we have got free will. Whether we have or not.

DAVID ERDOS: Pornography is a strong contender for being a by product of that free will, at least for those who make or consume it, rather than those who are consumed by it. Whether its as cure for loneliness, raison d'ctrc for thc intcrnet or salve for the darkness in all men (and women) as evidenced in the beauty and brilliance of *Lost Girls*.

ALAN MOORE: I'm so glad you liked *Lost Girls*.

DAVID ERDOS: I loved it. It thrilled me through its beauty and ideas. Again, something we waited years to see and that when it came more than satisfied the reader on all sorts of levels, a collision of the truly personal and the truly political impulse. I mean, one of the things I wanted to say at the start of this interview, and should have, but we just started talking, was that – and yes, I'm being self conscious again and I know its something that countless people have already said to you, but I just wanted to.. thank you for your work.

I'll do it again as I type up what we're saying now, and its not about just the past work, Alan, but I just want to look you in the eye and thank you for what you do.

ALAN MOORE: Well, cheers, man. You're welcome!

DAVID ERDOS: Its hard to sound pure as I say it but I feel that about this select group of my enthusiasms, whether its Heathcote, or Iain Sinclair's work, or Chris Petit. There's this vanguard:

ALAN MOORE: You mean like a kind of Justice League?

DAVID ERDOS: Yes! Of Seminalists who are really ringing the changes.

ALAN MOORE: Well, what I hope is that this is all something to do with the phenomenon of Coagula. Connecting up, almost like making neural connections between people because the counter culture hasn't gone anywhere. I am coming more to the conclusion that – it's actually something that Scroobius Pipps said when we did our 'Under the Austerity, the beach' counter culture event, he said that the thing about counter cultures is that they always fail. And I thought, yes that is true. They always fail because they're always assimilated by mainstream culture. So the thing to do is to make your counter culture either so toxic or so psychedelic that it cannot be assimilated without changing the culture that assimilates it. And I thought, well, this is how culture works, isn't it? Counter culture is a necessary part of culture. And probably vice versa. And it was only in the 1990's that counter culture suddenly stopped and we got Britpop, just in time for Tony Blair to get in and Noel Gallagher to shake his hand at Downing Street. We got this completely synthesised, phoney, top down, imposed form of culture, of union jack carrier bags and so forth and shit like that.

DAVID ERDOS: That's why I very consciously reconnected to progressive music in all its forms as it seemed the last bastion of the idea, with music being the superior art form, capable of saying and doing the most, emotionally and in terms of causing actual physical changes in the body. Someone like Eno being the prime example.

ALAN MOORE: Ah, Eno.

DAVID ERDOS: Yes, I know he's a great hero of yours.

ALAN MOORE: That was a real high point for me. Interviewing him.

DAVID ERDOS: Yes, that was a great radio and series and an important one; *Chain Reaction*. Stewart Lee interviewing you and then you interviewing Brian Eno. But you've now created a body of work that equals what Eno has produced. Forgetting even what you've produced in the past and now turned your back on. Will you now, in what you go on to do become more of a polemicist about these issues?

ALAN MOORE: Probably about the same. What I'm looking forward to doing is expanding into all sort of different areas. I'm probably not going to do another big novel for a while, though I wouldn't rule out some sort of novel in the future.

DAVID ERDOS: Is *Providence* (Moore's most recent comic series inspired by Robert Chambers *The King in Yellow*) the last comic, as such?

ALAN MOORE: No. It's nearly. Its getting on that way. *Providence* I finished quite a while ago, that will be wrapping up, probably by the end of the year. I just got the art for number 11 this morning. And then there is *Cinema Purgatorio*, that I'm doing with Kevin O Neill, which I'm very much enjoying. We both got excited by the material. I'm just reading a book that Kevin sent me about Todd Browning called 'Dark Carnival, ' because Todd Browning will be the next feature in *Cinema Purgatorio*. He was a strange character.

DAVID ERDOS: Well, people only ever refer to him in terms of (his film) *Freaks*, don't they?

ALAN MOORE: His actual personal life. Apparently he used to work in side shows. And in one of them he was the 'Hypnotic Corpse!' Where he would actually lay in a coffin, underground with a breathing tube for about 48 hours – and for the bloke who eventually did Dracula, that's quite an interesting balance! And then all these things in his early life. A very disturbed individual.

DAVID ERDOS: You were talking about other forms, so as a theatre man I was hoping you'd branch out into plays. Certainly some of the chapters of *Voice of the Fire* would make fantastic solo theatre pieces, and I know *Another Surburban Romance* started life as a theatre piece, didn't it?

ALAN MOORE: It was written for a musical play that was never finished but gave rise to a number of wonderful songs. In fact, everyone should check out the debut album of The Dandelion Set, who are mates of mine, The Mystery Guests, Mr Licquorish, who vanished for years and who then got in touch – it's him, its Glyn Bush from the Degotees, these are all old mates of mine who have suddenly connected up again and have done this album. They were doing the original music for Another Surburban Romance, so there's various bits on it. I've done some vocals on it. Yes, that was grasping towards something. And there is of course a chapter in Jerusalem which is actually a play. It's a Samuel Beckett play with Samuel Beckett in it. And Thomas a Becket as well, because they were both here, and its also a key part in the family story, in the Audrey Vernon story. And I've got John Clare there as well. I'd want people to get all of the proper context for it and that of course comes from the book itself. I don't know if it stands as a play on its own, although it might do, but I think it's a great thing to put in a novel. And it works well with the various narrative strands. So, I think that's its proper place. I have to say, though, discussing other forms, that I'm up for any programme. Its like the stuff with electric comics which was initially one of the embedded concepts in a recent performance piece, but is actually now a real thing in the real world. We were voted one of the best apps of the year –

DAVID ERDOS: That's great for a man who doesn't use the internet!

ALAN MOORE: Apparently so. And yet, the best digital comic of the year was my *Big Nemo*. Yes, I don't use this technology myself but at the same time I am thinking about it on a deeper level than many of the people who do. And also its from a level that's always going to be side on, as I'm not really engaging with this technology in the same way. It's a bit like what Eno said about recording equipment arriving in Jamaica and them not really understanding it and playing with it and inventing dub. And he said the moment he heard dub, he said that he just wanted to quit, as they'd sort of done what he set out to do. It's a naive mindset approaching a new technology and getting something completely unexpected out of it. At least that's what I hope I'm doing. In general there's lots of things opening up. Especially with the show and films such as *Jimmy's End* and the Showpieces DVD that we've been producing up here. We've got our own imaginary universe going, with uniquely fresh and new novelistic concepts. And so, I've invented lots of products to go into this world, a bit like the kind of thing with *Watchmen*. A parallel world down to every last detail, if you like. We were thinking we'd have restaurants and different styles of dress. So making a film actually changes things. In the film we have some teenagers drinking this energy drink, where the can is slightly narrower and slightly longer and is as bright, luminoius green. And the drink is called 'Fuelrods.' I thought that was funny. And then I had a message from Mitch Jenkins the Director of *Jimmy's End* saying he'd just got a message from one of the country's leading energy drink producers, saying if create that in the new film we're going to do, that they'd like to license it from us. And I thought, this is weird and potentially interesting, particularly as I think advertising is the work of Satan. I don't like it and I don't want to anything to do with it. However, this, would be like reverse product placement. You make up something in your imaginary world and then you export it to the real world. That would be fun.

DAVID ERDOS: Sounds great. The converse of that is this article in the paper yesterday about the Roald Dahl estate brewing the beer from *The Twits*, by using bits of the yeast from his writing chair, which would have tiny particles of Roald Dahl in it. Literary cannibalism in its most direct form!

ALAN MOORE: That's almost like transubstantiation. That is weird.

DAVID ERDOS: Bizarre.

ALAN MOORE: But what I thought was, to introduce an energy drink to the world, that's of no consequence, a bit of fun, but that principle of exporting from the imagination is key: Because what *couldn't* you do? So we've got things like a videogame that is causing a social panic like *Grand Theft Auto*, and is in all the papers, with people saying is this driving our kids to suicide? Is it making our kids mental? The game is called *Escapism*. We've got *Escapism* worked out. My daughter Amber who got her degree in computer technology, but realised about half way through that because the course was two years long and Moore's law says that computer processing power doubles every eighteen months by the time she got her degree it would be completely redundant. But she's done the game document and it's a completely different approach to the usual computer game.

DAVID ERDOS: It's a great family firm you have, Alan with Amber, Leah and John and Melinda all part of the cause and forging their own paths.

ALAN MOORE: Well, I have some talented people in my coterie. So there's *Escapism*, which is a great name for a computer game. And we're also introducing a made up counter culture. There's a group of teenagers who you see in the background of certain shots and they've all got a certain style and mode of dress and they're called The Post-Mods.

DAVID ERDOS (Laughs)

ALAN MOORE: And we've worked out their music, with the Jazz Butcher and others. And I also thought you could introduce a range of socially helpful institutions in the imaginary Northampton to the real one, and if they look sensible and look like they might work it would be almost irresistible to move them into reality.

DAVID ERDOS: Well, let a guest edited issue of IT by you, be an advert for some of that, that would be amazing.

ALAN MOORE: I'm sure there's lot of things we could do with IT. I'd love to do that. There's going to be all these new forms. And I'm sort of juggling with them. Because that's the other name for the magician: *The Jongleur*.

DAVID ERDOS: So is the revived arts lab all in service of this now?

ALAN MOORE: No. I just thought it would be good to have an arts lab, because where I came from, that's what taught me. And its what taught David Bowie. David Bowie couldn't have existed without the arts labs. It encourages this 'try everything, mix things up ethos.' With the arts lab I did the first gig of my *Mandrilifesto*, which I'm now taking with Kermit and Greg Wilson about doing it as a single, because its got some beats, you know!

DAVID ERDOS: You're down with the yout', Alan.

ALAN MOORE: I certainly am. With the next thing we're doing with the arts lab and this is a suggestion from the people in it, such as Megan Lucas, who is brilliant and can do anything - as I'm trying to take a backseat and not dominate - is to call our next event , 'The Annual General Meeting of a Medium sized firm of Accountants' and she just had an image of four to six desks on a stage. And I said, well what if you've got people sitting at those desks and you've got a spotlight moving between them and one of them will get up and say something or do something but everyone else will ignore them and carry on working, so this indicates its only happening in their mind. And you could explore all sorts of themes and have all sorts of different people in that simple context. We could have a whiteboard which would have a normal looking graph on it, but which would be projected, so the image could change and explore fantasy aspects. And we progress from there to a brilliant resolution that we've arrived at between us.

DAVID ERDOS: Ah, you've done it. The first play by Alan Moore. Its so exciting what you're saying there; The theatre is dead on its feet now in my opinion, because it has made itself a celebrity ridden vehicle going nowhere further than the Groucho Club. Its all bums and seats. And rich boys again. *Shakespeare in Love – The Play.*

ALAN MOORE: Terrible.

DAVID ERDOS: So theatre has to go back. Culture too. And Arts Labs clearly are the answer.

ALAN MOORE: Exactly. Its like what Will Shutes is doing with Test Centre; the books that are stab stapled. That makes me come! I love stab staples. That was when poetry was a real, vibrant culture. I finally got something in the last issue, the first poem I've written in quite a while, called 'The Town Planning in Dreams, ' which is a bit of obsession of mine. The town planning in dreams is always much more convenient and flooded with sunlight and there's always what seems to be a thirty second shortcut between any two points, even if one of them is at the other end of the country. There's a backway. Dreams as a feeling –

DAVID ERDOS: Permeating the day. Writing as atmosphere and the conjuring of alternative histories, which is what you're describing here with the film and theatre projects and is evidenced theatrically by Edward Bond and Howard Barker, whose works are primarily concerned with alternative viewpoints and heightened states. And of course its there from the start with you and in all of the most celebrated pieces. *Watchmen* is not about the Superhero – despite the fact it both kills and recreates that notion – nearly as much as it is about the story telling techniques and what you can do with them to put the ideas across.

ALAN MOORE: Exactly. Marvelman –

DAVID ERDOS: Which is almost the ur text for the comics work –

ALAN MOORE: Is a critique of the Superhero. I hadn't expected them to revitalise the genre in quite the way that they have. Where people are now saying, 'Yeah! If we make all superheroes miserable and pretentious they'll be kind of modern again!'

DAVID ERDOS: Its like people didn't listen. As they never do.

ALAN MOORE: Dead right.

DAVID ERDOS: When artists have something to say hoi polloi seem unable to access it. Stewart Lee has become the Peter Watkins of stand up comedy and you're the Samuel Beckett of comics!

ALAN MOORE: (*Laughs*) Its true. It seem to me now that the thesis Steve Moore and I put at the end of *The Moon and the Serpent Book of Magic* is to connect a revitalised and rethought form of magic up with art. This would be of immense benefit to all concerned as it means magicians would have something to show at the end of their rituals, like Austin Spare did, short of taking a Polaroid camera in there with you, that is the closest we're ever going to get to seeing what that realm looks like. Let the magicians and be artists and the artists be magicians as that would get rid of all of this vacuous conceptualism, or what passes for conceptualism – these demi ideas – I mean I thought the bling skull, and I'm probably a reactionary saying this, but there's nothing there. Its an insult.

DAVID ERDOS: Nothing. Its the death of the idea. Hirst and all like him are the fucking enemies of art, in my opinion. They're nothing more than the heroes of money.

ALAN MOORE: Yes. So why not give some vision, some magic, back to art? Connect them up. It would help both of them. Then connect magic with science. And that seems like a fairly easy thing.

DAVID ERDOS: You've taught people, if one were to try and sum up your work, not only the true value of an idea, but what an idea is, and how to use it. The irony of these mainstream films is that everyone makes superhero films to cover up the dearth of ideas, or they're displacements for that absence, and yet you've used the superhero form to explore the very ideas they are unable to appreciate. Your work is evolving all the time, while the rest is standing still. It seems to me that everything you go on to write now will be a gift in some form, separate to this evolved function as a sage and magus, pointing the way forward. I'm sorry if that sounds sycophantic. Heathcote does the same thing solely with the polemics and poetry. Like you he is one of the last examples of a truly sustainable talent. There's a new thing, poem or polemic every week, after fifty years.

ALAN MOORE: You've got to admire that.

DAVID ERDOS: So, you are now one of the select people starting a new culture, through this work.

ALAN MOORE: Well, thanks Dave, that would be nice. But the real work comes from the most contentious idea, which is to then, after art and science, connect magic up with politics, because then you would have evidence based government. Now wouldn't that be a magical thing?

DAVID ERDOS: It would. Thanks, Alan.

ALAN MOORE: Thanks, man. It's been a wonderful afternoon, Dave. I've really enjoyed it. And I'm very happy to do this for IT. I've been longing to see IT return for all these decades and now here it is. Anything I can do to help.

DAVID ERDOS: We'll make it happen. We must.

ALAN MOORE: Hey, did I tell you, I've actually got a bit of Timothy Leary on my altar at home?

DAVID ERDOS: Really? Which bit?

ALAN MOORE: Its actually a small part of his shin. Apparently, some of his ashes were blasted into space, by which we mean blasted into Nevada, because most of those things don't have enough escape velocity so they tend to end up in the desert. But some of the remaining ashes were given to friends including Brian Barrett who wrote 'Whisper' and who was told to scatter them on Stonehenge and allow anyone who caught them to give them to anyone who they thought deserved them. My friend John Higgs was there for the ceremony and at the end he noticed a tiny flake of bone left on the altar, so he gave it to me in this little reliquary and I put it on my altar. And so I asked my 'gentleman supplier,' 'Do people actually do acid these days?' I'm not sure I want to do any myself but I wanted to know and he came through with two little sugar cubes, so I put them in the reliquary with Tim, because I think that's what Tim would have wanted! And if I ever do get round to taking the acid I'm sure it will be infused with the spirit of the counter culture in its purest form!

DAVID ERDOS (*Laughs*) Just as in two hundred years time they'll be venerations of clippings from the Alan Moore beard!

ALAN MOORE (*Laughs*) Yes, though I think I'm up for being buried, a return to the source. Put it this way, if I were cremated people would be advised to stand downwind of the burning –

DAVID ERDOS: It'd be a hell of an explosion!

ALAN MOORE: Certainly an interesting wind! My carpet scrapings, man. They've got an instrinsic street value!

DAVID ERDOS (*Laughs*) But we're not talking about that, Alan. As I don't want you to go anywhere...

ALAN MOORE: Apart from on, into the Northampton of course.

DAVID ERDOS: Of course. Thanks so much, Alan.

ALAN MOORE: Its been lovely, it really has. It's like – I did an interview last night for Andy Warhol's Interview magazine on the phone- which is the same but without the Andy Warhol – so this has been like going back in time...

DAVID ERDOS: Which as we know now is just over there.

ALAN MOORE: It certainly is. See you soon.

IV: THE MAN IN ROOM FIVE

DAVID ERDOS: And with that he was gone, trailing love and respect in the distance. A man set on returning the shallow world to the deep. You need only read one comic or book by Alan Moore to grasp his essence but that leads you onto the next one, and that in turn to the next.

To have written:

Anon E Mouse, Maxwell the Magic Cat, Roscoe Moscow, The Emporers of Ice Cream, Future Shocks, Axel Pressbutton, Halo Jones, D.R and Quinch, Marvelman, V for Vendetta, The Bojeffries Saga, Captain Britain, Swamp Thing, Superman, The Killing Joke, Watch-

men, Promethea, Smax, Fashion Beast, From Hell, The League of Extraordinary Gentlemen, Wildcats, Top Ten, Neonomicon, and to move away from them all and then create projects like *A Small Killing, Big Numbers, Lost Girls, 20, 000 years of Erotic freedom, Americas Best Comics, Voice of the Fire, The Birth Caul, Snakes and Ladders, Angel Passage, The Highbury Working, Dodgem Logic, Providence, Cinema Purgatorio* and of course *Jerusalem* and the forthcoming *The Moon and The Serpent Book of Magic*, along with numerous musical and counter cultural happenings is to offer the world a series of new beginnings. From William Gull's explaining of Hawkmoor's mysticism of London to Coachman John Netley in Chapter 4 of *From Hell* to any page of Alan Moore you care to pick up you will see revelations and reverberations that if you have any richness in your soul at all, will stay with you for life. His work in all its forms is literally moving us on.

Although Alan has disowned his early work as it is all owned by others I will crave his and your indulgence in summing up. In chapter four of *V for Vendetta*, V has captured Lewis Prothero, the current 'Voice of Fate' for a dystopian Orwellian England and former commandant of the Larkhill Resettlement camp, set up to exterminate and experient on all of the country's political, sexual and artistic transgressives. V has recreated the camp within the confines of his Shadow Gallery HQ and has stolen Prothero's priceless collection of dolls. Dressed as inmates, Prothero's panic rises as he knows V will both destroy them and him. Before doing so, V takes the guilty man on a tour of his model invocation of the horror Prothero is responsible for. He arrives at a final corridor where the special cases were kept. Rooms one to five, each designated by the appropriate roman numeral. As we reach the final panel and see the V on the door and recognise as Prothero does that V is and was the man kept inside it, clearly the most horrific specimen the regime led by Prothero has encountered. At this moment, the full scope, horror and brilliance of the book, series and idea combine and converge, it has to be said, magically. We know that V is more than human, while being rendered less than it by the state; a child of madness, disfigurement and even deviancy but someone who is the ultimate challenger and changer of forms. That page changed me utterly when I read it as a twelve year old boy and helped form my own imagination. It stands now as merely the prototype for all of Alan Moore's efforts in both offering and creating solutions for the restrictions we have placed around ourselves along with those we have allowed to have been placed around us. How many other artists are there now who's work is not just about or informed by their own self regard? Whether shameful so called Conceptualist, or coke infused celebrity actor, none of them wish to break the bounds of their own being. Alan Moore shows a true and lasting alternative. We have traipsed down the corridors of our own horrors for too long. We must now seek true and lasting change through the true politics of liberation, the kind that comes from a return to the idea and what it alone can achieve.

In the magic of our own minds and in the places that form and shape us we can still deny the path our oppressors are intent on forcing us along. We can be the voice in our own private fire and seek and assist the new Jerusalem.

We must now be the man in the room five.

V: OVER TO YOU

DIVINE PASSENGER

A cinematic encounter between David Erdos and Seminal Artist, Musician, Poet, Shaman, Activist and Producer, Youth London, October 2016

Although it was a train brought me there it was a bus that contained us. The conversation started with music but ended around politics. As the Brexit Bus leaves the cliffs we are all left clutching at the handrails, hoping against hope for transcendence that will never come two at once. Life isn't art. Art is what we would like art to be like. And the thing that most stops us is of course politics. In discussing these things as you will see, Youth provides a wise counsel. He witnesses all as it happens as the music of the world fills his ears. Describing himself as a man 'who has a go' he has travelled, from Stonehenge to Rio, from Brixton to the Rio Grande. Youth has worked with them all, from Kate Bush to McCartney. From Pink Floyd's final languor right towards Killing Joke. From Punk, to jazz, via trance, dub, rock and reggae; from new age to the ancients and all the way back on his bus. He is the divine passenger who steers from the back with eyes narrowed. A joint in his hand, his exhaust pipe comes straight from the heart, pumping clear. And so the meet was arranged spurred by Claire P. And R. Rovers. An exchange of tea, books and laughter as the light outside painted days.

The film, available on the *International Times* website, is an edited conversation. It has been arranged into topics, seen at the left hand bottom edge of the screen. These detail some of the thoughts that passed between us. As the talk flowed like music, we made an album of sorts, here to see.

Youth is a man of discernment and yet he made me at home very quickly. He lives the communal idea but it's progress of an singular,if shared vision that takes place under his roof. In every room, albums form, or are being mixed or recorded. Paintings line the walls, album covers, family shots, shards of life. It is an organic house that gives the man his own bassline. A place to be he shares only with those he supports and can love. You could say this of anywhere, yes, but the atmosphere here is a temple. It is sacrosanct and yet busy with all of its deep prayers to art.

DIVINE PASSENGER

Youth is the c(h)ord that connects countless artists. He is the wasp, full with pollen and the passenger on each bus. He is an enviable man because of what he has been able to find and has given. He knows his place and shows others where it is they can go. We talked of art, politics, music, mood and transcendence. Two strangers connecting on a bus ride towards light and trust.

DEAD RINGERS

An appreciation of Josh Burton's debut film, *The Dead Truth*

Just as beauty belongs within the beholder, so does art finds position and residence in the eye. In Josh Burton's debut short film *The Dead Truth,* both are achieved through a combination of ambition and sincere effort. Written, directed, produced, filmed, edited and starring Josh Burton as triplet brothers confronting the issues and emotions that beset them all, after their mother's funeral, this fifteen minute film is an uncanny statement on both the aims of the individual when confronted with a sizeable industry as well as a statement on what the dreams of every actor, writer and creator should be.

By combining the various roles necessary to the production of films, Burton has demonstrated a masterly hold on technique and compassion, fusing the most charged of human experiences, with the most demanding of tasks. As the three brothers, each informed by a distinct personality move through a process of grief, recrimination and a concluding revelation, Burton the director of film allows them equal space to establish themselves. As an editor he provides effective juxtaposition of shots and therefore atmosphere, and his choices as a writer enable this one room setting to echo the confinement and perhaps sense of ensnarement that we all may face when having to deal with the great inevitability of death, in terms of what it leaves us with and where it leads us to.

The visual experience of watching the film is an extremely credible one and we are able to inhabit the space in a sensual and sub-textual way, alongside the characters, making us as viewers what all film goers should no doubt be; participants in the action and in the actions of the emotions or situation at play. We are encouraged to take a side or find a sympathy, only for that sympathy to be displaced and refocused. Burton as actor, allows for that crucial element in an actor's repertoire, freedom from likeability and the need for adoration, while still finding moments in which these desperate characters can find areas fit for compassion. Communication and connection are set up and then shattered by constant overturns of information and reaction. Eye-lines are wonderfully consistent and it is true that you could quite easily spend one watching of the film, praising its technical intelligence – but only after you have followed the unwinding story at play.

There could be different shades of characterisation employed and perhaps further nuances, along with flashbacks or outside footage of some of the situations mentioned, but these maybe for another film, one that continues this and extends the story. But that is not the point. The film captures a situation and a series of possible developments, just as a photograph of a flower may catch the unfolding of its petals. As a premiere project, the film's power is undeniable.

Today's filmmakers have a lot more control over technical innovations than previous generations, even if only in terms of accessibility. The wonder is, for an old pen, paper and Steenbeck man like myself, that it is now possible to make films of this stamp in a reasonably affordable way. I admire the time taken and the expertise with the laptop, just as I still wonder at the emergence of those early innovations in Meliere, Chaplin and Keaton. Film does possess a particular magic, even in its simplest forms, as I myself experienced in celluloid pieces I have made, when cutting from a corridor to another room, through the edit of a closing door. But here there is dazzle and flash in a believable and subdued fashion. The film feels organic rather than composed. This is not about an actor drawing attention to himself, but everything to do with a new artist attempting to tell his story. There is an argument that everyone who wants to act should at one time write and direct, for that is how you find out about these crucially connected areas of expertise and yes, of course, many do. But few with the intelligence and integrity shown here. I every much applaud the effort shown and encourage you to do likewise when the film is released.

Indeed, we are always keen to praise occasional examples of the multi/dual role approach, such as Brian Hegeland's recent *Legend*, featuring Tom Hardy's portrayal of the Kray twins, but that was a high budget project, possessed of so called star power, and the performances there were tightly maintained and controlled. Burton has gone out on a limb here – or perhaps twelve limbs – to make something bold and brash, filling his modest space with distinct characteristics and preoccupations. The film becomes an essay on grief in this regard, an exercise in character. While I'm sure Burton's aim is to capture reality, what I feel he does here to a sizeable degree, is to extend it. He allows us as participants to sympathise with his solo approach and asks us what we would do if we had the same drive and commitment that he has.

There is a fine Brian Eno quote about backing vocals in records being the song's invitation to the listener to sing. So it is here, with this approach. With the ideas and aims of one man so clearly displayed what can we add to the action and story we are being asked to take part in? How *much* information can we take in and at what rate and what is it *exactly* that we can or can't see? One thing is clear, with only man to watch we are all brought to listen, having to pay close attention to everything we are told. A transformation is shown (the root of all drama) as one actor undergoes all these changes, doing his utmost to achieve what each actor should: submersion in the sense of change and/or separation and what that transformation can give to us.

What truth is still out there for us (beyond the *X-Files*) to grasp? This film asks this question expertly and is a young man's challenge to us to find out. It is an important first step on what I suspect will be an equally important career, but it is also a provocation: How much effort do you put into the art you make and expect? If your answer is the same as what is shown in this film, I applaud you. If the commercial sector operated at the same level of intensity we would have a constantly evolving culture and not one half frozen by celebrity, albeit with a bubbling and at times aggressive sub-culture beneath it. Instead, we would all be part of a thriving ocean of transmogrification, one that both attacked the beach at the same time as reshaping and preserving it. We can only hope that this is what the future will bring to us all as practitioners and audiences and that projects like this one are part of a fresh and spectacular wave that re-invogrates the shores of perception and achievement. In this short film Josh Burton has started to ring his bright changes. Which one of you will swim with him and which one of you will hear first?

SING A SONG OF SIMON:

A birthday present reflection on the fiftieth anniversary of *The International Times* and my friend Simon Cash.

As October 15th 2016 marked the 50th anniversary of the official launch of IT at the Roundhouse, so it also marked the emergence of my close friend Simon Anthony Cash. The result of a full day of labour, his birth began around the time that McCartney, Miles, Hoppy and all were applying their silken scarves and in some cases, ramshackle glamour to take on the Camden night. Further up the road, Simon's mother, the actress, teacher and granddaughter of a former Mayor of Stepney, Susan Cash, was busily forming her own project, whose own sartorial flair and refinement would encompass more than his fair share of glamour, foppery and general fol-de-rol. Although untouched by the rumblings of the Floyd, Simon's belated embracing of the Beatles, after years of Mod-ery and flirtations with punk, has resulted in a state of affairs in which, should you have occasion to cut him open, you would find the words 'Paul McCartney' scored through him like the Brighton rock his beloved mods would once have munched. He is not so much a product of the counter culture as a result of the areas that it supports: fashion, lysergics, pop music in its purest form and a belief that somewhere in the society in which we inhabit, intelligence, common sense, informed questioning of the prevailing authority and dammit, decency must and should rise to the fore.

Like my other two almost brothers (Anthony and Ean), Simon is also the most generous and giving of people and the most encompassing of all of my friends. His time will be awarded to you at precisely the right moment. As a former Casanova of some standing, his understanding of the female mind is acute or goes as far as any man has the right or ability to reach and the subsequent wisdom comes to you sans hype, coloured only by balance and respect for the specific subject under concern or discussion. Indeed, his laid back, sometime joint infused stance is capable of resisting many of the pressures and neuroses most of us fall prey to. In this way he could perhaps be described as 'health in repose', one which arrives without any extra expenditure of effort. Indeed, while others run a mile, Simon gains his energy from watching his beloved cricket, football and cycling and no doubt his newly acquired vespa will serve to carry him around the provinces in the same way that his other model of style and musical achievement, Paul Weller, must have once surely cavorted.

Simon's still slender frame (how many 50 year old men are able to fit into the trousers they wore at 18!) resists all attempts at plastic renewal and his embracement of hedonism makes him a wonderous hybrid of both Jagger and Richards, facing the onset of aging with much of Mick's sheen and all of Keith's heady adoption of night. That alone is an inspiration, but the quiet power he asserts is also something that can be seen rippling through IT's historical and current pages. We were and are still attempting to alter the balance and repaint the mirror that society stands before and while we as a paper, site and presence can attempt that, individuals like Simon can live or exemplify it, in an every day way and in terms of their own lives and independence. The demise of the Independent newspaper was something of a blow to my friend as regardless of content and style its whole stance and philosophy was close to his own, as IT's is to all of its many contributors and handlers over the years.

Unlike mine and I suspect most of us, the moments of Simon's own moral or personal buckling have been rare and manageable to the extent that any of these things are, and indeed, in those cases he has been strongly supported by his devoted wife Cindy, son Jake, brother Pete, and vivacious parents Sue and Tony, not to mention his many friends, all of whom develop a soft spot for him, the hardening of which deepens no doubt through the years. It is this strength that again sisters that of what IT tries to represent and which makes Simon one of the many It-boys the last fifty years have given birth to, the pages of their stories rustling in the winds of history before being snagged on today's framing tree.

My first foray into the dramatic world was with Simon – a school production of *Fiddler on the Roof*, no less, the figure of whom, without stretching the joke too far, always seemed to me to be a kind of anarchist, commenting on the foibles of those below while sending his thoughts to the air - and while I am younger than Simon, I was merely childishly wooing his female contemporaries while he was applying the real.

A sense of liberation has always been part of Simon's character and this is what makes me ponder the connection between IT's founding forces of cultural anarchy and the small scale equivalents as lived by certain individuals in the mainstream. IT's strength was and is its usefulness as a mirror for a changing time. It offers responses, questions, actions and stances to be taken without a domineering didacticism, and hopefully allows for change, or the potential for change just as the seed on the wind begets the flower or weed in the pavement outside a hypocrite's house. So, too does my friend in his gentle but persistent probing of bullshit and obfuscation as it is presented to us daily.

Whilst working as a Computer Trainer, actor (a current Malvolio in his mother's production of *Twelfth Night* for the Pinner Players) not to mention fondler of the jazz cigarette, Simon is not the modernist or former hippy compromised into wearing his Zara bought suit by changing times and declining values, but rather someone whose air of rebellion is stitched through every fibre of his neatly tailored threads. He is in that way a pure fruit from the poisoned tree and one who blossoms brightly in a dimly lit age, living as freely as anyone can in this malformed democracy, uninfluenced by the controlling forces without making any grand statements about it; and secure to the extent that any of us is or can be, about his position and place in the world. As a father he sets clear boundaries for his son and allows him to grow in his own way as his mother Cindy guides and supports him, just as Sue and Dad (and former Captain of Industry), Tony showed him and his brother Pete how to be. Simon has had many enviable experiences along the way, and while this is not the place to reveal them, I can assure you, The Libertine lives!

But there is no sensationalism here. Instead there is the understanding of what life is actually for and how it can be lived. All of our friends set examples for us and that is why we choose them. There are emotional, intellectual and physical attractions that bind people together. We look to share the limited air that life gives us with those who make it taste sweeter or more interesting. Whether its the slick vape assisted high of Simon chuckling in the corner of my mind or a glass of rum at 3am, he is a fine companion against both the sun and the rain.

In that regard, Simon has always struck me as someone who has truly known himself - which is surely anyone's goal and perhaps the only real thing I can say about myself - and our friendship was re-ignited after twenty five years distance when moving back to the area in which I grew up after my mother's passing, and in which he and his family also returned to after Essex, Muswell Hill and Cuba, among other places. Since that time he and his beloveds have given me a place at their table, as indeed has IT and these happy synchronicities have allowed me to grasp both social and political standards that I can believe in at last and hang onto. That collision also inspires this short tribute to a person and to the idea or ideal that IT embodies.

On Friday the 14th October 2016, the current editorial board of the International Times met to decide to our continued direction and on Saturday the 15th as The Roundhouse launched their new website marking their fifty year history, of which IT played a huge part, I, along with Simon's friends and family danced through the night into the start of our own new chapters. We went to bed at 6am, as the dawn began its slow infiltration of the sky and this blurring of one day into the next seemed fitting as it marked Simon's own physical arrival and the sense that an isolated anniversary of this sort must now induce action on all levels. The song of becoming and of the human spirit of renewal and endeavour must now be sung if we are to breach the problems that face us in an age that is quickly shattering. If we and society ever needed a new glue, balm or paracetamol it is surely now. Let the music of recovery and change resume and play as loudly as the innovators and shamans of the 1960's always intended it to. As the party plates must be cleared, so must the oncoming time.

I commend you all in the songs you must form.

BETWEEN THE DRAGONS

An account of Christopher Stone's *Money Burning Walk Through The City Of London*, November 7th, 2016

Words on the wind. And in that wind, actions.
Thoughts snagged by people declaiming poetry into air.
The simple belief money burns into the heart
Of each conscience, and finds no warmth there
To soothe it or to truly solve human care.

By the two dragons we meet with the Thames
Stuck below us. London bridge blown by furies
Of the unrepentant gods who stare down.
Separate leaves in the wind. Activists and film makers.
Al on sound. Ben on camera. Susannah's rituals planned

Beside frowns. The day is against us? Not yet.
Christopher Stone arrives happy. In amongst the bricks
Of the city he will deconstruct as he builds. His word
Is his name, champion along with John Higgs and Jon Harris
Of all money burners and the reason why the pound

Can now yield. Christopher has a mission to save
The currency of desire. He and these others wish to
Reunite us all back to source. Arthur Pendragon stands,
King of all Druids. His proclamation strikes quickly
Into every heart, sharp as swords.

From the two dragons who stand at the edge of the city
We cross London Bridge in harsh weather to attain
Monument. The Druids vow is declared, as we hold hands
With strangers, while others pass they bear witness
To this, the new document. A ritual is invoked

As we prepare for the journey. Signified by new money
From King Arthur himself. A twenty three pound note made
By the ingenious Derek. It feels like the sanctified paper
That has so provoked our ill health. Money is all.

OIL ON SILVER

As Christopher says, it's desire. But it is also our Prison
And our founding stone. To break free of its hold
Should be where and how we aspire. We who are mighty
And are not trapped or alone. November the seventh, today
Is the Celtic New year, Stone informs us and therefore
The one day in which all debts can be cleared, or resolved.

As we gaze at the stone and the various statements
Of power, which as Christopher says are the buildings,
I catch a glimpse of what's real. The true and pagan
Belief in man's primal forces and not in that
Which would pull him so far away from the seal.

That and the covenant, too, but not the one of the Bible.
The agreement between people to cure themselves.
We must cure the wealthy ones of their wealth,
And the poor of their poverty also. We must relearn
What to value before we all sell ourselves.

And so we move on through the streets towards
The Bank of England, where Julian leads a ritual
That reconnects sacred signs. We draw the equalizer
On notes before they return to our wallets,
So that in time ancient magic can rifle and warp

Power lines. The spirit of Melusin is leased,
The ancient Goddess of money. Jacqueline Haigh dances
As her, setting her free from Starbucks. She is in the logo,
A Pun, as her unbroken skies of origin are re-invoked
Through our chanting until the commercial is what

In the end will stay fucked. Then at St. Paul's we are led
By John of the Crossbones Graveyard into a shortened
Long dance for Phatti, his sacred invocation of gain.
His passion fires and foams as we revolve in his incantation,
Summoning Blake as Policeman and Priest search for blame.

But there is none to be had. Only this offering
To the spirits. The wind bites. We're undaunted
As we question the search we all shield.

BETWEEN THE DRAGONS

With our bags at the heart of this magic circle,
Our possible baggage is grassfed on St. Paul's

Cold stone ground by Blake's fields.
We walk to Fleet Street towards the Royal Courts
Of Justice where the King of the Druids will proclaim
Once again. Money as root of the evil done to the equal
In which those with little can no longer feel true

Weight's gain. The Third Dragon stands, marking
The outer edge of the city. The fat cats are kept snarling
In a self conscious echo of it. But we have our own
Fire now as we burn the chains that have kept us,
Catching a glimpse of the golden in and among human shit.

7th November 2016

FIERCE UNDERSTANDING

An impression of The Guardian Live's *An Evening with Alan Moore and Stewart Lee*

There at the heart of London's theatre district,
Comes something real as the weather
Casts its torrid abstractions above.

A talk between friends and a set of commandments
To understand with compassion what we may hate
And still love. Alan Moore. Stewart Lee.

In conversation. The topic is Alan's
Jerusalem Novel, and how it expresses
A possible means to be free.

Stewart describes the book,
In his inimitable way, lit by humour.
But by scholarship also,

Schooled as he is in the word.
He captures this book of Spells
In which Moore conveys his family's magic

In ways that are truthful
And with a tongue that can
Nevertheless taste the absurd.

The book imagines Moore's home
As the Afterlife's garden.
The broken streets and lost buildings

Are the temples that death
Can rebuild. A stone angel speaks,
Along with the Devil.

Alan's brother Mike, as a ghost-child
Is also a featured after a brief

FIERCE UNDERSTANDING

Sojourn with those killed.

The laughter rings sharp
In this West End Theatre.
Deeper no doubt, with more reason

Than the usual pale joke expressed.
Now these art partners each support
Their combined assurance. Alan as Author,

And Stewart, reading had to call and wait
For Aviva insurance, which put his connection
With his good friend's book to the test.

The Lucia Joyce chapter wakes
Finnegan into a higher energy level.
Yet Alan's re-invention of language

Is not where his proper genius rests.
It is in the eloquence of his thought
And that his now white hair echoes

Snowy, his Great Grandfather Vernall
Who lived as he does in high realms.
To listen tonight was to somehow locate

A new season. One in the mind,
Fed by reading and how our love
Of what's there seems to meld

With what we are, what we need
And we what we want of each other,
And of the world and the weather

And the never quite found
Someone else, who will unlock what was kept
Behind our senses, but is all we feel

Sparked by the beauty of the book
He wrote. Its ourselves.

OIL ON SILVER

So many profundities come

Bidden by both style and substance,
A fierce understanding of all that we've done
Remains his. One feels Alan knows

(And Stewart Lee helps to serve this),
The path towards reformation.
And so this special book is a kiss.

As is all his work, from song to comic.
Alan now turns to poems
As the form to which he'll fix his name.

And he will write them, I know
Above these endeavours, knowing
That the work so far is a poem

And that there's poetry too
In each frame. We get the world we deserve
And the one we imagine.

The only one we can picture
With our somewhat limited view.
Alan soaks in his bath

And contemplates shadow.
'Lush' body products are his
Preferred balm for skin truth.

He loves them so much
'Lush' sought to market his essence.
And asked him, 'What was the fragrance,

Which aroma could hold and reflect
What he was, what he is, '
What was it he would summon?

'Hash and superiority' was the answer,
And indeed that is what we might expect.

FIERCE UNDERSTANDING

But beyond the flip lays the found

And in the found the forgiven.
Alan Moore knows the answer
And the location (Northampton)

Of where in the real sense
Jerusalem meets higher ground.

7th November 2016

DIVISIONS OF LOVE

*A Response to Chris Petit's new installation
In What's Missing Is Where Love Has Gone,
Decad, Berlin 14th March – 20 May, 2017*

Across splintered screens, the splintered soul, gathers
Newly assigned to the cosmos, the man who fell to earth
Spirals back. Chris Petit catches him, singed as he is
By the moon-glow; that electric eye, sourced by cameras
And by the mounted chill of re-birth.

In Gneisenaustrasse, Decad is a new home now for David,
Returning Jones/Bowie to a illuminated variation of self,
Another identity cast by Petit as Artist and Director,
Film's poet of detachment delivers the Thin White Duke
Back to health. Where Bowie once gazed down at the wall

To see those infamous lovers, Petit re-imagines the watcher
As his own kind of view. A host of images strewn across
The street and time's entertainment, as those in thrall
And grief chart the progress of a man who made
From shards of the past all that's new.

Radio on, Petit now broadcasts understanding
Of what constitutes image in his handling of frame and effect.
He muses on music's pull, in and beyond the known senses,
As if touch were soundtrack and scents the records
Of place we'd collect. His images talk through time,

As Bowie did and keeps doing. Petit's lugubrious language
Is there in the slowness of shot and smudged sound.
What do the adored do when they're dead
If not to make adoration, religion? And when do stars
Once they're fallen learn how to shine underground?

DIVISIONS OF LOVE

Petit dignifies Roeg who lost some of his vision, and then
Restores Newton at a time when the character has been smeared.
In 'Lazarus' the last breaths of the subsumed Bowie weathers,
But in this installation, the strangeness and charm's crystal clear.
Petit's camera cuts right to the heart of the image.

As he turns from film making, there is a visceral sense of his books;
In his photographs and his art and elegant fragments of poem,
The dead, re-imagined are teaching still life where to look;
This gaze is on what we first prized, and who we once placed
At our table; the ones we invited to colour our rooms with their art.

The actors, pop-stars and the fashionable icons, who children wore
On their jackets, until the imprint in time, stained their hearts.
In what is missing is where love has gone, Petit tell us,
And now David Bowie is missing but in the space he leaves
There's a mark. The image we have of the hope our love

Taught us; that there is in survival, another song we can chart:
What we remember of him and how that perception still changes,
As across the years different Bowies reflect that son of Kent
And our count; which is the number of years and the number
Of thoughts open to us, if we have the vision

On which not even age can bring doubt. Art must reflect.
One artist mirrors another. Petit takes Bowie back to the city
That in decadence kept him clean. Now Petit cleanses himself
As he wipes the surface free, he turns pages; clicks of the shutter
On which can be written the laws of love, life and dream.

15th March, 2017

Part Five:

GOLD STREAMING

(Tributes and Exercises in style)

Heathcote Williams photo and copyright by Elena Caldera

THE OXFORD MAGIC

FOR HEATHCOTE WILLIAMS ON HIS 75TH BIRTHDAY

What words can contain this lifetime of effort
In which the mutated seeds of his classic schooling
Have altered our vision and re-educated us all?
Firing word spears from his cot, infused first by Dylan
(the true one), Then the sixties' squats,
The Woolf's cupboard, and latterly his Oxford eyrie?

At Seventy-five he's undimmed in either word
Or intention. Writer, Actor, Magician
He re-orders sight for those closed. So many seminal works,
From Wet Dreams' angry word-sperm, bleeding back to stigmatics,
And starting of course with the Speakers
Who initially turned him on.

I have seen him laugh and confuse
At the primacy of the present. I have seen him draw
An electric light while still talking from the small return
Of his mouth. His is a generous muse and his sacred gift
Is still giving. His envelopes and his paintings
As much a part of him as his love.

His dazzle, his gaze shrouded in longjohns
And blue courdroy, remains diamond sharp as his tread
Is perhaps somewhat dulled. But the mind powers forth
As does the fountain pen also, as his calligraphic perfection
Reminds those he writes to, of a sacred time
In the past,

In which he would have been close
To the sanctified Marlowe, banishing Shakespeare
To the box room to sharpen quills and roll folds.
The voice above all who has inspired your heroes
And who spends his days and nights writing
The futures' return from the cold.

OIL ON SILVER

For Heathcote, the dream is still in the daytime.
We will do our best to maintain it.

Stre Mashe.
Stay transcendent.

As the light forms around you
And the air in the room keeps you bold.

15th November 2016

HIGH CHOIRS

(In memory of Leonard Cohen)

There are few equals now to your words
And in the sharp silence after.
The smoke in your song singes verses
As the secret to the chord has been lost.
Chastened, we turn towards an albino fire,
To find within its bleached colour the last golden
Traces from those richer shades you defined.

We are disconsolate now,
As we direct our gaze to the mountain,
Expecting you to walk down it in criss-crossing paths
Of damp grass. Your Buddhist robes catch the stems
Of unyielding flowers, which snag in the moisture,
Like the words you stalked through stone
To unearth. Your voice was the world

That soothed the rooms of the troubled.
In the misapprehensions rescinded,
A well placed word signalled truth.
Your breath kissed the flesh of more than
One hundred mothers, as you honoured yours
And your father after burying the collar
Of his shirt in the ground.

Dear Leonard, we call now to the inveterate choirs,
Beneath whom you rumble as we look for the God
You described. There will be the earth within earth
And a silent prayer, uncommanded
As all you embodied finds its evolution of sorts
In a cloud. The sun splinters. Skies break
As night claims the Rabbi. Tonight we sing for you

Incantatory oaths from religions whose corruptions
Of all you transformed. You are secular now
But you are also the spirit. Gifted to those

OIL ON SILVER

Who hymn to you and who you now leave, eloquently.
A new silence is set. And yet there are still
Those raised choirs who carry the words
You leave to us on the unrepentant air

Of your rest. For Suzanne, Marianne
And that famous blue raincoat,
For the books, songs and children,
The totems of your life on earth. There is a tower
To song along with your edifice of achievement.
It does not teeter, like Babel, but in its place
Is a bible for the adventurous heart to find worth.

The genius Jew, whose repose gained position.
The books are all open as your final poem becomes
All that you were for both men and in women,
And all you will be now, a new Lorca, albeit with a more
Profound turn of phrase. Your sigh and your song
Is now a part of the weather. I hear it now in high choirs
As we learn how to live the new day.

14th November 2016

BRANCHES OF THE YEWTREE

(Abused – The Untold Story, BBC1 April 11th 2016)

The BBC One show, ABUSED tells of the old victims horrors,
Twisted in youth to form puppets
Who have dangled and creaked throughout life.

They have at least found release from the tightness
Of thread wound across them, slick saccharine stains
Used to oil them, dried by the salted breath

Of warped cocks. Close to the end, a disguise
Placed over a boy/man fucked by (Chris) Denning,
Both appals and detaches with the stark strangeness shown.

CGI on the hair, his eyes as well, cartoon eyebrows.
The nose, oddly painted, his girlfriend
Also badly adapted, beside.

This does not serve or assist, or provide
The seclusion, wanted no doubt by the victim
Who shares the same name as mine.

Instead, it renders these old crimes extinct,
As if perpetrated perhaps
By Bugs Bunny, whose overbite and charisma

De-emphasise ancient signs.
The investigation persists, but somewhere out there,
'They' continue; In the semi-priviliged jail cell

And an infamous lair, undisclosed.
How do those old Devils live in their declining skin
And desire? Withering on but reviving

Small explosions of blood on love's rose.

OIL ON SILVER

To these men, the ability to perform Unnatural acts
Became natural; The kiss on a cousin

Related to the use of a tongue on a child.
Orality with your love as a generation's morality
Lessens, is in conversation divided

Between those favouring the accepted
Norm and the wild. The programme reports
But it resolves very little;

The evil die, like the victims, who,
So much younger endeavour to linger on
Under storms. But whether convicted, or dead,

Or ruining their reputations, those we've uncovered
Are never in the broken dark asking why.
It is only when we accept that the bitter tree
Is still growing. And that its roots sparked within us
Are trimmed by the wrong gardeners
That we will have the chance to reform

And to recognise the great weakness
That allows truth to blossom and stops
The ground beneath our shame hardening.

BOLESKINNING

On the hopeful salvation of Boleskin House.

photo and copyright by Max Crow Reeves

The house of former frequency sits, emptied of sound
An endangered. Where once blood like magic weathered its stone,
Fate affronts. Crowley coursed through its rooms,
Summoning shade, leaving entrails of goat and ghost.
He saw daemons bleeding through walls to become.

The Guardian Angels seek rest in the beams of the house.
Chords announce them. Sounds carved in the future,
When Crowley's acolyte Page set to play.
Boleskin House, like a state for which reality
Is re-ordered, commands your attention

OIL ON SILVER

And the dedication we need to convey
The wounds of the past and the glistening promise
Still gifted. The kind that sets tongues afire,
Even those singing through rock to transform.
Once celebrated by Maugham and refered to as Skene,

The skin of the house shelters secrets.
These the MacGillivrays could not rescue
Due to the ravage and scars on each beam.
All of the house's power is spent and now it needs
Fresh investment. A kind of faith formed by darkness

Which in seeking salvation turns its face
Towards forces that may well have to be heaven sent.
Where are the places we prize,
And must the homes we revere all be holy?
As the light breaks and shimmers,

We hear the feedback of history as it chimes.
The buzz of the cable connects to the singing stone,
Which surrounds us. The structure itself sighs,
As Crowley, or an Usher of sorts, finding voice.
Fire speaks. Magic too; a chorus of wall and encounter,

The only chance we have in us to connect to the past
And find choice. We can remain as we are, continually
Moving forward to nowhere, or learn from those trying
To change all that's seen. Whether as a challenge
To the charts or to the map of man's progress,

Boleskin House stands as a totem
To an experiment across forms. We must not allow
These old stones on magick sites to slide
From us. Times' fire tortures until we learn to decipher
That first and seminal frequency.

BOLESKINNING

photos and copyright by Max Crow Reeves

THE STOCKHOLM SEQUENCE

Written between 1pm Monday 19th December and 7pm Tuesday 20th December 2016 In the changing hours between London and Sweden

ONE: AT AN AIRPORT

While early on, it was breasts and backsides
(And of course always faces), these days,
Seeing women I direct my gaze to left hands.

I am looking out for the ring, while hoping of course
For its absence. As if, phantom wrapped
Round the finger true happiness could be won.

At this age, chance declines, fattening
Close beside you. Faded beauty fleshed over
Is the tiring song that's still sung.

And yet, the heart, wearing thin, still finds
Thick clothes for fresh mornings. Warming itself
Through short hours before love's last reprieve

Has begun.

THE STOCKHOLM SEQUENCE

TWO: TAKING OFF

While the concerns multiply I am currently
Above weather. Moving away from the missing
And the securing of my heart across stone.

The wing of the plane sisters cloud, turning the world
To one colour. Washing clean for two hours
The slate wedged between well worn states.

To be at this point with you far and somewhere
Else on the planet, masked by the slick rain
Of England as I am suddenly struck by new sun,

Is to recognise love may well be defined
By a passport and at such a remove, free from
Options, I could learn to receive anyone.

For this interim, there will be a small time
Of freedom. Before your love cages
And my need for the cell becomes one.

OIL ON SILVER

THREE: IN FLIGHT

There is that particular point in the flight
Where the plane does not appear to be moving,
As if the sky was stalled. Your fate blocked and balanced
Before its own check-in gate. Time's idiot tale
Is falsified in that instant. As the wing's dip
Reveals patterns that immediately seem alien.

You are all too quickly displaced, as looking up,
Space awaits you. The Earth's edge, black paper
That the whiteness of God can write through.
All that binds you to the real is the technology
Of the present. And the fact, that despite face
Or figure the Air Stewardess has a glamour

That her tight blouse and skirt can't undo.
You are flying from the sharpness of day
Into an afternoon softness. Time cut by scissors
And the propulsion of blades across heat.
What you know of the world is absurd if it can be
Altered so quickly, as if the lives we all lead

Are just fragments that can be rearranged constantly.
The day has been pinched. When it should be lunch,
Its now evening. Have I been force-fed into aging,
Or do these splinters of day resist span?
All that remains is the trail of thoughts. Spent Graffiti;
Scrawls on the ceiling, scratched by sky fed ancient man.

THE STOCKHOLM SEQUENCE

FOUR: A SUDDEN OUTBREAK OF COMMERCE

Flight is a shop. They lull you with lunch
Then sell at you. A death in the sea may await you,
Or a terrorist coup, God forbid.
People passing others on, exchanging them
For new countries. An act of being, translated
Into a barter of steps on new ground.

FIVE: OUTSIDERING

The flutter of wind on the wing, like a film
Of the air's conversation; the numerous vapours
Bemoaning this artificial slice through their realm.

Or perhaps, the joining of airs, as man apes
Bird distinctions. Flight's swift persuasion
Of the ghost within cloud, served by steel.

SIX: O, SUPERWOMAN

Dominatrix.
Nurse.
Maid.

For me, the Air-Stewardess truly has it.
She offers promise.
Her sex with the sky defies ground.

This fleeting truth is revealed
In the way that she wears her hair up,
As if her own life were lifted,
And her independence revealed.

Its profound.

The other fantasies stall,
Tied as they are to the bed-post.

The mile high club needs no toilet
When desire's new course
Has been found.

THE STOCKHOLM SEQUENCE

SEVEN: ARRIVAL

Stockholm, in rain looking not unlike Milton Keynes,
Or worse, Watford; An iridescent food palace.
Princesses of sex sell kebabs. I wander, struck dumb,
Fooled by the first taxi driver. Sixty euros down,
In-some panic, I exchange the fifty I have left
For Kronor. I forego a sumptuous Chinese meal
To fall for Burger King's morphine, numbing the shock
With thin pleasure when I know the result will be fat.

I should have pushed the boat out *this* far, having located it between
Plane and taxi, to taste all that's different, despite the fact
All's the same. Life is not at all what it was, but then again,
Was it ever? Hoping to meet The One I'll pass through here
Without having the chance to meet *her*. Time is no time
Because we do not know how to judge it. Walking abroad,
New perspectives are in a poignant way, narrowing.

EIGHT: SWEDISH TV

What sets each nation apart
Is often the hair of its actors.
In Sweden, egg baldness
Is surrounded by a low curtain of hair.
As if the head itself were the play,
Or theatre perhaps for emotion,
The male actors pall, academic
While their younger comrades lengthen fringe.

There is nothing wiry. All flows.
There is the expected *efficiency* of it.
Even in grease, all is shining as if the cold and the snow
Brothered sun. The actresses and presenters, though pale,
All wear leather trousers.
ABBA meets Bergman as the Scandi-Noir risks a smile.

Naturally, this is all seen through half closed eyes
And untrusted. The real greets presumption
As the lumps of light summon night.

THE STOCKHOLM SEQUENCE

NINE: BREAKFAST

Sweet curling ham that could almost be bacon.
Eggs scrambled lightly, to within an inch of a cloud.
Wolkshnapke cheese, the truth of its name
In its texture. The slim, crispy wafer as an alternative
To blood-breads. A breakfast that deigns
To meet the mouth of the tourist. But which retains,
Through precision a thoroughly regal state.
Eating it, we succumb to the monarchy of the present.
Among these Japanese and Norweigans
My empire is mapped on warm plates.

TEN: EUROPA, O

Europe concedes to the brits even as we reject them.
Will the oncoming days house our language,
Or leave the Brexiting fools bastardised?

We should be silenced for all we have done
With our voices; English and Americans also
Who have placed the shining shit as their prize.

Now in the murk we scour for gold through
Excrescence, for some small expression
That may convince the world's hosts that our lies

Are not everyone's. The pig has run free
Of the farmer. Intelligent once, it resembles
The man in a wig with dead eyes.

There is the sound of hollow guffaws in the trees
As trotters tickle The Button. Abomination sits expectant
As hell meets its handcart and the rivers beneath duly dry.

ELEVEN: TO BOLDLY GO

Casting thought across space to consider life
On strange planets, one need only visit new countries
To garner some of what that experience is.

The breathing of other airs, coupled with an outsider's view
On decorum. The feeling within a Swedish train carriage,
Or on a Russian street. A French kiss.

We are all travelling if only to the Tabac
Or the churchyard. Each of us fused to a cosmos
in which the Utgang and Hiss are so far.

The breath or beards of young men
With an ice-cream scoop hairstyle, or a woman
Who was once small doll pretty, pierced so she shines

As a star. Each remains alien.
This universe swells as I travel. And I am badly travelled.
Yet look at these steps. Void; procure.

TWELVE: JUST CHECKING

Is masturbation alone
In a foreign hotel room

Any more wistful

Than in a place of one's own?

Or is that touch an appeal
For someone to find you?

A small signal's fire
Across a sea or field,

All seed sown?

OIL ON SILVER

THIRTEEN: PREPARATIONS

After a night's arrival, two meals, a look through town,
I am leaving. My imprint is flushed in an instant
To be replaced by fresh stains. I was not even history here,
More of a moth; one day's lifeline. Quickly rewritten
As I rest on the bed, dreading bags.

Soon I will fly, caked in my sweat and my burden,
As I negotiate custom through the lengthening traditions
Of me. Not even enough spare cash for a beer,
As Stockholm is expensive. I am a parched prisoner,
Marked by travel, the withdrawal of which sets me free.

The cold is making everything ache, as I smell
The small machine rusting in me. I will need to cleanse
It all later, as opposed to oil. Musn't eat. The year ends
With a slide from a temporary reformation.
The old shape is about me and one I was keen to avoid.

This wasn't ideal but I will still be paid, thanks to David,
My friend in business, Jewishness and in name.
We have walked brothered paths, though his has been
More exotic. My orphaned field still surprises
Despite my knowing well its terrain.

It has rained here all day. My face looks young.
Half my body. While the other is aching for someone else's
Warm family. Perhaps its too late. The thoughts accrue.
Scant cohesion. Or is such fragmentation the subject
When a man is beset by three pains?

That of the heart, mind and skin. We each of us chase
Our solutions. As I return now to London whatever remains
Soon begins. Does this little notebook reduce or expand
What I'm feeling? All writers' pads are their gravestones,
Charting new births, marking deaths.

THE STOCKHOLM SEQUENCE

FOURTEEN: WHAT ICARUS TAUGHT

The stress of the check-in soon smears
Some of the peace I located. My own holiday moments
Have never totally stretched to a day.

And so the rigmarole fries, part of a far greater ritual,
In which the official pettiness bred by terror
Has made the getting to your seat a mind-bomb.

The woman's rejection of the bag and the possible exile
Promised. The lack of concern is a scandal
As long as this process is performed.

People can be left, or luggage lost. Its what happens.
As long as the phoenix rises, preferably free from flame.
You must bow. You must bend to achieve your diagonal

In ascension. Just as Icarus struggled, so must you,
With your case. As the sun melted him, so the time sculpts
Your patience. Chipping it slowly, before releasing

Irregular shards into flight. The slow bird greets the dark
Of an already ancient evening. It is only 6pm but these hours
Weather and knock at the bone. Everything snags.

Especially the noises of others. Passengers appear like depression;
A black line's offence at my eye. I long for the ease of the flight
While I loathe the disease of preparing. To exist in such moments

Is to know how that wing-struck one learnt to die.

FIFTEEN: REPRIEVE AND REPRISE

Another sex stewardess on the return and reverse.
This one, younger. Her body's explosion dressed up
As a tribute to glory's full compliment.

SIXTEEN: PRIVATE, THEN PUBLIC CONCERNS

Privately loving someone as I do at a proximity to obsession,
A growing contempt for the public on a crowded plane or train
Still appals. That I can contain these extremes
Is not something fit for admittance, and yet the inane conversations
And selfishness shown makes skin crawl. Where then, can it go?
Maybe an atom's worth in extension.
Could that alteration affect human nature's quantum?
I doubt it. If so, I certainly couldn't see it.
I would hope that this small shift in conscience
Might see the science of love and hate quite undone.
But then of course, there's a view, ignorant, uninvited,
And love's deepest horror is a shelter of sorts from the norm.

THE STOCKHOLM SEQUENCE

SEVENTEEN: ANOTHER LOOK AT STEWARDSHIP

Is boredom brewing this?

The glaze at her eye as the announcement precludes her.
She is staring ahead, through her portal, in a melancholy pout, eyes declined.

Heavily mascared, false lashed, dark, frizzing hair, jutting, irish,
She works in a region not even the inevitable boyfriend can breach.

Look how the air offers her, casting her across oceans,
Like a coin tossed and tested, her currency unexchanged.

They care and don't care. Why are the men homosexual?
As if there have to be types here, like Nurses,

Trained to watch us all through thick glass.

EIGHTEEN: GSOH

God loves the gathering speed and then that sharp elevation,
As the plane climbs, He's reminded of the firefly's lustful leaps.

Or how the Biblical lost once tried to find him;
Scaling trees, seeking height,
And believing each cloud to be solid.

Then snagging it, like some anchor.
God wets Himself.

Turbulence.

NINETEEN: 200SEK X 24

Stockholm, once stronghold
Of the great Ingmar Bergman – who now graces a 200 sek banknote.

For 4, 800 Kronor you could revive him
In a one second flickbook of his filmic return from the dead.

THE STOCKHOLM SEQUENCE

TWENTY: THE BOOK I'M READING

Job cancelled, I am only coming home the next day
And yet it feels like a fortnight,
Thanks to the body's aches, melancholy
And a confirmed lack of sleep.

Odd how everything in me needs tea
On account of caffeine withdrawal.
Strength sapped, will politeness
Guide me past the guardians at the gate?

This wrong-footing through time,
Truncating and then retrieving lost hours
Has accordioned my squat body
And left some of the air seeping through.

B. Catling's Vorrh has been the only thing
To sustain me, its incantatory dreamscape
Will assist from within my return.
Tsungali's bow made from Este,

Using fibres gleaned from her body
Is as common to me now as the time drag
That has been wrenching me out of shape.
Travel broadens the mind

But it traumatises the main-frame,
As the blurred picture shimmers
Before settling to mixed shades of grey.
Hair, suit, skin, hope.

Can grey hope ever help you?
Ask that of Muybridge whose faded kills split design.
My body is also in parts, murdered by flight
For sleep's surgeon to somehow restore me

And the story resume. I read on.

OIL ON SILVER

TWENTY ONE: REFLECTIONS ON

As I approach home, these thoughts:
A cigarette's worth of concerns resume smoking.

And yet the coming year proffers promise.
Here's to what I take in and exhale.

A year's work ending blank with shadows of hope
Through the paper. What awaits, death or taxes?

Love or success? Who will fail?
A trip of two days forms some sort of coda.

A book's white endpapers
On which can be told the new tale.

LILIAN

(Lilian Ray Erdos, 28/12/1938 – 10/2/2012)

I won't write about how you sailed from this part of the world
To another; a hospital bed as your vessel,
Medicine's imposition your sail.

Of how your tiny voice sang, catching the wind in small doses,
And of how I waved you off from the distance
Of that hospital chair and bed-rail.

Of how you are gone. And of how long
You had waited, as I strove to reach you
With you in turn reaching out.

Of how you twisted and turned, so thin to me,
A small daughter; you, my own Mother,
One eye to the wall, one in cloud.

Of how your finger's small wipe
Across my desperate hand keen to keep you;
Of the final look that you gave me,

Drowning in drugs, death and sleep.
Of the times we can't have,
And the ghosted days I will look for,

Of your skeletal skin, my huge body,
And the terrible weight of this dream.
Of the specific moment you'd gone,

To be simply replaced by mechanics;
The slow machine slowing,
The passage of breath closing doors.

Of how I loved you, and will,
Of how I sat with your body,

OIL ON SILVER

Of this long not-believing
That will bring me no reprieve or reward.
Of wanting to know and not knowing at all
Where you've gone to;

I can't and won't write about you
For fear of reducing you still.
And yet I sit now with words

Which I throw to the night: can you hear them?
How will I know, Mum? Please tell me,
Unless I am to not of course know until –

The end of the wind and the tiny song
I'll be singing;
Lilian, will you listen? It will take me
The rest of my life to begin.

GRIEFLAND
(Tamas Erdos, 26/7/1938 – 10/2/1994)

I

Dead, then.

Still dead,
            With the gathering winds
Out of London,
And the cars in their coughing
On the too long absent road.

Dead,
      With no sound.
And no voice to speak of this.
With no brief arms to signal,
No face and no order
Without view or feeling
On the plight we're condemned to,

Dead,
      And with peace now,

OIL ON SILVER

Just like flowers,
Around.

I see you here,
In my minds eyes, still living.
Observing, or mindful of the surplus tears
At our side. Sighing perhaps,
At the opportunities wasted,
Or for the future which lingers
One moment dreadful, then strange.

Here, then, am I
And are there words you can offer?
Is there anything you can show me?
Deathly signals? Night moves?
When will you come and with a fresher face
For the morning
Appear, and smile at me from the confines of your room?
I long for that now with all of the breath in my body,
With all of the breath you had stolen,
From the remaining air of your life.
And in that longing, relax into a cold kind of crying;
A past point, or passing recollection of you.

II

The ships of the past are now just dying wood on the water,
They seem to float like dead birds do, a half wing half sinking
While a fat, lifeless chest is pointing up with beak empty
To a seared, sightless looking beyond the bleared frame of the sky.
Is that boat your home, and just what is it, this sailing?
Did you repay your life's tarry to the strange Ferryman?
Or is there just ash, the flash of a worm on ants breakfasts?
Did you receive fresh perspectives, or the unlikely shimmers of God?
It's unlikely a God would be so cruel as to steal you.
So cruel as to see you at such a sad turn in your life.
Or perhaps it is good, and entails a lifting off of your hardships,

To gather you in and protect you, providing you with the Father
That you of course, were denied.
Or perhaps, it's just bad. As much of a sign as Crows landing.
As much of a sign as Christ dying for all of the poor Christians.
Or perhaps it is like the way the day creates evening;in it's own
image, different through what it shows has been lost.
For all of these things, I will say it now, I'd reclaim you.
And I would draw you close to me in the tapering sheets of fast
thought. I would struggle through strands at some distant part of
the morning, a Father Baby clutched to me – Oh, yes – a miniature
you...Plucked from time, placed at the point of beginning,
Snatched from God, granted from the powerful entrails of Grief.

III

Be born again, and in a crowd I would know you.
In your second Pram I will know you and steal you too, from that
seat! Outside the shop, the swimming pool, by the Bus Stop,
Beneath the bag of your Mother, newly given, assigned.
Come back to me and we will both split the difference;
Two halves of the apple, the banana skin peel duly peeled.
So that there, at the cusp of where the flesh greets the flower
Will be the sense of you, handled, will be the thick sense of
You.

IV

I peel back the skin and see my own self inside you.
Beneath your olive skinned background, behind your Jew's sacrifice.
And in looking, still feel that I have born despite conscience
And am not of sperm, nor of shadow,
Not of whiteness,
Or bone.
But rather, the fruit, the tired skin of your being.
My own life the proof of your passing
Which occurs without value and which leaves me
No time to speak, or to seek definition
For the place you have left now

And from where I still grow.

Close to the spell of you name my own existence continues.
Despite the sweat and the bleeding, my own small cuts
Were earthed. And held in the salt of the tears we've shed
And your eating is the breath I give birth to
With every day left of life.

V

Dead,
    And the sound of the boats
In the harbour
Of the birds above cities
And of the blood in your shoes.

Dead,
    And the sound
Of the faraway Steamer
That you stole and rode on
At the tender age of Eighteen.

Dead,
    And you lay
In a small bed, uncovered
Without soft soil or pillow
But rather on the air within ash.

Dead,
    And the sound
Of your arms in a burnt smoke
Of your wide smile in tapers
Of sky headed mist.

Words and their use seem to fly about me like insects.
Like minute irritations that have their own kind of life.
If only such words could be used now, despite that.
If they in some way could witness this sad experience now.
And if only there was just a small chance to see you,

GRIEFLAND

For one moment of meeting, so as to in some way decide.

If only the old things;
The floodlights, the Cathedrals
Could glorify people
The way that these words have run.

Too soon passing Man, your dark and curls,
Your sunglasses
Are small machines to catch morning
Over the sad smile of grief.

Let everything end if there is no more to do with you.
If there is nothing left now to hold you,
And not one thing to remind.

Let everything end,
As the life you gave passes to me,
And the breaths which came too fast
Now appear to be mine

To command.

6 4 SNOO

ONE: IN MEMORIAM, ANDREW 'SNOO' WILSON,

2nd August 1948-3rd July 2013

Snoo, there are no words to describe
The particular voice that you mastered;
No specific masks to uncover the uncanny
Faces you pulled;composed and sneering
Perhaps at the new Hampstead fashion,
While locating new countries in harbours
Without parallel. Ideas rampaged through,
Borne on vibrant winds by host figures;
The collection of Sprites, Progs and Demons
Who gargled and belched through your Plays.
And how boisterous you were, and how tenderly
Measured;and how the smallest spark
Of endeavour placed all of your heart
Into flame. Where now are the walks –
All too few in number – that we took
Across Hackney, with Frieda the Dog
Pulling you? Where are the waters, the drinks
And that V&A trip in April?
Where are the new Revelations in theatre?
How will the eyebrows raise without you?

Andrew from Reading you blazed,
And reading you fires pleasure.
In dark times to come let us treasure
The magicks you carved from the blue.

TWO: SNOO'S SONNET

You meet a man by a brook
Whose work you first read as a youngster.
You walk, spend an hour,
He directs you through the west of the sun.

And in no time at all
That uncertain stream is a river,
And then that river an ocean,
Or part of the sea, close to home.

After a nuclear dawn, what will be the things
We remember? Spectacular visions and language
To charm broken bone? Then later, we'll wake

And attempt another way to make culture,
And your individual voice will inspire,
And the hidden heart find it's home.

THREE: REMNANTS REMAIN

I find that the books haunt me now,
As the hands that wrought cannot make them.
The books become forms of echo, like squares of light,
Falling through. Or a handprint perhaps,
On an otherwise wall-less building;
Whose chambers, though empty
Still contain the precious remnants of truth.

OIL ON SILVER

FOUR: AT A WORD

At an (unthinkable) word, you are gone
Leaving a Pinteresque silence. (And you know
I loved Pinter as much as I valued you.)
But whereas Harold's work paused
To find an everlasting conclusion,
Yours is still yapping, barking your laugh
At the dark. Your work will return
Held by your strong undercurrent,
For just as the mainstream fills oceans,
So the rarefied taste leaves it's mark.

FIVE: TO A FALLEN COMRADE

Comrade, exchange all of your goods
at the border;
        Sacrifice Solstice
For a new term of leave,
Without sun.

Or with a whole other light
That those of us left cannot filter;
Hunched in the dark we chase endings
While somewhere new and strange,

You've begun.

SIX: FINAL EXCHANGE

Scratching these words of friendship and love with a South London
Biro on a wind cast summer's evening that you now cannot see,
I think of the sheen that your countenance gave us,
And of the colourful weather spun from your work, wild and free.

Out of fashion you fell. True ideas resist fashion.
Instead, it is fashion that will slowly encumber the dead.
Snoo, your vitality thrives, and it will endure across seasons,
Expertly baking a future in which the pleasures of words become bread.

HOARSE LATITUDES
A Dramaticule

SCENE: A Paris doorway. Night. Distant sounds of the city. But this street is silent, replete as it is with old ghosts. The two shades hunker down, JIMI's garish clothes have long faded. JIM is bearded, large bellied, his matted shirt and trousers are stained.

JIMI. There's too much rubbish here...

JIM. Merde.

JIMI. Where are we now?

JIM. Not inseine, but in merde!. We're in the wrong part of Paris. I told you not to roam, man..

JIMI. I got these LP legs, I extend.

JIM. Or you did.

JIMI. It's the air. I like to feel it rip all around me. In a high breeze, distortion. The music I felt. Days of old.

JIM. There's not even a whore here..

JIMI. Whose whore? You couldn't fuck if you wanted.

JIM. Because I'm dead?

JIMI. You're too drunk, man.

JIM. You know where you are with the booze.

JIMI. You mean you know where you were and that it's now a place you can't get to. The drunk lose their purpose, like a face in the crowd you loved once.

JIM. And the stoned?

JIMI. They relax. I never had any problems. I worked.

JIM. Bee-busy. You seemed to fuckin' buzz everywhere.

JIMI. Its why I needed my tabs and its why I needed my pussy.

JIM. You were an animal, Jimi.

JIMI. Man, I was allowed! I'm the way.

JIM. Was.

JIMI. Arguable. These days they still need me. People have lost all direction..

JIM. Including us. Its cold here.

JIMI. Way cold.

JIM. Too cold. Especially if the phantoms can feel it.

JIMI. You want to rush back to Oscar?

JIM. Fuck, no.

JIMI. He digs you!

JIM. He digs you! I know. He likes them pretty.

JIMI. Pretty far out if you ask me..

JIM. He just likes sharing the flow. He's Ok.

JIMI. But a bore, no?

JIM. Who's not? Live like that, you're defensive. So, you want to walk back?

JIM. We'll get back there. First signs of dawn, there's no choice.

(Silence.)

JIMI. Stinks here.

JIM. Smells odd.

JIMI. The French have got trouble. Have their cleaned these rues since the sixties? I smell trouble rising. Gasoline, fire.

JIM. Cars.

JIMI. Bombs, Jim. Try bombs. Nearly forty years later. They got themselves some new trouble.

JIM. So, what do you wanna do, play a solo?

JIMI. Baby, we're outta tune. I'm not playing and I ain't got no guitar. I was walking around just last week and I saw one laying there, on the roadside. I just stood and stared at it. Battered but loved. Playable. It was an accident, sure. But it looked like a sacrifice to me. If I had seen it in Soho, I may have very well picked it up. But it was here. I flew here. I landed here. I was walking. It shone, a reminder.

JIM. A gravestone, you mean?

JIMI. Possibly. They place flowers on roads where deathly accidents happen.

JIM. What would they place for me, a wine bottle?

JIMI. Either that or a lizard. But for me, I kept walking. I've lost the touch, anyway.

JIM. I still write.

JIMI. Huh..

JIM. In my head. Like a report from the mirror. But who's there to listen with all that special glass in the way.

JIMI. That's life, James.

JIM. The glass..

JIMI. You're on the other side, baby. You see reflections, but the subject has gone, lost to light.

JIM. My throat's sore.

JIMI. From drink?

JIM. From trying to recite what I'm writing. It's like the words are embedded and I can't get them out. They don't know where they are.

JIMI. Right.

JIM. Or why they'd be spoken. For an audience who can't listen while playing out from a record broadcast on the wrong frequency.

JIMI. Death is the real tuning out, even while the concert keeps playing. We could play well together. Those screams you always did..

JIM. Your high wail. Yeah, I know what you mean, but what good would it do us? We've been drowned out by decades, and those who'd want to hear cannot see.

JIMI. Dark night.

JIM. Dark times. Do you know the Brecht poem?

JIMI. Berthold, I know it..

JIM. In the dark times/Will there also be singing?/Yes, there will also be singing -

JIMI. - About the dark times...

JIM. Yeah.

JIMI. That's profound.

JIM. Nobody knows what will be. The American Prayer has been cancelled. Look what they got now. Devil in a wig.

JIMI. Its no wig.

JIM. And the other guy, too, who won't fade, from London. Another cartoon for the rising.

JIMI. Yeah, that fucker's own hair is a wig.

JIM. A mask, you mean?

JIMI. Yeah.

JIM. As the sickness starts, there's a searching. All the options are fizzing like germs in a slide, but none fix.

JIMI. All the old ghosts return who might have provided the answer.

JIM. The tomb doors are open and the heavy earth all gives way.

JIMI. But people are scared of the lizard king and the cactus..

JIM. The little wing isn't flying as she who calls Mary finds herself snagged on the wind.

JIMI. It's a good time to be dead. Fuck knows what will happen. Though, I'd still like to ask her..

JIM. Ask who?

JIMI. Fuck. She's my friend.

(The two of them laugh. There is a guitar howl and a screaming. The sounds of the city are rising as what is left of the light fades away.)

JIMI. Did you ever fuck her, your Ma?

JIM. Its getting dark.

JIMI. That's no answer.

JIM. When it gets dark, that's what happens. Nobody ever knows what to say.

(Silence.)

JIMI. My balls ache.
JIM. That's death. The body keeps trying. But it never gets there.

(Pause.)

JIMI. So, where are we now?
JIM. Silence, James.

COMEBACK: A PLAY IN A PAGE

A MODEL poses while ANDERSON films her. J. enters, darkskin.

Model. Who's this?

J. I've returned. I'd like to know if you're ready.

Anderson. She is..

J. Forgive me. They said at the gate to come through. I was told you're in charge and that you have the means to announce me..

Anderson. To who, son? I'll film you, if you're one of the cocks I've just booked. I thought there'd be more. I asked for a batch of gangbangers from Corby. But you'll do.

Model. I like him.

Anderson. Got all your tests?

J. Failed first time. I came back.

Anderson. Everyone needs a chance and coming again's what we're after. What about her, get you going?

Model. You never know, Max..the rumour, with luck on our side, might be true.

Anderson. I hope so..

J. It will.

Anderson. Where are you from, son?

J. Judea.

OIL ON SILVER

Model. Don't they make furniture?

J. Yes. I am here for your comfort. Take me back. I can help you. I can support everyone. I have come to forgive. As has been writ ten. The cost is faith..

Anderson. You get fifty, plus fifty again if you come. Oh, I forgot: you've come back. Well, I don't pay up front, that's for certain. Come on, then..let's see it..*(Gestures)* Let's see what you've got..

(J. attempts understanding and lets his trousers fall.)

Model. Jesus Christ..!

WITH THANKS

A Dramaticule

SCENE: *A Suburban bedroom or lounge. Night. Don and Vi, a dowdyish couple sit reading. There is a long silence before Vi turns to Don.*

VI. Darling, did you put the cat.. down?

DON. Not yet. I'm just going to finish this chapter..

(He reaches across for matches or lighter and sets the book alight.)

VI (*Dreamily*) Oh, look, Donald: fire..

DON. One gets what one wants when one waits.

(He throws the book into a nearby wastebin where it continues to burn. Silence.)

VI. I was thinking..

DON. Oh, yes?

VI. You don't want to let them go, do you, darling?

DON. What do you mean?

VI. Well, I wondered..

DON. Darling, why would I? They're useful. You're such a Worry wart tonight, little pet.

(She slaps him.)

Thankyou.

VI. I don't mean to worry. But I want it right..

DON. Always.

VI. And you know I couldn't go on without you.

(A silence. They smile. She kisses him, lightly.)

VI. How about a glass of piss before bedtime?

DON. I didn't know we had any..

VI. Plenty.

DON. Any particular flavour tonight?

(She gets up and goes into the bathroom or kitchen. He sits back, relaxes and also reflects.)

We've had a wonderful time. It's just such a shame doors are closing. I even remember the first one, seeing you there, framed by light.

(She returns, carrying two vials or glasses and passes him his.)

VI. Framed by what?

DON. Light.

VI. Whose?

DON. Everlasting.

VI. Donald, sometimes you're silly.

DON. Then I'm silly for you, Violet, dear.

(She slaps him.)

WITH THANKS

VI. Thankyou.
DON. Of course..

VI. I remember another occasion. We were somewhere I think near an orchard. There were certainly apples and trees everywhere. birds, too, of course. Yes. Vociperous birds. Very noisy. We were both arranged by a picnic but I don't think we ate anything. I was in a long summer dress, my underwear burning behind us. The equally long light was dappled, cast I suppose by the trees. Suddenly, one of these birds just landed there between us both, on the blanket. It simply stood there, stuck, stupid and I remember you pulled it apart with your hands. You were much younger then and had such a wonderful presence. You were my man, boy, my soldier. My Somebody Who. You were gold. With the birdblood on your hands I knew in a blink we'd be married. I was seventeen.

DON. Yet we waited..

VI. Such power you had on that day. I knew right away it was you. That you were my life, love, my future..

DON. I remember it too.

VI. I'm so happy.

(He puts his hands to her throat.)

Thankyou, love.

(Fade to End.)
—

THE CURE FOR CANCER

A clinical looking room in any city. Kelly and Dr. Kearns at a table. She's dressed like a patient and anything between 16 and 20. Kearns is much older, in anonymous suit and tie. Their joint focus is placed on a single green apple. They scrutinise it. It is like a light in the room.

KEARNS. Is it loaded?

KELLY (*laughs*) Not yet. Or not in the way you imagine..

KEARNS. Then in what way?

KELLY. It's heavy. It's got the sins on the world packed in there. Adam, then Eve. The Holocaust. Human worry. Or the serpent who sits under culture and sucks away at it's root. It's a bomb in waiting, of course. But worse: this bomb's patient...

KEARNS. Patient?

KELLY. It's choosing. Yes, it's choosing it's moment..

KEARNS. Is it? (*he pauses*) How did you find it?

KELLY. It's mine. I've always had it. It was given to me. It was granted. It's a form of inheritance.

KEARNS. Oh.

KELLY. An Heirloom.

KEARNS. I see.

KELLY. I don't think you do. It's the secret.

KEARNS. This?

KELLY. Yes.

KEARNS. What is it?

KELLY. Above everything else it's the grail. The grail's not a cup. It's not some..fucking tankard. The Grail's emblematic of what Christ or whoever he thought he was - represents.

KEARNS. The sins of the world..

KELLY. That's right.

THE CURE FOR CANCER

KEARNS. As might be held in one apple..

KELLY. In <u>the</u> apple..

KEARNS. Truly?

KELLY. My family were all gardeners. They cross pollinated like Bees, moving between nations. They ended here but they started back in the homeland, back in his Middle East. Each generation in turn began to move sideways. They married next to their culture instead of right inside it. Geographical love, spanning the world in hot congress. From country to country and from –

KEARNS. What?

KELLY. Cunt to cunt.

KEARNS. I don't think you should say that.

KELLY. Why not? Extreme times, extreme feeling. The people of the world as one person. Isn't that what Christ wanted most? Or Mohamed. Or –

KEARNS. What?

KELLY. Who are the other ones?

KEARNS. Does it matter?

KELLY. No. But it happened. My roots, my people were the first Guardians...

KEARNS. But your name's..?

KELLY. Kelly.

KEARNS. Yes, quite. (*smiles*) It's hardly Biblical.

KELLY (*proving point*:) David.. Paul.

KEARNS (*proving his*:) Yes.. Goliath.

KELLY. Sarah..

KEARNS. Moses.

KELLY. What does it matter? It's mine. Here and now, at this moment. Names are just titles for whatever type of object we are. I have been here before. I've been here always. And besides, you couldn't pronounce it..

KEARNS. Pronounce what?

KELLY. My true name.

289

(silence)

The first. The one before judgement. The one after judgement. Every word you have now is made up.

(he stares at her.)

KEARNS. Well.

KELLY. Well indeed. I'm not sure you know what has happened. Everything here's an invention. Time and tablecloths. Buildings. The buckle you have on your belt. Your wristwatch marks time, but it's only time marked by sunlight. What about darkness. What about –

KEARNS. What?

KELLY. The first things. (*she addresses the apple*) Nature is here, inside of that, all of nature. The growth of the world forms around it and also decays just as fast. What's that book by that man, the one who died from the blowjobs..

KEARNS. From the - ?

KELLY. Oscar Wilde!

KEARNS. Blowjobs?

KELLY. Dorian Gray! Yes, that's it! This is the painting but here, it's everything else that starts aging. This keeps its freshness. This remains natural. *(she pauses.)* Why don't you take a bite of it?

KEARNS. No.

KELLY. Why don't you have a bite?

KEARNS. I'm not hungry.

KELLY. Then why don't you just bite it to test it, if you don't believe what I say?

KEARNS. I didn't say that..

KELLY. Oh, right..

KEARNS. I'm quite prepared to believe you..Afterall, we all want it..

KELLY. An apple a day?

KEARNS. No. A cure.

KELLY. For cancer.

KEARNS. That's right. And you're saying it's here. In this apple..

KELLY. Yes. I am saying because I know the entire thing stretches back. This is the start. This begat human nature. Temptation, torture. All of it springs from this. There's so much in there, in fact, I don't really think you'd believe it. It's practically quantum; heavier in than looks out. It's pan dimensional too. This is all we can see in our context..

KEARNS. So, you're saying that this is all apples?

KELLY. Better than that. It's all *Trees*.

(pause)

KELLY (*cont*) And of course there's a cure. All cures begin in the illness. The illness begats them, before it's replaced or mutates. You cure a cold by watching the bacteria happen. The means to cure cancer is to study it's appetite.

KEARNS. We need to understand it.

KELLY. Do you?

KEARNS. I'm not that sort of Doctor.

KELLY. No. You've been granted.

KEARNS. I have.

KELLY. You're assigned.

KEARNS. Perhaps.

KELLY. Christ's true gift to the world was the one they rejected: a true embrace and acceptance of everything beyond their control. A surrender to fate. And a belief in the silence. No word comes. There's no message. None that anything other than Dogs could well hear. (*of the apple*:) This is the key. This unlocks human nature. One sweet surrender to illness and death and then cure. Home. Where we grow. Where the seeds are all started. Where the earth is rich. Taste it. The worms and the buds bursting forth. (*pause*) I dare you. Taste it.

(*silence*)

KEARNS. Now?

KELLY. Yes.

KEARNS. Well, now you're playing Eve to my Adam.

KELLY. If I take off this smock they'll arrest you..

KEARNS. Do you really think so?

KELLY. I know so. No smock without fire is there?

KEARNS. Not on this ward. Or not in this lifetime.

KELLY. Who says that matters?

KEARNS. You mean when there's more?

KELLY. When there's none. What if we stop? What if all there is is just darkness? A time and place without measure. A time and place without sense. All we have is the now and the now is dead as we say it. And so we must savour of suffer. Everything ends in regret.

KEARNS. Regret?

KELLY. That it hurt, regret that it ever happened. Regret that it's over. Why couldn't it just stay with us? This is a warning for you and yet it is also a present. You could be someone different. You could be the one with the cure.

KEARNS (*takes a moment*). I contemplate cure. I consider it's reasons..

KELLY. I consider you. You've been chosen.

KEARNS. Chosen for what?

KELLY. This one chance.

KEARNS (*laughs*) Kelly..please..

KELLY. What?

KEARNS. You're very..

KELLY. Yes?

KEARNS. Entertaining..

KELLY. If God made the so called garden for Adam why, after woman did he then make the snake?

(he smiles and stands)

KEARNS. I like you, you know. I liked you the moment I saw you. As soon as you came in I noticed there was something delightfully *bold* about you. You're not like other girls, girls of your age, are you, Kelly? You're somehow special. And I mean that, you know. I'm sincere.

KELLY. Good.

KEARNS. But I mean, all this fuss..those things you said and did in the papers. All to – what? Draw attention? Attention to this –

KELLY. Apple, yes.

KEARNS. But how is it proved? We need more than opinion. It looks like it came from the Grocers. It's remarkably well preserved. You've made lots of claims. You've exhibited yourself in the papers. A girl of your age.

KELLY. I've a body. If I can use it for good, then I will.

KEARNS. You don't sound naïve..

KELLY. I know what this is. I know what it can do. It's full meaning. I know the reason why it was gifted and given to me, at this time. It's been entrusted to me, to teach this generation a lesson. We no longer care. We're a people who self preserve, at all costs. The culture dumbs down. The Political system collapses. Finances are squandered. Books are replaced. The old, freeze.. This represents hope. This is the thing they've been wanting..

KEARNS. Who?

KELLY. The Time-Draggers. The Occultists and yes, the insane. *(she pauses)* That's what you think I am.

KEARNS. No, I don't. I think you're a stunning young woman.

KELLY. Does that mean you want to fuck me?

KEARNS. No, thankyou. But I need to talk to someone else. Please wait here.

KELLY. Why would I leave? I'm Guardian to the secret.

KEARNS. Kelly, please.

KELLY. (*of the apple:*) It's fine. I'll keep waiting. Because any minute now it will speak.

CONDEMNATION

SCENE: Present, or past? A chill descends on the theatre. A back entrance opens. Noose limp round his neck, THE CONDEMNED MAN trails a rope.

CONDEMNED MAN:

To my detractors, just this: you will not be forgiven. To all of those who would judge me, you can suck on the wronged cock of God. For God has been wronged if you think you pleasure him with your image. God has been slandered, with the kiss you exchanged, turned to mud. I've made my decision right here, a place of ill-defined shadow, where the light, while intrusive reveals nothing worth much insight. Where the light I'll direct fails to grant you much substance; all of you who are copper, set in a world primed for gold.

You'll be surprised or detached from what you might see as invective. These words have no context other than the air they slice through. Soon they will be all that remain and the previous misunderstandings shall flourish. I could not convince you to take me at my word, so I screamed. You might want that now. But I shall not scream. I am singing. It is in these final moments that I can at last testify. The song begins at the heart but the coursing blood forms a chorus until the emotion is an orchestra from the skin.

Your scaffold frames the sky, a prison of sorts. Your directive..firing me like a cannon ball to shatter wind and splice clouds. It is as high as my death and your ignorance, my propulsion. But my last word is unwritten with its authorship in *your* sin.

You misconstrue, you destroy, extract the pips and keep eating. Believing yourselves to be better, you cast away men like me. Men who have tried to successfully honour the forces but who were beaten down by the shallow: Why cross an ocean when you can idle away in a stream?

You think yourselves found. You believe yourselves full of purpose. But you have no purpose and your faces are smoke and thin glass... I see through you. I know. I tried to love between borders. I tried to show them an *actual* way to believe. God can't be kissed. He can't be touched, felt, or conjured. True God is a sickness that only some can contract. Then God speeds through them, re-ordering rules and commandments. The needs for these alter as time rushes on. My supposed blasphemies will be tied to the flesh of the future. And my indiscretions will form a fresh bible code. Decipher me. Understand. Here is the line to be written.

(Like a tail, he casts the lengthy rope to those watching.)

At the end of this he is waiting for both you and I to pull through.

MUSE ON MONDAY

SCENE: An anonymous room, half made/decorated. A beautiful young woman poses as the light grows on her. She moves languidly, as if through a series of stages. She comes to rest and seems perfect, albeit slightly dreamlike somehow. Throughout the piece she will attempt to discard this. This small journey concerns the girl who is worshipped climbing down from her pedestal.

THE MODEL:

Mondays are Painters. They come with a gaggle of brushes, talking themselves onto canvas or onto those slack little pads. Sometimes these overturn, or they move around with them, making a mark as they do so, eager to see what there is from all sides. Or what I am. My side. They're trying to capture me from an angle. Trying to take a small statement from me in order to make something large enough of their own. And yet the subject persists. Clearly they don't know what they're doing. The brushstrokes grow abstract. The pencil lines are soon rubbed. To capture a curve you have to a good deal more than just follow. You have to imagine..You have to feel the weight and shape and size in your hand. Then the eye follows suit. And then the suit finds the armchair. Clothes, like air rising, then collapsing back down like a sigh..

What do they want, these odd men? Most of the time they look filthy. Jackets and jeans torn about them, the remains of a meal on their shirt. Their arms all seem thin, and yet their gaze commands substance, as if through their looking something inside them grows fat..Maybe their ego. Their drive. Their lust. Their erection. By covering me with their colours they want all sorts of things to come back.

It never happens of course. I do my best work as an image. Get too close and I frighten. Intimidation comes from a touch. I sit and watch them ignite and see the possibilities forming. Their lips move, their hunger practically becomes visible. But I just recline. Perform whatever pose they imagine. Detach myself from them. Distance myself from the dream. It's theirs after all, which I suppose they take from my body. The smooth shape inspires all manners of shade in their minds. The fingers draw but don't touch. I am fondled and held through the pencil. Tickled and stroked by a paintbrush, patted and smacked through soft clay. They take their cue from my smile and my stare fascinates them. What am I thinking? Men will never know. They can't know. All they may do is dream and hope that I will unravel. A woman sheds her clothes like a secret, and then dressing again rewrites it. We may allow them a night, or not even a night, a few minutes – and in that time let them read us, let them scour the skin like found words. But the language is ours and they as yet, have no grammar. And so they stumble like tourists, or a drowning man grabbing water in the futile hope of support. All Desire is dumb. Desire is just muscle shouting. But the love that they wish to capture is hidden within, with no tongue. You don't want to be seen. Or to be seen as an object. You want to be special. But special to whom? That's the point. Not to them, anyway. It's an act of theft, all that capture. Drawing you into an image defined as it is by their hands. And yet they never see it. Their art is what keeps them separate. All they can ever do is reflect me, but they will never own me at all. Imprints that fade and an endless repeat of old shadows, stretching ahead into darkness, into the receding day, the long night. Soon enough you're a dream, and soon to be replaced by another. Who once more is a shadow, of whatever they first saw in you. The Model. The Muse. Only ever meant for a Monday. As their week continues, yours smudges and smears, into stains. You're not what you were, because they know they can't have you. And so they distort you. You're turned into a Picasso, a fast jarring line, a strange square.

Mondays are hard. But they're just there to get through them. In time, the day changes and you get to try again, somewhere else.

(She finally drops the pose and starts undressing.)

No, you close your eyes now. Start dreaming. From this moment on you imagine what shapes you must chase through the dark..

(Darkness..)

(Lights rise. The scene slightly altered. A studio setting with a back projection perhaps. The Muse's costume has changed - she is more of a type, more exotic - As has her manner. She is more direct now, stronger.)

THE IMAGE:

Tuesdays are film. Usually a bullshit commercial. A branded drink or insurance, made to seem glamourous. Put a girl in it quick and see if works for boys watching. Sex sold for Tesco, bottoms and breasts for Waitrose. Here, they'd never admit to the need because this is just about business. And yet they do need you. They need you to be more than you. Or more you than you could ever imagine. What they want is the secret that unlocks the worrying nerve in the need.

It's usually the same man each time. Or the same sort of man. The same faces. Overweight or a Hippy, hair always too long for their age. And then all of the extras of course, the various hands on a film set. Hands with eyes staring, emotionless through the glare. There's a dazzle of lights and the smell of tea and fried bacon. The smell of sweat that climbs higher, gardenia green on the wall. The hours of boredom and push when they suddenly decide they are ready, only to stop when the traffic three miles away threatens sound.

Commercials steal souls. They take all of the profoundity from you. You are there to do nothing for nothing that in the long run will last for no time at all. You're a subliminal turn, a particular twist to the senses. Lucky as hell if those who are watching recall or remember anything else but your tits. You're the girl in the frame. The dream in the dress. You're the object taking human form for an instant before disappearing into white noise. In amongst all the shit you are the final bloom of the species. The last rose, or flower that the dribbling earth gobbles back.

You're an accessory to. Or the womanly take on a handle. A smile in a bra and a wiggle. A wobble of faith they can't see. But of course they like using you, because as a muse you're compliant. You concede and move calmly in amongst bump and rush.

Then they're done with you just like that and you're supposed to recede without problems. Only to appear again if they need you looking even more beautiful. More inspiring. More. So that they can find something extra. Or reshoot the answer in order to find a better question perhaps. Nobody knows. The entire thing becomes fragile. Film is a fragment which makes no acceptable sense frame by frame. Only when spun, when conjured or run through the camera. Projected of course in the old days, a series of ghosts flicked to life. Frozen moments thawed by the heat and glare of attention. The lights of the cinema burning just as they did Joan of Arc.

I feel that sacrifice. True. Everytime when on camera. Their gaze is the fire for which the slaughtered kebab lamb is sliced. I am that faun. That slaughtered lamb, that meat turning..and they are the fire sending makeup and nails into ash.

Got to change this somehow..
Got to climb down from the pyre...
Look, how the pedestal topples when the bum you so love starts to break..

(Silence. She seems to weaken slightly.)

Forgive me, the heat..
I've been in these heels hours...
Where do you want me? And how long do you need me for?

(She waits as the lights fade or fall.)
(Music. A chord. Followed on by another. A guitar strummed a piano tries to capture a tune..)

(Lights rise. She sits, her look now far more natural. A simple dress. She looks sweeter, and carefully placed on a stool. The music fades in and out as a song is attempted. She taps her foot, listens, willing the songwriter on.)

THE SUBJECT:

Wednesdays are song. The middle of the week gives you balance. Words dance around me, while fingers that fall capture me. Forming chords, keys and strings are shaped to contain me. Veins tense. Throats widen as a chorus of cores summon forth. The heart opens. The soul is placed within structure. The various chimes are colliding. A committee of air is convened.

(*sings*) Hey, did you happen to see/The most beautiful girl in the world..?

Of course, it's not me. Oh, no. I'm just one of the muses..But I represent them, because the girl that they sing for is somehow improved when they sing. She grows prettier. Her figure becomes more attractive. Her skin appears softer..her hair is - what? Summer long? Rhymes court the air like distant birds or slow motion. Clouds form. Are they moving or is that just the world spinning round? A number of questions resound but the delirious phrase chases closure. How may they win you, these makers of song, these key thieves? They want the key to your heart and the open back door to your knickers. They amuse you with rhymes then let poems worm their slick way towards tears..

But Isn't Music The Form? Songs are designed for seduction. The major change to the minor encourages love to break forth. And yet after them..sex. Songs in that sense are betrayals. They win you with words, harmonise you, then rhythm you back into bed. Melody captivates and in that sense is distraction. From the matter at hand they divert you by a convenient truth, shaped and paced. In no time at all – sometimes as little as two or three minutes, your world is turned, your cloud fashioned and all of your sky tidied too. Your landscape is clear, defined by the things they have conjured..the popular tropes; bays and bedrooms, walks through the park, rain and stars. Songs sung for you and then making a world out of music. These are the motions for which the desire to dance will be sparked. Dance is sex standing up. Dance is sex without touching. Drums are blood pumping as the guitarring gates open up.

(Pause.)

Jolene.
Peggy Sue.
Oh, Diane.
Deanna.
Lady Jane, or Madonna.
Angie.
Oh, Carol!
Mother.
Or...Oh. So many names. So many types. So many forms of desire.
The mouth wide or sneering, hoping to fit the girl in. When they sing now they –
Well..
When they sing..let me tell you..
What I feel –
What – Listen – What I'm trying to tell you is..
Oh.

(Silence)

Or..oh..Suddenly I feel – I feel –
Silence..
Why can't I hear them?
Where are all the songs summoned forth?

(She spins round.)

Where is?
Oh –
Oh -
Or What have I - Where – ? In the silence?
So is no-one now –
No-one..?
Then why am I..
Am I..?
Oh.

(The music has stopped. She examines the silence.)

So all of the songs have been written and all we have left is the drums.

(Darkness.)

(Lights rise. She sits at a desk, business like and surrounded by papers. Handwritten notes and typed pages which she now rifles through. She reads and compares before looking at us through her glasses. She seems slightly furtive as if she shouldn't really be there at all.)

THE REPRESENTATIVE:

Thursdays are Novelists. Work. The weekend is not yet upon us. Now there is progress. So much should or still needs to be done. We need this full day to let the rest of the week find it's anchor. So we can describe, be expansive. Plan or plot out the details. They take a lot more time when they come to lift what they want from my shoulders. They talk to me or cajole me, or try to understand me – that's worse! They do all they can to squeeze out all the details, examining the sweat and the pores as if it were gold dust that had been scattered or found in their hand.

And yet they do so much work! They spend so much time thinking of you. Teasing you out. Twisting, trying. Moving you around back and forth. They try to represent you somehow without ever knowing you really. A character is the thing they do in reaction to whatever it is people say...

Theatre Plays are the same. Books dragged on stage for an audience of lazy readers, those for whom the theatre of the mind needs a platform and an exorbitant ticket prize. The Theatre play shows while the written book tells you. Two sides, or sisters;the in and the outside perhaps. But the men are the same. The Novelists and the Playwrights. Male or female they're placing the butterfly you in their net. You mirror for them some of their own private darkness, allowing them to find distance if they ascribe it to you.

"Oh, no the character says!"
"So it must come out by instinct!"
"Is isn't me! No! It's Mary!"
Or whoever the fuck she is..Little Me.
They assume it's inspiration. It's not. It's just slim recognition. Selective choice as they dredge up something they first smelt in themselves. Well, I've had enough. I'm nobody's Hedda Gabbler. I'm not Ophelia either, although you'd be driven half mad with all that!
I'm not Eskimo Nell..and I'm certainly not Little Dorritt!
And I'm not a Gangster's moll in a Copshow that wouldn't know it's arse in bad light!

(Pause.)

I'm..undefined.
I'm about to be.
I'm sequential.
I'm missing chapters..
I'm undecided..
Am I?

(Silence.)

This is how panic starts. This is when you want them to shape you. Defined for years by your body, you hide out in parts you don't know...Darknesses. Dreams. Fantasies. Bollocks.Because you've become what they show you, you start to believe you don't know.

Where is the poem of you, the exact soul of you, where is essence? Where are you hiding when all of the light falls or fades?

That's when you're out with the cats, and the hunters at night, Doggers, Rapists..

That's when you're water that the wrong end of night tries to stain.

(She stares as the light fades or falls.)

(Lights rise. A class, or something like it. Desks, books and papers and a painted window, now seen. She looks more neutral now, having removed some makeup. She is fresher now, natural, ready to be someone else.)

THE MUSE:

Friday is Poets Day. Laugh! It's a working class joke. Have you heard it? Piss Off Early, Tomorrow's Saturday. As an acronym it *so* works. Playing with words, which is poetry's function. Playing for someone the curious ode of the heart. You start again with new words. You try to become something different. Another eye claims you. Another heart flowers forth.

The Poets are sweet. Or try to be sweet. They're pretending. Those that go about it all as a living are already removing whatever their first impulse was. They are experts on form, so turn their full gaze to my body. They clothe it in strict tersa rima, or whatever the actual term is..but their technique glares through, smearing the blush and shine of the flower. That first flesh that opens and lets their waspish hearts fuck and feed. I don't trust poetry, but I suppose I love the poetic. I admire the pure observation that comes before the mouth starts to form. That sigh beyond words in which the love to be born can find colour. The prize that remains uncollected. The message you write in the sand.

Poetry is the key. You can hide your truth deep inside it. Like a clenched fist the poem is only revealed in the palm. We come to it blocked but then open it with each finger, examining meanings as we extrapolate the condensed. These are my thoughts, recognised as I tell you. In this I'm discovered. Suddenly I feel and almost find what I am.
My own thoughts. My need to capture substance..I'm in the palm there and so much more than my face.

They could write me a poem of sex, but that makes them pure oxymorons; those who write about fucking are basically those who can't fuck. It's the love after sex;the glow or the scent of the body. The way that one sets the other, unlocking the heart or the cunt. With the cock as the key, or with the clitoris trigger, love's combination is only revealed afterwards. Is fresh sex the start? Is each new bout confirmation? Or is one affirming how this relationship ends?

Having been used for so long I seem to have found my perspective. Dare I say I'm the Poem that they all try to write?

I'm better than them. Well, girls are. Because we understand nature. Because we are nature. Seasons move under our hands every month. Elevated at Ten, or sometimes even younger – into womanhood we're sent flying towards our ultimate truth. Boys and men stumble on. They never really grasp their true function. And so use bravado to patch up the holes that wear thin. Men are blank space that creative skills try to fathom. Women are water that powers the ground, that dry earth...

Men wank. Women bleed. And that's the distinction. Women masturbate also, but we know why! That's the point! Men are animals, grunts made from strained sperm explains them. They're the fruit that keeps falling but we of course are the tree! We are the place that they all emerge from! We are the destination, they are just the need to move! To find something else that they will of course not be given.. because they have no power, or simply no proper understanding of power – because they are the asking and we the very question itself! The parallel in our worlds grows evermore distant! We collide all too rarely, just often enough to seem close! But we're on different paths..our singular truths are divergent; theirs is just about their own motive, while ours is about everything! Children study the failings of men in their History classes! But the real story is womans! We should study Herstory instead! We are the Muse! We are the need to write Poems! We are the Poems! We are THE POETRY. The Poetics of sex. The Poetics of beauty. The curve of the guitar or the piano that echoes the hips, arse and breasts! In this we are free! This is how we accept them! What we allow will define us in the final and great compromise! How women must live with the love men afford them...

MUSE ON MONDAY

Which is barely love, which is conquest, or simple desperation at best! That is our song. That is our story! Our Play. Our painting;the knowledge is clear seen on our face! We are characters in a film that will always deceive us, because the illusion of movement helps to gloss over the truth!

Which is that we see you.

I see.

And I know all about you. As you reward, as you worship, as you place me on your pedestal..I look down on you, because I am beautiful to you. And it is that, that decision that shows the separation of you. The space between us. The ways in which we are divided. The corridor I can walk down if I am at last, to be free.

You want me for yourself because there is not enough in you. Because there is not enough of you to properly know yourself. So you fill it with love. Or what you think is love. With desire. You summon your Muse on a Monday, hoping she will last the full week. But then you waste the full day with your wronged decisions. You waste the days and grow weaker. And so you call to her again. Only now it's enough. That Pedestal bites. Or it topples. And it's time to stand low beneath it, and find my own way to go on. I have to show you what you are by moving so very far away from you. I have to take away all the beauty. I have to take away sex to find truth.

The simplicity of the room. The bareness of the world all about you. The world not as you wish it, but as you have made it to be. That's what you have. That is the mate made to please you. That is your partner, not some spectacular mouth you might kiss. Not my body, my flesh that you want pushed against you. Not the curve of my bottom, or my breath on your neck. Not my kiss. Just the feel of the air with no sense of promise. Just the light shining on you, showing the marks on your face...

Your ugliness.

Or your own form of beauty.

Intelligence. Lack of talent. Loneliness too, in it's way.

This is my Poem to you.

This is your Muse musing. If I send it now, would you see it, my message of light through the dark?

(She stands there. She waits, examining her audience as she does so.)

You see, no-one answers, because nobody knows what to say.

(Darkness.)

(Lights rise – but only partially. There is music. Distant and clublike and strangely mixed with birdsong. We just glimpse her now. She lets the dark hide her. We never see her face again. She stays hidden through these final scenes.)

THE FELT:

On Saturdays I just walk, hoping that no-one will notice. By day I prowl country lanes and an antique shops, while in the evenings I appear anonymously in bright bars..I appear in cities and towns as one of the shapes out there walking. Once more, mine are the breasts you brush harshly as you sidle your way to the bar..

My breath crests the smoke. My lipstick appears on the wine glass. Mine is the body which failing to score you look to. When you wake in the dark and wish that she was beside you. I am her image. Mine is the face you would see. For a moment – a flash – it's me you see. I don't know you. But suddenly you are dreaming and I am the sense memory. Something about me, my skin. The contours and shape of my body; the softness that flows around women that the roughness of men can't abide. They don't understand it always, this irresistible hunger. But they feel it there..and they want it, they want all of it to themselves. Always and on. And forever after. They cry out in their dreaming and express themselves through the sheets. Into Kleenex and dreams that will haunt their days ever after. Into the feeling that they will never receive what they want. Or that they lost something once that can never be regained, never fathomed. That they will be forever now falling into the waiting arms of the dark...

I will miss it. I will. I will honestly miss it. For a while. As I'm moving, before I become something else.

I am shedding my skin. Soon you'll find an empty dress on the dancefloor.

Look at me. I am leaving, the ache in your heart's influence.
It is time to become your own muse or to try to find it in others.

The lesson is over. As is the week.

The world starts.

Where is your world? Because it's not with me, baby.
Grow up and discover the love that you need on your own.

(The music builds suddenly.)

Saturday night's almost over. When you wake tomorrow, your conquest will leave empty sheets...

You will be alone. Be alone. Because that's how you learn to love others. Especially those who have left you. On their buses home. Or to death. There is only you. Now there is only you, starting. A whole week's creation crumbles to dust on your breath.

Do not be afraid. Everyone loves you. The only thing is they don't know it. So what will you do to convince?

(The Music cuts. The light falls. Darkness. The sound of a distant bell tolling.)

THE REMEMBERED:

On Sunday.. escape from design.

(Lights rise. The Room or series of rooms as we saw them. Interspersed now with music, the song or the sounds we have heard: we see every one and each one without her. Her voice is heard talking to us, from a hidden corner or even on tape.)

THE LOST:

Today is Monday. Day One. Now it is time to get started. This is the room where you found me. And this is the space I escaped.

(Silence. last room. The Muse has absconced. The lights remain glaring until the audience learn when to leave.)

HER COLLECTION

A Short Film for the reader to make.

Note: All Female roles to be played by the same actress

BLACK.

CREDITS/TITLE: HER COLLECTION

FADE IN:

1 EXT. LONDON HOUSE. STREET. DAY.   1

PETER, an older man stands with flowers. He consults a small piece of paper and then approaches the door. His hand goes for the bell but then the door opens. CASSIE, a dishevelled party girl, stumbles out.

          CASSIE.

Do you live here?

          PETER.

What? No..I was looking for –

          CASSIE.

Christmas? Or a Prince? Something..
What's the name of this street? Do
you know? (FEELS HERSELF:) Fuck!

          PETER.

Is something - ?

CASSIE.

What? Fuck! Where the fuck are my knickers!
Have you got my knickers?
Where are my fucking knickers? Oh! Fuck!

She darts back inside leaving PETER standing.
She is heard shouting and banging on a higher floor.

CASSIE (OOS)

LET ME IN, YOU PIG! SAL! OR WHATEVER
YOUR NAME IS! LET ME IN! DO YOU HEAR
ME! I SAID LET ME IN! LET ME IN!

PETER stands at the door. He peers in, uncertain.
Cassie approaches. She pushes past him and out.

CASSIE.

Spanish twat.

PETER looks after her. He stands, disconcerted.

2 INT. HALLWAY. DAY.   2

PETER enters. He closes the front door as a Flat door opens.
CARA (thick accent) stands staring at him..

CARA.

What was noise?

PETER.

That? Oh..I think it was one of the tenants..

CARA.

Was not you?

PETER.

I'm no tenant. I was looking for –

Cara shuts the door.

Nevermind.

PETER walks on. He puts down the flowers. Another door opens. CAROL, dowdy and fearful is looking though the crack.

CAROL.

Who are you?

PETER.

Hello..hi..

CAROL.

Are you from the landlord? I've got mice in here somewhere. I can hear them pick and scratch through the walls. They didn't say there were mice when they asked me to stay here. Plus they said there'd be carpets, but there isn't even that. And it's cold. I can't go out. Are you –

PETER.

No. I'm actually looking for someone..

CAROL.

Who?

PETER.

Oh, my sister. My sister Emma.

CAROL.

I'm Carol.

PETER.

Hello.

CAROL.

Do you know the landlord?

PETER.

No.

CAROL.

Can't you help me? You see, I'm being driven mad by this mouse..!

PETER.

I'm sorry..

He walks to the stairs. She watches after.

CAROL.

Don't tell the landlord! This isn't my fault! None of this!

She slams the door shut as Peter continues.

3 INT. CAROL'S ROOM. DAY.   3

CAROL turns back inside. A BODY is laying, seemingly dead in the foreground. She looks at it, impassive.

CAROL.

It isn't. And more..never could.

4 INT. STAIRCASE.   4

PETER passes patches on the wall where information has been.

5 INT. LANDING. DAY.   5

Another door to a flat. PETER knocks. There is no answer. He knocks. Then continues knocking.

6 INT. 2nd ROOM. DAY.   6

The knocking from outside continues. CATHY, an executive type woman turns to regard it. She turns back to the person that she's been addressing. She takes a gun from her handbag and points it at this person. We do not see him unless in OS shot.

CATHY.

If you answer that door I'll have you, Derek. Can you imagine that, Mr Walters? I'll murder you. It's like a film, this. All this. What you might call an extreme situation. But it took time to find you and now I want to play it out, properly. Wicked Stepdads are shit. I'm sure they give off an odour. You do, for certain. They can smell you in here through the walls! And where are we now? Quite near town...

CATHY (CONT))

Living in shit on my Mother's money. You couldn't even waste her cash wisely, like you wasted me, years ago. (BEAT) I'm going to kill you, you cunt.

7   INT. LANDING. DAY.   7

Another door, slightly open. PETER peers in.

8   INT. 3rd ROOM. DAY.   8

CANDY, a buxom prostitute is greasing her hands with petro leum jelly. We glimpse the outline of a man lain before her.

CANDY.

Rollover, your Highness. Crack to.

9   INT. LANDING. DAY.   9

PETER straightens. Walks on and takes the staircase to the higher floor.

10 INT. 2ND LANDING. DAY.   10

More doors ahead. PETER stands there, uncertain. Suddenly a door opens and CLAIRE comes out. She is a bright, breezy girl, dressed for work. Calm and cheerful. Her hair is dyed a strong colour. Her makeup reminiscent of punk or goth.

CLAIRE.

Oh, hello!

PETER.

Hi.

CLAIRE.

Are you Avon calling?

PETER.

No, I'm not.

CLAIRE.

Pity. I could do with a cure for my nails. You look lost.

PETER.

It's my —

CLAIRE.

What?

PETER.

I've been trying to find my kid sister. She ran away.

CLAIRE.

There's no children —

PETER.

No, she ran away years ago. My Dad. Our Dad.
He — I don't suppose you —

CLAIRE.

What? (*She smiles cooly.*) There's no kids.

PETER.

Her name's Emma.

CLAIRE.

There isn't an Emma. Not here.

PETER.

I have this address. Carlton Road. Queensway.

CLAIRE.

This is Carlton Road. This is Queensway.

PETER.

It's all that was sent.

CLAIRE.

Let me see.

He shows her.

Weird.

PETER.

Yes.

CLAIRE.

Someone's playing games with you..

PETER.

Thinks so? I used to play games with my sister

when she was kid.

CLAIRE.

Oh? What sort.

PETER.

Cryptic stuff.

CLAIRE.

Ah.

PETER.

She twisted me round her finger. She was a minx.

CLAIRE.

Was she really.

PETER.

A real little minx.

CLAIRE.

Aren't they all? And I'm late for work..

PETER.

Look, I'm sorry: this house..How many rooms are there?

CLAIRE.

God knows. There's lots of people. But I mean, it's mostly girls, girls in here.

She smiles.

OIL ON SILVER

It's a kind of refuge.

PETER.

I see.

CLAIRE.

Yes, this was a safehouse.

PETER.

Was? Something happen?

CLAIRE.

I said I was late. So I'm gone.

She goes, passing him very quickly, she practically runs down the stairs. He stares after.

Another door opens. A BEATEN WOMAN WITH A BRUISED FACE stares at him.

The front door slams.
PETER moves back to the staircase.

PETER.

EMMA!

He runs to the landing window to see the street below him.

11 EXT. STREET. DAY.   11

CLAIRE/ EMMA is running. Her face is fearful.
She disappears down the street.

DISSOLVE TO:

12 Same shots of each woman (CASSIE/CARA/CAROL/CATHY/ CANDY/CLAIRE) running. They have all been the same person, each one victimised by her Father and Brother and any number of men. The image repeats, each time superimposing until image definition and the truth blurs from view..

FADE TO BLACK.

CREDITS. END.

A CHILDREN'S STORY

Hamlyn. It was spring and all of the children had died. The survivors had tried to keep them alive but the air had proved itself full of toxins, and so the elderly folk sighed and shuffled, eyes suitably sad, hearts declined. In the village that year the after-effects had proved costly and so the young were relinquished, tucked into the ground like warm beds. Some of the Eighty year old Mothers sat numbed, while their Ninety year old husbands kept drinking, filling the small bars and cafes with talk of the past and the sea. The ocean itself bartered on, battering the coast in sharp clashes, before things were settled, resolving away to thrashed foam.

Ice marked the streets with dark glass. Some of the older women had slipped and this is where the lost progeny had proved useful. Their soft skins were buffers and had seemed designed for protection, as if the purpose of their full existence was to keep the elderly inhabitants safe. There had of course always been teenage buoys, bobbing about in the water and indeed, their effusions had proved a valuable line of control. When some of the older Debutantes strayed, their milk deprived arms would deter them, subduing their language and shaming the inadequate marks on each face. Then the women would turn, spurning the youth that would taunt them, to swim home, like plump ducklings, their fleshy arms waving flag like, as if mirroring the stirred sea. As they lumbered back up the sand, numerous six year old girls would be waiting, ready with towels to embrace them, as the wonders of wool produced warmth. The old girls would then coo as their own voluptuousness brought them comfort. And so the liminals soothed and patted, impressed by the women's curves, size and rumps. Now, all was gone and the village would have to begin a new process. The Octogenarian wives smiled and fluttered while the Seventy year old men cleared their throats.

CODA: THE VIEW FROM UXBRIDGE

Out in zone 6 the borders are frozen. The not so dumb blonde sucks the suburbs for another half pint of blood to go on. The man I'd happily kill strides from privilege to position in which the ice sheets housing Parliament's member urinates on tax payers who become his Members of Purgatory. His food smeared trousers fall and excrescence cold-acid-rains down on us all.

We are close to the lost in the Uxbridge environ, and soon to be kept in a gulag of moralless, slumped vacancy. As the crypto fascist cunt fucks us back, Heathrow's new runway divides us. For those who were living in Sipson it levels their tender hopes to the ground. There are no dreams here just scarves tightly binding expression. As the cold bites we hunker somewhere further down in ourselves. To elect out of hate, or unproven suspicion is to live the new fashion that currently clogs shops and shelves. London is lost and is chasing itself between stations. As the signals block like a prostate the cancerous worm catches hold. What we do not know we won't test, for now experiment is beyond us. The laboratory walls have been sundered and the virus is out on the streets. The ignorant shift, happy they thought for the moment, before the winded breath taken from then blackened the United States with warped gold. Almost everywhere now will be subject to Tsunamis. Waves of Rightwing action rearguard and then forefront and foreclose. The Druids of old will be summoning lost gods to assist them while the dirty doggers fuck numbly as U-KKK-IP goons now walk proudly into the next Laundromat.

Is London lost? Occupy raged but was peaceful. The ruling forces have gassed them with the perilous decisions of (Theresa) May. As winter takes hold will there be a spring to greet warmly? Or will we all burn in summer before the dead leaves of autumn crackle like poems the brutalists throw to flames? Beneath us the ground is already shifting. The rain smoothed pavements are biscuit as we no longer know what to taste.

This is the fear if not the reality for the moment. Resist all you can. The left wing is still flapping. Release the bird quickly for the skies now above us are going to need fresh colouring.

Everywhere looks like anywhere now. Our hearts are all made of cardboard. What we think and write now is crucial. It is the only blood that will stain. From these places not change, but I hope education. For these are the boundaries in which the encampment and the open field look the same.

The football thugs are in force. And not all of them can play football. The breakfast cafes are burning and the shopping malls are to blame. Rise up London and see what you truly are as a city. We are just streets and slices which the hungry foxes are prowling. Even the dogs have grown doubtful. For God or our children's sake we must question, or in the long run lose every right we have or ever had, to a name.

14th November 2016

ON THE FADING OF STARS (for Heathcote Williams)

When one of the great voices fades
The world no longer knows how to listen;
Pictures are splintered and what was clear
In a cloud is wrenched loose.
Shining through it all is the light
That was initially formed to dare darkness;
Prising it open, like malnourished hands
On sweet fruit.

A special man has just died who I saw
Fashion light from his laughter;
A small electric bulb conjured
By the dexterous hands that wrote spells;
Dense invocations of words
And comprehensive poetics,
Erudite interrogations of the systems
And codes the failed sell.

And yet his was always success,
From early days, each endeavour;
Word photographs of the speakers
Or the stigmatics rage below stairs,
Then the spraying of truth
Across Ladbroke Grove, stars and places,
The saviour grace for the homeless
Whose continued torrent of language
Drowned out defeat and changed air.

The genius in the room with his
Fountain pen and mind water; the source
Of all rivers for those that he befriended
And loved. A man whose clear life
Captured the fog found in others,
Crystallising intention before posting to hell,
Or above. The journalist of the heart,
And Poet of the eye, whose voice music
Fused word and meaning and turned

OIL ON SILVER

Disasters birds into doves.

From ravens to stars he flew with all
Through his writing; Now that a new
Migration has started and we will be
Watching the sky that's now his.
We will see the perfect calligraphy
Of his lines in those streaks of dawn
And torn sunsets. Let each new thought
Now be his thought and our time with him
This life's gift.

July 1st 2017